Withdrawn

SEP 19 2015

Northville District Library
212 W. Cady Street
Northville, MI 48167-1560

THE
GREAT SWINDLE

THE GREAT SWINDLE

PIERRE LEMAITRE

TRANSLATED FROM THE FRENCH
BY FRANK WYNNE

MacLehose Press
New York • London

MacLehose Press
An imprint of Quercus
New York • London

© 2013 by Pierre Lemaitre
First published in the United States by Quercus in 2015

English translation © 2015 by Frank Wynne
First published in French as *Au revoir là-haut* by Editions Albin Michel, Paris, in 2013

All rights reserved. No part of this book may be reproduced in any form or by any electronic or mechanical means, including information storage and retrieval systems, without permission in writing from the publisher, except by reviewers, who may quote brief passages in a review. Scanning, uploading, and electronic distribution of this book or the facilitation of the same without the permission of the publisher is prohibited.

Please purchase only authorized electronic editions, and do not participate in or encourage electronic piracy of copyrighted materials. Your support of the author's rights is appreciated.

Any member of educational institutions wishing to photocopy part or all of the work for classroom use or anthology should send inquiries to permissions@quercus.com.

ISBN 978-1-62365-903-5

Library of Congress Control Number: 2015940794

Distributed in the United States and Canada by
Hachette Book Group
1290 Avenue of the Americas
New York, NY 10104

This book is a work of fiction. Names, characters, institutions, places, and events are either the product of the author's imagination or are used fictitiously. Any resemblance to actual persons—living or dead—events, or locales is entirely coincidental.

Manufactured in the United States

10 9 8 7 6 5 4 3 2 1

www.quercus.com

Let us make a date to meet in heaven
where I hope God will reunite us.
Good-bye till there, my darling wife . . .

Last words written by Jean Blanchard,
December 4, 1914

NOVEMBER
1918

I

Those who thought the war would soon be over were all long dead. Killed by the war. And so, in October, Albert treated reports of an impending armistice with a healthy dose of skepticism. He gave these rumors no more credit than he had the propaganda at the beginning of the war that claimed that the bullets of the Boches were so soft they burst against French uniforms like overripe pears, leaving soldiers roaring with laughter. In four years, Albert had seen his fair share of guys who died laughing from a German bullet.

He knew all too well that his refusal to believe in this armistice was a sort of conjuration: in order to ward off ill fortune, the more a man hopes for peace, the less inclined he is to believe the news that it is imminent. Yet day after day, the news came in ever-increasing waves, and everywhere people were beginning to say that the war truly was coming to an end. He even read speeches he could scarcely believe about the need to demobilize the older soldiers who had been on the front lines for years. When, finally, the armistice seemed a credible prospect, even the most pessimistic souls began to nurture the hope they might get out alive. Consequently, no one was particularly keen to mount an offensive. There was talk of the 163rd Infantry Division attempting to mount an attack and cross the Meuse. A few officers still talked about fighting to the death, but seen from the ranks, from the position of Albert and his comrades, since the Allied victory in Flanders, the liberation of Lille, the rout of the Austrian army, and the capitulation of the Turks, the ordinary soldiers felt rather less frenzied than the officers. The successes of the Italian offensive, the British at Tournai, the Americans at Châtillon . . . it seemed clear the worst was behind them. Most men in the unit began to play for time, and there was a clear distinction between those, like Albert, who were prepared to wait out the war holed up in their trenches, smoking cigarettes and writing letters home, and those eager to make the most of the last few days to gut a few more Krauts.

This demarcation line exactly corresponded to the one separating officers from ordinary soldiers. Nothing new there, thought Albert. The commanders want to take control of as much terrain as they can to be in a stronger position at the negotiating table. They will insist that gaining another hundred feet could decide the outcome of the war, that it would be even more worthwhile to die today than yesterday.

This latter position was the one espoused by Lieutenant d'Aulnay-Pradelle. When talking of him, everyone dropped the first name, the nobiliary particle, the "Aulnay," and the hyphen, referring to him simply as "Pradelle" since they knew very well how much this riled him. They could afford to do so, since Pradelle made it a point of honor never to express personal animus. An aristocratic reflex. Albert did not like the man. Perhaps because he was handsome. Tall, thin, elegant, with a cascade of dark brown curls, a straight nose, thin, perfectly shaped lips. And eyes of deepest blue. A face that Albert considered typical of an upper-class twat. Moreover, he seemed to be permanently angry. He was impetuous, he had no cruising speed: he was either accelerating or braking; there was no middle ground. He walked quickly, one shoulder forward as though to push obstacles aside; he bore down on you at speed and even sat down briskly: this was his normal rhythm. It made for a curious combination: with his aristocratic bearing, he seemed at once terribly civilized and utterly brutish. A little like this war. Which was perhaps why he felt so at ease here. To top it all, he had an athlete's build—rowing, probably, or tennis.

The other thing Albert did not like was the hair. Pradelle had thick dark hair all over, even on his fingers; great tufts sprouted from his shirt collar just below his Adam's apple. In peacetime, he probably had to shave several times a day so as not to look disreputable. There were certainly some women who were attracted by that wild, hirsute, faintly Spanish look. Even Cécile . . . But even without thinking of Cécile, Albert could not abide Lieutenant Pradelle. And most of all he feared the man. Because Pradelle liked to charge. He genuinely enjoyed going over the top, storming, attacking.

In fact, recently he had been less high spirited than usual. The prospect of an armistice depressed him; it undermined his patriotic zeal. The idea that the war might be over was killing Lieutenant Pradelle. He was showing disturbing signs of impatience. He found the lack of team spirit worrying. As he strode through the trenches and spoke to the men, his passionate zeal and his talk of crushing the enemy, of a final surge that would be the *coup de grâce*, was met with vague mutterings; the soldiers would nod, staring down at their boots. It was not just the fear of dying, but the fear of dying now. Dying last was like dying first, Albert thought to himself; it was rank stupidity.

But this was exactly what was about to happen.

Whereas until now they had been able to while away the uneventful days waiting for the armistice, now, suddenly, things were gearing up again. Orders had been received from on high, demanding that they approach enemy lines to find out what the Germans were up to. Despite the fact that it did not take a *général* to know that they, like the French, were waiting for the end. Even so, they had to go and see. From this point, no one was able to piece together the sequence of events.

It was difficult to know why Lieutenant Pradelle assigned the reconnaissance mission to Gaston Grisonnier and Louis Thérieux, an old man and a kid. Perhaps he hoped to combine youthful vigor with mature experience. Neither quality proved useful, since the two men were dead within half an hour of being allocated the task. In theory, they did not have to advance very far. They only needed to follow a line about six hundred and fifty feet to the northeast, cut through the wires, crawl to the second line of barbed wire, have a quick look, and then hightail it back to say everything was fine, because everyone knew there was nothing to see. And in fact, the two soldiers were not worried about approaching the enemy lines. Given the state of affairs in recent days, even if they were spotted, the Huns would let them reconnoiter and go back; it was little more than a distraction. But the moment they started to advance, crouching as low as they could, the two scouts were shot like rabbits. There was the sound of gunshots, three of them, and then silence; as far as the enemy was concerned, the matter was settled. There was a frantic attempt to see where they were, but since they had left from the north side, it was impossible to tell where they had fallen.

All around Albert everyone stood in stunned silence. Then suddenly there were shouts. Bastards! They're all the same, the fucking Boches! Savages! To gun down an old man and a kid! Not that this made any difference, but to the men in the trenches the Boches had not simply killed a couple of French soldiers; they had slaughtered two symbols. There was pandemonium.

In the minutes that followed, with a promptness no one thought them capable of, the rear gunners began pounding the German lines with 75mm shells, leaving the men in the front line wondering how they knew what had happened.

So began the escalating spiral of violence.

The Germans returned fire. It did not take long to mobilize everyone in the French trenches. They would show the fucking Boches a thing or two. It was November 2, 1918. Though no one knew it, this was scarcely ten days from the end of the war.

And to launch an attack on All Souls' Day, the Day of the Dead . . . Try as one might to ignore the omens . . .

Here we go again, thought Albert, getting ready to climb the scaffold (this was what they called the stepladders used to scramble out of the trenches—a cheering thought) and charge, head down, toward the enemy. Lined up in Indian file, the men were swallowing hard. Albert was third in line behind Berry and young Péricourt, who turned around as though to check that the men were all present and correct. Their eyes met, and Péricourt gave him a smile like a little boy about to play a prank. Albert tried to return the smile but failed. Péricourt turned away again. The feverishness was almost palpable as they waited for the order to attack. Shocked by the outrageous behavior of the Boches, the French soldiers were now seething. Above them, shells streaked the sky in both directions, causing the very bowels of the earth to shake.

Albert looked over Berry's shoulder. Perched on his little outpost, Lieutenant Pradelle was peering through binoculars, surveying the enemy lines. Albert returned to his position in the line. Had it not been for the deafening racket, he would have been able to think about what was worrying him. The shrill whistle of the shells increased, punctuated by booming explosions that shook the men from head to foot. Try concentrating in such conditions.

Just now, the men are standing, waiting for the signal to advance. It seems an apt moment to study Albert.

Albert Maillard was a scrawny boy of a somewhat lethargic disposition, reserved. He spoke little, was good with figures. Before the war, he was a teller in a regional branch of the Parisian Banque de l'Union. He did not much enjoy the work but stuck it out because of his mother. Mme Maillard had only one son, and she loved managers. She was ecstatic at the prospect of Albert as a bank manager and convinced that "with his intelligence" he would soon rise to the top. This inflated taste for authority she had inherited from her father, an assistant to the deputy chief clerk at the Ministère des Postes who considered the ministerial hierarchy a metaphor for the universe. Mme Maillard loved all leaders without exception. She was not particular about their virtues or their provenance. She had photographs of Clemenceau, of Maurras, of Jaurès, Joffre, Briand[1] . . .

Since the death of her husband, who had commanded a squadron of uniformed guards at the Louvre, exceptional men had inspired extraordinary sensations in her. Albert was not keen on the bank but allowed himself to be persuaded—with his mother this was always the best policy. But he had begun to make plans. He had longed to escape;

he dreamed of running away to Tonkin, though his plans were rather vague. At the very least, he would quit his job as a bank teller and do something else. But Albert was not a man in a hurry; everything took time. Then, shortly afterward, he had met Cécile, had fallen passionately in love with Cécile's eyes, Cécile's mouth, Cécile's and, before long, Cécile's breasts, Cécile's ass—how could he be expected to think about anything else?

Nowadays, at five feet eight, Albert Maillard would not seem especially tall, but in those days it was tall enough. There was a time when he had turned girls' heads. Cécile's in particular. Well . . . , it would be more accurate to say that she turned Albert's head and, after a while, the fact that he stared at her all the time meant that she noticed his existence, and she in turn began to stare at him. He had a face that could melt your heart. A bullet had grazed his temple during the Battle of the Somme. He had been terrified, but he came through with nothing more than a scar shaped like a parenthesis, which tugged his eye slightly to one side and gave him a dashing air. When he was next home on leave, Cécile dreamily, curiously, caressed the scar with her forefinger, which did little for his morale. As a child, Albert had had a pale, round face with drooping eyelids that made him look like a mournful Pierrot. Mme Maillard would go without food so that she could feed him red meat, convinced that his pallor was caused by lack of blood. Though Albert told her a thousand times that there was no connection, his mother rarely changed her mind. She would find examples, new reasons; she could not bear to be in the wrong. Even in her letters she would dredge up events from years gone by; it was exhausting. One might wonder whether this was why Albert enlisted as soon as war was declared. When she found out, Mme Maillard let out a loud wail, but as she was a demonstrative woman it was difficult to distinguish genuine fear from sheer theatrics. She had screamed and torn her hair, but she quickly pulled herself together. Since she had a conventional view of war, she persuaded herself that Albert—"with his intelligence"—would stand out from the crowd and soon be promoted; she could picture him on the front lines leading an assault. In her imagination, he would perform some heroic feat and immediately ascend to the officer class to become *capitaine*, *commandant*, or even *général*—such things happened in war.

With Cécile, things were very different. War did not frighten her. First, because it was a "patriotic duty" (Albert was surprised . . . he had never heard her utter the words before). Second, there was no real reason to be frightened; the outcome was a formality. Everyone said as much.

Albert, for his part, had his doubts, but Cécile was rather like Mme Maillard: she had fixed ideas. To hear her talk, the war would not last long. Albert almost believed her; no matter what she said, Cécile, with those hands, those lips, could convince Albert of anything. It's impossible to understand if you don't know her, thought Albert. To us, Cécile would seem like a pretty girl, nothing more. To him, she was different. Every pore in Cécile's skin was a molecular miracle, her breath had a rare perfume. She had blue eyes, and that might not seem much to you, but to Albert those eyes were a precipice, a yawning chasm. Take her lips, for example, and try to put yourself in Albert's shoes. From these lips he had known kisses of exquisite warmth and tenderness, kisses that caused his stomach to lurch, his whole being to explode. He had felt Cécile's saliva flow into him and had drunk it passionately; Cécile was capable of such wondrous feats that she was not merely Cécile . . . She was . . .

And so, when she insisted the war would be a piece of cake, Albert could only think of those lips and imagine he was that piece of cake . . .

Now he saw things rather differently. He knew that war was nothing more than a gigantic game of Russian roulette, and that to survive for four years was little short of a miracle.

To be buried alive when the end of the war was finally in sight would truly be the icing on the cake.

And yet, that is exactly what is about to happen.

Little Albert, buried alive.

"Hap and mishap govern the world," as his mother would say.

Lieutenant Pradelle turned back to his troops, his eyes boring into the men to left and right, who gazed back as though he were the Messiah. He nodded slowly and took a deep breath.

A few minutes later, half-crouching, Albert is running through an apocalyptic landscape as shells rain down and bullets whistle through the air, pressing onward, his head drawn in, clutching his rifle as hard as he can. The ground beneath his heavy boots is muddy because it has been raining now for several days. All around him there are men howling like lunatics, drunk on their own bravado, steeling themselves for battle. Others, like him, are concentrating hard, their stomachs in knots, their throats dry. All of them are converging on the enemy, armed with righteous rage and the thirst for vengeance. In fact, this may be a perverse result of the rumored armistice. They have suffered for so long that to see the war end like this, with so many of their friends dead and so many enemies still alive, they have half a mind to massacre the enemy, to put an end to this war once and for all. They are prepared to slaughter anyone.

Even Albert, terrified at the thought of dying, is ready to gut the first man he encounters. But there are many obstacles along the way; as he runs, he veers toward the right. At first, he advanced along the line indicated by the lieutenant, but as the bullets whined and the shells droned, he had no choice but to zigzag. Especially since Péricourt, directly ahead of him, has just been hit by a bullet and crumples at his feet so suddenly that Albert scarcely has time to step over him. He loses his balance, staggers a few yards more, carried forward by momentum, only to stumble upon the body of old Grisonnier, whose unexpected death triggered this final, bloody slaughter.

Despite the bullets whistling all around, when Albert sees him sprawled there, he stops in his tracks.

He recognizes Grisonnier by his greatcoat, because the old man always wore something red in his buttonhole, "my *légion d'horreur*," he called it. Grisonnier was not a great wit. He was not exactly subtle, but he was a brave man, and everyone loved him. There could be no doubt that it was him. His huge head was buried in the mud, and the rest of his body looked as though he had fallen headlong. Next to him, Albert recognized the kid, Louis Thérieux. He, too, is partly covered by mud, huddled up in a fetal position. It is heartbreaking to die at such an age, in such a way . . .

Albert does not know what comes over him, but instinctively he grabs the old man's shoulder and heaves. The dead man topples over and lands heavily on his belly. It takes several seconds for the penny to drop. Then suddenly the truth is glaringly obvious: when a man is advancing toward the enemy, he does not die from two bullets in his back.

Albert steps over the body and takes a few paces, he is still half-crouching though he does not know why, since a bullet can strike whether a man is standing or stooping, but instinctively he offers as small a target as possible, as though war were constantly waged for fear the sky should fall. Now he stands before the body of young Louis. The boy's hands, clenched into fists, are pressed against his mouth, and in this pose he seems so young; he is barely twenty-two. Albert cannot see his face, which is caked in mud. He can see only the boy's back. One bullet wound. With the two bullets in the old man, that makes three. And only three shots were fired.

As he straightens up again, Albert is still shaken by what he has discovered. By what it means. A few days from the armistice, the men were in no hurry to take on the Boches; the only way to goad them into an attack was to start a fight: so where was Pradelle when these two men were shot in the back?

Dear God . . .

Shocked by the realization, Albert turns and sees Lieutenant Pradelle bearing down on him, moving as fast as his heavy pack will allow, his head held high. What Albert most notices is the lieutenant's stare, his bright, cold eyes. He is utterly single minded. Suddenly, the whole story becomes clear.

It is at that moment that Albert realizes he is going to die.

He tries to move, but everything in him refuses to obey: his mind, his legs, everything. Everything is happening too quickly. As I said, Albert was never a man in a hurry. In three swift strides, Pradelle is upon him. Next to them is a gaping hole, a crater made by a shell. The lieutenant's shoulder hits Albert square in the chest, winding him. He loses his footing, tries to stop himself, but falls back, arms spread, into the void.

And, as he falls into the crater, as though in slow motion, he sees Pradelle take a step back, and in his expression Albert sees the extent of his defiance, his conviction, and his provocation.

Albert rolls as he hits the bottom of the crater, his momentum barely slowed by his pack. His legs become tangled with his rifle, but he manages to struggle to his feet and quickly presses himself against the muddy slope as though ducking behind a door for fear of being surprised. Leaning his weight on his heels (the compacted clay is as slippery as soap), he tries to catch his breath. His fleeting, tangled thoughts keep returning to the cold, hard look in Pradelle's eyes. Up above, the battle seems to have intensified; the sky is strung with garlands of smoke. The milky vault is lit by blue and orange haloes. The shells fired from both sides rain down as they did at the Battle of Gravelotte[2] in a deafening thunder of whistles and explosions. Albert looks up. There, standing on a ledge, overhanging the crater like the angel of death, is the silhouette of Lieutenant Pradelle.

To Albert, it seems as though he spent a long time falling. In fact, barely six feet separate the men. Probably less. But it makes all the difference. Lieutenant Pradelle stands above, feet apart, his hands firmly gripping his belt. Behind him, the flickering glow of battle. Calm, motionless, he looks down into the hole. He stares at Albert, a half smile playing on his lips. He will not lift a finger to help him out. Albert is shocked, he sees red, he grabs his rifle, stumbles but manages to right himself, raises the weapon, and suddenly there is no one standing on the edge of the pit. Pradelle has disappeared.

Albert is alone.

He drops the rifle and tries to get his second wind. He cannot afford to waste time, he should scramble up the side of the crater and run after Pradelle, shoot him in the back, grab him by the throat. Or find the others, talk to them, scream at them, do something, though he does not know what. But he feels so tired. Exhaustion has finally overtaken him. Because this is all so stupid. It is as though he has just set down his suitcase, as though he has arrived. He could not climb the slope even if he wanted. He was within a hair's breadth of surviving the war, and now here he is at the bottom of a shell crater.

He slumps rather than sits and takes his head in his hands. He tries to assess the situation, but his confidence has suddenly melted away. Like an ice cream. Like the lemon sorbets Cécile loves, so sour that she clenches her teeth and screws her face up in a catlike expression that makes Albert want to hug her. When was it that he last had a letter from Cécile? This is another reason for his exhaustion. He does not talk about it to anyone, but Cécile's letters have dwindled to brief notes. With the end of the war in sight, she writes as though it were already over, as though there is no longer any point in writing long letters. It is not the same for those who have whole families, who are constantly getting letters, but for Albert there is only Cécile . . . There is his mother, too, of course, but she is more tiresome than anything else. Her letters have the same hectoring tone as her conversation, as she tries to make his decisions for him. These things have been wearing Albert down, eating away at him; and then there are all his comrades who have died, the fallen friends he tries not to think about too much. He has experienced these moments of abject despair before, but this one comes at a bad time. Just when he needs to summon all his strength. He could not say why, but something inside him has suddenly given way. He can feel it in his belly. It is a vast weariness, as heavy as stone. A stubborn refusal, something utterly passive and detached. Like the end of something. When he first enlisted and, like so many men, tried to imagine what war would be like, he secretly thought that, if the worst came to the worst, he would simply play dead. He would collapse, or, for the sake of credibility, he could scream and pretend he had just taken a bullet through the heart. Then all he would need to do was lie there and wait until all was calm again. When it was dark, he would inch toward the body of a fallen comrade, someone who was really dead, and steal his papers. After that, he could continue his reptilian crawl for hours on end, stopping and holding his breath whenever he heard voices in the darkness. Taking a thousand precautions, he would carry on until he came to a road, and he would head north (or south, depending). As he trudged, he would learn the details of his new identity by heart. Then he would fall in with a lost unit, whose *caporal-chef*, a heavyset man with . . . As you can see, for a bank teller Albert has a vivid imagination. Perhaps he was influenced by Mme Maillard's flights of fancy. In the beginning, this romantic vision of warfare was one he shared with many of his comrades. He would imagine serried ranks of soldiers in their striking blue-and-red uniforms marching toward the terrified enemy. Their fixed bayonets would sparkle in the sunshine as the plumes of smoke from a few carefully aimed shells confirmed the enemy had been routed. In his heart, Albert had signed up for a war from the pages of Stendhal only to be confronted by a banal, barbaric slaughter that claimed a thousand lives a day for fifty months. To get a sense of the carnage, one had only to peer out over the lip of a trench and survey the scene: a wasteland devoid of any plants, pockmarked by thousands of craters, littered with hundreds of rotting corpses exuding a putrid stench that made your stomach lurch again and again. At every lull in the fighting, rats as large as hares would scurry hungrily from one corpse to another, fighting the blowflies for the worm-eaten remains. Albert knew all this, because he had served as a stretcher bearer at the Battle of the Aisne and, when he could find no more wounded men whimpering or howling, he collected bodies in various stages of decomposition. He knew everything there was to know. It was a difficult task for Albert, who had always been tenderhearted.

And, to make matters worse for a man who is about to be buried alive, Albert is a little claustrophobic.

As a child, the very thought that his mother might inadvertently close the bedroom door after she said goodnight had made him feel sick. He would simply lie there. He never said anything. He did not want to trouble his mother, who was always telling him she had troubles enough already. But the night and the darkness frightened him. Even quite recently, when he and Cécile were rolling around in the sheets, whenever Albert was completely covered, he found it difficult to breathe and felt a panic rising in him. Especially since Cécile would sometime wind her legs around him and hold him there. Just to see, she would say with a laugh. Suffocation is the form of death he most fears. Fortunately, he is not thinking about this because next to what is about to happen, being trapped between Cécile's silken thighs will seem like paradise. If he knew what lay in store, Albert would want to die.

Which would not necessarily be a bad thing, since that is what is going to happen. Though not just yet. In a little while, when the fateful shell explodes a few yards from his shelter, raising up a wave of earth as high as a wall, which will collapse and cover him completely, he will not have long to live, but it will be just long enough to realize what is happening to him. Albert will be seized by that desperate desire to survive, a primitive resistance of the sort that laboratory rats must feel when picked up by their hind paws, or pigs about to have their throats cut, or cattle about to be slaughtered . . . We will have to wait a while before this happens . . . Wait for his lungs to whiten as they gasp for air, for his body to tire of his desperate attempts to free himself, for his head to feel as though it will explode, for his mind to be engulfed by madness, for . . . let's not get ahead of ourselves.

Albert turns and looks up for a last time; it is not very far when he thinks about it—it is simply too far for him. He tries to summon his strength, to focus on nothing but scrambling up this slope, getting out of this hole. He picks up his pack and his rifle, steels himself, and begins to climb. It is not easy. His feet slip and slide in the mud; he can get no purchase. He digs his fingers into the clay, lashes out with the toe of his boot, trying to create a foothold, only to fall back. So he drops his rifle and his pack. If he had to strip naked, he would not hesitate. He presses himself against the muddy hill and begins to crawl on his belly. His movements are like those of a squirrel in a cage: he scrambles at the empty air, falls, and lands in the very same spot. He pants, he groans, and then he howls. Panic is getting the better of him. He can feel tears welling; he beats his fists against the wall of earth. The edge of the crater is almost within reach, for Christ's sake; when he extends his arms he can almost touch it, but the soles of his boots skid, and every inch he gains is just as quickly lost. I have to get out of this fucking shell crater! he screams to himself. And he will do it. He is prepared to die, someday, but not now; it would be too stupid, too senseless. He will get out of here and hunt down Lieutenant Pradelle. He will go looking in the German trenches if necessary; he will find him, and he will kill him. It gives him courage, the thought of gunning that fucker down.

For a moment he ponders the miserable notion that, despite trying for more than four years, the Boches have failed to kill him; it is a French officer who will do the job.

Shit.

Albert kneels and opens his pack. He takes everything out, slips his canteen between his legs; he will spread his greatcoat over the slippery slope and dig anything and everything that might serve as a crampon into the sodden earth. He turns, and at precisely that moment he hears the whine of the shell above him. Suddenly worried, Albert looks up. In his four years at the front he has learned to tell a 75mm shell from a 95mm, a 105mm from a 120mm . . . This time he hesitates. Perhaps because of the depth of the crater, or perhaps because of the distance, the shell is heralded by a strange, new sound, at once quieter and more muffled than usual, a sort of dull roar that rises to a piercing shriek. Albert's mind just has time to form a question. The explosion is immeasurable. The earth shakes with terrible spasms, emits a deep, mournful groan, and then erupts like a volcano. Thrown off balance by the blast, Albert is surprised to look up and see that the world has suddenly gone dark. A dozen yards above his head, where the sky should be, he watches as, in slow motion, the dark earth furls into a great wave whose shifting, sinuous crest is surging toward him, about to break and engulf him completely. A light, almost indolent rain of pebbles, clods, and assorted rubble heralds its arrival. Albert curls into a ball and holds his breath. This is not a good move, on the contrary, he should stretch himself out as much as possible, as anyone who has been buried alive will tell you. There follow two or three suspended seconds during which Albert stares up at the mantle of earth that hovers in the sky, seemingly deciding on the time and place of its fall.

In a moment, this blanket will crash down and cover him.

To give you an idea, under normal circumstances Albert looks rather like a Tintoretto self-portrait. He has always had rather hangdog features with finely delineated lips, a protruding chin, and dark rings around his eyes accentuated by his arched black eyebrows. But in this moment, as he looks up at the sky and sees death bearing down on him, he looks more like Saint Sebastian. Suddenly he looks haggard. His face is creased by pain and fear into a kind of prayer, which is all the more useless since Albert has never believed in anything in his life, and, given the misfortune about to befall him, he is not going to start believing in something now. Even supposing he had the time.

With a thunderous crack, the sheet of clay collapses on him. One might believe that the impact would kill him on the spot, Albert would be dead, it would all be over. What happens is worse. The pebbles and stones continue to rain down on him, then comes the soil, covering him with a blanket that grows heavier and heavier. Albert is pinned to the ground.

Gradually, as the earth piles up above him, he is engulfed, compressed, crushed.

Light flickers out.

Everything stops.

This is a new world, a world in which Cécile no longer exists.

The first thing he notices, just before panic overtakes him, is that the noise of the war has stopped. As though everything had suddenly fallen silent, and God had blown the final whistle. Of course, if he stopped to think, he would realize that nothing has stopped, that the noise is simply muffled by the weight of the earth above him, almost inaudible. But just now, Albert has more pressing concerns than listening for whether the war is still going on, because all that matters is that, for him, it is about to end.

The moment the din abated, Albert was trapped. I'm under the earth, he thinks, though it is a somewhat abstract concept. It is only when he thinks "I am buried alive" that it becomes appallingly concrete.

And when he realizes the extent of the catastrophe, the nature of the death that awaits him, when it becomes clear that he is going to choke to death, to suffocate, Albert goes insane: instantly, utterly insane. Everything in his head becomes confused, he screams and with that scream squanders what little oxygen he has left. I'm buried alive, he thinks over and over, and his mind is so consumed by this terrible conclusion that he has not even thought to open his eyes. He tries to move. Every last ounce of strength, every wave of the panic surging through him is transformed into muscular exertion. As he struggles, he uses up incalculable energy. And it is all in vain.

Then, suddenly, he stops.

Because he has just realized that he can move his hands. Only slightly, but he can move them. He holds his breath. As it fell, the sodden clay fashioned a sort of shell around his arms, his shoulders, his neck. The world in which he lies almost petrified affords him a few scant inches here and there. In fact, the layer of earth covering him is not very deep. Albert knows this. Sixteen inches, perhaps. But he is underneath and this blanket is enough to paralyze him, to inhibit all movement, to condemn him.

All around him, the ground is trembling. Above him, in the distance, the war rages on, the shells continue to pound and shake the earth.

Albert opens his eyes, warily at first. It is dark but not pitch dark. Infinitesimal rays of sunlight are managing to filter through. A faint, pale glow, a flicker of life.

He forces himself to take short, halting breaths. He moves his elbows a few inches and manages to spread his legs a little, packing the soil by his feet. Taking infinite precautions, and struggling to contain the panic he feels mounting in him, he tries to lift his face so he can breathe. Immediately a slab of earth collapses like a bubble bursting. Instinctively, he tenses every muscle and curls his body into a ball, but nothing else happens. How long does he lie in this perilous position as the air around him grows thinner, imagining the death that awaits him, trying to understand what it means to be deprived of oxygen, to have every vessel in him burst like a balloon, his wide eyes staring as though searching for the air he lacks? Moving as slowly as possible, while he strives not to breathe more than necessary, not to think more than necessary, not to picture the position he is in, his hand inches forward, feeling the ground. Unexpectedly, his fingers encounter something, but the faint glow, though brighter, is not enough to make out his surroundings. He runs his fingertips over something soft; it is not dirt, not clay, something silky, almost velvety.

It takes him some time to work out what it is.

As his eyes adjust to the darkness, he gradually sees what is in front of him: a pair of huge lips oozing some viscous liquid, great yellow teeth, huge blue-gray eyes that seem to melt . . .

A horse's head, enormous, repulsive, a monstrous thing.

Albert cannot help but shrink back. His head slams into the roof of his cave, which collapses in a muddy shower around his neck. He arches his shoulders to protect himself, then waits, unmoving, not even daring to breathe. The seconds tick past.

As it buried itself in the ground, the shell had unearthed one of the countless old nags rotting on the battlefield and had served the head up to Albert. Face-to-face, the young man and the dead horse are so close they could almost kiss. The collapsing soil has freed Albert's hands, but the soil weighs heavily on him, crushing his rib cage. He begins to breathe again in short, shallow bursts; his lungs are already fit to burst. He feels tears begin to well, but manages to hold back. To cry now, he thinks, would mean accepting death.

He might as well give up, because it will not be long now.

It is not true that at the moment of death our whole life flashes before our eyes in an instant. But there are a few flickering images. Pictures from his childhood. His father's face, so stark, so clear that Albert could swear that he is with him here, beneath the earth. Perhaps because that is where they are destined to meet again. Albert sees him as a young man, as young as he is now. A little over thirty, obviously, but it is that "little" that counts. He is dressed in the uniform he wears at the museum; his mustache is carefully waxed, as in the photograph on the chest of drawers at home; he is unsmiling. Albert is beginning to suffocate. His lungs ache, and his body is convulsed with spasms. He would like to think calmly. It is no use: a crippling dread overtakes him; the terrible fear of death gnaws at his guts. The tears begin to flow in spite of himself. Mme Maillard gives him a disapproving look. That Albert, he will never learn—falling into a hole, I ask you!—because to die when the war is almost over is one thing, it's foolish, but these things happen, but to be buried alive like a man already dead! This is Albert all over, couldn't just be like everyone else, never quite up to scratch. And anyway, if he didn't die in the war, who knows what would have become of the boy? Mme Maillard finally smiles. With Albert dead, at least she will have a hero in the family, so it is not so bad.

Albert's face is almost blue; his temples are pounding at an unimaginable rate as though every vein is about to burst. He calls Cécile. He wishes he were trapped between her thighs with her squeezing as hard as possible, but Cécile's features do not come, as though she is too far away to reach him, and this is what hurts most, not being able to picture her in this moment, not having her with him. There is only her name, Cécile, because in the world into which he is slowly sinking there are no bodies, only words. He wants to beg her to come with him, he is terribly afraid to die. But it is futile; he will die alone, without her.

And so good-bye, good-bye till up there, Cécile, a long time from now.

Then even the name Cécile fades, giving way to the face of Lieutenant Pradelle with his insufferable smile.

Albert thrashes around. He can barely fill his lungs now, they wheeze as he strains. He starts to cough. He grips his stomach. No air.

He clutches the horse's head, manages to grasp the slimy lips but the flesh gives way beneath his fingers. He grabs the huge yellow teeth and, with superhuman effort, pries open the mouth, which belches fetid air that Albert gulps down, filling his lungs. In doing so he gains a few scant seconds, his stomach churns, he vomits. Once again his whole body begins to tremble; he struggles to turn over, desperately seeking a mouthful of air, but it is hopeless.

The soil above is heavy, the light has almost faded, there is nothing now but the shudder of the earth as above him the shells continues to rain down; then there is nothing more. Nothing but a death rattle.

He feels a great peace flooding through him. He closes his eyes.

He feels faint, his heart fails, his mind flickers out, he founders.

Albert Maillard, *soldat*, has just died.

2

Lieutenant d'Aulnay-Pradelle, a determined, brutish, primitive man, was running across the battlefield toward the enemy lines with the single-mindedness of a charging bull. It was impressive, his utter lack of fear. In truth, there was little courage involved, much less than one might think. He was not especially heroic, but he had become convinced that he would not die here. This war, he was certain, was destined not to kill him but to offer him opportunities.

In this rash assault on Hill 113, however, his fierce determination stemmed from the fact that he nursed a boundless hatred of the Germans, a hatred that was almost metaphysical, and also from the fact that they were nearing the end of the war and there was not much time left to profit from the opportunities such an exemplary conflict could offer a man like him.

Albert and the other soldiers had sensed this: the guy behaved like a country squire from a washed-up family. In the three previous generations, the Aulnay-Pradelles had been cleaned out by a series of bankruptcies and failures. Of his former ancestral glory, all that remained was a crumbling family home, la Sallevière, the prestige inherent in his name, a few distant ancestors, a couple of vague relations, and a determination bordering on fury to make a place for himself in the world. His perilous situation he considered a grave injustice, and his sole ambition, the consuming passion for which he was prepared to sacrifice everything, was to regain his position in the aristocracy. His father had shot himself through the heart in a seedy provincial hotel after squandering what little fortune remained. Legend had it that his mother, who passed away a year later, had died of a broken heart, though the rumor had no basis in fact. Having no brothers or sisters, the lieutenant was now the only Aulnay-Pradelle, and being "the last of his line" lent an urgency to his obsession. After him, there was nothing. His father's inexorable decline had long since persuaded him that the restoration of the family fortunes rested squarely on his shoulders, and he knew that he had the will and the talent necessary to succeed.

Add to this the fact that he was passably handsome, if one found bland beauty attractive. Nonetheless, women desired him, men envied him; the signs were unmistakable. Anyone will tell you that a man in possession of such good looks and such a name must be in want of a fortune. This was certainly the lieutenant's view, and indeed his only concern.

It is not difficult to understand why he had gone to such lengths to set up the charge that Général Morieux so ardently desired. To the top brass, Hill 113 was like a wart, a tiny blemish on the map that daily plagued them, the sort of fixation that becomes all consuming.

Lieutenant Pradelle was not prone to such fixations, but he too wanted to take Hill 113, because he was on the bottom rung of the hierarchical ladder, and because the war was almost over and in a few short weeks it would be too late to distinguish himself. That he had risen to the rank of lieutenant in three years was not bad. A grand gesture now and the matter would be sealed: he would be demobilized as *capitaine*.

Pradelle was pretty pleased with himself. For having goaded his men into launching an assault on Hill113, for persuading them that the Boches had gunned down two of their comrades in cold blood, knowing it would spark a glorious wave of vengeful fury. It had been a masterstroke.

When the attack was launched, he had tasked one of his *adjudants* with leading the first charge. He had deliberately lagged a little behind . . . he had a few things to attend to before rejoining the unit. Once they were settled, he could race toward the enemy lines, overtake his men thanks to his natural athleticism, and be among the first to get there and slaughter as many Boches as God allowed.

At the first blast of his whistle, as the men went over the top, he had taken up a position on the right to prevent the soldiers from wandering in the wrong direction. He felt his blood boil when he saw one of his men—what was his name again? the guy with the miserable face and mournful eyes who constantly looked as though he was about burst into tears, Maillard, that was it—suddenly stop dead, over to the right. Pradelle wondered how the stupid fucker had ended up there.

Pradelle had watched the soldier stop, retrace his steps, kneel down, and turn over the body of old Grisonnier.

The lieutenant had been keeping an eye on that particular corpse from the moment he launched the attack, because he needed to deal with it, needed to make it disappear as soon as possible. In fact, this was why he had brought up the rear. To make sure . . .

And now this stupid fucking soldier stops and looks at the bodies of the old man and the kid.

In an instant, Pradelle charged—like a bull, as I said. Albert Maillard was just getting to his feet again. He looked shaken by what he had just discovered. Seeing Pradelle bearing down on him, he panicked and tried to run, but his fear was no match for his lieutenant's rage. By the time he had realized what was happening, Pradelle was already upon him. A hard blow to the chest, and the soldier toppled into a shell crater and rolled to the bottom. Granted, it is no more than six feet deep, but it will be difficult to climb out, it will take energy, and before he can do so Pradelle will have dealt with the matter.

Afterward, there will be nothing to say, since there will be no problem.

Pradelle stands on the lip of the muddy crater and stares down at the soldier, hesitating over the best way of tackling the problem, but he feels calmer now, knowing that he has the time he needs. He turns away and takes a few steps back.

Old Grisonnier is lying on the ground, a stubborn look on his face. The advantage of the situation is that, in turning him over, Maillard has moved him closer to young Louis Thérieux, which will make the task easier. Pradelle glances around to ensure that no one is watching, and he sees the extent of the carnage. At this point it is clear that the assault will cost him dearly in terms of men. But this is a war, and he is not here to philosophize. Lieutenant Pradelle pulls the pin from his grenade and carefully sets it down between the corpses. He just has time to retreat to a safe distance and clap his hands over his ears before he feels the explosion that obliterates the bodies of the two dead soldiers.

Two fewer fatalities in the Great War.

Two more missing in action.

Now he needs to go and deal with the soldier in the bottom of the crater. Pradelle takes out a second grenade. He knows his stuff: two months ago, he herded a dozen Boches who had just surrendered into a tight circle. The prisoners stared at each other, mystified; no one understood what was happening. With a flick of the wrist, he threw a grenade into the circle two seconds before it exploded. An expert toss. Four years practice playing *pétanque*. Impeccable precision. By the time the Boche prisoners realized what had landed at their feet, they were already on their way to Valhalla. The bastards can go and play around with some Valkyries.

This is his last grenade. He will have nothing now to toss into the German trenches. Pity, but there it is.

At that moment, a shell explodes, and a vast wave of earth rises, crests, and breaks. Pradelle stands on tiptoe, the better to watch. The shell crater is completely covered.

Perfect timing. The guy is buried under all that mud. Stupid fuck.

The bonus for Pradelle is that he did not have to squander his last grenade.

Suddenly fired up again, he begins to run toward the front line. He feels an urgent need to tell the Boches a few home truths. To give them a little parting gift.

3

Péricourt was mown down as he ran. The bullet had shattered his leg. He howled like a wild animal and crumpled into the mud; the pain was unbearable. As he writhed and screamed on the ground, his hands gripping his thigh, he had a sudden fear that a piece of shrapnel might have severed it completely. By sheer force of will, he managed to struggle to his feet and, in spite of the terrible shooting pains, felt a surge of relief: his leg was still attached; it was still in one piece—he could see the foot at the end of it. The damage was just below the knee. It was pissing blood. He could still move his foot a little, it hurt like hell, but it moved. In spite of the thunderous roar, the shriek of bullets and shrapnel, at least I've got my leg, he thought. He felt reassured, because he did not like the thought of going home with one leg.

He was often jokingly referred to as "petit Péricourt" because, for a child born in 1895, he was extremely tall—in those days six feet was exceptional. Especially since he was not simply tall, but scrawny. He had reached his full height by the age of fifteen. At his private school, his classmates called him "the giant"—and not always affectionately; he was not especially well liked.

Édouard Péricourt, the kind of guy fortune smiled on.

At the schools he attended, all the boys were like him, rich brats from noble families, born into a world of absolute certainties, gifted with an arrogant self-assurance inherited from generations of moneyed forebears. In Édouard, such traits seemed even more objectionable since, to add insult to injury, he was blessed with good luck. And a man may be forgiven anything—his wealth, even his talent—but not good luck, which seems too unfair.

In fact, Édouard Péricourt's good luck stemmed mostly from a keen sense of self-preservation. Whenever danger threatened, whenever events conspired against him, he would sense it; he had a keen intuition, and he would do whatever it took to carry on without getting his fingers burned. Obviously, seeing Édouard Péricourt sprawled in the mud on November 2, 1918, with one leg blasted to a pulp, one might reasonably think his luck had changed, and not for the better. But no, not quite; he will keep his leg. Though he will walk with a limp for the rest of his days, he will still have both his legs.

He took off his belt and fashioned a makeshift tourniquet, pulling it tight to stop the bleeding. Then, exhausted from the effort, he lay down again. The pain subsided a little. He could have been blown to pieces by an exploding shell, or suffered a worse fate . . . At the time, there were frequent rumors that at night the Germans would crawl out of their trenches and hack the wounded to death.

To ease the tension in his muscles, Édouard tilted his head back into the mud, savoring the coolness of the soil. From this angle, everything is upside down. As though he were lying beneath a tree out in the countryside. With a girl. This is something he has never done, not with a girl. His only experience of women were those who worked in the whorehouses along the rue des Beaux-Arts.

He had little time to stroll down memory lane before he spotted the stiff figure of Lieutenant Pradelle. Moments earlier, as he was rolling around in agony and trying to fashion his tourniquet, Édouard had left his comrades racing toward the enemy lines yet here, thirty-three feet behind him, Lieutenant Pradelle was standing motionless, as though the battle were already over.

Viewed upside down and in profile, the lieutenant stands with his thumbs hooked into his belt, staring at his boots, looking for all the world like an entomologist studying an anthill. In the midst of the chaos he is imperturbable. Olympian. Then, as though he has completed his study or has suddenly lost interest, he vanishes. It is so astonishing to witness an officer stopping in the middle of a charge and staring at his feet that, for a moment, Édouard forgets his pain. Something strange is going on. That Édouard should wind up with a broken leg is strange enough; he has come through the war until now without so much as a scratch, so there is something odd about finding himself sprawled on the ground with one leg smashed to a pulp, but this is war, and for a man to be injured is in the nature of things. But for an officer to stop amid the hail of shells and stare down at his feet . . .

Péricourt relaxes and allows himself to fall back, tries to catch his breath, his hands clasped around his knee above the makeshift tourniquet. Some minutes later, curiosity gets the better of him and he arches himself again and stares toward the spot where Lieutenant Pradelle was standing moments earlier . . . Nothing. The officer has disappeared. The front line has moved forward, the explosions are now farther away. Édouard could dismiss the thought, concentrate on his injury. He might, for example, consider whether it is better to wait for help to come to him or to try to make it back to his own lines; instead, he lies there, his body arched like a fish out of water, still staring at the spot.

Finally, he comes to a decision. Now the difficult work begins. Still lying on his back, he heaves himself up on his elbows and awkwardly begins to crawl. His right leg now useless, he inches backward using all the strength in his forearms, his left foot providing traction, dragging his other limb through the mud like a dead thing. Every yard requires a grueling effort. And Péricourt does not quite understand his actions, he would be incapable of explaining, but for the fact that there is something disturbing about Lieutenant Pradelle. No one in the unit can stand him. Pradelle is living confirmation of the old cliché that the real threat to a soldier is not the enemy, but his commanding officer.

Though Édouard is not sufficiently politicized to argue that it is the nature of the system, his thoughts tend in that direction.

Abruptly, he is stopped dead. Hardly has he crawled twenty-five feet when a shell of unimaginable caliber explodes, pinning him to the ground. Perhaps being so close to the ground amplifies the blast. Péricourt's whole body immediately stiffens; even his right leg cannot resist the impulse. He looks like an epileptic in the throes of a fit. He is still staring at the place where Pradelle was standing moments before when a vast spray of earth shoots up, a powerful, violent wave that curls into the air. It seems so close that Édouard is terrified of being buried alive, but it falls back with a horrible thud, a muffled sound like an ogre's sigh. The exploding shells, the whistling bullets, the flares blossoming in the sky are as nothing compared to this wall of earth crumpling all around. He squeezes his eyes shut, paralyzed by fear, the ground beneath him shudders. He curls into a ball and holds his breath. When finally he dares to reemerge and realizes he is still alive, it seems like a miracle.

The wall of earth has disappeared. Immediately, with a surge of strength he cannot explain, he sets off again, scrambling like a rat in the trenches, crawling on his back, drawn inexorably to the place he has been staring at. All of a sudden he realizes that he has reached the spot where the wall of earth collapsed and sees a glittering shard of steel that pierces the powdery soil. A few inches at most. It is the tip of a bayonet. The significance is obvious. There is a soldier buried underneath.

Péricourt has heard tales of soldiers being buried alive, but it is not something he has ever personally witnessed. In the units he fought with, there were sappers with picks and shovels ready to dig out men who found themselves in that terrible position. They always arrived too late and when they were dragged out, the soldiers' faces were blue, their eyes bulging. The thought of Pradelle flickers for a moment through Édouard's mind, but he dismisses it.

He has to act fast.

He rolls over onto his belly and howls in pain as the ragged wound in his leg gapes open and is pressed into the stony ground. His hoarse scream has scarcely died as he feverishly scratches at the muddy ground, his hands hooked into claws. Tools that are pitifully inadequate if the buried man is already struggling for air, something Édouard soon realizes. How deeply is the soldier buried? If only he had something he could use to dig with. Péricourt glances to his right. His eye falls on the two corpses; there is nothing else, nothing he might use as a tool, nothing. The only solution is somehow to detach the bayonet and use it to dig, but that will take hours. He thinks he can hear the man screaming. But even if the man were not buried too deeply, it would be impossible to hear him screaming over the thunderous roar of battle—it is merely a figment of Édouard's imagination, his mind is racing, he knows that time is of the essence. If those buried alive are not dug out quickly, they come out dead. As he scrambles with his fingernails at the dirt either side of the bayonet, he wonders if he knows this man; he mentally conjures up the names, the faces of the men in his unit. Given the circumstances, it seems incongruous: he wants to save his comrade, he wants it to be someone he knows, someone he likes. This thought helps him work more quickly. He glances left and right, desperately searching for help of some kind, but nothing comes, his fingers ache. He has managed to dig out a hole about four inches on either side, but when he tries to extract the bayonet, it does not move at all, it is as well rooted as a healthy tooth, he feels discouraged. How long has he been working, two minutes, three? The guy is probably already dead. His shoulders begin to hurt because of his awkward position. He cannot carry on much longer, he feels a creeping doubt, a mounting weariness, his movements become slower, his breathing more labored, his biceps cramp, he pounds the earth with his fists. Suddenly, he is sure he feels it move! He begins to weep, great wrenching sobs, he grabs the steel shaft with both hands and tugs with all his might, wiping away the tears blurring his vision with the back of his hand, the work now suddenly effortless, he stops tugging and returns to digging, then plunges his hand into the hole and tries to extract the bayonet. He lets out a howl of victory as it comes loose. He pulls it out and, for a brief instant, he stares at it in disbelief, as though this is the first time he has seen such a thing, then angrily plants it in the soil, screaming and roaring, stabbing at the earth. Using the blunt edge, he carves a wide circle; then, turning the blade so it is horizontal, he hacks away at the dirt, sweeping it aside with his free hand. How long does it take? The pain in his right leg is excruciating now. But finally he sees something, he reaches down and feels a patch of fabric, a button; he burrows like a lunatic, like a hunting dog, he reaches down again and feels a uniform jacket, he is using both hands now, both arms, the wave of earth clearly collapsed into some sort of shell crater, his fingertips brush against things he does not recognize. Then he feels the polished surface of a helmet, he follows the curve, and just beneath he finds his buried comrade. "Hey!" Édouard is still sobbing, still shouting even as his arms whirl, propelled by some unknown force, churning away at the muddy soil. Finally the soldier's face appears less than a foot away. He looks like he is sleeping. Édouard recognizes him—what was his name again? He is dead. The realization is so devastating that Édouard Péricourt stops and stares down at his fallen comrade, and in that moment, he feels as though he, too, is dead, that what he is contemplating is his own death, and the pain of it is vast, overwhelming . . .

Still sobbing, he digs out the body, moving quickly now: there are the shoulders, the torso, the waist. Lying next to the face of the dead soldier is the head of a horse. It seems curious that they should have been buried together, thinks Édouard, face-to-face. Through his tears, he cannot help but imagine sketching the scene. The work would be easier if he could stand up or shift position, but even so he carries on, talking aloud, blubbering like a child and babbling inanities—"Don't worry, pal"—as though the man can hear him. He wants to huddle up against him and finds himself muttering things he would be ashamed to say if they were overheard, because deep down it is his own death he is mourning. He is weeping for the fear he can now finally admit he has felt for the past two years, the terrible dread that one day he would be the dead comrade of a soldier who was merely wounded. The war is ending. These tears for his comrade he sheds for his own childhood, his own life. He has been lucky. Crippled for the rest of his days, dragging his right leg behind him. But so what? He is alive. With large, sweeping gestures he finally digs out the body.

The name comes back to him: Maillard. The man's first name, he never knew: he was always Maillard.

With it comes a doubt. He brings his face close to Albert's, longing to hush the world that is exploding all around so he can listen because he cannot help but wonder: is he really dead? From his position sprawled next to him, it is not easy, but he slaps the man's face and watches as Maillard's head follows the movement without flinching; it means nothing, and it is a terrible idea for Édouard to imagine that the soldier is not completely dead, an idea that will only cause him more pain, but there it is. Now that there is a doubt, he has no choice but to make sure, and for us who are watching, it is a terrible thing to witness. We want to scream, "Let it go, you did your best," to take his hands, grip them tightly so that he will stop moving, stop trembling, to say the sort of things one might say to a child having a tantrum, to hold him until his tears run dry. To comfort him, in a word. But there is no one, not you, not me, to show Édouard the way, and from somewhere in the depths of his mind, a notion develops that perhaps Maillard is not really dead. Édouard saw it happen once, or heard the story from someone who did, it is a myth of the front lines, one no one ever actually witnesses, the story of a soldier everyone thought was dead who came back to life, whose heart began to beat again.

While he is thinking this, and in spite of the agonizing pain, Édouard manages to stand on his good leg. He sees his right leg, trailing uselessly behind, but sees it through a mist of fear mingled with exhaustion, pain, and despair.

He gathers his strength.

For a fleeting second he manages to stand on one leg like a heron; balancing precariously, he glances around then, taking a quick, deep breath, he lets his full weight fall onto Albert's chest.

There is an ominous crack of crushed and breaking ribs. Édouard hears a groan. Beneath him, the ground shifts and he slips down, as though falling off a chair, but it is not the earth rising up. It is Albert turning over, spewing his guts and coughing. Édouard cannot believe his eyes, he feels tears welling up again. You have to admit, Édouard has the luck of the devil. Albert carries on vomiting, and Édouard cheerfully pats him on the back, laughing and crying at the same time. There he sits on the ravaged battlefield beside a horse's severed head, one leg bent backward and bleeding, feeling he might pass out from exhaustion, while next to him this man who has returned from the dead is throwing up . . .

Even for the end of the war, it was curious scene. An arresting image. But it was not the last. As Albert Maillard slowly regains consciousness, spluttering hoarsely as he rolls onto his side, Édouard, his body ramrod straight, is hurling abuse at the heavens as though smoking a stick of dynamite.

It is at this point that a sliver of shrapnel as big as a soup plate comes hurtling toward him. A thick shard and moving at a dizzying speed.

The gods, it would appear, have answered him.

4

The two men came to in very different ways.

Albert, having returned from the dead and spewed his guts, gradually became aware of a sky streaked with shells, a clear sign that he had come back to the real world. He could not know it yet, but the charge initiated and led by Lieutenant Pradelle was already almost over. In the end, Hill 113 had been easily captured. After a brief but forceful resistance, the enemy had surrendered and been taken prisoner. From beginning to end, the operation had been a formality that left thirty-eight men dead, twenty-seven wounded, and two missing in action (the Boches were not included in these calculations). In short, an excellent result.

When the stretcher bearers found him on the battlefield, Albert was cradling Édouard Péricourt's head in his lap and singing softly, in a state his rescuers described as "delusional." Every one of his ribs was fractured, cracked, or broken, but his lungs were undamaged. He was in terrible pain, which, all in all, was a good sign, a sign that he was alive. He was not, however, in the greatest health, and was forced to postpone thinking about the issues raised by his situation.

By what astonishing miracle, by the grace of what higher power, by what improbable chance was it that his heart had stopped beating only a few short seconds before Soldat Péricourt attempted his highly individual method of resuscitation? All Albert could say for certain was that the engine had started up again—stuttering and jolting, and with a few backfires—and that the essentials were intact.

Having bandaged him up securely, the doctors announced that the limits of their skills ended there and consigned him to an enormous general ward where some soldiers lay dying, others were gravely wounded, a handful had been crippled in some way, and the able-bodied played cards, peering through their bandages.

Thanks to the taking of Hill 113, the field hospital, which had stood almost idle for weeks while waiting for the armistice, geared up for action again, but, since casualties of the offensive had not been too numerous, doctors could work at the sort of unhurried pace they had four years earlier. A period when nurses could take time to attend to a man dying of thirst. When doctors did not have to give up treating soldiers long before they were indeed dead. When surgeons who had not slept for three days were no longer writhing with cramps from hours spent hacking through femurs, tibias, and humeri.

As soon as he was brought in, Édouard had undergone two rudimentary procedures. His right leg had been fractured in several places and suffered ruptured ligaments and tendons; he would limp for the rest of his life. The most serious operation consisted of exploring his facial wounds to remove foreign bodies (as far as a front-line field hospital was equipped to do so). They had vaccinated him, cleared his airway, taken steps to deal with the risk of gas gangrene, debrided the wounds to prevent them from becoming infected; the rest—which is to say the most essential treatment—they would have to leave to a better-equipped hospital in the civilian zone, and only then—assuming the patient did not die—could he be sent to a specialist facility.

An urgent transfer was ordered for Édouard, and in the meantime Albert—whose tale had been retold and embellished all over the hospital—was allowed to remain at his comrade's bedside. Fortunately, it had been possible to place the patient in a private room in the south wing of the building, where he was not surrounded by the groans of the dying.

Powerless to help, Albert watched Édouard recover consciousness by gradual stages, though he scarcely understood the process. Sometimes he noticed a gesture, a facial expression that he thought he could interpret, but they were so fleeting they had vanished before Albert could find a word to describe them. As I have said, Albert never had been particularly bright, and the ordeal he had been through had not helped matters.

Édouard was in agony from his wounds; he screamed and thrashed so wildly that he had to be strapped to the bed. It was then that Albert realized that the choice of a room in the empty wing had not been for Édouard's comfort, but so that other patients would not have to endure his constant screams. Four years of war were not enough; Albert's naivety was still boundless.

He spent hours sitting, wringing his hands, listening to his comrade's cries, a litany of moans and howls and wracking sobs that spanned the whole gamut of what a man may express when he finds himself at the very limit of pain and madness.

From a man incapable of holding a conversation with his assistant manager at the bank, Albert was transformed into a passionate advocate, pleading that the hunk of shrapnel lodged in his comrade was no splinter wound. By his own standards, he acquitted himself well and felt he had been effective. In fact he had simply been pathetic, though that proved to be sufficient. Since there was nothing more to be done while they waited for a transfer, the young surgeon agreed to prescribe morphine for Édouard's pain on condition that he was given the minimum dose and gradually weaned off it. It was unimaginable that Édouard would be here for much longer. His condition required prompt specialist care. His transfer was classed "urgent."

Thanks to the morphine, Édouard's slow recovery was less brutal. His first conscious sensations were jumbled: cold, heat, faint sounds he could not make out, voices he did not recognize; more difficult were the shooting pains through his chest and upper torso that seemed to keep time with his heartbeat, an unending series of waves that became unbearable as the morphine wore off. His head was like a resonance chamber; each wave ended with a muffled thud like the sound of a ship's mooring buoys colliding with the jetty as it docks.

He could feel his leg, too. The right leg that had been shattered by a stray bullet and which he had further damaged when he went to save Albert Maillard. But this pain, too, was tempered by the drugs. He was vaguely aware that he still had his leg, which was true. Granted it was smashed to a pulp, but it was still capable (at least partially) of performing the tasks expected of a leg returning from the Great War. For a long time, his awareness of what was going on was murky, drowned out by a flood of images. Édouard was living in a confused dream world where, in no particular order, he was assailed by everything he had seen, heard, and felt.

His brain conflated reality, sketches, paintings as though his life were no more than one more mixed-media masterpiece in the museum of his imagination. The evanescent beauty of a Botticelli and the palpable fear of Caravaggio's *Boy Bitten by a Lizard* were succeeded by the face of a street merchant on the rue des Martyrs, whose solemn expression had always attracted Édouard's attention, and—who knows why?—by his father's detachable collar, the one with the slightly pinkish tinge.

Out of the grayness of everyday objects, of characters from Bosch, of nudes and savage warriors, came the recurring image of Courbet's *L'Origine du monde*. He had only ever seen the painting once, a reproduction secretly glimpsed at the home of a family friend. It was a long time ago, long before the war, he would have been eleven, perhaps twelve. He would still have been studying at the Institution Sainte-Clotilde at the time. Sainte Clotilde, daughter of Chilperic and Carétène, an out-and-out slut . . . Édouard had sketched her in every possible position: being mounted by her uncle Godegisel, taken doggy-style by King Clovis and, sometime around AD 493, giving the king of Burgundy a blow job with the bishop of Reims taking her from behind. This was what led to his third—and final—suspension.

Everyone agreed it was extraordinarily detailed; indeed, they wondered, given his age, where he had come by the models. There were individual details . . . His father, who considered art to be a degenerate depravity, remained tight lipped. In fact, long before he started school at Sainte-Clotilde, things had not been going well for Édouard. Especially when it came to his father. Édouard had always expressed himself through drawing. In every school he attended, all his teachers would sooner or later find a caricature a yard high scrawled on the blackboard. It might just as well have been signed; it would be classic Péricourt. Over the years, his inspiration, which had focused on the schools in which his father, using his connections, managed to have him enrolled, shifted to encompass other themes, what one might call his "religious period," culminating in the scene in which the music teacher, Mlle Juste, in the guise of a voluptuous Judith, held up the severed head of a Holofernes who was the spitting image of M. Lapurce, the math teacher. Everyone had known they were doing it. Until their final parting, as depicted in this splendid decapitation, Édouard had kept a visual record, a series of sometimes shocking tableaux sketched on blackboards, walls, and scraps of paper that even the teachers, when they confiscated them, passed around among themselves before handing them to the principal. Anyone watching the diffident mathematics teacher loping across the playground could not but see him as a lecherous, preposterously well-endowed satyr. Édouard, at the time, was eight years old. This biblical scene earned him an interview in the principal's office. The conversation did little to improve matters. When the principal, holding the sketch at arm's length, made some outraged reference to Judith, Édouard felt the need to point out that, although in the drawing the young woman was holding the severed head by the hair, it was resting on a salver, consequently she might well be Salome rather than Judith and the head therefore of John the Baptist rather than Holofernes. Édouard was something of a pedant, the sort of know-it-all who could be profoundly irritating.

Unquestionably his greatest inspiration, what one might call his "efflorescent" period, began when he learned to masturbate, at which point his work teemed with imagination and inventiveness. His paintings now presented all of the staff—including the servants, something that offended the dignity of the teachers at the school—in epic panoramas where the sheer number of characters made possible the most remarkable sexual configurations. Everyone laughed, although confronted with this erotic imaginative world, they could not help but reconsider their own lives, and the smartest saw in it a troubling predilection for—how to put it?—questionable relations.

Édouard was forever drawing. People said he was wicked because he liked to shock—and he invariably succeeded—but the sodomy of Sainte-Clotilde by the bishop of Reims deeply upset the school authorities. And his parents. Outraged them. His father, as always, offered to pay whatever was necessary to avoid a scandal. Nothing would persuade the school to acquiesce. On the subject of sodomy, they remained obdurate. The whole world was against Édouard. Excepting a few friends, particularly those who found his drawings titillating, and his sister, Madeleine. She found the whole thing hilarious—not the bishop of Reims shafting Sainte Clotilde, that was ancient history, but imagining the expression on the face of Father Hubert, the principal . . . She had attended the girls' school at Sainte-Clotilde, she knew exactly what it was like. Madeleine would laugh at Édouard's nerve, his insolent remarks. She loved to tousle his hair—though only when he let her, because, though several years her junior, he was so tall . . . He would bend down and she would bury her fingers in his thick curls, and tickle him so hard that he would eventually beg for mercy. It would not have done for their father to catch them doing this.

To get back to Édouard. As far as his education was concerned, everything turned out for the best because his parents were very wealthy, but it was not an easy road. Even before the war, M. Péricourt had been earning pots of money, he was one of those men who flourish in a crisis, as though such things are intended for them. No one ever spoke of Maman's fortune, there was no need; one might as well ask how long has the sea been salty. But since Maman died of heart trouble at a young age, Papa was left solely in charge. Since his time was wholly taken up by his business interests, he delegated the education of his children to institutions, teachers, and private tutors. To servants. Édouard, everyone agreed, had been gifted with an uncommon intelligence, an extraordinary natural talent for drawing—even his teachers at the Beaux-Arts were astonished—and the luck of the devil. What more could he have hoped for? This, perhaps, was why he had always been so provocative. Knowing one had nothing to lose, that everything can be worked out, leads to a lack of inhibitions. You can say what you like, however you like. The fact is that M. Péricourt rescued his son from every situation, but he did so for selfish reasons, because he refused to allow his name to be tarnished. And this was no easy matter since Édouard was deeply rebellious; he relished causing a scandal. Édouard took advantage of his father's lack of interest in his future to enroll at the École des Beaux-Arts. A loving and protective sister, a powerful reactionary father who habitually rejected him, an undeniable talent, Édouard had just about everything he might need to succeed. Of course, we know that things are not going to be quite so straightforward, but as the war is coming to an end, this is how it seems. Apart from his leg. Which is horribly mutilated.

Of such things, of course, as he checks and changes Édouard's linen, Albert knows nothing. The only thing he knows for certain is that, whatever it might have been, Édouard Péricourt's trajectory changed radically on November 2, 1918.

And that his shattered leg will soon be the least of his worries.

Albert spent all his waking hours by his friend's bedside, working as a voluntary assistant for the nurses. The nurses took charge of all care intended to limit the risk of infection, his feeding (he was fed through a tube with a concoction of milk whisked with eggs or gravy); Albert did everything else. When he was not wiping Édouard's forehead with a damp cloth, or helping him to drink with the precision of a jeweler, he would change the draw sheets. At such times he would have to hold his nose, turn, and look away, reminding himself that his friend's future probably depended on such disgusting duties.

His attention was wholly occupied by these two tasks: trying vainly to find a way to breathe without moving his ribs, and keeping his comrade company while they waited for the ambulance.

Over and over, he saw Édouard Péricourt half-sprawled on top of him when he returned from the dead. But what haunted him was the image of that bastard Pradelle. He spent countless hours imagining what he would do when next he ran into the lieutenant. He could still see Pradelle on the battlefield, charging toward him, could feel the almost physical way the shell crater had sucked him in. But it was still difficult for him to think for long periods of time, as though his brain had not yet managed to return to its normal speed.

But shortly after he returned to the land of the living, a phrase occurred to him: someone had tried to kill him.

It sounded bizarre, but not unreasonable; after all a great war was merely attempted murder on a continental scale. The difference in his case was that he had been personally targeted. Sometimes when he looked at Édouard Péricourt, Albert found himself reliving the moment when the air grew thin, and he seethed with rage. Two days later, he, too, was ready to commit murder. After four years fighting a war, it was high time.

When he was alone, he thought about Cécile. She had grown more distant, and he missed her terribly. The force of events had thrust Albert into a different life, but since no life was possible unless Cécile was part of it, he clung to his memories, gazed at her photograph, enumerated her countless flawless features, eyebrows, nose, lips all the way down to her chin, how was it possible that something as perfect as Cécile's mouth could exist? It was being taken from him. One day, someone would come and take it. Or she would leave. Would realize that Albert was not worth much, whereas she, her shoulders, just her shoulders . . . It killed him to think about it; he spent inconsolable hours. All this for that, he thought. Then he would take out a sheet of paper and try to write her a letter. Should he tell her everything, she who wanted to hear nothing more about the war, who wanted it to be over and done with?

When he was not thinking about what he should write to Cécile, or to his mother (first Cécile, then his mother if he had the time), when he was not working as a volunteer nurse, Albert brooded.

He often thought, for example, about the horse's head he had discovered buried beside him. Curiously, as time passed, it no longer seemed so monstrous. Even the stench of the putrid air that had belched from its mouth no longer seemed foul and fetid. While the image of Pradelle standing on the lip of the shell crater still had the exactness of a photograph, the image of the horse's head, which he would have liked to remember, gradually melted, the details blurred. Despite his efforts, the picture faded, and Albert felt a sense of loss he found obscurely worrying. The war was drawing to a close. This was not the time for reckonings, but the terrible moment when one must survey the extent of the damage. Like those men who had spent four years crouched under a hail of bullets and would, literally, never stand tall again but would go through life with their shoulders bowed by an invisible weight, Albert was convinced that one thing at least he would never recover: serenity. For several months, since he was first wounded at the Somme, since the interminable nights spent working as a stretcher bearer, scuttling around, terrified of being hit by a stray bullet, looking for wounded men on the battlefield, and even more since he had returned from among the dead, he knew that he would forever be inhabited by an indefinable, pulsing, almost palpable fear. This had been made worse by the devastating effects of having been buried alive. Some part of him was still buried in the earth, his body had emerged, but some captive, terrified part of his brain had remained trapped below. The experience was seared into his flesh, his actions, his eyes. Panicked at the thought of leaving the room, he was alert to the faintest footstep, put his head around a door before fully pushing it open, hugged the walls as he walked, often imagining a presence shadowing him, studied the features of those he talked to and was careful always to be close to an exit just in case. Whatever the circumstances, his eyes were perpetually shifting this way and that. When sitting by Édouard's bed, he sometimes felt the need to get up and look out of the window because he found the room oppressive. He was permanently on the alert; anything and everything made him suspicious. Serenity, he knew, was gone forever. He had to learn to live with this animal fear, just as a man who inadvertently discovers he feels jealous realizes he must reconcile himself to this new disease. This saddened him.

The morphine did its work. Though the doses would be regularly reduced, for the moment Édouard was allowed one ampoule every five to six hours. He was no longer writhing in pain; his room no longer echoed with monotonous whimpers punctuated by blood-curdling howls. When not dozing, he seemed to float, but he had to remain strapped to the bed in case he tried to scratch his open wounds.

Albert and Édouard had never been friends; they had seen each other, run into each other, said hello, smiled perhaps, but nothing more. Édouard Péricourt, a comrade like so many others, close yet terrifyingly anonymous. Now, to Albert, he is a puzzle, an enigma.

The day after their arrival at the field hospital, he noticed that Édouard's belongings had been put at the bottom of a wardrobe whose doors creaked and swung open at the slightest breeze. Anyone could come in and steal them. Albert decided to put them somewhere safe. Picking up the burlap sack that contained Édouard's personal effects, Albert realized that the reason he had not done so before was because he would not have been able to resist the temptation to rummage. He had not done so out of respect for Édouard; that was one reason. But there was a second reason. It reminded him of his mother. Mme Maillard was the kind of mother who rummaged. Albert had spent his childhood coming up with ingenious ruses to hide his—obviously trifling—secrets, which Mme Maillard would eventually discover and wave under his nose, while unleashing a torrent of criticism. Whether it was a photograph of a cyclist clipped from *L'Illustration*, three lines of a poem copied from an anthology, or four marbles and a taw won from Soubise during playtime, Mme Maillard considered every secret a betrayal. On days when she was particularly inspired, she might brandish a postcard of the "Tree of the Rocks in Tonkin" given to Albert by a neighbor and launch into an impassioned diatribe that ranged from the ingratitude of children in general to the particular selfishness of her own child and her fervent desire to join her dead husband as soon as possible so that she might finally get some peace; you can guess the rest.

These painful reminders faded when, having opened Édouard's knapsack, Albert almost immediately came on a battered hardcover notebook closed with an elastic band that contained nothing but sketches in blue pencil. Albert sat there cross-legged on the floor facing the creaking wardrobe, hypnotized by these drawings, some clearly hastily sketched, others carefully reworked with dark shadows of cross-hatching as dense as torrential rain. All of the pictures—a hundred or so—had been sketched here at the front, in the trenches. They depicted everyday scenes: soldiers writing letters, lighting pipes, laughing at a joke, preparing for an assault, eating, drinking, things like that. From a single stroke one could make out the weary profile of a young soldier, three lines and the whole face emerged, the sunken eyes, the haggard features—it was gut wrenching. From almost nothing, a line that seemed effortless, casual, Édouard captured everything, the fear and the pity, the monotony, the despair, the exhaustion; the sketchbook was like a manifesto of fate.

Leafing through it, Albert felt sick at heart. Because in these pages there were no pictures of the dead. Nor the wounded. There was not a single corpse. Only the living. And that made it more terrible, because every drawing seemed to scream the same message: these men will die.

He packed away Édouard's belongings, overcome with dismay.

5

On the subject of morphine the young doctor was resolute: things could not carry on like this, people become dependent on such drugs, which can lead to terrible problems, you have to understand we simply cannot carry on, we have to stop. From the day after the operation, he began to reduce the dosage.

As he resurfaced and gradually became more conscious, Édouard found himself in terrible pain, and Albert began to worry about the transfer to Paris, of which there was still no sign.

When questioned, the young doctor threw up his hands helplessly; his voice dropped to a whisper.

"Thirty-six hours he's been here . . . I don't understand, he should have been transferred already. Obviously, the ambulances are overstretched. But it's really not good for him to be here . . ."

Worry was etched into his face. From that moment, a panicked Albert focused himself on a single goal: having his comrade transferred as soon as possible.

He did everything in his power. He set about questioning the nurses, who, though the hospital was quieter now, still scuttled around the corridors like mice in an attic. This tactic was useless: this was a military hospital, which meant it was almost impossible to find out anything, including the names of those who were in charge.

Every hour, he would come back to Édouard's bedside and sit with him until he fell asleep. The rest of the time he spent lurking around the offices and the corridors that led to the main buildings. He even went to the general headquarters.

Coming back from one such mission, he ran into two soldiers cooling their heels in the corridor. From their immaculate uniforms, their freshly shaved faces, and the halo of confidence that surrounded them, it was clear they were from HQ. The first handed him a sealed envelope while the second, perhaps to give himself an air of authority, laid a hand on his pistol. Such anxious reflexes, Albert thought, were not entirely unfounded.

"We did go in," the first soldier said almost apologetically, jerking his thumb toward the door. "But we decided it was better to wait out here. The stench . . ."

Albert went into the room, dropping the letter he had been opening, and rushed to Édouard's bed. For the first time since being admitted, the young man's eyes were open. He had been propped up on pillows—by a passing nurse, probably. His hands, still strapped to the bed, were covered by the sheet. He nodded his head slowly, uttering guttural sounds that trailed off into gurgles. Put this way, it does not sound like much of an improvement, but until now Albert has only seen his comrade's body racked by spasms and terrible howls or lifeless almost to the point of coma. What he now saw was infinitely better.

It was difficult to know what mysterious current had passed between the two men in the days while Albert sat dozing in a chair, but as soon as Albert laid his hand on the bed, Édouard jerked frantically at his restraints and managed to grab him by the wrist and hold on like a drowning man. What precisely this gesture meant, no one is in any position to say. In it were condensed all the fears and all the hopes, all the pleas and all the questions of a twenty-three-year-old man who is wounded, unsure of the seriousness of his condition, and suffering so greatly he cannot locate the source of his pain.

"Finally decided to wake up, then, friend," Albert said, attempting to put the greatest possible enthusiasm into his words.

A voice from behind made him start.

"We have to head back . . ."

Albert turned.

The soldier held out the letter he had picked up off the floor.

He spent almost four hours sitting on a chair waiting. Time enough to go through all the possible reasons why a humble solider like himself might be summoned to the office of Général Morieux. Aside from being decorated for acts of bravery regarding Édouard's condition, it is anyone's guess.

The result of these hours of cogitation melted away in an instant when, at the far end of the hallway, he saw the tall, thin figure of Lieutenant Pradelle appear. The officer stared him in the eye and swaggered toward him. Albert felt the lump in his throat drop into his belly and was overcome by an urge to retch he barely managed to suppress. Except for the speed, this was the same swagger that had pushed him into the shell crater. The lieutenant tore his eyes away when he drew alongside Albert, pivoted on his heels, knocked on the *général's* door, and disappeared inside.

It would have taken Albert some time to digest this information, but time he did not have. The door reopened, he heard his name barked, and, faltering, he stepped into the holy of holies, which smelled of brandy and cigars; perhaps they were celebrating the coming victory early.

Général Morieux seems terribly old and looks like all those old men who have sent generations of their sons and grandsons to their death. Combine the portraits of Joffre and Pétain with those of Nivelle, Gallieni, and Ludendorff[3] and you have Général Morieux: walrus whiskers, rheumy eyes sunken in his ruddy face, deep wrinkles, and an innate sense of his own importance.

Albert stands, frozen. Impossible to say whether the *général* is alert or half-asleep. There is an air of Kutuzov[4] about him. Sitting behind his desk, he is poring over his papers. Standing facing Albert, with his back to the *général*, Lieutenant Pradelle does not move a muscle as he glares at him, looking him up and down. Feet apart, hands behind his back as though on inspection, he is rocking gently on his heels. Albert gets the message and stands to attention. He holds himself stiffly, arching his back until it aches. The silence is heavy. Finally the walrus lifts his head. Albert feels obliged to throw his shoulders back even further. If he carries on, he'll end up bent double like a circus acrobat. Under normal circumstances, the *général* should put him at ease from this uncomfortable position, but no, he stares at Albert, clears his throat, glances down at a document.

"Soldat Maillard," he enunciates slowly.

Albert should say "Yes, sir" or something of the kind, but slow though the *général* is, he is too fast for Albert.

"I have in front of me a report . . . ," he continues. "During an action carried out by your unit on November 2, you deliberately attempted to shirk your duty."

This is something Albert has not expected. He has imagined various scenarios, but not this. The *général* reads aloud:

"You 'took shelter in a shell crater in a cowardly attempt to avoid your obligations' . . . Thirty-eight of your valiant comrades gave their lives during that attack. For their country. But you are a scoundrel, Soldat Maillard. In fact, in my personal opinion you are a bastard!"

Albert's heart is so heavy he could almost weep. Weeks and weeks he has been waiting for this war to be over; so this is how it will end . . .

Général Morieux is still staring at him. He finds this cowardice utterly deplorable. Furious at the moral degeneracy this pathetic soldier represents, he concludes:

"But desertion does not fall within my remit. I deal with war. You will be dealt with by the military tribunal, Soldat Maillard, the court-martial."

Albert is no longer at attention. His hands by his sides begin to tremble. This means death. Everyone has heard of cases of desertion, of fellows shooting themselves to get away from the front lines. It is nothing new. There was much talk of courts-martial, especially in 1917, when Pétain was called in to put the shambles in order. Many were sent to their deaths; on the matter of desertion, the tribunal made no concessions. Very few faced the firing squad, but all of them were executed. And quickly. Speed in execution is part of the execution. Albert has three days left to live. At best.

He needs to explain; this is a misunderstanding. But Pradelle's expression as he stares him down leaves no room for a misunderstanding.

This is the second time he has sent Albert to his death. With luck—a lot of luck—a man might survive being buried alive, but not a court-martial . . .

Sweat trickles between his shoulder blades, down his forehead, blurring his vision. His trembling gets steadily worse, and slowly, as he stands there, he starts to piss himself. The *général* and the lieutenant watch as the stain spreads from his zipper toward his boots.

Say something. Albert racks his brain but can think of nothing. The *général* goes on the offensive again; going on the offensive is something he knows about, being a *général*.

"Lieutenant d'Aulnay-Pradelle is positive. He personally saw you throwing yourself into the mud. Is that not so, Pradelle?"

"Absolutely, sir. With my own eyes, sir."

"Well, Soldat Maillard?"

It is not for want of searching for words that Albert cannot utter a single one. Eventually he mutters:

"It wasn't like that . . ."

The *général* frowns.

"What do you mean 'wasn't like that'? Did you fight with your unit to the end?"

"Er . . . no."

He should say "No, sir," but in such situations it is difficult to think of everything.

"You did not take part in the assault," the *général* roars, pounding the desk with his fist, "because you were in a shell crater, am I correct?"

It is difficult to explain. All the more so since the *général* pounds the desk again.

"Yes or no, Soldat Maillard?"

The lamp, the inkwell, the desk blotter hover in the air. Pradelle is staring at Albert's boots, where piss has spread to stain the threadbare carpet.

"Yes, but . . ."

"Of course I'm right! Lieutenant Pradelle saw you, did you not, Pradelle?"

"With my own eyes, sir."

"But your cowardice was not rewarded, was it, Soldat Maillard?"

The *général* wags a vengeful finger.

"In fact your cowardice almost cost you your life . . . And a good thing too!"

In life, there are certain moments of truth. Granted, they are rare. In the life of Albert Maillard, the next second will be one such moment. It hangs on three words that encapsulate all his faith.

"It's not fair."

Had he uttered some grandiloquent phrase, some attempt at self-justification, Général Morieux would have dismissed it with a petulant wave, but this . . . The *général* glances down. Seems to be thinking. Pradelle is now staring at the bead of sweat poised on the end of Albert's nose, which, given he is standing to attention, he cannot wipe away. The droplet dangles miserably, wavers, grows longer, but still it does not fall. Albert snuffles loudly. The droplet trembles but clings fast. But it is enough to rouse the *général* from his cogitation.

"Thing is, your service record is not bad . . . ," he says, giving a helpless shrug. "Can't get my head around it."

Something has just happened, but what?

"Camp de Mailly," the *général* reads aloud, "La Marne, mm-hmm . . ."

He is bent over his papers. Albert can see only the *général*'s white hair, balding to reveal his pink pate.

"Wounded at the Somme . . . mm-hmm . . . And again at the Battle of the Aisne! Stretcher bearer . . . mm-hmm . . ."

He shakes his head like a half-drowned parrot.

The droplet on the end of Albert's nose finally decides to fall, and as it bursts on the carpet, it triggers a revelation: this is all horseshit.

The *général* is bluffing.

Albert's neurons survey the terrain, the report, the facts, the situation. When the *général* looks up at him, he knows, he understands; the response does not come as a surprise.

"I am prepared to take your service record into account, Maillard."

Albert sniffles. Pradelle is crestfallen. In filing a complaint with the *général*, he was trying his luck. If it worked, he would be rid of Albert Maillard, an embarrassing witness. But he made the wrong choice: at this stage of the war, no one is being shot. But Pradelle is a good loser. He bows his head and champs at the bit.

"You had a fine year in '17," the *général* carries on, "But now . . ." He shrugs again, saddened by the whole affair. It is obvious he thinks the world is going to hell in a handcart. For a military man, there is nothing worse than the end of a war. The *général* has done his best, cudgeled his brains, but he has to face the facts; though this is a flagrant case of desertion, it would be impossible to justify a firing squad a few days before the armistice. It is simply not done. No one would support his decision. Indeed, it would be seen as counterproductive.

Albert's life hung by a thread: he will not be shot, because, this month, firing squads are *passé*.

"Thank you, sir," he babbles.

Morieux greets these words with stoic resignation. At any other time, to thank a *général* would almost be an insult, but these days . . .

The matter is settled. Morieux shoos them away with a disgruntled wave. Dismissed!

What has got into Albert? Who knows? He has come within a hair's breadth of facing the firing squad, but apparently that is not enough.

"I have a request I'd like to make, sir," he says.

"Really? Well go on, go on . . ."

Curiously, the *général* is pleased at the thought of this request. It means he is still useful. He raises a questioning eyebrow to encourage the soldier. He waits. Standing next to Albert, Pradelle stiffens and looks grave.

"I'd like to request an investigation, sir," Albert says.

"Oh, you would, would you? And what would be the subject of this investigation, dammit?"

Because much as he appreciates requests, the *général* has no time for investigations. He is a military man.

"Two soldiers, sir."

"And what's the problem with these soldiers?"

"They're dead, sir. And it would be good to know how they died."

Morieux knits his brow. He does not like suspicious deaths. In war, people want deaths that are clean, heroic, and conclusive, which is why, though the wounded are tolerated, no one really likes them.

"Hold your horses . . ." The *général*'s voice quavers. "First of all, who exactly are these men?"

"Soldat Gaston Grisonnier and Soldat Louis Thérieux, sir. People want to know how they died."

The objective "people" is a stroke of genius; it just came to him. Albert is more resourceful than he appears.

Morieux shoots Pradelle a questioning look.

"The two men reported missing in action on Hill 113, sir," snaps the lieutenant.

Albert is dumbfounded.

He saw them on the battlefield, they were dead, but very much present. He even rolled the old man over; he can still see the bullet wounds in his back.

"That's impossible . . ."

"Good God, man, the lieutenant here has just told you they are missing in action! . . . Isn't that so, Pradelle?"

"Missing In Action, sir. No question, sir."

"Horsefeathers," the old man snarls. "You're not going to come in here and create a ruckus over a couple of missing soldiers."

This is not a question, it is an order. He is livid.

"What is this damned foolishness?" he mutters to himself.

But he needs a little support.

"Well, Pradelle?"

He is calling him as witness.

"Absolutely, sir. We can't have people kicking up a stink over a couple of MIAs."

"You see!" the *général* barks, glaring at Albert.

Pradelle is staring at him, too. Is that a flicker of a smile he can see on the bastard's lips?

Albert gives up. All he wants now is for the war to end so he can go back to Paris. In one piece, if possible. Which thought brings him back to Édouard. He hardly takes the time to give the old fogey a cursory salute (he does not click his heels; he casually brings one finger to his temple like a laborer finishing his shift and heading home), then, avoiding the lieutenant's gaze, he takes to his heels, running through the hallways, seized by the sort of intuition parents have. He is out of breath and panting as he flings open the door of the room.

Édouard has not shifted, but he wakes when he hears Albert approach. He points weakly toward the window beside his bed. It's true the room reeks to high heaven. Albert opens the window a little. Édouard watches intently. "More," the injured man insists, his fingers signaling "a little more," or "a little less." Albert complies, opens the window a little wider and, by the time he realizes, it is too late. Having struggled to say something and found he could produce only a gurgling sound, Édouard needed to know. Now he can see his reflection in the windowpane.

The exploding shell ripped away his lower jaw; below his nose is a gaping void; his throat, his palate, his upper teeth are visible, beneath them is a pulp of crimson flesh and something deep within that must be his epiglottis. There is no tongue; his gullet is a red-raw hole . . .

Édouard Péricourt is twenty-three years old.

He blacks out.

6

The following morning at about 4:00 a.m., just as Albert loosened his restraints so he could change the sheets, Édouard tried to throw himself out of the window. But as he got out of bed, finding his right leg could no longer support his weight, he lost his balance and collapsed on the floor. By an immense effort of will he managed to get to his feet; he looked like a ghost. He lumbered heavily toward the window, eyes bulging from their sockets, arms outstretched, howling in grief and pain. Albert took him in his arms and stroked the back of his head, sobbing, too. Albert felt a maternal tenderness toward Édouard. He chattered away to fill the silence.

"Général Morieux is a stupid cunt," he would say. "I mean, he's a *général*. And he was happy to have me court-martialed. And Pradelle fucking standing there, the bastard . . ."

Albert talked and talked, but Édouard's eyes were so vacant that it was impossible to tell whether he understood what was being said. The reduction in the doses of morphine left him awake for longer and longer periods, meaning Albert did not have the time to try and get news of the transfer, which had still not arrived. When Édouard started to groan, he did not stop; his voice grew louder and louder until finally a nurse would come and give him another injection.

Early the following afternoon, having come back empty handed—it was impossible to find out whether the ambulance had been requested—he found Édouard screaming in terrible pain, his gaping throat red-raw and mottled here and there with oozing pus; the stench was increasingly unbearable.

Albert ran out of the room to the nurses station. No one. He shouted down the hallway, "Anyone here?" No one. He was running again; then suddenly he stopped, retraced his steps. Surely he wouldn't dare. Would he? He glanced left and right along the corridor, the howls of his comrade still ringing in his ears urged him on, he stepped into the room, he knew where everything was kept. He took the key from the right-hand drawer, opened the glass cabinet. A syringe, rubbing alcohol, a few ampoules of morphine. If he was caught, he would be finished: theft of military materials, he could see Général Morieux's ugly mug looming and behind him the baleful figure of Lieutenant Pradelle . . . Who would take care of Édouard, he wondered anxiously. But no one came. Albert emerged from the nurses station bathed in sweat, hugging the spoils of his raid. He did not know whether he was doing the right thing, but Édouard's pain was unbearable.

The first injection was an adventure in itself. Albert had often helped the nurses, but when it came to actually doing it . . . First the bedsheets, then the stink, now the injections . . . As if stopping a man from throwing himself out the window isn't enough, he thought as he prepared the syringe, wiping his ass, breathing his stench, giving his injections . . . what had he got himself into?

He had pushed a chair against the door to avoid any unexpected arrivals. It did not go too badly. Albert had carefully calculated the dose; it would tide Édouard over until the next injection from the nurse.

"Just give it a minute, you'll feel a lot better, you'll see."

And it was true, Édouard relaxed and fell asleep. Even while he was asleep, Albert kept talking to him. Kept brooding over the matter of the phantom transfer. He came to the conclusion that he would have to go to the source: the personnel office.

"I hate to do this when you're calm," he explained, "But I can't be sure that you'll be sensible . . ."

Reluctantly, he strapped Édouard to the bed and left.

Outside the room, hugging the walls, ever on the alert, he ran as fast as possible so that he would not be gone too long.

"Well, that's the best one I've heard all year!" the officer said.

His name was Grosjean. The personnel unit was a cramped office with a tiny window and shelves groaning under the weight of bulging files. Behind a desk piled high with documents, lists, reports, Caporal Grosjean looked overwhelmed.

He opened a huge ledger, ran a nicotine-stained finger down the columns, mumbling to himself:

"I tell you, the number of wounded we've had through here, you can't imagine . . ."

"I can."

"You what?"

"I can imagine."

Grosjean looked up from the register and stared at him. Albert realized he had made a mistake, tried to think of some way to make amends, but Grosjean had already gone back to his search.

"Shit . . . I recognize the name . . ."

"Obviously," Albert said.

"Of course, obviously, the point is where the fuck . . ."

Suddenly he yelped.

"Here we go!"

It was clear that he had won a great victory.

"Péricourt, Édouard! I knew it! I knew I'd seen it somewhere!"

He turned the book around toward Albert, the stubby index finger jabbing at the bottom of the page. He was determined to prove he had been right.

"So?" Albert was confused.

"So, your friend has been registered."

He emphasized the word "registered." From his lips it had a ring of triumph.

"You see, didn't I tell you I remembered the name? I'm not soft in the head just yet, damn it."

"So what?"

The guy squeezed his eyes closed with sheer pleasure. He opened them again.

"He was registered here" (he tapped the ledger with his finger). "Once that's done, we write out a transfer slip."

"And where does it go, this transfer slip?"

"The logistics unit. They're the ones who make the decisions about vehicles . . ."

Albert would have to go back to the logistics unit. He had already been there twice and they had no memo, no transfer slip, no document relating to Édouard Péricourt . . . it was enough to drive one mad. He checked his watch. He would have to leave it for now, he had to get back to Édouard, give him something to drink, the doctor had recommended that he drink a lot. He turned on his heel, then changed his mind. Shit . . . , he thought.

"So you the deliver the transfer slips yourself?"

"Yep," Grosjean said, "or someone comes to collect them, it depends."

"You don't remember who collected the slip for Péricourt?"

Albert already knew the answer.

"Affirmative. A lieutenant, I don't know his name."

"Tall, thin man . . ."

"Exactly."

". . . with blue eyes?"

"That's the one."

"The fucker . . ."

"I can't comment on that . . ."

"So, how long does it take to issue a new slip?"

"A duplicate, they call it."

"All right, a duplicate, how long does it take?"

Grosjean was in his element now. He pulled the inkwell toward him, picked up a pen, and waved it high.

"Consider it done."

* * *

The room reeked of rotting flesh. Édouard needed to be transferred quickly. Pradelle's strategy might just work. Scorched-earth policy. Albert had narrowly escaped being court-martialed, but for Édouard the cemetery was beginning to loom. A few more hours, and he would rot where he lay. Lieutenant Pradelle did not want any witnesses to his heroism.

Albert personally delivered the duplicate to the logistics unit.

Nothing before tomorrow, he was told.

The wait seemed interminable.

The young doctor had finished his stint at the hospital. No one knew who would replace him. There were other surgeons, other doctors who Albert did not know, one of whom popped in to visit and stayed only briefly, as though it were not worth his while.

"When is he being transferred?" he asked.

"It's being processed. There was a problem with the transfer slip. I mean, he had been registered, but . . ."

"When?" the doctor cut him short, "because the way things are going . . ."

"They said tomorrow . . ."

The doctor rolled his eyes. He had seen it all before. He nodded, he got the picture. "Well, I've got work to do . . ." He patted Albert's shoulder and turned to leave.

"And open a window, for God's sake," he said, "this place stinks!"

By dawn the following morning, Albert was camped outside the logistics unit. His chief fear was encountering Lieutenant Pradelle. The man was capable of anything. Albert simply needed to keep his head down. And get Édouard out of here as soon as possible.

"Today?" he said.

The man liked Albert. He thought it was great that he was taking care of his comrade. We see too many here who don't give a shit, only think about themselves, am I right? But no, he was sorry, not today. Tomorrow definitely.

"Do you know what time?"

The officer scanned his various lists.

"Thing is," he said without looking up, "the garbage collection—I'm sorry, friend, that's just what we call them around here—anyway, the ambulance should be here early afternoon."

"Absolutely, definitely?"

Albert clung to this hope—all right, tomorrow then—but he was angry with himself for being so slow, for not realizing earlier. Édouard would have been transferred by now if he had had a brighter friend.

Tomorrow.

Édouard no longer slept. Propped up on a pile of pillows Albert had filched from every other room, he rocked himself for hours, moaning pitifully.

"Are you in pain, is that it?" Albert would ask.

But Édouard never answered. Obviously.

The window was always half-open. Albert slept in the chair in front of it, his feet propped up on another chair. He smoked a lot, partly to keep himself awake to watch over Édouard, partly because the room stank.

"You're a lucky bastard, you've got no sense of smell anymore . . ."

Shit, what would he do if he wanted to laugh? A guy with his lower jaw missing probably did not have much cause to laugh, but even so the questions nagged at Albert.

"The doc . . . ," he ventured.

It was about two or three in the morning. The transfer was scheduled for later in the day.

"The doc, he said that when you get there they can fit a prosthesis . . ."

He had no idea what such a thing might look like, a prosthetic lower jaw, and this might not be the time to discuss it.

But at the mention of this, Édouard perked up, he nodded his head and made wet gurgling noises. He made a sign—Albert had never realized he was left-handed. Remembering the sketchpad, he foolishly wondered how Édouard could have done such drawings with his left hand.

This was what he should have suggested earlier: sketching.

"You want your sketchbook?"

Édouard looked at him, yes he wanted his pad, but not so that he could draw.

It is funny, this scene in the middle of the night. Édouard's eyes, so wide, so alive in that gouged swollen red face, were fiercely intense. Almost frightening. Albert is overawed.

Balancing the pad on the bed, Édouard scrawls in large clumsy letters; he is so weak he seems to have forgotten how to write, the pencil seems to move of its own volition. Albert studies the letters, whose risers and descenders trail off the page. The writing takes a long time, and he is dead on his feet. By a phenomenal effort, Édouard manages to draw one letter, then two. Albert tries to guess the word, concentrating all the energy he can muster. Another letter, and another, and when the word finally comes, the message is still a long way off. He has to decrypt the meaning. It is taking an age, and Édouard, who tires quickly, falls back on the bed. But after less than an hour, he tries again, picks up the notepad, as though something is urging him on. Albert shakes himself, gets up from his chair, lights a cigarette to wake himself up, and goes back to playing hangman. Letter by letter, word by word.

At around 4:00 a.m., Albert has come to this point:

"So, you want to go back to Paris? But where will you go?"

They start again. Édouard is feverish now, hacking at the notepad. Letters gush forth onto the page, so large they are unrecognizable.

"Calm down," Albert says. "Don't worry, we'll get there."

He is not at all certain that they will, because it seems extremely complicated. He perseveres. With the first glimmer of dawn, he has confirmation that Édouard does not want to go back home. Is that what you're saying? Édouard writes "yes."

"But that's normal," Albert tries to explain. "At first, you don't want anyone to see you in this state. We all feel a bit ashamed, that's always the way. I mean even me, I swear, when I took that bullet at the Somme, for a while I was convinced that Cécile would turn her back on me! But your parents love you, they won't stop loving you because you were wounded in the war, don't worry."

Rather than calm him, his little speech succeeds in sending Édouard into a rage, guttural groans bubble from his throat in a torrent, he struggles so hard that Albert is forced to threaten to strap him down again. Édouard manages to control himself, but he is still agitated, even angry. He brutally rips the sketchpad from Albert, as he might a tablecloth during an argument. He goes back to his attempts at writing. Albert lights another cigarette and considers the young man's demand.

If Édouard does not want his family to see him in this state, it may be because there is a Cécile involved somewhere. To give her up would be more than he could bear. Albert can understand that. Cautiously, he makes the case.

Édouard, focused on the page, jerks his head dismissively. There is no Cécile.

But there is a sister. It takes forever to work out what he is saying about his sister. He cannot make out her name. They give up, after all, it is not that important.

Besides, this is not about his sister, either.

And in fact it hardly matters; whatever Édouard's reasons, Albert has to attempt to persuade him.

"I understand," Albert says. "But you'll see, once you have the prosthesis, things will be different."

Édouard gets angry again, the pain is coming back, he gives up any attempt at communicating and goes back to howling like a madman. Albert holds out as long as he can; he, too, is at the end of his tether. Eventually, he gives in and gives him another injection of morphine. Édouard starts to doze; he has endured a lot these past days. If he pulls through, it is because he is made of steel.

In the morning, when he is being changed and fed (Albert does as he has been shown, inserting the rubber tube into the gullet, pouring slowly into the funnel so the stomach does not resist), Édouard becomes frantic again, tries to get up, cannot lie still. Albert is at his wits' end. The young man grabs the pad and starts scrawling letters as illegible as those the night before. He jabs the pencil on the paper. Albert tries but fails to decipher them. He frowns . . . what is this, an *E*? *B*? Then suddenly, unable to stand it any longer, he explodes:

"Listen, there's nothing I can do, *mon vieux*! You don't want to go home, I don't really understand why, but in the end I don't get to decide. It's shitty, but there's nothing I can do!"

Then Édouard grabs his arm and squeezes incredibly hard.

"Hey," Albert yells, "you're hurting me."

Édouard digs his nails in. The pain is fierce. Then the pressure eases, and Édouard wraps his arms around Albert's neck, hugs him hard, shaking with sobs and whimpering cries. Albert has heard cries like this before. At a circus, little monkeys in sailor suits riding bicycles, whimpering fit to bring you to tears. Such grief is harrowing. Whether or not he gets a prosthesis, what has happened to Édouard is so final, so irreversible . . .

"You don't want to go back home," Albert says, "I get that."

In the crook of his neck, he feels Édouard's head shaking, no, he does not want to go back. No, no, he repeats it over and over.

As he hugs the young man, Albert realizes that, like everyone else, Édouard spent the war thinking only of coming out alive, but now it is over and he is still alive, all he wants is to die. If even the survivors have no greater ambition than to die, what a waste . . .

Finally Albert understands: Édouard no longer has the strength to kill himself. It is over. If he had managed to throw himself through the window that first day, it would all be over, the misery and the tears, the time, the interminable time to come . . . it would all have ended there in the courtyard of a field hospital, but the opportunity has passed. He will not have the courage to try again; he is condemned to live.

And it is Albert's fault . . . it is all his fault. It has been from the start. Everything. He, too, feels overwhelmed; he could almost weep. What terrible loneliness. In Édouard's life, Albert now occupies all the space. He is his one and only recourse. The young man has delegated his existence to Albert, offering it because he cannot carry it alone it nor rid himself of it.

Albert is aghast, devastated.

"Okay," he mutters, "I'll see what I can do."

He says this without thinking, but instantly Édouard's head jerks upright as from an electric shock. His face is an almost complete blank, no nose, no mouth, no cheeks, just a pair of blazing eyes that pierce you to the quick. Albert is cornered.

"I'll see . . . ," he repeats inanely, "I'll work something out."

Édouard squeezes his hands and closes his eyes. Then he slowly lies back against the pillows. Calm, though still in pain, he moans weakly, bringing blood-flecked spittle bubbling from his windpipe.

I'll work something out.

Saying "a little too much" is a constant in Albert's life. How many times, by dint of excess enthusiasm, has he got himself embroiled in disastrous situations? It's easy: the number of times he regretted not taking time to think. Albert is often guilty of an impulsive generosity, of yielding to the moment, but until now his rash promises have only ever concerned minor problems. His promise today is very different; a man's life is at stake.

Albert pats Édouard's hands, looks at him, tries to soothe him.

It seems terrible that he cannot remember the face of the boy he knew simply as Péricourt, who was always smiling, always laughing, always sketching; he can see him in profile, can picture the back of his head in the moment before the attack was launched on Hill 113, but of the face, he can remember nothing. He remembers Péricourt turning to him at that moment, but he cannot summon the image, the memory has been eaten away by the bloody, gaping void he sees now; it pains him that he cannot remember.

He looks down at the sheets, at the notepad lying there. The word he could not decipher earlier is suddenly obvious.

"Father."

The word plunges him into an abyss. His own father has long been nothing more than a yellowing portrait that hangs above the sideboard, but if he still nurses a grudge against his father for dying so young, he guesses that having a father who is still alive must make things even more complicated. He would like to know, to understand, but it is too late: he has promised Édouard he will "work something out." Albert no longer knows what he meant by the phrase. As he watches over his sleeping comrade, he ponders the idea.

Édouard wants to disappear, so be it, but how do you make a living soldier disappear? Albert is not a lieutenant, he knows nothing, he has not the first idea how to do such a thing. Would it mean creating a new identity?

Albert may not be brilliant, but, having been an accountant, he is logical. If Édouard wants to disappear, he realizes, the obvious thing to do is give him the identity of a dead soldier. Make a swap.

And there is only one possible solution.

The Personnel Unit, Caporal Grosjean's office.

Albert attempts to imagine the consequences of such an act. Having escaped court-martial by the skin of his teeth, he is now planning—always assuming he is capable of it—to tamper with official documents, to sacrifice the living and resurrect the dead.

This time, it would certainly mean the firing squad. Best not to think.

Overcome by exhaustion, Édouard is sleeping soundly. Albert glances at the clock on the wall, gets up, opens the wardrobe door.

He rummages in Édouard's knapsack and takes out his military record.

It is almost noon; four minutes, three, two . . . Albert sets off, heading along the corridors, hugging the wall, knocks on the door of the office, and goes in without waiting for an answer. Above Grosjean's overloaded desk: one minute to noon.

"Hello," Albert says.

He is going for joviality. But this close to lunchtime on an empty stomach, bonhomie is unlikely to succeed. Grosjean snorts. What does he want now, especially at this time of day? To say thank you. That appeases Grosjean. He had raised one buttock from his chair, preparing to slam shut the ledger, but "thank you" is something he has not heard since the beginning of the war. He does not know how to react.

"Uh . . . don't mention it . . ."

Albert ratchets things up, ladles it on.

"Your idea of a duplicate was a stroke of genius. My friend's being transferred this afternoon."

Grosjean perks up, he gets to his feet, wipes his hands on his ink-stained pants. Flattered though he is by these compliments, it is lunchtime. Albert moves into the attack:

"I'm trying to trace two other friends . . ."

"Oh . . ."

Grosjean pulls on his jacket.

"I don't know what's happened to them. Someone told me they were missing in action. Someone else said they'd been wounded and transferred . . ."

"Well then, how do you expect me to know!"

Grosjean steps past Albert, making for the door.

"Surely it would be in your register . . . ," Albert says nervously.

Grosjean throws open the door.

"Come back after lunch," he says. "We'll see what we can find."

Albert's eyes grow wide suddenly, as though he has just had a great idea.

"If you like, I could look while you go to the mess hall?"

"Oh, no, I couldn't do that. I have my orders."

He pushes Albert ahead of him, locks the door, and then stands, motionless. Albert knows when he is not wanted. He says thanks, see you later, and sets off down the corridor. Édouard's transfer is only an hour or two from now. Albert wrings his hands, *shit, shit, shit,* he mutters over and over, crushed by the weight of his own helplessness.

A few yards on, he turns back halfheartedly. Grosjean is still standing in the hallway, watching him and waiting. Albert turns toward the courtyard, and as he does an idea begins to germinate: Grosjean standing in front of the office door waiting . . . waiting for what? By the time he has worked out the answer, Albert has already turned on his heel and is hurrying back; he will have to be quick. As he comes to the office he sees a soldier in the distance. Albert stands, petrified—it is Lieutenant Pradelle. Fortunately he walks on without turning and disappears around the corner. Albert breathes a sigh of relief. He hears other sounds, hurrying footsteps, laughter, shouts, voices heading toward the mess hall. Meanwhile Albert reaches up, runs his fingers along the doorframe, feels the key, grabs it, slams it into the lock and twists, opens the door, and quickly closes it behind him. He keeps his back to the door, as in a trench. In front of him, the records. Tons of records stacked from floor to ceiling.

Albert is familiar with ledgers from his work at the bank, the gummed labels, the spidery handwriting in blue ink that fades over time. Even so, it took him twenty-five minutes to locate the files he is looking for. He was flustered, glancing frequently toward the door, expecting it to open at any moment. He had no idea what he might say.

It was 12:30 by the time he had lined up the three record books. In each, the writing was in several different hands, some of it already fading; it is astonishing how quickly a name can die. Almost another ten minutes to find what he is looking for, at which point—it is in his nature—he began to waver. As though the choice made any difference . . . Take the first one, he thought. He looked from the clock to the door as though they had suddenly grown and now took up all available space. He thought about Édouard, alone and strapped to the bed . . .

12:42 p.m.

He was scanning the list of the dead whose next of kin had not yet been informed. The last entry was for October 30.

Boulivet, Victor, born February 12, 1891. Killed in action October 24, 1918. Next of kin, parents, Dijon.

In this moment, it was not so much qualms that made him hesitate, but the precautions he needed to take. Albert knew that he was now responsible for his comrade's welfare; he could not afford to make a mistake. He had to do things properly, professionally. But if he were to give Édouard the identity of a dead soldier, then the soldier would be alive again. His parents would be waiting. They would ask for news of him. There would be an inquiry; it would not be difficult to trace things back. Albert shook his head as he imagined the consequences, for Édouard and for himself, if they were charged with forgery and the use of forged papers (and who knew how many other infractions).

Albert began to shake. This was how he often reacted before the war when he was afraid. He seemed to quiver. He looked up at the clock. Time was slipping away: he wrung his hands, turned the pages of the register.

Dubois, Alfred, born September 24, 1890, died October 25, 1918, married, two children, family lives in Saint-Pourçain.

What the hell could he do? It was not as though he had actually promised Édouard anything. He had said, "I'll see what I can do." It was not a firm undertaking. It was . . . Albert groped for the word as he continued to turn the pages.

Évrard, Louis, born June 13, 1892, died October 30, 1918. Next of kin: parents, Toulouse.

That was his problem, he never thought things through, never planned ahead. He just blundered in like a lunatic, full of good intentions, and then . . . His mother was right . . .

Goujou, Constant, born January 11, 1891, died October 26, 1918, married. Place of residence: Mornant.

Albert looked up. Even time was against him, it seemed to have speeded up, how else could it already be one o'clock. Two fat drops of sweat trickled onto the register, he looked for a blotter, then back to the door, no blotting paper, he turned the page. Any moment now the door will open, what will he say?

Then, suddenly, there it is.

Larivière, Eugène. Born November 1, 1893. Died October 30, 1918, on the eve of his birthday. Eugène was twenty-five, or almost. Contact: Public Health Department.

It is a miracle. No parents, just the state: in other words, no one.

Earlier, Albert had spotted the boxes containing military records. They are well organized, and it takes only a minute or two to locate the one marked Larivière. It is 1:05 p.m. Grosjean is tall, big-boned and has a paunch—he obviously likes his food. No need to panic . . . he will probably not leave the mess hall before 1:30 p.m. Even so, better to act fast.

Attached to his military record is one half of Larivière's name tag; the other half will be buried with the body. Or nailed to the cross. It does not matter. In the photograph, Eugène Larivière looks like a very ordinary young man, with the sort of unremarkable face that would be unrecognizable if the lower jaw was blown away. Albert slips the military record into his jacket. He grabs two more at random and slips them into his other pocket. To mislay one record might pass for an error, to lose several requires chaos, something the army is known for and will therefore be more convincing. He opens the other register, flips the cap off the inkwell, picks up a nib pen, takes a deep breath to stop himself shaking and writes "Édouard Péricourt" (he checks the birthdate and notes it down together with his regimental number) then adds: "Died, November 2, 1918." He puts Édouard's military record in the box with the dead. Right on top. With one half of the metal tag on which are stamped his name and number. In a week or two, his family will be informed that a son, a brother, was killed in action. It is a standard-issue letter. It requires only the name of the deceased, making it simple, practical. Even in the chaos of war, sooner or later, bureaucracy manages to catch up.

1:15 p.m.

The rest takes very little time. He has watched Grosjean working and knows where he keeps his counterfoil book. He checks: in the current book, the last entry is the duplicate request for Édouard's transfer. Albert rummages around and finds a blank book. No one ever checks the numbers. By the time anyone notices a counterfoil book is missing from the bottom of the pile, this war will be over and there will have been time to start another. In a heartbeat, he makes out a transfer request in the name of Eugène Larivière. As he adds the final rubber stamp, he realizes he is bathed in sweat.

He quickly tidies away the registers, looks around to make sure he has left nothing behind, then presses his ear to the door. The only sounds are faint and distant. He steps out, locks the door, puts the key back where he found it and slinks away.

Édouard Péricourt has just died for France.

And Eugène Larivière, resurrected from the dead, has a long life ahead of him.

Édouard was having trouble breathing, he was twisting and turning and, but for the straps at his wrists and ankles, would have been rolling from one side of the bed to the other. Albert gripped his shoulders, his hands, talking quickly. Explaining. Your name's Eugène. Hope you like it—it was the only one left in the shop. But getting Édouard to see the funny side . . . Albert is still curious as to how he will cope later if he ever feels like laughing.

Then, finally, it arrived.

Albert knew as soon as the truck belching smoke pulled up outside. Albert ran to the door, hurtled down the stairs and, seeing an orderly waving a form and looking around for someone, shouted:

"Is this about the transfer?"

The man seemed relieved. The ambulance driver arrived. They tramped up the stairs carrying the stretcher—the canvas sheet wrapped around the poles—and followed Albert along the corridor.

"I have to warn you," Albert says, "it stinks in here."

The taller stretcher bearer shrugs; they are used to it. He opens the door.

"You aren't kidding . . ."

It is true that even Albert, when he has been away and come back to the room, finds the stench stomach churning.

They laid the stretcher on the floor. The big man, who was obviously in charge, set the form down on the bedside table and went to the other side of the bed. It was quick: they undid the straps, one of them took Édouard's legs, the other took his head: "on three . . ."

"One," they steeled themselves.

"Two," they lifted him.

"Three," just as they were laying the wounded man on the stretcher, Albert snatched the duplicate from the bedside table and replaced it with the one marked "Larivière."

"Do you have any morphine you can give him?"

"Don't worry, we've got everything we need," the shorter man said.

"Here, these are his papers," Albert said, "I wanted to give them to you personally, you know, in case his stuff gets mislaid."

"Don't worry," said the other man, taking the papers.

They reached the bottom of the stairs and moved out into the courtyard. Édouard's head lolled as he stared into space. Albert climbed into the back of the ambulance and bent over him.

"Come on, Eugène, buck up, everything will be fine, you'll see."

Albert felt like crying. Behind him, the stretcher bearer said:

"Sorry, friend, we've got to go . . ."

"Of course, of course . . ."

He took Édouard's hands. This is what he will always remember, his eyes in that moment, wet, vacant, staring up at him.

Albert kissed his forehead.

"See you soon, all right?"

He clambered down from the truck, and before the door was closed, he shouted.

"I'll come and see you!"

As he fumbled for a handkerchief, Albert looked up. Framed in an open window on the second floor, Lieutenant Pradelle, reaching for his cigarette case, was watching the scene.

The ambulance moved off.

It pulled out of the hospital grounds and vanished into the clouds of black smoke that hung in the air like smog from a factory. Albert turned back to the building. Pradelle had disappeared. The window on the second floor was closed.

A gust of wind whipped away the smoke. The courtyard was empty now. Albert, too, felt empty, hopeless. He snuffled and patted his pockets looking for a handkerchief.

"Shit!" he said.

He had forgotten to give Édouard back his sketchpad.

In the days that followed, a new anxiety blossomed in Albert's mind that would not to let him sleep. If he were dead, would he want Cécile to receive an official notification—in other words, a brusque, unconditional form letter informing her he was dead and nothing more? As for his mother, he could not even bear to think about her. Whatever the means by which she learned of his death, she would weep noble tears and then hang his picture in the living room.

This question of whether or not he should contact Édouard's family had been nagging him ever since he found at the bottom of his bag one of the other military records he had filched when stealing a new identity for Édouard.

It was in the name Évrard, Louis, born June 13, 1892.

Albert could no longer remember the date this soldier had died: in the final days of the war, obviously, but when? He did, however, remember that the man's parents lived in Toulouse. He had probably had a thick accent. In a few weeks, a few months, since no one would be able to find any trace of him and his military record was missing, he would be listed as missing in action, and Évrard, Louis, would vanish as though he had never existed. When, in turn, his parents died, what would remain of Évrard, Louis? Were there not already enough dead, enough missing, without Albert muddying the waters? And all those poor parents condemned to shed tears into the void . . .

Take Eugène Larivière on the one hand, Louis Évrard on the other, and put Édouard Péricourt in the mix, give it all to a soldier like Albert Maillard, and you have a recipe for utter heartache.

He knew nothing about Édouard Péricourt's family. They lived—he had seen it in the files—in a fancy neighborhood. He knew nothing more. But when dealing with the death of a son, where one lived hardly mattered. The first thing the family received was often a letter from a comrade, since the wheels of bureaucracy, though swift in sending men to their deaths, is rather slower when it comes to communicating that same death . . .

Albert could have written such a letter—he knew he could find the words—but he could not get past the fact that it would be a lie.

How could he bring such grief to people, telling them that their son was dead when in fact he was alive? But what else was there? He was faced either with a lie or with regret. The kind of dilemma capable of keeping him brooding for weeks.

It was while leafing through Édouard's sketchbook that he came to a decision. He kept it on his table and often flicked through it. These sketches had become a part of his life, but the book did not belong to him. He had to give it back. As carefully as possible, he tore out the last pages—those they had so recently used to communicate.

Though he knew he was not expressing himself very well, one morning, he began.

Madame, Monsieur,

My name is Albert Maillard, a friend of your son Édouard, and it is my sad duty to inform you that he died on November 2 last. The administration will officially inform you, but I can tell you that he died a hero, storming the enemy in the defense of his country.

Édouard left me a sketchpad to send to you in case anything should happen to him. I am enclosing it now.

I hope it will be of some comfort to know that he is buried in a little cemetery he shares with other comrades, and let me assure you that every care has been taken so that he is at peace there.

I remain . . .

7

Eugène, dear comrade . . .

He could not be sure whether there was still official censorship, whether letters were still opened, read, redacted. Being uncertain, Albert had taken the precaution of addressing him by his new name. A name Édouard was already accustomed to. In fact, it was a strange twist in the story. Though he did not like to think about such things, memories flooded back in spite of himself.

He had known two boys called Eugène. The first had been in his primary school, a skinny boy with freckles who mumbled unintelligibly, but he was not the one who mattered; that was the other Eugène. They had met at an art class Édouard was taking unbeknownst to his parents and quickly became inseparable. Almost everything Édouard did, he had to do behind his parents' backs. Luckily, his sister, Madeleine, worked everything out—at least everything that could be worked out. Eugène and Édouard, because they were lovers, had applied to the École des Beaux-Arts together. Eugène was not quite gifted enough and his application was not accepted. After that, they had lost touch; in 1916 Édouard heard that he was dead.

Eugène, dear comrade . . .

I truly appreciate the fact that you have kept in touch, but in the past four months, you've sent nothing but drawings, not a word, not a line . . . I'm sure it is because you don't like to write, and I can understand that. But . . .

Drawing was easier because the words simply would not come. Had it been down to him, he would not have written at all, but this boy, Albert, was enthusiastic, and he had done everything he could. Édouard did not blame him for anything. Well, maybe a little . . . After all, it was in saving Albert's life that he had ended up this way. He had done it willingly, but—how to put it?—try as he might, he could not find words to express what he felt, the unfairness of it . . . No one was to blame and everyone was to blame. But facts are facts and had it not been for Soldat Maillard contriving to bury himself alive, he would be at home now, in one piece. When he thought about this, he cried, he could not help himself; yet it hardly mattered, there was a lot of crying where he was, it was a literal vale of tears.

Whenever the pain, the anguish and the grief subsided for a moment, they gave way to thoughts in which the figure of Albert Maillard melted away and was replaced by that of Lieutenant Pradelle. Édouard did not understand the whole story about being summoned to appear before a *général* and narrowly escaping a court-martial . . . This episode had taken place the day before his transfer, when he had been doped up on painkillers so what little he could remember was vague and full of gaps. What was crystal clear, on the other hand, was the image of Lieutenant Pradelle, standing motionless amid the hail of shells and shrapnel, staring at his feet, then moving away, and then a wave of earth rising up and breaking . . . Even if he did not understand why, Édouard had no doubt that Pradelle was somehow involved in what had happened. Anyone else would be seething with rage. But, although on the battlefield he had mustered all his strength so he could go to the aid of a comrade, now he had no strength left. His thoughts now were frozen images, distant and yet tenuously connected to him. There was no place for anger or for hope.

Édouard was profoundly depressed.

... and I have to say it's not always easy to know what is going on in your life. I don't even know whether you are eating properly, whether the doctors talk to you sometimes and whether, as I hope, there is now the possibility of the graft I was told about, the one I mentioned ...

The graft ... That was ancient history now. Albert had been wide of the mark; his understanding of the situation had been purely theoretical. All these weeks in the hospital had served only to contain the infection and to do a little "replastering," to use the words of Professeur Maudret, chief surgeon at the Hôpital Rollin on the avenue Trudaine, a lanky, red-headed man with boundless energy. Six times he had operated on Édouard.

"You might say we're intimate, you and me ..."

Each time he explained in detail the reasons for the procedure and its limitations, had "put it into the context of the overall strategy." Not for nothing was he a military doctor. He was a man blessed with unshakeable confidence, the result of hundreds of amputations and resections performed day and night in field hospitals, sometimes even in the trenches.

Only recently had they finally allowed Édouard to look at himself in a mirror. Obviously to the nurses and the doctors, having taken in a man whose lower face was little more than a bleeding wound where nothing remained but the uvula, the windpipe, and a miraculously undamaged set of upper teeth, the sight of Édouard gave them a certain satisfaction. They spoke about it optimistically, but their satisfaction was usually swept aside by the abject despair such men feel when, for the first time, they are faced with what they have become.

Hence the little homily about the future. Essential to the morale of victims. Several weeks before Édouard was allowed to look in a mirror, Maudret had recited his maxim:

"I need you to remember that who you are today is nothing like who you will be tomorrow."

He emphasized *nothing*; it was an immense nothing.

He expended all the more energy because he could feel that he was not getting through to Édouard. Of course the war had been unimaginably brutal, but on the positive side it had made possible significant advances in maxillofacial surgery.

"Extraordinary advances, I would say."

They showed Édouard dental devices for mechanotherapy, plaster heads equipped with steel shafts, a wide range of gadgets that looked like medieval torture implements but which represented the most modern advances in orthopedics. Bait is what they actually were: Maudret, being a skilled tactician, adopted a strategy of encirclement where Édouard was concerned, gradually leading him toward the grand finale of his therapeutic plans.

"The Dufourmentel graft!"

Strips of skin were harvested from the scalp and grafted onto the lower part of the face.

Maudret showed him photographs of wounded men who had been "replastered." There you go, thought Édouard, give a military surgeon a soldier whose face has been completely mangled by a bunch of other soldiers, and he'll give you a perfectly presentable gnome.

Édouard's response was understated.

"No," he wrote in large letters on his notepad.

And so, against his better judgment—curiously, he hated such devices—Maudret talked about prostheses. Vulcanite, lightweight metal, aluminum, they had everything they needed to make a new jaw for him. As for his cheeks . . . Édouard did hear him out before grabbing his books and once again writing:

"No."

"What do you mean, no?" the surgeon asked. "No to what?"

"No to everything. I stay as I am."

Maudret closed his eyes with a knowing air; he understood: in the early months refusal was a common reaction, a result of post-traumatic depression. It was something that would pass in time. Even the disfigured sooner or later become realistic again. That is how life is.

But four months later, after a thousand attempts at persuasion and at a point where every other patient, without exception, had agreed to put their trust in the surgeons to mitigate the damage, Soldat Larivière still stubbornly refused: I am staying like this.

And his eyes as he said it were fixed, glassy, obdurate.

They called in the psychiatrists again.

That said, from your drawings I think I have a sense of what's happening. The room you're in now seems bigger and more spacious than the one before, am I right? Are those trees I can see in the courtyard? Obviously I'm not foolish enough to think that you're happy there, it's just that I don't know what I can do to help, being so far away. I feel completely helpless.

Thank you for the sketch of Sister Marie-Camille.

Before now, you always managed to draw her from behind or in profile and now I understand why you wanted to keep her to yourself, you old rogue, because she is very pretty. In fact, I have to say that if I didn't already have my Cécile . . .

In fact, there were no female nuns in the hospital, only civilians, kindly women of great compassion. But he had to find something to say to Albert, who sent letters twice a week. Édouard's first sketches were clumsy; his hand shook convulsively and he could hardly see. To say nothing of the fact that after every operation he was in terrible pain. It was Albert who saw a "young nun" in the barely sketched face in profile. Let's say she's a nun, Édouard thought, what difference does it make? He called her Marie-Camille. From his letters, Édouard had formed a certain sense of Albert, and he tried to give his imaginary nun the sort of face he thought Albert would probably like.

Though united by a shared experience in which each had taken his life in his hands, the two men did not know each other, and their relationship was complicated by a murky combination of guilt, solidarity, resentment, diffidence, and comradeship. Édouard nursed a little grudge against Albert, but it was tempered by the fact that his comrade had found him a new identity so he did not have to return home. He had not the first idea what he would do with himself now that he was no longer Édouard Péricourt, but he welcomed any life in which his father did not have to see him in this state.

Speaking of Cécile, I had a letter from her. Like me, she thinks the end of the war is taking too long. We talk about the good times we'll have when I get back, but from her tone I can tell that she is tired of the whole thing. In the beginning, she used to visit my mother a lot, but she doesn't really go much now. I can hardly blame her. I told you about my mother, she's a real character, that woman.

Thank you so much for the horse's head. I know I went on and on about it . . . I think it's perfect now, very expressive, the way you've drawn the bulging eyes, the half-open mouth. It's stupid, you know, but I often wonder what that horse was called. It's as though I need to give him a name.

How many horse's heads had he drawn for Albert? They were always too scrawny, the head should be turned to the side . . . no, actually, the other side, and the eyes should be more . . . I don't know how to describe it . . . No, they were never quite right. Anyone but Édouard would have chucked the whole thing up, but he could sense how important it was for his comrade to dredge up, to remember the head of the old nag that had probably saved his life. Albert's request masked a deeper, more troubling issue that concerned Édouard, one that he could not put into words. Édouard set to work, dashing off dozens of sketches, trying to follow the ham-fisted instructions Albert—between profuse apologies and gratitude—offered in each new letter. Édouard was just about to give up when he remembered a sketch da Vinci had done of a horse's head for a statue—a red chalk drawing if he remembered rightly—and he used this as a model. When he got the picture, Albert had literally jumped for joy.

Reading those words, Édouard finally understood what Albert was going on about.

Now that he had given his comrade his horse's head, he set down his pencil.

He would never draw again.

Time drags here. Do you realize, the armistice was signed last November, it's February already and there's still no sign of us being demobilized? Weeks we've been sitting around doing nothing . . . They've given us all sorts of different reasons to explain the situation, but there's no way of knowing what's true and what isn't. It's just like the trenches here, rumors travel faster than news. Apparently, Parisians will soon be going on sightseeing trips with Le Petit Journal to visit the battlefields near Reims while we're still moldering here in conditions that—like us—are going from bad to worse. Sometimes, I swear, we wonder if we weren't better off being shot at—at least we felt useful, at least we thought we were winning the war. I feel ashamed to be complaining about my petty gripes to you, my poor Eugène, here I am whining on and you're probably thinking I don't know how lucky I am. And you're right, it's amazing how self-centered people are.

Sorry if this letter is a bit rambling (I never could stick to a subject, it was the same at school), maybe I'd be better off taking up drawing . . .

Édouard wrote to Docteur Maudret saying that he refused any cosmetic treatment whatever and requesting to be returned to civilian life as quickly as possible.

"With a face like that?"

The doctor was livid. He was clutching the letter in his right hand while his left gripped Édouard's shoulder, forcing him to look in the mirror.

For a long time Édouard stared at this swollen magma of flesh in which he could just make out faint vestiges of the face he had known. The folds of flesh formed pale, milky pads. In the middle, the hole, partially scarred over where the skin had been strained and stretched, formed a sort of crater that seemed more remote than it had previously, though it was still as crimson. It looked like the face of a circus contortionist who could suck in his cheeks and swallow his lower jaw, but could not reverse the process.

"Yes," Édouard nodded, "with a face like this."

8

It is pandemonium. Thousands of soldiers coming and going, hanging around, piling in, all crammed together in unimaginable chaos. The Center for Demobilization is crammed to the gills; the men are supposed to be demobilized in waves of hundreds at a time, but no one knows what to do. Orders are given only to be countermanded; the entire setup keeps changing. Exhausted and frustrated, soldiers clutch at any straw of information, and within minutes, the rumor swells, a roar goes up, almost a threat. Beleaguered noncommissioned officers stride through the crowd, snarling irritably to no one in particular: "What do you want me to say? I don't know any more than you do!" Suddenly whistle blasts sound. Everyone turns to look, the focus of frustration shifts, there is a guy at the far end yelling, all anyone can hear is "Papers? What fucking papers?" and another voice, "What do you mean my military record?" Instinctively, the soldiers all pat their breast pockets or their back pockets, look at each other quizzically. "Four fucking hours we've been waiting here!," "Think yourself lucky, me, I've been here three days." Someone else says, "Where did you say I should go for the boots?" But apparently they only have larger sizes. "So what am I supposed to do?" The guy is overwrought. He is a lowly *soldat de première classe*, yet he is addressing a *capitaine* as if he were a servant. He is fuming. "So, what the hell am I supposed to do?" he says again. The officer stares down at his list, ticking off names. The *première classe* turns on his heel and stomps off, muttering something that is inaudible but for the word *bastards* . . . The *capitaine* pretends not to hear. His face is flushed, his hands are shaking, but the place is so packed that that the insult is carried away on the crowd like a fleck of sea foam. Elsewhere, two men are arguing, punching each other on the shoulder. "I told you, it's my damn jacket," yells the first man. "Fuck," says the other man, "that's all I need." But he lets go of the jacket and walks away; he tried his best; he can try again. There are so many thefts here every day that they need to open a special office to deal with them. Can you imagine setting up counters for every type of complaint . . . it would be impossible! So say the men lining up for soup. Lukewarm. It has always been like that. It makes no sense: the coffee is scalding; the soup is stone cold. Ever since they've been here. When they are not lining up for something or other, they try to get whatever information they can. ("But the train for Mâcon is listed there on the board!" one man says. "Yeah, sure, it's listed, but it's not here, so what the hell do you expect me to do?")

Yesterday, finally, a train left for Paris, forty-seven carriages, room enough for fifteen hundred men, but more than two thousand soldiers piled inside, packed tight as sardines but happy. Carriage windows were broken, noncommissioned officers showed up and muttered darkly about "criminal damage." Everyone had to get off, and the train—already ten hours late by then—was delayed another hour. When eventually it shuddered and moved off, there were shouts from everywhere, from those leaving and those left behind. And when all that could be seen was a plume of smoke over the flat countryside, those who were left behind shuffled forward, searching for a familiar face in the hope of picking up some crumb of information, asking the same questions: which units were being demobilized, in what order . . . surely there must be someone in charge here, for Christ's sake. But in charge of what? No one seems to know anything. They wait. Half the soldiers have been sleeping on the floor in their greatcoats; they had more room in the trenches. Granted, it's not the same, but if there are no rats here, there are lice aplenty, because the little creatures travel with you. "Can't even write home to say when we'll get there," one soldier moans, an old man with craggy features and vacant eyes; despite his grumbling, he is resigned. There were rumors that an extra train was being dispatched, and amazingly it actually arrived, but rather than taking the three hundred and twenty waiting men, it brought two hundred new arrivals, and there is nowhere to put them.

The chaplain tries to weave his way through the lines of soldiers stretched out on the floor; he is jostled, half his coffee spills, a little guy winks at him—"You'd think the Good Lord would take care of his own!"—and laughs. The chaplain grits his teeth and tries to find space on a bench; apparently they are sending more benches, but when, no one knows. In the meantime, anyone who has a seat is under constant siege. The chaplain only finds a space because the men bunch up; if it were an officer, he could go to hell, but a priest . . .

Being in such a crowd was not good for Albert's anxiety. He was permanently on edge. It was impossible to find a place to sit without being jostled or elbowed by someone. And the noise, the incessant shouting upset him, boring into his head, at the slightest thing he found himself flinching and turning this way and that. Sometimes, as though a trapdoor had been closed, the roar of the crowd would suddenly fade to be replaced by faint echoes like the muffled blast of shells heard by a man buried underground.

Such moments had been recurring more frequently since he spotted Lieutenant Pradelle at the far end of the hall. Standing feet apart—his favorite position—and hands clasped behind his back, he observed this pitiful spectacle with the solemnity of a man dismayed but unscathed by the mediocrity of others. As he thought about Pradelle, Albert glanced at the soldiers around him and felt a sudden surge of panic. He did not want to talk to Édouard about Lieutenant Pradelle, but it seemed to Albert that he was everywhere, like an evil spirit, constantly hovering close by ready to swoop.

And you're right, it's amazing how selfish people are. Sorry if this letter is a bit rambling . . .

"Albert!"

It's just that, well, the thing is we're all a little crazy. When you have . . .

"Albert, for Christ's sake!"

The angry *caporal-chef* grabbed his shoulder, shook him hard, and pointed to the sign. Albert quickly gathered up the scattered pages and rushed off, scrambling as best he could to organize his things, clutching his papers as he pushed through the line of waiting soldiers.

"You don't look much like your photo."

The *gendarme* was a man of about forty, self-satisfied (potbellied, practically obese . . . it made you wonder where he had managed to find so much food these past four years) and suspicious. The sort of man who has a sense of duty. There was a seasonal fluctuation in this sense of duty. Since the armistice, for example, there seemed to be a surfeit. Besides, Albert was an easy target. Not much of a fighter. Desperate to get home. Desperate to get some sleep.

"Albert Maillard . . . ," the *gendarme* said, studying the military record.

He was tempted to hold it up to the light. His suspicions were confirmed as he studied Albert's face: "does not resemble photograph." On the other hand, the photograph was four years old, dog eared, washed out . . . For a dog-eared, washed-out guy like me, it's perfect, thought Albert. But the official was unlikely to see things in the same light. There were so many cheats, con artists, and swindlers these days. He nodded his head, looking from Albert to the picture and back again.

"It's a photo from before," Albert said.

Though the *gendarme* was a skeptic and a petty bureaucrat, the notion of "before" was one he understood. For everyone, the meaning of "before" was clear as day. All the same.

"Fair enough," he said, "I'm happy to go with 'Albert Maillard.' Trouble is now I've got two Maillards."

"You have two Albert Maillards?"

"No, two 'A. Maillards,' and *A* could easily stand for *Albert.*"

The *gendarme* seemed proud of this deduction, which he felt confirmed his sophistication.

"Yes," Albert agreed, "or it could stand for Alfred. Or for André. Or for Alcide."

The *gendarme* eyed him warily, then screwed his eyes up like a big cat.

"And why would it not stand for Albert?"

Of course. Albert had nothing with which to counter this indisputable hypothesis.

"So where is he, this other man named Maillard?" he said.

"Well, that's the problem: he left the day before yesterday."

"You let him leave without asking his first name?"

The *gendarme* closed his eyes; it was painful to have to explain such simple procedures.

"We had his first name, but we don't have it anymore, the files were transferred to Paris yesterday. Once they've left, all I have is this list here." (He prodded a peremptory finger at the list of surnames.) "See, 'A. Maillard.'"

"So if you can't track down the paperwork, I have to carry on fighting the war on my own?"

"If it was down to me, I'd let you through," the *gendarme* said, "but I've got my orders . . . If someone gets demobilized and turns out to be the wrong guy, who gets it in the neck? Me, that's who. You wouldn't believe the number of line cutters we get. Not to mention how many of you seem to lose your papers. If you knew all the guys who've lost their pay book so they can claim the allowance twice . . ."

"And it's really that serious?" Albert said.

The *gendarme* frowned as though suddenly realizing he was dealing with a Bolshevik.

"Since that picture was taken, I've been wounded at the Somme," Albert explained to calm things down. "Maybe that explains it . . ."

The *gendarme*, delighted to have to use his expertise, scrutinized the photograph and the face in turn, looking from one to the other faster and faster, and eventually announced, "It's possible." And yet it still seemed as though there was something missing. Behind Albert, the other soldiers were beginning to get impatient. The commotion was muted still, but before long there would likely be a full-scale riot . . .

"Is there a problem?"

Albert was pole axed at the sound of this voice: like a breath of poison, it seemed to exude evil. From the corner of his eye, at first all he noticed was an officer's belt and a *capitaine*'s stripes. He could feel himself beginning to shake. Don't piss yourself.

"See, the thing is . . ." The *gendarme* handed over the papers. Albert finally forced himself to look up and, like a knife wound, felt the cold caustic stare of Capitaine d'Aulnay-Pradelle. Still tanned and hirsute, with a swaggering self-confidence. Never taking his eyes off Albert, Pradelle reached out and took the papers.

". . . Thing is, I've got two guys named 'A. Maillard.' And, well, looking at the photo, I had my doubts . . ."

Pradelle still did not look at the document. Albert bowed his head and stared at his shoes. He simply could not hold the *capitaine*'s gaze. Another five minutes, and a bead of sweat would be dangling from his nose.

"I know this man . . . ," Pradelle said casually. "Know him well, actually."

"Really?" the *gendarme* said.

"This is Albert Maillard . . ."

Pradelle spoke with infinite slowness, as though putting his whole weight behind each syllable.

". . . No doubt about it."

At the *capitaine*'s arrival, the commotion had instantly ceased. The soldiers lining up behind Albert fell silent as though surprised by an eclipse. There was something about him that chilled the blood, something reminiscent of the vile Inspector Javert in *Les Misérables*. With a face like that, he clearly had guardian angels in hell.

I wasn't sure whether to say anything about it, but I've decided I should all the same; I've had news about A.P. You'll never guess: he's been promoted to capitaine! So you see, in war it's better to be a shit than a soldier. And he's here, he's running some section of the demob. center. I can't tell you what it was like, seeing him again . . . You wouldn't believe the nightmares I've had since I ran into him.

"We do know each other, don't we, Soldat Maillard?"

Albert eventually looked up.

"Yes, Lieut . . . yes, Capitaine. We know each other."

The *gendarme* said nothing; he simply stared down at his lists and his rubber stamps. The air was thick with malice.

"In particular, I am aware of your heroism, Soldat Maillard," Pradelle said with the flicker of a condescending smile.

He looked Albert up and down scornfully, taking his time, then focused on his face. Albert felt as though the ground were slipping away beneath him, as though he were standing on quicksand, and it was his panic that made him react.

"That's the, uh . . . the thing about war," he stammered.

All around them there was a deafening silence. Pradelle tilted his head over this notion.

"Every . . . every man reveals his true nature," Albert managed to complete his sentence.

A half smile played on Pradelle's thin lips which, most of the time, were merely a horizontal line that twitched like an automaton. Albert realized why he felt uneasy: Capitaine Pradelle did not blink, ever; this was what gave him that corrosive stare. Animals like that have no tears, he thought, then swallowed hard and looked away.

Sometimes, in my dreams, I kill him, run him through with a bayonet. Sometimes we're both there, you and me, and we give him what for, I can tell you. But sometimes I find myself in front of the court-martial and then the firing squad, and I know I should refuse the blindfold, that I should be brave, I suppose. But I don't, I take the blindfold, because there is only one man on the firing squad and it's him, and he smiles smugly as he aims his rifle . . . Even when I'm awake, I dream of killing him. But mostly when I hear that bastard's name, I think about you, my friend. I know I shouldn't say these things . . .

The *gendarme* clears his throat.

"Right, well . . . If you're prepared to vouch for him, *capitaine* . . ."

The clamor of voices starts up again, soft at first, but growing louder.

When Albert finally looks up again, Pradelle has disappeared, and the *gendarme* is once again hunched over his lists.

Since morning, everyone has been yelling and screaming. The Demobilization Center has been a bedlam of shouts and angry roars. Then, as the day waned, this great dying organism seemed overcome by despair. The counters closed, the officers went to eat while tired non-coms, slumped on sacks, blew on their coffee out of habit though it was barely lukewarm. The desks were cleared away. Until tomorrow.

The trains that had not come would not arrive now.

Nothing more would happen today.

Maybe tomorrow.

But actually, that's all we've been doing since the end of the war: waiting. Being here is a bit like being in the trenches. There is an enemy we cannot see, but one that weighs on us. We're dependent on that. They're much the same, the enemy, the war, the bureaucracy, the army, they're all things that no one understands and no one can stop.

Soon, it was dark. Those who had already eaten sat daydreaming and digesting, sparked up cigarettes. Exhausted from a day spent struggling like the very devil for precious little, they felt patient, magnanimous; now that everything was calm, they shared the blankets, gave away bread when there was some left over. They took off their shoes, and though it may have been the light, their faces seemed more drawn. Everyone had aged. The weariness, the interminable bureaucratic process, it seemed as though they would never be done with this war. Some started up a card game, wagering boots two sizes too small that they had been unable to exchange; they laughed, told jokes. They were heavyhearted.

. . . this is how war ends, my poor Eugène, with an oversized dormitory full of worn-out men the army can't even fucking manage to send home. No one to talk to you or even shake your hand. The newspapers promised us triumphal arches; instead we're crowded into barns open to the four winds. The "sincere thanks of a grateful France" (I read that in Le Matin, word for word, I swear) has turned into endless wrangling: they try to bilk us out of fifty-two francs of our savings; they begrudge us the clothes, the soup, the coffee. They treat us like thieves.

"Back where I'm from, when we get home," one man said, relighting his cigarette, "there'll be one hell of a party . . ."

No one said anything. Everyone was uncertain.

"Where you from?"

"Saint-Viguier-de-Soulage."

"Oh . . ."

No one had ever heard of the place, but it had a nice ring to it.

I'll leave it at that for today. I'm thinking of you, my dear comrade, and I can't wait to see you, it's the first thing I plan to do when I get back to Paris—after I go to see my Cécile, obviously, I'm sure you understand. Take care of yourself and write if you can, if not I'm happy with the drawings—you know I've kept them all? Who knows, when you're a great artist, I mean a famous artist, maybe they'll make me rich.

A hearty handshake from your friend,
Albert

After a long night spent in resignation, morning came, and everyone stretched. Day had hardly broken and already the noncoms were hammering away, nailing up new placards. Everyone rushed to see. Trains were confirmed for Friday, two days from now. Two trains for Paris. Men scanned the lists for their own names and those of their comrades. Albert bided his time as soldiers elbowed him in his ribs, trod on his feet. Eventually he pushed through the crowd and ran a finger down the first list, then the second, shuffled sideways, third list, and finally, there he was, Albert Maillard, that's me, night train.

Friday, departing 2200 hours.

Given the time it would take to have his transportation papers stamped and get to the station with the others, he would have to leave at least an hour before. He thought about writing to Cécile but quickly changed his mind. There was no point. There were already too many false reports.

Like many soldiers, he felt a surge of relief. Even if the information was later contradicted, even if turned out to be wrong, it felt good.

Albert left his belongings with a Parisian who was sitting writing a letter so he could go out and make the most of a sunny spell. The rains had stopped during the night, and the men wondered whether maybe the weather was taking a turn for the better; they scanned the clouds and everyone offered a forecast. And that morning, though they still had more than enough to worry about, every man was conscious of how good it was to be alive. Along the barriers erected to mark the boundaries of the camp, dozens of soldiers were already standing around, as they did every morning, chewing the fat with the villagers who came to see what was going on, with the kids who wanted to touch a real rifle, with strangers who showed up God knows how from God knows where. With people. It felt strange, standing around like that chatting over the barricades with real people. Albert still had a little tobacco, something he was never parted from. Fortunately, since a lot of the men were exhausted, lying around on their greatcoats, trying to summon the energy to get up, it was easier to get a hot drink now than later in the day. He wandered over to the barriers and stood, smoking a cigarette and sipping his coffee. Above him, white clouds scudded across the sky. He walked as far as the entrance to the camp, chatted a bit with the men here and there. But he steered clear of the bulletin boards, determined to wait calmly until his name was called, he was tired of rushing around, they would have to send him home eventually. In her last letter, Cécile had enclosed a telephone number where he could leave a message when he knew the day he would be arriving. Ever since she had sent it, he has been itching to call the number, to talk to Cécile, tell her how much he longed to be home, to be with her at last, to tell her so many other things, but the number was just a means of getting a message to her, the telephone belonged to Monsieur Mauléon, who owned the ironmongers on the corner of the rue des Amandiers. Besides, first he would have to find a telephone in order to make the call, and he would be better off going home first.

There was a good crowd at the barriers. Albert allowed himself a second cigarette and strolled around. There were people from the nearby town gossiping with the soldiers. They had long faces. Women searching desperately for their son, their husband, holding out photographs; they might as well hunt for a needle in a haystack. The fathers, when they came, hung back. It was always the wives who did the hard work, asked the questions, persevered in their silent struggle, getting up every morning with a small sliver of hope still to be used up. The men had long since stopped hoping. The soldiers were evasive, they nodded vaguely, all the photographs looked the same.

Albert felt a hand on his shoulder. He turned, and instantly he felt his gorge rise, his heart begin to hammer.

"Ah, Soldat Maillard, I've been looking for you!"

Pradelle grasped his arm and forced him to walk.

"Follow me!"

Albert was no longer under the command of Pradelle, but such was his air of authority, he trotted after him clutching his bag.

They walked along the barriers.

The young woman was shorter than they were. Twenty-seven, twenty-eight, perhaps, Albert thought, not particularly pretty, but she had a certain charm. Actually, it was difficult to tell. Her coat looked like ermine; Albert could not be sure. Cécile had once shown him a coat just like it in the window of some high-priced shop, and he had felt miserable that he could not go in and buy her one. The young woman was wearing a matching muff and a cloche hat with a wide brim. The sort of woman with the means to dress simply without looking poor. She had an open face, a network of fine wrinkles at the corners of her large dark eyes, long lashes, and a small mouth. Not pretty, no, but well presented. And besides it was immediately clear that she was a strong-minded woman.

She was upset. In her gloved hands she held a piece of paper that she unfolded and held out to Albert.

To hide his nervousness, he took the page and pretended to read, though there was no need: he already knew what it was. A form letter. His eye caught the words "died for his country." "CAUSE: injuries received on the field of battle. . . ." "Interred nearby."

"Mademoiselle was asking about one of your comrades who was killed in action," the *capitaine* said coldly.

The young woman handed him a second piece of paper. He almost dropped it but caught himself in time. She let out a little "oh!"

It was his own handwriting.

Madame, Monsieur,

My name is Albert Maillard, a friend of your son Édouard, and it is my sad duty to inform you that he died . . .

He handed the letters back, and the woman held out a soft, cold hand.

"My name is Madeleine Péricourt. I am Édouard's sister . . ."

Albert nodded. She looked a lot like Édouard. Something about the eyes. Neither of them knew what to say next.

"I'm so sorry," Albert said.

"Mademoiselle came to see me at the suggestion of Général Morieux," Pradelle explained and turned to her. "He is a great friend of your father's, I believe?"

Madeleine acknowledged this with a curt nod, not taking her eyes off Albert, whose stomach lurched when he heard the *général*'s name; in a wave of panic he wondered how this would end and instinctively clenched his buttocks and tried to control his bladder. Pradelle, Morieux. The trap was about to snap shut.

"In fact, Mlle Péricourt would like to visit her brother's grave. But she doesn't know where he is buried . . ."

Capitaine d'Aulnay-Pradelle laid a heavy hand on the shoulder of Soldat Maillard, forcing him to turn and look at him. It looked like a friendly gesture, Madeleine probably thought he was terribly compassionate, this bastard who was staring at Albert with a smile as muted as it was menacing. Mentally, Albert made the connection between the names Morieux and Péricourt and the phrase "a friend of your father." It was obvious that the *capitaine* was reinforcing his contacts and it was therefore in his best interests to please this woman rather than to tell her the truth he was all too aware of. He had caught Albert in his lie about Édouard Péricourt's death, and from his manner, it was clear that he intended to exploit the situation for as long as it was to his advantage.

Mlle Péricourt had eyes only for Albert; she gazed at him in wild hope, knitting her brow as though urging him to say something. He shook his head wordlessly.

"Is it far from here?" she asked.

A pretty voice. And when Albert did not reply, Pradelle said patiently:

"The lady asked whether it's far from here, the cemetery where you buried her brother Édouard."

Madeleine gave the officer a questioning glance. Is he a simpleton, this soldier? Does he understand what we are saying? She crumpled the letter in her hand. Her eyes darted from Albert to the *capitaine* and back again.

"Quite far . . . ," Albert said.

Madeleine looked relieved. "Quite far" clearly meant not too far. It also meant: I remember where he is buried. She took a deep breath. Someone knew. He could tell it had taken great effort on her part to get this far. She did not allow herself to smile—obviously, it would not have been appropriate—but she was calm.

"Could you tell me how to get there?"

"The thing is . . . ," Albert said quickly, "It wouldn't be easy to find . . . It's out in the countryside, there are very few landmarks . . ."

"Maybe you could take us there then?"

"Now?" Albert said anxiously, "It's just that . . ."

"Oh, no, not right now . . ."

Madeleine Péricourt's response had been too quick, and she regretted it immediately. She looked to Capitaine Pradelle for support.

And at this point, a curious thing happened: suddenly everyone knew what this was really about.

One ill-judged word now, and it was all over. And that cast a very different light on everything.

Pradelle, inevitably, was quickest off the mark.

"The thing is, Mlle Péricourt would like to take some time to reflect by her brother's graveside . . ."

He stressed every syllable as though each contained some independent meaning.

To reflect. Well, well. And why not now?

Why wait?

Because what she wanted to do would take time, and most of all it required discretion.

For months now, families had been asking for the return of the remains of soldiers buried at the front. Give us back our children. But there was nothing to be done. There were too many of them. The north of France was dotted with makeshift, hastily dug graves because the dead could not wait; nor would the rats. As soon as armistice was declared, the families began to clamor, but the government stubbornly refused to concede. Thinking about it, Albert could see it was logical. If the government authorized private exhumations, within a few days hundreds of thousands of families armed with shovels and spades would have dug up half the country—imagine the chaos—to say nothing of transporting thousands of rotting corpses, shipping coffins through railways stations, loading them onto trains that, at the moment, ran barely once a week between Paris and Orléans—it was impossible. And so, from the beginning, the answer had been no. But it was a difficult decision for the families to accept. The war was over; they did not understand, they persevered. For its part, the government could scarcely manage to demobilize the soldiers who had survived. It could not begin to consider organizing the exhumation and transportation of two hundred, three hundred, perhaps even four hundred thousand bodies, no one knew exactly. For the families, it posed a dilemma.

There were those who sought refuge in their grief—relatives who had crossed the country to stand by graves in godforsaken cemeteries and who found they could not bring themselves to leave.

But other families remained stubbornly determined; they refused to be swindled by a government of incompetents. They took a different approach. Édouard's family was one such. Mme Péricourt had not come to reflect at her brother's graveside.

She had come to fetch him.

She had come to dig him up, to take him home.

Albert had heard stories. There was a whole traffic in such things, people who specialized. All one needed was a truck, a shovel, a pick, and a strong stomach. You found the grave, went there at night, worked fast.

"So, when might it be possible for Mademoiselle Péricourt to go and reflect by her brother's grave, Soldat Maillard?" Capitaine Pradelle said.

"Tomorrow, if you like," Albert said in a toneless voice.

"Tomorrow would be perfect," the young woman said, "I have a car. How long do you think it will take to get there?"

"Difficult to say. An hour, maybe two . . . Maybe longer . . . ," Albert said. "What time would suit you?"

Madeleine hesitated. And since neither Albert nor the *capitaine* reacted, she said her piece.

"I could come and pick you up at 6:00 p.m. What do you think?"

What did he think?

"You want to visit the grave at night?"

The words had slipped out. He had not been able to stop himself. It was cowardly.

Seeing Madeleine lower her eyes, he regretted it. Not that she was embarrassed by his question, no, she was calculating. She was young, but she had her feet firmly planted on the ground. And, since she was rich—that much was obvious from the ermine, the little cloche hat, the perfect teeth—she was soberly considering the situation and wondering how much she should offer for the soldier's help.

Albert felt sick to his stomach that anyone might think he would accept money for such a thing . . . Before she could open her mouth, he said:

"All right. Tomorrow."

He turned and made his way back to the camp.

9

And honestly, I'm sorry to bring this up again . . . But I need you to be absolutely sure. Sometimes we make decisions in the heat of the moment, out of anger, or disappointment, or grief, sometimes our emotions get the better of us, you know what I'm saying. I'm not even sure how we might do it now, but I know we could find a way . . . What we have done can probably be undone. I'm not trying to influence your decision, I am just asking that you think about your parents. I feel sure that if they saw you as you are now, they would love you as much as ever, if not more. Your father, I'm sure, must be a brave and a loving man, imagine the joy he would feel if he knew you were alive. I'm not trying to sway you. Whatever you decide is what we will do, I simply think that these are decisions not to be taken lightly. You sent me a sketch of your sister Madeleine, she is a lovely young woman, think what pain she must have felt when she heard that you were dead and what a miracle it would be for her now . . .

It was a futile thing to write. There was no way of knowing when the letter would arrive, it could take two weeks, it could take four. Besides, the die was cast. Albert was writing this purely for himself. He did not regret helping Édouard change his identity, but unless he saw things through to the end, he found it difficult to imagine the consequences, which, he suspected, were dire. He lay on the ground, wrapped in his greatcoat.

He tossed and turned most of the night, nervous, fretful.

In his dreams, a body was being exhumed, and Madeleine Péricourt immediately realized that it was not her brother, he was too tall or too short, sometimes it was immediately obvious because the face was that of an old soldier, sometimes it was the body of a man with the head of a dead horse. He could see the young woman take his arm and say, "What have you done with my brother?" Capitaine d'Aulnay-Pradelle was gleeful, of course, his blue eyes shone so brightly they lit up Albert's face like a torch. His booming voice was that of Général Morieux. "Answer the woman, Soldat Maillard! What have you done with her brother?"

It was from one such nightmare that he woke with a start sometime before dawn.

While the whole camp was sleeping, Albert brooded, and as the minutes ticked past in the gloom of the vast hall, as he listened to the muffled breathing of his comrades and the rain hammering on the roof, his thoughts grew darker, gloomier, more menacing. He did not regret what he had done until now, but he could not bring himself to go further. He kept picturing that young woman crumpling a letter filled with lies. Was it cruel, this thing that he was doing? Was it even possible to undo what had been done? There were as many reasons to go on as to turn back. After all, he thought, I am not going to dig up bodies to cover up a lie I told out of the goodness of my heart! Or out of weakness, it amounts to the same thing. But if I don't dig him up, if I reveal everything, I'll be court-martialed. He did not know the dangers he risked, simply that they were serious; the whole thing had taken on terrifying proportions.

When day finally broke, he had still not come to a decision, endlessly deferring the moment when he must resolve this terrible dilemma.

He was awakened by a kick in the ribs. Dumbstruck with astonishment, he scrambled to sit up. By now, the whole hall was buzzing with the sound of voices and commotion, Albert looked around, utterly lost, unsure where he was, when suddenly from above, he saw the harsh, cruel face of Capitaine Pradelle swoop down and stop inches from his own.

The officer stared at him for a long moment, gave a heavy sigh, and slapped his face. Albert instinctively brought his hands up to protect himself. Pradelle smiled. A broad smile that boded nothing good.

"Well, Soldat Maillard, you learn something new every day. So your comrade Édouard Péricourt is dead? It came as a shock to me, I can tell you . . . Because the last time I saw him . . ."

He frowned, as though trying hard to remember.

". . . I do believe it was at the military hospital. And I have to say, at the time, he seemed very much alive. Well, I'll grant you he didn't look his best . . . In fact, I'd say he looked a little drawn. Tried to stop a shell with his teeth, a very rash decision, now if he'd asked my advice . . . But I certainly did not expect him to die, Soldat Maillard, the thought never even occurred to me. But there seems little doubt that he is actually dead, you even sent a personal letter to his family to inform them, and such style, Soldat Maillard, such old-fashioned gallantry!"

When he pronounced the name *Maillard*, he had a disagreeable manner of giving it a derisory and contemptuous drawl that made *Maillard* sound like *merde* or something very like it.

He lowered his voice almost to a whisper, like an outraged man trying hard to contain himself.

"Now, I don't know what has happened to Soldat Péricourt, and I don't want to know, but Général Morieux has instructed me to help the family, so obviously I can't help but wonder . . ."

The statement sounded almost like a question. Up until now, Albert had not been able to speak, and Pradelle had no intention of allowing him to do so now.

"There are two possible solutions, Soldat Maillard. We tell the truth and settle the matter. If we do that, you will be had up for identity theft. I don't know how exactly you went about it, but I can guarantee it would land you in jail for fifteen years minimum. On the other hand, if that happens, you'll start demanding an inquiry into the assault on

Hill 113 . . . So, for both of us it is the worst possible solution. Which leaves only one: the family have asked for a dead soldier, we provide them with a dead soldier, case closed. You may speak now."

Albert was still attempting to piece together the beginnings of this speech.

"I don't know . . . ," he said.

In situations like this, Mme Maillard would explode: "That's you all over, isn't it, Albert! When you're called on to make a decision, to be a man for once in your life, there's no one at home! It's always '*I don't know . . . We'll see . . . Maybe . . . I'll think about it . . .*' Come on, Albert, make a decision! If you honestly think you can get through life, etc., etc."

Capitaine Pradelle shared some of Mme Maillard's characteristics. But he was quicker to cut to the chase.

"I'll tell you what you're going to do. You're going to get off your ass and, tonight, when Mlle Péricourt comes back, you're going to produce a corpse neatly tagged 'Édouard Péricourt,' have you got that? A day's work and you can leave here with a clear conscience. But you'd better think fast. Because, if you'd rather be sent to prison, I'm just the man to do it . . ."

Albert asked a number of his comrades, and they talked about the various graveyards nearby. They confirmed what he already knew: the largest cemetery was nearly four miles away at Pierreval. This would offer the greatest choice. He set off on foot.

At the edge of a wood were dozens and dozens of graves dug seemingly at random. In the beginning, they had been dug in neat rows but later, as the war churned out more and more bodies, they were buried in a slapdash manner as they arrived. There were graves everywhere, some with crosses, some without; on some the crosses had already rotted away. Here a name. There the words "a soldier" crudely carved on a wooden plaque. There were dozens that simply bore the words "a soldier." On others, an upturned bottle had been planted in the ground containing a scrap of paper with the soldier's name scrawled on it in case someone later wanted to know who was buried there.

Albert could easily have spent hours wandering among the crude tombs in Pierreval cemetery before finally choosing, the victim of his sempiternal indecisiveness, but reason finally prevailed. All right, he thought, it's getting late, and it's a long walk back to the Demobilization Center, I have to make a decision. He glanced around, spotted a grave with a cross that bore no name, and said to himself "That one."

He had taken some nails from a placard ripped from the barrier at the Center, now he looked around for a rock, hammered the broken half of Édouard Péricourt's name tag onto the cross, memorized the location, and then, like a wedding photographer, he took a few steps back to consider the overall effect.

Then he headed back, racked with fear and guilt because, even when well intentioned, lying was not in his nature. He thought about the young woman, about Édouard. He thought about the soldier whom fate had chosen to take Édouard's place and who would never now be found, a soldier who, until now, was unidentified, had vanished forever.

As he walked away from the cemetery back toward the Demobilization Center, the immediate risks occurred to him, flashing through his mind like falling dominos. It would all be fine, thought Albert, if all she wanted to do was pray. A sister wants to visit her brother's grave, so I find her a grave, what matter if it's her brother's or another man's, it's the feelings that matter. But things are more complicated now she wants to dig. Go looking at the bottom of a hole and who knows what you'll find. No papers, well that's one thing; a dead soldier is a dead soldier. But when you dig him up, what will you find? Some personal trinket? A distinctive mark? Or even simply a corpse that is too tall or too short?

But the choice has been made, he said "That one," and his fate is sealed. For better or worse. It has been a long time since Albert has trusted fate.

He arrived back at the Center exhausted. To make sure he catches his train to Paris—and he cannot miss it (assuming there is a train)—he will need to be back by 9:00 p.m. at the latest. The Center was already bubbling with excitement, men hopping around like fleas, their knapsacks packed hours ago, shouting, singing, yelling, clapping each other on the back. The worried noncoms are fretting about what they will do if the scheduled train does not arrive, as has happened all too often . . .

Albert left the hall. Standing in the doorway, he stared up at the sky. Would it be dark enough?

Capitaine Pradelle was looking dashing. A preening peacock. Freshly pressed uniform, freshly polished boots; all he lacked was a row of shiny medals. A few strides and already he was thirty feet away; Albert still had not moved.

"Well, are you coming?"

Just after six o'clock. Behind a large truck, a limousine was idling, its engine making a hushed purr as smoke streamed almost tenderly from the exhaust. Albert could have lived for a year on the price of a single tire for this car. He felt as poor as he was miserable.

When he got to the truck, the *capitaine* did not stop but walked on to the limousine, and Albert heard the car door closing softly. The young woman did not appear.

A driver with a thick beard who stank of sweat was sitting behind the wheel of the brand-new truck, a Berliet CBA worth thirty thousand francs. Business was obviously booming. It was clear that this was not his first job and that he trusted only himself. He stared at Albert through the rolled-down window, looked him up and down, and then took him aside. His fearsome fist gripped Albert's arm hard.

"If you're coming along, then you're implicated, you know that?"

Albert nodded. He turned toward the limousine, which was still exhaling its sweet, soft fumes. God, how cruel that warm breath seemed after so many years of suffering.

"So . . . ," the driver whispered, "how much are you stinging them for?"

Albert sensed that to this kind of man, a disinterested act would not go down well. He did a swift mental calculation.

"Three hundred francs."

"Fool!"

But there was a certain satisfaction on the face of the driver that he had played a better hand. A small-minded man, he got as much fulfillment from watching others fail as he did from his own little triumphs. He twisted around to look at the limousine.

"You not seen her? Strutting around in fur coats, living in the lap of luxury! You could have pushed her to four hundred, easy. Five hundred, even!"

The driver seemed about to reveal what he had negotiated, but discretion prevailed and he let go Albert's arm.

"Right, come on, we've not got much time."

Albert turned back to the car, the young woman had still not emerged to—I don't know—to say hello, to thank him . . . nothing, he was a servant, an underling.

He climbed into the truck, and they drove off. The limousine followed some distance behind, thereby reserving the option of overtaking and disappearing should the *gendarmerie* suddenly appear and start asking questions.

It was now pitch dark.

The truck's yellow headlights lit up the road, but inside the cab, Albert could not see his feet. He put his hand on the dashboard and peered through the windshield at the landscape. Now and then he said "turn right," or "this way," scared of losing his way, and the closer they came to the cemetery, the more his fear mounted. And so he made a decision. If it all goes wrong, I'll take off on foot through the forest. The driver won't come running after me. He'll get back in the truck and head for Paris, where he probably has other clients waiting.

Capitaine Pradelle, on the other hand, might well come after him; the bastard had already proved he had quick reactions. What could he do, Albert wondered. He felt a desperate urge to piss, and held it in with all his strength.

The truck climbed the last hill.

The cemetery extended almost to the edge of the road. The driver maneuvered the truck to park facing down the hill. When they left, he would not even need to use the accelerator, just release the brake and coast.

When the engine stopped, a strange silence descended, like a cloak falling around them. The *capitaine* immediately appeared at the door of the truck. The driver was to stand lookout while the body was unearthed, carried to the truck, and loaded into the back; then it would all be over.

Mlle Péricourt's limousine looked like a white animal crouching in the darkness ready to pounce. The car door opened, and the young woman appeared. She seemed tiny. To Albert, she seemed even younger than she had the day before. The *capitaine* made as if to stop her but did not have time to open his mouth; she walked on resolutely. Her presence in such a place at such a time was so preposterous that the men were speechless. With a curt jerk of her head, she signaled for them to set off.

They started walking.

The driver was carrying two shovels, Albert was dragging a large rolled-up tarpaulin in which to pile the soil, making it easier to fill in the grave. The *capitaine* strode ahead. Among the dead, he had always had a confident swagger. Scurrying after him, between Albert and the driver, came the young girl, Madeleine. It was a name Albert was very fond of. His grandmother's name.

"Where is it?"

They had been walking for a long time, first on one path, then another . . .

It is the *capitaine* who asks the question. He has turned around nervously. Though he is whispering, he cannot hide his irritation. He wants this thing over and done with. Albert looks around, raises his arm, realizes he is mistaken, tries to get his bearings. They can see him thinking, no, not that way.

"Over there," he says finally.

"You sure?" the driver sounds skeptical.

"Yes," Albert says, "It's over there."

They are still talking in whispers as though this were a ceremony.

"Get a move on, man!" The *capitaine* is getting angry.

At last, they are there.

Nailed to the cross, the broken name tag: Édouard Péricourt.

The men withdraw. Mlle Péricourt steps forward. She sobs discreetly. The driver has already dropped the shovels and gone back to keep watch. The night is inky black; they can barely see each other. Just the fragile figure of this young girl. Behind her, they bow their heads respectfully, though the *capitaine* continues to glance around anxiously. It is an awkward moment. Albert takes the initiative. He reaches out and gently places a hand on Madeleine Péricourt's shoulder, she turns and looks at him, she understands and steps back. The officer hands Albert a shovel, the young woman stands aside. They dig.

The ground is muddy, and digging is slow work. Near the front lines where there was little time to dig, graves were seldom deep; sometimes they were so shallow that rats had discovered them by morning. They would not have to dig long before they found something. Albert, now in a blind panic, stops regularly to listen. He can sense Mlle Péricourt's presence, standing stiffly next to a withered tree, as tense as he is. Nervously, she smokes a cigarette. Albert finds it striking that a woman like this would smoke cigarettes. Pradelle, too, glances at her, then come on, man, we haven't got all night. They get back to work.

What takes patience is digging without striking the corpse that lies beneath. Earth piles up in shovelfuls on the tarpaulin. What will the Péricourts do with the body, Albert wonders. Bury it in the garden? At night?

He stops.

"About fucking time!" hisses the *capitaine*, leaning down. He says it softly, he does not want the young woman to hear. Part of the body is visible, though it is difficult to see exactly what. The last part of the digging must be delicate; they need to scoop out the soil so as not to do any damage.

Albert works carefully. Pradelle is impatient.

"Get a move on, come on, it's not like you can hurt him now."

The shovel rips part of the greatcoat that served as a shroud and, instantly, the smell rises, nauseating. The officer turns away.

Even Albert takes a step back, though he has smelled his fair share of rotting flesh during the war, particularly when he worked as a stretcher bearer. Not to mention when Édouard was in the hospital. Thinking of him suddenly, Albert looks up toward the young woman who, though she is some distance away, is holding a handkerchief to her nose. She must truly love her brother, he thinks. Pradelle shoves him viciously and climbs out of the hole.

In a bound, he is standing beside the young lady, he lays his hands on her shoulders and turns her away from the grave, leaving Albert alone in the pit, in the stench. The young woman demurs, she shakes her head, she wants to stand at the grave. Albert stands, frozen, unsure how to react as the figure of Pradelle towers over him. Being in a hole, however shallow, he finds himself sweating despite the chill air, he is in a crater, the *capitaine* is standing on the edge, it all comes flooding back, he feels his throat tighten, terrified he is about to be buried alive, he starts to shake, but he thinks about his comrade, about Édouard, and forces himself to bend down and go back to his task.

These things can break your heart. With the tip of the shovel, Albert cautiously scrapes at the dirt. The heavy clay, the body carefully wrapped in the greatcoat, all this has slowed the process of decomposition. The thick fabric sticks to the gummy mud, the man's chest appears, the yellowish ribs, scraps of black putrid flesh crawling with maggots because there is still much left to eat.

From above, there is a cry, Albert looks up. The young woman is sobbing. The *capitaine* consoles her but gestures irritably to Albert over her shoulder, hurry up, what are you waiting for?

Albert drops the shovel, climbs out of the hole and starts to run. His heart is heaving, this whole thing makes him sick, the poor dead soldier, the driver trading on other people's grief, the *capitaine* who doesn't care which body goes in the coffin as long as it is done quickly . . . And the real Édouard, horribly mutilated, smelling like a corpse, strapped to a hospital bed. It is devastating to think that this is what they have fought for.

Seeing him arrive, the driver heaves a sigh of relief. In the blink of an eye, he has opened the canvas flap at the back of the truck, grabbed an iron hook, hitched it to the handle of the coffin and dragged it toward him. With the driver leading the way and Albert behind, they trudge back to the grave.

Albert is gasping for breath, the driver is walking quickly, he has done this before, while Albert struggles to keep up and more than once almost trips and drops the casket. Finally, they come to the grave. The stench is horrendous.

It is a beautiful oak coffin with gilded handles and an iron cross set into the lid. A cemetery is the most natural place for a coffin, but this one looks oddly out of place, too ornate for this bleak setting. It is not the sort of coffin used in wars and looks more suited to the good burghers who die in their beds than to these nameless young men shot to pieces. Albert does not have time to complete this fine philosophical thought. Everyone is eager for this to be over.

The lid of the casket is removed and set next to it.

The driver steps into the pit where the body lies, bends down and, with his bare hands, grabs both ends of the greatcoat then looks around for someone to help. It falls to Albert. Who else? He steps forward, climbs down into the hole, and immediately feels the same wave of panic; the terror is written in his face, because the driver asks:

"You going to be all right, boy?"

Together they stoop, the rotting stench hits them full in the face, they grab the thick fabric, and with a grunt—one, two—they swing the body up onto the side of the grave. It makes a mournful squelching sound. It is not heavy, what they have to lift. The remains weigh barely as much as a child.

The driver quickly climbs out and Albert is only too happy to follow. Together they gather up the edges of the greatcoat and lift everything into the coffin. This time, the sound is a dull thud, and in an instant the driver has replaced the lid. There may still be a few stray bones in the grave, but it does not matter. In any case, both the driver and the *capitaine* clearly think what they have is more than enough, given what they plan to do with the body. Albert looks around for Mlle Péricourt but she has already headed back to her car. He can hardly blame her, what she has suffered is unimaginable, seeing her brother reduced to a pile of writhing maggots.

They cannot nail down the lid down here, too much noise; they can do it later, on the drive back. For the time being, the driver uses two large canvas straps to hold the lid in place so that the smell will not leak into the truck. They walk back quickly through the graveyard, Albert trailing behind, the two others in front. The *capitaine* has lit a cigarette and is calmly smoking. Albert feels shattered; his back has borne the brunt of it.

They load the casket into the back of the truck, the driver and the *capitaine* take the front, with Albert still bringing up the rear: this, clearly, is where he belongs. They lift, and with a grunt, they push it inside, the wood scrapes against the metal flooring and echoes for a moment, but it is done, they cannot hang around. Behind them, the limousine is purring.

The young woman appears for a fleeting instant.

"Thank you, *monsieur*," she says.

Albert wants to say something. There is no time. Already, she has grabbed his arm, fumbled for his wrist, pressed a wad of notes into his hand, she squeezes it closed with her own; the effect of this simple gesture on Albert . . .

She is already walking back toward her car.

The driver lashes the coffin to the slats so that it does not move around, and Capitaine Pradelle signals to Albert, gesturing toward the cemetery. The hole has to be filled in quickly, because if the *gendarmes* find an empty grave, there will be an inquiry and that is something they don't need.

Albert picks up a shovel and runs between the graves. Then, suddenly wary, he stops and looks back.

He is alone.

One hundred feet away, he hears the limousine drive off and then the engine of the truck starts up as it rolls down the hill.

NOVEMBER
1919

10

Sprawled in a big leather armchair, Henri d'Aulnay-Pradelle casually slung one leg over the armrest as he held a large glass of vintage cognac at arm's length, studying it in the light. He listened to the conversations of those around him with studied detachment, to show that he was a man who "knew the ropes." He was fond of such slightly uncouth expressions. Were it up to him, he would go further still and be downright vulgar; he would take great pleasure in casually spouting obscenities in front of civilized people who could not afford to feel outraged.

For that, he would need five million francs.

With five million he could laze with complete impunity.

Pradelle visited the Jockey Club three times a week. Not that he particularly liked the place—in fact, given his expectations, he found the standard rather disappointing—but it was a symbol of his upward social mobility that never failed to thrill. The mirrors, the drapes, the carpets, the gildings, the calculated obsequiousness of the staff, even the exorbitant annual dues gave him an immense satisfaction, which was enhanced by the countless opportunities it offered for making contacts. His membership had been approved four months earlier, though only just—the great and the good of the Jockey Club found him suspect. But if they were to blackball all the *nouveaux riches*—given the calamitous fall in membership over recent years—the club would become an elegant waiting room. Besides, Pradelle had a number of influential sponsors, chief among them his father-in-law, who was impossible to refuse; also his friend Ferdinand, the grandson of Général Morieux, a dissolute young ne'er-do-well, but one with powerful connections. To discard a single link might mean forfeiting the whole chain, which was unthinkable, and besides the shortage of men sometimes made such compromises necessary . . . At least Aulnay-Pradelle had a name. The mind of a brigand, perhaps, but some measure of noble lineage. And so, in the end, he had been admitted. In fact, M. de La Rochefoucauld, the serving president, felt he rather blended in, this lanky young man who strutted around the rooms in a peremptory fashion. With an arrogance that confirmed the maxim that a conqueror is an ugly thing. Vulgar he might be, but he was a hero. And heroes are like pretty women; polite society always requires a few. And, at a time when it was difficult to come by a man of his age who was not missing an arm or a leg or indeed both, Pradelle was passably decorative.

So far, Aulnay-Pradelle had nothing but good things to say about the Great War. As soon as he was demobilized, he had got into buying and selling military surplus. Hundreds of French and American vehicles, engines, trailers, thousands of tons of wood, canvas, tarpaulin, tools, scrap iron, and spare parts the state no longer needed and was impatient to offload. Pradelle would buy up whole lots that he resold to railway and transport companies and agricultural businesses. Dividends were all the greater since the materials were stored in areas controlled by security guards open to bribes and all kinds of baksheesh so that, once inside, it was easy to haul away three truckloads instead of one and five tons instead of two.

The patronage of Général Morieux and his personal status as a national hero had opened many doors for Aulnay-Pradelle, and his role in the Union Nationale des Combattants—who had proved their usefulness by successfully breaking the most recent strikes—had brought him many more supporters. Thanks to whom he had already gained access to extensive markets of liquidated stocks where, for tens of thousands of borrowed francs, he could buy whole lots that, when sold, realized hundreds of thousands worth of profits.

"Hello, old chum!"

Léon Jardin-Beaulieu. A man of considerable merit, but one who was born short—four inches shorter than the average man, which was both not much and too much, but a catastrophe for him, since he craved respect.

"Hello, Henri," he said, walking with a swagger because he believed it made him look taller.

To Jardin-Beaulieu, being allowed to address Aulnay-Pradelle by his first name is an exquisite pleasure for which he would have sold both father and mother, as, indeed, he has. He affects the same tone as others so as to seem like them, thought Henri as he proffered a limp, almost careless hand and asked in an anxious whisper:

"So?"

"Nothing," Jardin-Beaulieu said, "not a word yet . . ."

Pradelle raised a peevish eyebrow; he had a talent for communicating wordlessly with his lackeys.

"I know," Jardin-Beaulieu apologized, "I know . . ."

Pradelle was impatient.

Some months earlier, the government had taken the decision to entrust the exhumation of the soldiers buried at the front to private companies. The plan was to rebury them in vast military necropolises; the ministerial directive stipulated "the construction of the smallest possible number of the largest possible cemeteries." The problem was, they were everywhere, these buried soldiers. In makeshift graveyards a few miles, sometimes barely a few yards, from the front lines. In ground that now needed to be restored to farmland. For years, almost since the beginning of the war, families had been demanding the right to visit the graves of their children. The planned mass burial grounds did not preclude the possibility of returning the bodies of soldiers to those families who wished to claim them, but the government hoped that, once created, these huge cemeteries where heroes might rest "next to comrades who were killed in action" would do something to temper their anger. And avoid burdening the government with the cost of individual exhumations, to say nothing of the thorny issue of sanitation, which was bound to prove costly at a time when the coffers were empty—until Germany repaid its debts.

The vast honorable and patriotic venture of bringing together the bodies of the dead involved a whole series of gratifyingly lucrative operations. There were hundreds of thousands of coffins to be made, since most soldiers had been buried in the bare ground, wrapped only in their greatcoats; hundreds of thousands of exhumations to be done by hand (the decree specifically insisted that the greatest possible care be taken); countless trucks to transport the coffins to the nearest train stations; and as many reburials in the new military cemeteries . . .

If Pradelle could secure a small part of this business, for a few centimes apiece his Chinamen would dig up thousands of bodies, his trucks would ferry the thousands of rotting corpses, his Senegalese workers would rebury them in rows of neat new graves each with a pretty cross at a premium price—in less than three years there would be enough money to renovate the family home at la Sallevière, which at present was a crumbling ruin.

At eighty francs per corpse, and assuming an actual cost of about twenty-five, Pradelle expected to make a net profit of two and a half million.

And if, besides, the ministry should approve various mutually agreed-upon orders, even allowing for the necessary bribes, it could come to five million.

The bargain of the century. To an entrepreneur, war represents significant business opportunities, even after it is over.

Kept well informed by Jardin-Beaulieu, whose father was a *deputé*, Pradelle was ahead of the game. No sooner had he been demobilized than he founded Pradelle & Cie. Jardin-Beaulieu and Morieux's grandson had each contributed fifty thousand francs together with their invaluable connections, and Pradelle had personally invested four hundred thousand. So that he would be the boss. And so that he could claim eighty percent of the profits.

The Adjudication Committee dealing with procurement contracts was meeting today; it had been in conclave since 2:00 p.m. Thanks to his contacts and the little matter of a hundred and fifty thousand francs in bribes, Pradelle had it in his pocket: three committee members, two of whom he controlled, were to evaluate the various proposals and decide—completely impartially—that Pradelle & Cie had submitted the most competitive quotes, that the sample casket they had delivered to the Graves Commission had been the one most suited to the dignity of those who had died for France and the exigencies of the treasury. In consideration of which, Pradelle would be accorded a number of contracts, a dozen if things went well. Perhaps more.

"And the ministry?"

Jardin-Beaulieu's face creased into a broad smile; he had an answer . . .

"It's in the bag!"

"Yes, yes, I know that," Pradelle snapped irritably. "But when?"

His worries did not merely concern the deliberations of the Adjudication Committee. The War Graves Commission, which came under the direct responsibility of the Ministère des Pensions, was authorized, in emergencies or when necessary, to award contracts by simple agreement, without issuing an invitation to compete. If this should happen, Pradelle & Cie would have a virtual monopoly and could charge whatever they wished—as much as 130 francs per corpse . . .

Pradelle feigned the aloofness that great minds adopt when faced with fraught situations, but in fact he was in a highly nervous state. Alas, Jardin-Beaulieu did not yet have an answer to this question. His smile shriveled.

"We don't know . . ."

He was ashen. Pradelle turned away, effectively dismissing the man. Jardin-Beaulieu beat a retreat, pretended to spot a friendly face, and scuttled pathetically to the other end of the vast room. Pradelle watched him go; the man was wearing shoe lifts. A pity—were it not for his Napoleon complex, which meant he lost all dignity, the man might have been intelligent. But it was not for his intelligence that

Pradelle had brought him on board. Jardin-Beaulieu had two invaluable advantages: a father in parliament and a fiancée who, though penniless (why else would she be with such a midget!), was ravishing, a girl with dark-brown hair and a pretty mouth, whom Jardin-Beaulieu was to marry in a few months. From the moment they were introduced, Pradelle sensed that this girl was suffering in silence from this expedient alliance that demeaned her beauty. The sort of woman who would feel the need to exact her revenge, and as he watched her move around the Jardin-Beaulieus' drawing room—Pradelle boasted an unerring instinct for women and for horses—he was willing to wager that, if he played his cards well, she would not even wait until the ceremony.

Pradelle returned to contemplating his glass of cognac and, for the umpteenth time, considered the best strategy to adopt.

To make so many coffins, he would have to subcontract work to a number of specialized companies, something strictly forbidden by his contract with the government. But if he were careful, no one would look too closely. Everyone had a vested interest in turning a blind eye. What mattered—opinion on this was unanimous—was that, within a reasonable delay, the country would be able to boast a small number of extremely large cemeteries, making it possible for everyone finally to file this war among its other unpleasant memories.

And Pradelle would have earned the right to wave his snifter of cognac and belch loudly in the Jockey Club without anyone disapproving.

So absorbed was he in his thoughts that he did not notice his father-in-law come in. It was the quality of the silence that told him he had made a social gaffe, the tremulous hush that greets a bishop entering a cathedral. By the time he realized, it was too late. To remain in this languorous position in the presence of the old man signified a lack of respect he would not be forgiven. To change his posture too quickly would be to acknowledge his subservience to the old man in front of everyone. Neither solution was palatable. To avoid provocation, Pradelle opted for the least damaging indignity. He arched his back as casually as he could, brushing an invisible speck from his shoulder. His right foot slipped to the floor and he settled himself upright in his chair, mentally adding this humiliation to the list of scores he would one day settle.

M. Péricourt strolled into the Jockey Club with an easy grace. He pretended not to notice his son-in-law's maneuver, mentally adding the incident to the list of debts to be repaid. He moved between the tables, stopping here and there to bestow the flaccid handshake of a benevolent monarch, uttering the names of those present with the dignity of a doge—Good morning, dear friend; Ah, Ballanger, Frappier, I didn't see you there; Evening, Godard,—occasionally hazarding a trace of irony—well, well, Palamède de Chavigne, if my eyes don't deceive me—and, as he drew level with Henri, he simply lowered his eyes with the knowing air of a sphinx and walked on toward the fireplace, extending his hands with exaggerated satisfaction.

Turning around, he could observe his son-in-law from behind. It was a deliberate strategy. It must be deeply irritating to be watched from behind. From the way the two men maneuvered, it was clear their little chess game had only just begun and there was everything to play for.

Their mutual antipathy had been instantaneous and unruffled, almost serene. The promise of slow-burning hatred. Péricourt had immediately recognized Pradelle as a scoundrel but had done nothing to discourage Madeleine's infatuation. There were no words to describe it, but one only had to see them together to know that Pradelle was very attentive to her pleasures, and that she wanted him, wanted him desperately.

M. Péricourt loved his daughter—after his fashion, of course, which had never been overly demonstrative—and would have been happy to know she was happy had she not become foolishly besotted with Henri d'Aulnay-Pradelle. Being extraordinarily wealthy, Madeleine Péricourt had been coveted by many men and, though only passably attractive, had had her share of suitors. She was no fool, quick tempered like her late mother, she was a strong-willed woman who did not easily lose her composure nor succumb to temptation. Before the war, she had been quick to spot them, the parvenus who found her plain of face but delightful of dowry. Her manner of dismissing them was as effective as it was discreet. So many proposals of marriage had made her confident—too confident. She had been twenty-five when war was declared, thirty by the time it was over, and she had suffered the devastating loss of her younger brother. In the meantime she had begun to age. This, perhaps, was the explanation. She met Henri d'Aulnay-Pradelle in May; they were married in July.

Men could not see what it was in this Henri that had that justified such unseemly haste; he was handsome enough, granted, but even so . . . So much for the men. Women, on the other hand, could see it right away. They had only to look at him, those thick curls, the pale-blue eyes, the broad shoulders, that complexion, and they understood why Madeleine Péricourt had been drawn to sample such delights, why she had been captivated.

M. Péricourt had not insisted, the battle was lost before it was begun. He made do with judiciously imposed limits. Among the bourgeois, this is known as a marriage contract. Madeleine had made no objection. The dashing son-in-law, on the other hand, had sulked when he saw the draft drawn up by the family lawyer. The two men had stared at each other without uttering a word, a sensible precaution. Madeleine would remain sole heir and possessor of her property and would enjoy joint ownership of all assets accumulated during the marriage. She understood her father's reservations about Henri, of which this contract was irrefutable proof. To those with great fortunes, prudence becomes second nature. She smiled at her husband and told him it did not change anything. Pradelle, for his part, knew that it changed everything.

He felt cheated at first, poorly rewarded for his efforts. In the lives of many of his friends, marriage had settled their problems. It could be difficult to negotiate and required skillful maneuvering, but when achieved, it was a godsend: once married, a man could do as he pleased. For Henri, on the other hand, marriage had changed nothing. Granted, from the point of view of status, he had to admit it had been a boon, but Henri was a poor man with immoderate tastes. From his personal businesses he had quickly pocketed a hundred thousand francs, which he immediately invested in refurbishing the family house, but there was so much to do . . . the whole estate was collapsing.

Henri had not found his fortune. But the deal had been far from a failure. First, the marriage would finally put an end to the incident on Hill 113, which had been causing him some anxiety. If it were to resurface (and incidents that might seem long forgotten sometimes did resurface), it was no longer a risk, since he was now rich, even if only by proxy, and allied to a family as powerful as it was prestigious. Marrying Madeleine Péricourt had made him almost invulnerable.

Second, he had gained an extraordinary advantage: access to the family contacts. (He was the son-in-law of Marcel Péricourt, an intimate of M. Deschanel, and friend of M. Poincaré, M. Daudet, and many others.) And he was very satisfied with the initial return on investment. In a few months, he would be able to look his future father-in-law straight in the eye: he was fucking his daughter, he was exploiting his contacts, and three years from now, if all went as planned, he would loll in an armchair any way he pleased when the old man came into the smoking room.

M. Péricourt kept himself abreast of how his son-in-law was making his money. There was no doubt the young man was swift and efficient: he managed three companies that, in a few short months, had already returned profits totaling almost a million. Seen from this perspective, he was a man admirably adapted to his times, but M. Péricourt instinctively mistrusted his success. Too sudden, too questionable.

He had quickly attracted supporters and clients: great fortunes invariably attract courtiers.

Henri watched his father-in-law at work. He was impressed. There was no doubt the old curmudgeon was a master. He had style. With discriminating munificence he dispensed advice, approval, and endorsements. His entourage had learned to consider his suggestions as orders and his reservations as vetoes. He was the sort of man with whom it was impossible to be angry when he refused to grant a favor, since it was within his power to take away whatever you had left.

At that moment, Labourdin finally rushed into the smoking room pouring sweat, fluttering a large handkerchief. Henri suppressed a sigh of relief, drained his brandy, got to his feet, and taking the man by the shoulder, steered him into the next room. Labourdin scampered alongside on fat stubby legs, as if he were not sweaty enough . . .

Labourdin was a fool made great by idiocy. In him, it manifested itself as an indomitable tenaciousness, something of a virtue in politics, though in his case it was due to his absolute want of imagination and a complete inability to change his mind. Mediocre in everything, invariably ridiculous, Labourdin was the sort of man one could safely appoint to any position; he was a loyal beast of burden, one could ask anything of him. Everything about him was written on his face: his affability, his love of food, his cowardice, his insignificance, and, especially, his prurience. Incapable of resisting a filthy joke, a lewd remark, he stared at every woman with unbridled lust, especially maidservants, whose *derrières* he fondled whenever they turned their backs, and was formerly in the habit of visiting brothels three times a week. "Formerly" because, as his reputation spread beyond the boundaries of the *arrondissement* of which he was mayor, many women clamored for his attentions, and there were always one or two prepared to spare him a trip to the whorehouse in exchange for an authorization, a favor, a signature, a rubber stamp. One only had to look at him to know Labourdin was happy. A full belly and a full pair of balls, he was always ready for the next meal or the next piece of ass. He owed his election victory to a small group of influential men over whom M. Péricourt presided.

"You are about to be nominated to the Adjudication Committee," Pradelle told him one day.

Labourdin loved being appointed to commissions, committees, delegations, considering it proof of his importance. And since the news came by way of his son-in-law, he assumed he had been nominated by M. Péricourt himself. In a large, spidery scrawl, he had carefully noted down the instructions he was to follow. When he had finished issuing orders, Pradelle gestured to the piece of paper.

"Now, get rid of that list," he said. "You don't want to see it plastered up in the window of the Bon Marché!"

For Labourdin, this had been the beginning of a nightmare. Terrified at the thought of failing in his mission, he had spent sleepless nights memorizing the instructions one by one, but the more he recited them, the more confused he became; the nomination was by now torment, the commission his *bête noire*.

During the course of today's meeting, he had had to expend every ounce of concentration, he had had to deliberate, to make pronouncements; he had emerged exhausted. Exhausted but happy, he emerged with the satisfaction of having done his duty. In the hansom cab, he had been practicing what he considered "elegant turns of phrase," of which his favorite was "My dear friend, without wishing to boast, I think I can safely say . . ."

"How many in Compiègne?" Pradelle interrupted.

Hardly had the door to the smoking room swung shut than the wild-eyed young man was haranguing him, leaving him no time to speak. Whatever Labourdin had imagined, it was not this, which is to say that, as always, he had not imagined at all.

"Well, I, uh . . ."

"How many?" Pradelle thundered.

Labourdin could not remember. Compiègne . . . He put down his handkerchief and quickly rummaged through in his pockets, found the folded slips of paper on which he had noted the results of the decisions.

"C . . . Compiègne . . . ," he stammered, "Compiègne, let's see . . ."

Nothing was ever fast enough for Pradelle, he tore the piece of paper from Labourdin's hand and stepped to one side, staring at the list of figures. Eighteen thousand coffins for Compiègne, five thousand for Laon, more than six thousand for Colmar, eight thousand for the district of Nancy and Lunéville . . . The figures for Verdun, Amiens, Épinal, and Reims were yet to come . . . The results were better than he had dared to hope. Pradelle could not suppress a satisfied smile, which did not go unnoticed by Labourdin.

"We're meeting again tomorrow morning," the mayor said, "and again on Saturday."

He fancied that the moment had come for his fine turn of phrase.

"So you see, my dear friend, without wishing to . . ."

But at that moment, the door was flung open, a voice called, "Henri!" . . . there was a commotion in the next room.

Pradelle strode out.

At the far end of the room, next to the fireplace, a small crowd was bustling about while others rushed over from the billiard room, the smoking room . . .

Pradelle heard raised voices, took a few more steps, more curious than concerned.

His father-in-law was sitting on the floor, leaning against the fireplace, his legs stretched out, his eyes closed, his face waxen, his right hand clutching his chest as though trying to hold in or rip out an organ. "Smelling salts!" cried a voice, "Give him some air!" said another, the club steward arrived and asked everyone to make room.

"Well now, Péricourt, what's all this fuss?"

Then, turning discreetly to Pradelle.

"You'd better send for a car at once, my friend, this is serious."

Pradelle hurried away.

My God, what a quirk of fate.

The day he became a millionaire, his father-in-in law looked set to go and meet his maker.

Such extraordinary luck was scarcely believable.

II

Albert's mind was a complete blank, it was impossible to string two notions together, to imagine what was going to happen; he tried to organize his thoughts but could not. He walked quickly, constantly stroking the blade of the knife in his pocket. The minutes ticked by, the métro stations and the streets flashed past, and still he had not a single constructive idea. He could scarcely believe what he was doing, yet he was doing it nonetheless. He was determined; he would stop at nothing.

This dependence on morphine . . . From the beginning it had been a problem. Édouard could no longer do without it. Until now, Albert had managed to provide for his needs. This time, although he had scraped together everything he could, there was simply not enough money. And so when, after days spent in agony, his comrade had begged Albert to kill him because he could no longer stand the pain, an exhausted Albert had acted on instinct, he had grabbed the first kitchen knife he could find and gone downstairs, like an automaton, taken the métro to Bastille, and headed along the rue Sedaine into the Greek quarter. He was determined to get morphine for Édouard, if necessary, he was prepared to kill for it.

A thought finally occurred to him when he set eyes on the Greek, an elephantine man of about thirty who walked with his feet set wide apart, panting at every step, sweating in spite of the November chill. As Albert stared in panic at the huge paunch, the heavy breasts bouncing beneath the sweater, the bovine neck, the sagging jowls, he thought the knife he had brought was useless, he needed a blade of at least six inches. Maybe twenty. The situation now seemed far from auspicious, and the realization that he had come so ill equipped depressed him. "Always the same," he could hear his mother say, "never could organize yourself. Never could see beyond the end of your nose, boy . . . ," and she would roll her eyes to heaven, calling God as her witness. In front of her new husband (this was a figure of speech, they were not actually married, but Mme Maillard liked everything to be just so), she would complain bitterly about her son. Meanwhile, his "stepfather"—a department head at La Samaritaine—would study his shoelaces, but the contempt was there, too, just the same. Faced with them, even if he could summon the energy, Albert would have been unable to defend himself because every day he did a little more to prove them right.

Everything seemed to be conspiring against him; these truly were difficult times.

They were to meet next to the public urinal on the corner of the rue Saint-Sabin. Albert had no idea how such things were done. He had made contact with the Greek by telephoning a café, saying he had got the number from a friend of a friend; since the Greek spoke barely a dozen words of French, he had asked no questions. Antonopoulos. Everyone said Poulos. Even himself.

In fact, he said "Poulos!" as he arrived.

For a man of such exceptional corpulence, he moved with surprising agility in short, rapid strides. The knife was too short, the guy was moving too quickly . . . Albert's plan was truly pathetic. Having glanced around, the Greek grabbed Albert's arm and dragged him into the urinal. There had been no flush for some time, and the air was unbreathable, something that did not seem to bother Poulos at all. This fetid place was a little like a waiting room. To Albert, who had a fear of confined spaces, it was a double torture.

"Cash?" the Greek demanded.

He wanted to see the money and jerked his chin toward Albert's pocket, not knowing that it contained a knife whose blade, now that the two men were squeezed together in the urinal, proved to be even more derisory. Albert turned slightly to expose his other pocket, from which several twenty-franc bills conspicuously emerged. The Greek nodded.

"Five," he said.

This was what had been agreed on the telephone. The Greek turned to leave.

"Wait," Albert cried, grabbing his sleeve.

Poulos stopped and looked at him nervously.

"I need more . . . ," Albert whispered.

He enunciated excessively, gesturing with his hands (when talking to foreigners, Albert often spoke as though they were deaf). Poulos knitted his thick brows.

"Twelve," Albert said.

He flashed the whole wad of bills, though he could not spend them since this was all they had to live on for the next three weeks. Poulos's face lit up. He jabbed a finger at Albert and nodded.

"Twelve. You stay!"

He made to leave.

"No!" Albert stopped him.

The stomach-churning stench of the *pissotière* and the prospect of getting out of this cramped space where, with every passing minute, he felt his panic mounting helped him adopt a more persuasive tone. His only stratagem was to convince the Greek to let him come along.

Poulos shook his head.

"All right," Albert said and stepped past him.

The Greek grabbed him by the sleeve, hesitated for a moment. Albert was pitiful. Sometimes it was his great strength. He did not have to make an effort to look pathetic. Eight months back in civilian life, and he was still wearing the clothes he had been given when he was demobilized. When he was discharged he had been given a choice between a greatcoat and fifty-two francs. He had taken the coat because it was cold. In fact, the government was simply trying to offload hastily dyed military greatcoats. That evening it rained, and the dye began to run in great miserable streaks. Albert had gone back and said that he had thought about it and would rather have the fifty-two francs, but it was too late, he should have thought earlier.

He had also kept his army boots, which were by now half worn out, and two army-issue blankets. All these things had left their mark, and not just dye marks; he had that haggard, exhausted face one saw in so many demobilized men, that expression of defeat and resignation.

The Greek studied his careworn features and made a decision.

"Come, quick," he whispered.

In that moment, Albert was stepping into the unknown.

The two men walked up the rue Sedaine as far as the passage Salarnier. When they reached the alley, Poulos pointed to the pavement and said again: "Stay!"

Albert surveyed the deserted streets. At just after 7:00 p.m., the only lights were those of a café a hundred yards away.

"Here!"

The command was unequivocal.

The Greek strode off without waiting for a response.

He turned back more than once to ensure that his customer was obediently waiting where he had indicated. Albert watched helplessly, but as soon as the man suddenly entered a building on the right, he broke into a run, racing down the alley as fast as he could, never taking his eyes off the spot where he had seen Poulos disappear, a ramshackle building from which wafted the smell of cooking. Albert pushed open the door and made his way down a hall. He took the few steps leading down to the basement. A faint glow from the streetlight filtered through the grimy panes of a window. He saw the Greek crouching on the floor, his left arm fumbling in a recess cut into the wall. On the floor next to him he had set down the small wooden hatch that covered it. Albert did not break his stride, he ran across the cellar, grabbed the hatch—much heavier than he had expected—and, with both hands, brought it down on the Greek's head. The blow echoed like a gong; Poulos crumpled. Only then did Albert realize what he had just done and was so terrified that all he wanted to do was run away . . .

He pulled himself together. Was the Greek dead?

He bent down and listened. Poulos was breathing heavily. It was difficult to tell whether the man was seriously hurt, but a thin line of blood trickled from his scalp. Albert felt so dizzy he thought he might black out. He balled his fists, repeating, "Come on, come on . . ." He hunkered down, thrust his arm into the cubbyhole and pulled out a shoebox. A miracle: it was full to the brim with morphine ampoules, twenty and thirty milligrams. Albert recognized the dosages; he had been doing this long enough.

He closed the box, struggled to his feet, and as he did so he saw Poulos's arm sweep around in a wide circle . . . Unlike Albert, he was well equipped, a switchblade, with a razor-sharp blade. It slashed across Albert's hand so quickly that he felt only a brief, burning sensation. He whirled around, one foot in the air; the heel of his boot caught the man's temple. His head struck the floor with a dull clang. Still clutching the shoebox, Albert stamped on the hand holding the knife, then set the box down, picked up the wooden hatch again, and began beating the Greek over the head. He stopped. He was panting from the effort, from fear. He was bleeding heavily from the deep cut on his hand, and his greatcoat was badly stained. He had always been terrified by the sight of blood. It was now that the pain finally hit, reminding him he needed to take emergency action. He searched the cellar, found a dusty piece of cloth, which he wound around his left hand. Fearfully, as though stealing up on a sleeping beast, he went back and bent over the body of the Greek. His breathing was heavy and regular; he obviously had a hard head. Trembling, Albert staggered out of the building with the shoebox tucked under his arm.

Given this injury, he had to abandon the idea of taking the métro or the tram. Covering his improvised bandage and the bloodstains on his coat, he caught a taxi at Bastille.

The driver was much the same age as Albert. As they drove, he brazenly stared at his passenger, who was pale as death, perched on the edge of his seat, hugging his left hand to his stomach. He became worried when Albert rolled down the window because in the cramped car he was beginning to feel a panic he could barely contain. The driver thought the man was about to throw up.

"You're not feeling sick, are you?"

"No, no," Albert said, with what little cheerfulness he could muster.

"'Cos if you're feeling sick, you can get out right here!"

"No, no," Albert said, "I'm just tired."

Despite this reassurance, the driver had misgivings.

"You sure you've got the fare?"

Albert took a twenty-franc bill from his pocket with his good hand and waved it. The driver felt relieved, but only for a moment. He was an old hand, he had seen it all, and this was his taxi. And being a businessman, he would stoop to anything.

"Sorry, friend! It's just that, lads like you, they . . ."

"What do you mean 'lads like me'?" Albert said.

"You know, men who have just been demobilized . . ."

"Because I suppose you haven't been demobilized?"

"No sir, I spent my war right here. I'm asthmatic and I've got one leg shorter than the other."

"A lot of guys would have enlisted anyway. And a lot of them came back with one leg a lot fucking shorter than the other."

The driver did not take kindly to this, ex-soldiers were all the same, forever going on about their war, forever giving little homilies, people had had just about enough of heroes. The true heroes were dead! Now they really had been heroes. Besides, there was something suspicious about guys who were always going on about the trenches, most of them had spent the war sitting behind a desk.

"So you're saying that we didn't do our duty, is that it?"

Besides, what did men who had just been demobilized know about the hardships ordinary people had had to endure? Albert had heard the spiel before, he knew it by heart, the price of coal and the price of bread, it was the sort of information he remembered. This was something he had realized since being demobilized: to live in peace, it was best to put away the victor's stripes in a drawer.

The driver dropped him on the corner of the rue Simart, asked for twelve francs, and before he would leave, insisted Albert give him a tip.

There were hordes of Russians living in the area, but the doctor was a Frenchman named Martineau.

Albert had met him in June when the first attacks started. No one knew how Édouard had managed to get his hands on morphine while he was in the sanatorium, but he had become terribly dependent. Albert tried to reason with him: it's a slippery slope, old man, you can't carry on like this, we need to get you well. Édouard would not listen and proved as stubborn as he had been about the graft. Albert did not understand. I know a legless cripple, he would say, the man who sells lottery tickets on the rue Faubourg-Saint-Martin, he was treated at the Hôpital Février in Châlons, and he told me about the sort of grafts surgeons can do these days, all right, the patients don't come out looking handsome, but at least they have a human face. But Édouard was not even listening, it was always no, no, no, then he would go back to playing patience at the kitchen table and smoking cigarettes through his nostril. He gave off a putrid smell, which was hardly surprising with his gullet wide open to the world . . . He drank through a funnel. Albert had managed to get him a second-hand masticating device (from a surgical patient who had died when his graft failed to take, a real stroke of luck!), which made his life a little simpler, but even so, everything was complicated.

Édouard had been discharged from the Hôpital Rollin in June and a few days later began to display worrying signs of anxiety: his whole body would shudder, he sweated profusely, vomited what little he managed to eat . . . Albert felt helpless. The first seizures brought on by morphine withdrawal were so violent Albert had had to strap him to the bed—as he had in the field hospital in November . . . so much for the war being over—and stop up the door so the other tenants would not come and put Édouard out of his misery (and theirs).

A skeleton possessed by a demon, Édouard was terrifying to behold.

Eventually, Docteur Martineau—a surly, distant man who claimed to have performed twelve amputations in the trenches in 1916—had agreed to give him an injection, and Édouard did become a little calmer. It was Docteur Martineau who had put Albert in touch with Basile, who became his supplier. Basile obviously made his living breaking into pharmacies, hospitals, and clinics; he could get any medication you wanted. Shortly afterward, Basile had offered Albert a grab bag of morphine ampoules he needed to offload; it was a clearance sale of sorts.

Albert carefully recorded the each injection, together with the day, the time, and the dosage, to help Édouard cope with his dependence, and he would lecture him in his feeble way, though it had little effect. But at least for the moment, Édouard appeared to be on the mend. He no longer cried for hours on end, but he no longer drew, despite the sketchpads and the pencils Albert had brought him. He seemed to spend his time lying on the sofa staring into space. September came around, the stock of morphine was exhausted, and Édouard was still not weaned. In June, he had been taking sixty milligrams a day; three months later he needed ninety milligrams, and Albert could see no end of it. Édouard lived as a recluse; he barely communicated. Albert, meanwhile, spent his time desperately trying to find money to pay for the morphine, to pay for the rent, the food, the coal—new clothes were out of the question, much too expensive. Money ran through his fingers at an alarming speed. He had pawned everything he could, he had even fucked Mme Monestier, the fat manageress at L'Horlogerie Mécanique for whom he stuffed envelopes and who, in return, put a little more in his pay packet (this was how Albert saw it, he liked to play the martyr. In fact, he had rather enjoyed the opportunity, after six months of being without a woman . . . Mme Monestier had huge breasts, he never knew quite what to do with them, but she was kind and had every reason to cheat on her husband, an arrogant bastard who had been on the home front and claimed that any soldier who had not been awarded an Iron Cross was unworthy of the name).

Most of Albert's budget was spent on morphine. The price was soaring, the price of everything was soaring. Morphine was just like everything else, the price was linked to the cost of living. Albert deplored the fact that a government who, to stem inflation, could introduce the *costume national,* a cheap suit that cost a hundred ten francs, could not introduce an *ampoule national* of morphine for five francs. They could also have implemented "national bread," "national coal," "national shoes," "national rent," and even a "national job"; Albert wondered whether these were not precisely the measures that led to Bolshevism.

The bank had not taken him back. Gone was the time when members of parliament were wont to declare, hand on heart, that the country "owed a debt of gratitude to *les chers poilus* who had fought in the trenches." Albert had received a letter explaining that the state of the economy made it impossible to rehire him; that to do so would mean laying off men who, during "the fifty-two months of this brutal war, had provided singular service to the company . . ." etc.

For Albert, getting money had become a full-time occupation.

The situation had become yet more complicated when, in an ugly scene, Basile was arrested with his pockets stuffed with drugs and spattered with the blood of a local pharmacist.

Finding himself without a dealer overnight, Albert took to hanging out in seedy bars and asking for addresses. But finding morphine proved to be less difficult than expected; with the cost of living spiraling, Paris had become a hub for trafficking of every kind; a man could find anything he needed—Albert had found the Greek.

Docteur Martineau disinfected the wound and sutured it closed. Albert winced and gritted his teeth.

"A fine knife," the doctor muttered and said nothing more.

He had opened the door without comment or question. He lived on the fourth floor in an apartment that was unfurnished save for a sofa tucked in one corner, the curtains were permanently drawn, the floor littered with crates of books, paintings were stacked against the wall; two chairs facing each other in the hallway served as a waiting room. He could have been mistaken for a lawyer but for the adjoining room, which had a hospital bed and surgical equipment. His fee was less than Albert's taxi fare.

As he left, Albert thought of Cécile, though he did not know why.

He decided to go the rest of the way on foot. He needed to keep moving. Cécile, the life he had once had, the hopes he had once nurtured . . . It seemed foolish, succumbing to maudlin nostalgia, but as he wandered through the streets with his shoebox under his arm, his left hand bandaged, thinking about all those things that had so quickly faded to memories, he felt like a stateless person. And, as of tonight, a thug, perhaps a murderer. He had no idea how this vicious cycle would end. Barring a miracle. And even then . . . Albert had experienced a miracle or two since being demobilized, and each had turned into a nightmare. Take Cécile, since Albert was just thinking about her . . . This problem with Cécile had begun with a miracle made possible by his new stepfather. Albert should have been suspicious. After the bank declined to rehire him, he had searched and searched, applied for every job he could; he had even taken part in the rat extermination program. But as his mother pointed out, at twenty-five centimes a rat, he was not about to make a quick fortune. In the end, all he had come away with was a rat bite, which was unsurprising, he had always been a clumsy boy. All this to is say that, three months after being demobilized, he was as poor as Job—not much of a catch for a girl like Cécile. Mme Maillard felt for the girl. And it was true: what future could he give the delicate, graceful Cécile. It was clear that, in Cécile's shoes, Mme Maillard would have done the same. And so, after three months spent doing piecemeal work and waiting for the "demobilization bonus" that everyone had talked about but the government could not afford to pay, the miracle happened: his stepfather found him a job as an elevator attendant at La Samaritaine.

The management would have preferred a veteran with rather more medals to flaunt, "for customer relations," but they would take what they could get; they took Albert.

He operated a handsome wrought-iron elevator and announced the floors. Though he never said as much to anyone (although he mentioned it in a letter to Édouard), he did not much enjoy the work. He did not quite know why. The realization finally came one afternoon in June when the doors opened and he saw Cécile in the company of a square-shouldered young man. They had not seen each other since her last letter, to which he had simply replied, "As you wish."

That first second had been his first mistake; Albert had pretended not to recognize her and busied himself with the control panel for the elevator. Cécile and her friend were going to the top floor, which seemed to take an eternity given that the elevator stopped at every floor. It was an ordeal. Albert's voice croaked as he announced each floor. Despite himself, he inhaled Cécile's new perfume: elegant, chic, reeking of money. Her friend also reeked of money. He was young, evidently younger than Cécile, which Albert found shocking.

What he found humiliating was not so much the unexpected meeting as being seen in his ridiculous uniform. Like a tin soldier. With fringed epaulets.

Cécile lowered her eyes. It was obvious that she was embarrassed for him, she wrung her hands and stared at her feet. For his part, the square-shouldered young man marveled at the elevator, plainly dazzled by the wonders of modern technology.

Albert had never known minutes so interminable, excepting those he had spent buried alive in a shell crater; in fact to him the two incidents felt obscurely similar.

Cécile and her friend got out at the lingerie department; they did not even exchange a look. Back on the ground floor, Albert deserted his post at the elevator, took off his uniform, and left without even asking for what he was owed. A week's work for nothing.

Some days later, moved, perhaps, by seeing him reduced to such a menial post, Cécile returned his engagement ring. By mail. Albert wanted to send it back, he did not want charity, had he really looked so poor in that garish flunkey's uniform? But times were hard, with Caporal cigarettes selling for one franc fifty apiece, savings had to be made, coal prices had gone through the roof. He took the ring to the pawnbroker. Since the armistice, people called it the *Crédit Municipal*, it sounded more republican.

He had so many things there waiting to be redeemed, but he had written them all off.

After this incident, the only job Albert had been able to find was as a sandwich man, traipsing the streets carrying advertising boards strapped to him front and back; the thing weighed more than a dead donkey. Advertisements promoting the prices at La Samaritaine or the quality of De Dion-Bouton bicycles. He dreaded the thought of running into Cécile again. Being seen in fancy-dress uniform was bad enough, but the thought of being seen covered in advertisements for Campari was unbearable.

He might as well throw himself into the Seine.

12

M. Péricourt did not open his eyes until he was sure that he was alone. All that fuss . . . All those people milling around the Jockey Club. As though fainting in public were not embarrassing enough . . .

And then there had been Madeleine, his son-in-law, his housekeeper, all standing at the foot of his bed wringing their hands, and the telephone in the hall ringing and ringing, and Docteur Blanche with his drops and his pills, his voice like a curate and his ceaseless prating advice. Not that he had found anything wrong, he talked about heart trouble, exhaustion, anxiety, the unwholesome air of Paris, he talked a lot of nonsense—the man was well suited to a university position.

The Péricourt family owned a vast town house overlooking the parc Monceau. M. Péricourt had given over most of it to his daughter, who, after her marriage, had the third floor, where she and her husband lived, redecorated to her taste. M. Péricourt confined himself to a six-room apartment on the top floor, though he only really used the vast bedroom—which also served him as a library and a study—and a bathroom, which, though small, was adequate for a single man. As far as he was concerned, the whole mansion was reduced to this apartment. Since the death of his wife, he had rarely set foot in the other rooms, except the immense ground-floor dining hall. Had such things been left to him, receptions would have been held at Voisin, and that would be an end to it. His bed was set in an alcove curtained in dark-green velvet; he had never brought a woman here—he went elsewhere for such things—this was his space.

Earlier, when he was brought home, Madeleine had sat patiently with him for a long time. When, finally, she took his hand, he bridled.

"It's like a damn wake!" he said.

Anyone but Madeleine would have protested; she simply smiled. The opportunities for them to spend time alone together were rare. She really is not a pretty girl, Péricourt was thinking. He looks old, thought Madeleine.

"I'll leave you in peace," she said, getting to her feet.

She gestured to the bell pull, he nodded, yes, fine, stop worrying, she checked the glass, the bottle of water, the handkerchief, the tablets.

"Turn the light out, would you?" he said.

But he quickly regretted his daughter leaving.

Though he felt better—the bout of apoplexy at the Jockey Club was already a distant memory—he suddenly experienced the same strange malaise that had struck him down earlier. It started in his belly, coursing through his chest to his shoulders, his head. His heart pounded wildly, as though trying to escape. Péricourt reached for the bell pull, then changed his mind; something told him that he was not dying, that his time had not yet come.

The bedroom was bathed in a dim glow, he stared at the book-shelves, the paintings, the pattern on the carpet as though seeing them for the first time. He felt terribly old, perhaps because everything around him, every tiny detail, seemed unexpectedly new. The feeling of suffocation was so intense, the sudden tightness in his throat so brutal, that tears sprang to his eyes. He began to weep. A flood of simple, honest tears, a sadness more overwhelming than he could remember ever feeling—except perhaps as a child—but one that brought with it a strange relief. He surrendered to it, allowed the tears to trickle unashamedly, warm, comforting. He wiped his face with a corner of the sheet, caught his breath, but it was no use;

the tears kept coming, the grief engulfed him. Am I going senile, he wondered, though he did not really believe it. He propped himself up on the pillows, picked up a handkerchief, and blew his nose, burying his head beneath the covers so no one would hear, so no one would worry, so no one would come. Was he ashamed someone might see him crying? No, that was not it. True, he would not have liked it, it was degrading for a man his age to be seen sobbing like child, but mostly he wanted to be alone.

The vise around his throat loosened, though his breathing was still labored. Gradually the tears subsided, leaving a terrible emptiness. He felt exhausted, but sleep refused to come. All his life, sleep had come easily; even when his wife died and he had been unable to eat, he had still slept soundly. He had loved his wife, a wonderful woman, so many admirable qualities. And to be taken so young, it was unjust. But being unable to sleep was unusual and worrying for a man like him. It's not my heart, thought Péricourt, Blanche is an idiot. It's anxiety. Something heavy and ominous was looming over him. He thought about his work, about his meetings that afternoon, searching for an answer. He had been out of sorts all day. It could hardly be the conversation with the stockbroker, there had been nothing there to worry him, nothing out of the ordinary, this was his business, he had crushed dozens of stockbrokers in the course of his career. On the last Friday of every month he held the customary financial review with bankers, brokers, and middlemen all standing to attention before him.

Standing to attention.

These words left him suddenly devastated.

The sobs returned as, suddenly, he realized why he was crying. He bit down on the covers and let out a long, muffled roar of rage and despair, convulsed by a grief more intense, more terrifying than he could imagine. A feeling all the more terrible because he . . . he . . . He could find no words, his thoughts seemed to dissolve, as though melted by this unendurable pain.

He was grieving for his son.

Édouard was dead. Édouard had just died at this very moment. His little boy, his son, was dead.

This thought had not occurred to him even on Édouard's birthday, the image had flickered through his mind, everything had swelled within him ready to explode today.

Today, a year exactly since Édouard's death.

The enormity of his grief was multiplied by the fact that this was the first time that Édouard truly existed for him. Suddenly, he understood how much, dimly, grudgingly, he had loved his son; understood it at precisely the moment he realized he would never see him again.

But no, even that was not the worst, he could tell from the tears, the vise crushing his chest, the blade against his throat.

It was something worse: he had been guilty of greeting the news of his son's death as a deliverance.

He lay awake all night, remembering Édouard as a child, smiling at memories that had been so deeply buried they seemed new minted. There was no logic to it, he could not say whether the memory of Édouard dressed as cherub (though he had Satan's horns, even at the age of eight he was incapable of taking anything seriously) had come before the interview with the principal about his drawings. My God, his drawings, the shame. And yet, what talent.

M. Péricourt had kept nothing, not a toy, not a sketch, not a painting or a watercolor, nothing. Maybe Madeleine . . . ? No, he would never be able to bring himself to ask.

He spent the night remembering and regretting, he saw Édouard everywhere, as a baby, as a toddler, as a boy and that laugh, such a laugh, such irrepressible joy, if only he could have behaved differently, if only he had not had that taste for provocation . . . M. Péricourt had never been at ease with his son, he had always had an abhorrence of excess. It was something he got from his wife. In marrying into her fortune (she had been born a de Margis, of the powerful mill-owning family), he had married into her values, which held certain things to be calamities. Artists, for example. Ultimately, though, he might have been able to get used to his son's artistic dabblings, after all, there were people who made a living daubing canvases for city halls and government departments. No, what M. Péricourt had been unable to forgive his son was not what he did, but what he was: Édouard's voice was high pitched, he was too thin, too attentive to his clothing, his gestures were too . . . It was not difficult to see, the boy was really effeminate . . . Even in his heart of hearts, M. Péricourt never dared to think the words. He was ashamed of his son in front of his friends, because he could read those words on their lips. He was not a cruel man, but one who had been hurt and humiliated. His son was a living, breathing insult to the modest hopes he had nurtured. Though he never admitted it to anyone, the birth of his daughter had been a bitter disappointment. He considered it normal that a man should want a son. There was a secret, intimate bond between father and son, he thought, since the latter is the successor of the former, the father builds and bequeaths, the son inherits and augments, life has been so since the dawn of time.

Madeleine was a pleasant child; he quickly came to love her, but he remained impatient.

No son came. There were miscarriages, tragic incidents, time passed, M. Péricourt became almost irritable. Then Édouard arrived. At last. Péricourt considered the birth the result of sheer will on his part. Indeed, when his wife died shortly afterward, he saw this as a sign. In those first years, he invested such efforts on his son's education. He nurtured such hopes, and felt buoyed by the presence of the child. Then came the disappointment. Édouard was about eight or ten when he finally had to face the facts. The boy was a failure. M. Péricourt was not too old to start a new life, but he was too proud to do so. He refused to countenance failure. He retreated into bitterness and resentment.

Now that his son was dead (he did not even know how he had died, he had never asked), the bitter reproaches came flooding back, the harsh, irrevocable words, the doors he had closed, the heart he had closed. M. Péricourt had closed off every avenue for his son, leaving him only the war that was to kill him.

Even when he learned of Édouard's death, he had said nothing. He could still picture the scene. Madeleine, prostrate with grief. He, laying his hand on her shoulder, showing her the way. Dignity, Madeleine, dignity. He could not tell her, did not even realize himself, that Édouard's death was the answer to a question that had been troubling him for years: how could a man such as himself endure such a son? Now it was over, death had drawn a line under the question, there had been justice. Balance had been restored. The death of his wife had seemed to him unjust, she had been too young to die; he had felt no such qualms about his son though he had died even younger than she.

The dry sobs returned.

No tears, he thought, I am dried up inside. He wished he might die. For the first time in his life, he felt for someone other than himself.

The following morning, having lain awake all night, he was exhausted. Grief was etched on his face, but since he never showed emotion, Madeleine did not understand and felt afraid. She leaned over him. He kissed her forehead. There were no words to express what he felt.

"I'm going to get up," he said.

Madeleine was about to protest, but seeing his drained, determined face, she withdrew without a word.

An hour later, M. Péricourt emerged from his apartments dressed and freshly shaven, having eaten nothing. Madeleine could see he had not taken his pills, he looked weak, his shoulders hunched, his face was chalk white. He was wearing a coat. To the astonishment of the servants, he sat in the hallway on the chair on which visitors' coats were left if they were staying only briefly. He gestured to Madeleine.

"Have the car brought around, we're going out."

How much there was in these few words . . . Madeleine gave the orders, ran up to her room, and came back dressed. Beneath her gray coat, she wore a smock of black silk twill that draped about her waist and a cloche hat in the same color. "She loves me," M. Péricourt thought when he saw his daughter; he meant "she understands me."

"Let us go . . . ," he said.

Out on the street, he informed the chauffeur his services would not be needed. He did not often drive himself, it was not something he cared for, except when he wanted to be alone.

He had been to the cemetery only once. For his wife's funeral.

Even when Madeleine had brought her brother's body back to be buried in the family vault, M. Péricourt had not been present. She had been the one who wanted to "bring her brother home." He would not himself have taken the trouble. His son had died for his country, had been buried with his comrades; that was the nature of things. But Madeleine had insisted. He had firmly explained that it was unthinkable that "a man in his position" should allow his daughter to do something so absolutely, categorically forbidden—and when M. Péricourt resorted to more than one adverb, it was not a good sign. Even so, Madeleine had not been daunted, she said never mind, she would take care of things, and if something unforeseen should happen, he had only to say that he knew nothing; she would confirm this, she would accept full responsibility. Two days later, she had come across an envelope containing the money she needed and a discreet letter of introduction to Général Morieux.

In the darkness, she had shared out the money between the men, the guards at the Parisian cemetery, the undertaker, the driver, the laborer who had opened the family crypt; two men had taken down the coffin, and the door had been resealed. Madeleine stood for a moment in prayer until someone roughly took her elbow—the dead of night was no time for such things; now her brother was here, she could come as often as she liked, but right now, it was best not to attract attention.

M. Péricourt knew nothing of this, he had asked no questions. As he drove with his silent daughter toward the cemetery, he remembered the thoughts that had kept him awake at night. Having previously not wanted to know anything, he was now eager to know every detail . . . Every time he thought about his son, he felt the urge to cry. Mercifully, his self-respect swiftly prevailed.

For Édouard to be buried in the family vault, he had had to be exhumed, M. Péricourt thought. He felt his chest tighten at this thought. He tried to imagine Édouard lying dead, but each time he pictured a civilian death, Édouard in a suit and tie, his shoes spit polished, with candles all around. It was ridiculous. He shook his head, annoyed with himself. What did a corpse look like after so many months? How had they gone about it? Images came to him, commonplace images, and from them arose a question his sleepless night had left unanswered, a question he was surprised had not occurred to him before: why had he felt no shock that his son had died before him? It was not in the nature of things. M. Péricourt was fifty-seven. He was rich. Respected. He had not fought in any wars. Everything had worked out well for him, even his marriage. And he was alive. He felt ashamed of himself.

Curiously, it was this precise moment, here in the car, that Madeleine chose. As she gazed out the window at the houses rolling past, she gently laid her hand on his as though she understood. She understands me, M. Péricourt thought. This cheered him.

Then there was his son-in-law. Madeleine had gone to fetch her brother from that far-flung field where he had died and had come back with this Pradelle, whom she had married that same summer. Though it had not struck him at the time, M. Péricourt now saw a strange equivalence between these two events. He associated the death of his son with the appearance of the man he had been obliged to accept as his son-in-law. He could not explain it; it was as though he blamed this man for his son's death; the idea was preposterous, but he could not help himself: one had appeared just as the other had disappeared, the idea of cause and effect had occurred automatically, which, to him, meant logically.

Madeleine had tried to explain to him how she had met Capitaine d'Aulnay-Pradelle, how considerate, how tactful he had been, but M. Péricourt did not listen; he was blind and deaf to everything. Why had his daughter married this man rather than another? It was still a mystery to him. He had understood nothing about his son's life, nothing about his death, and deep down understood nothing about his daughter's life, nothing about her marriage. On a human level, he understood nothing. The guard at the cemetery gate had lost his right arm. Seeing him, M. Péricourt thought, in my case it's my heart that is crippled.

The graveyard, given the hour, was thronged with people. Being a businessman, M. Péricourt could not help but notice that the street hawkers were having a field day selling sprays and bouquets of chrysanthemums. Good seasonal trade. Especially since this year, the government had decreed that all commemorations should take place on All Souls' Day, November 2, at precisely the same time all over France. As one, the whole country went to honor the dead. From his limousine, M. Péricourt watched the preparations, people hanging up ribbons, setting up barriers, brass bands in civilian clothes silently rehearsing, the pavements had been scrubbed, the carriages and automobiles were moved on. M. Péricourt had watched all this dispassionately, his grief was entirely personal.

They parked the car outside the gate. Arm in arm, father and daughter walked quietly toward the family vault. The weather was bright; the chill, pale-yellow sunlight set off the flowers that were already strewn on the graves to either side of the path. M. Péricourt and Madeleine had come empty handed. Neither had thought to buy flowers though there had been an embarrassment of choice at the gates.

The tympanum of the family crypt was surmounted with a cross, and above the studded iron door was the inscription "FAMILLE PÉRICOURT." On either side were carved the names of those interred there, beginning with M. Péricourt's parents, since the family's wealth dated back less than a century.

M. Péricourt kept his hands in the pockets of his greatcoat and did not doff his hat. The thought did not even cross his mind. All his thoughts were with his son. The tears returned, he had thought he had no more to shed, flickering images of Édouard as a child, as a young man, and suddenly he found that the very things he had despised he missed terribly: Édouard's laugh, his cries. The night before, he had recalled long-forgotten scenes from Édouard's childhood, a time when he had had only faint suspicions about his son's true nature and could allow himself a measured, moderate enthusiasm for his drawings, which, he had to admit, showed an uncommon maturity. He could still picture some of them. Édouard had been a child of his time, his imagination filled with exotic images, locomotives, airplanes. M. Péricourt had been struck one day by a sketch of a racing car at top speed, which seemed astonishingly realistic though he had never seen such a car. What was it about this frozen image that it could give an impression of such speed that it seemed as if the car were about to take off? He did not know. Édouard had been nine years old. His drawings had always had a lot of movement. Even his flowers gave a sense of the breeze. He remembered a watercolor—flowers, again, though what kind he did not know—the petals seemed so delicate, that was all he could say. And framed in a very particular way. M. Péricourt, though he knew little about art, realized that there was something original about it. Where were they, he wondered, those sketches? Had Madeleine kept them? But he did not want to look at them again, he preferred to hide them away inside, he did not want these images to ever leave him. Of the images that had surfaced in his memory, he particularly remembered a face, Édouard had sketched faces of every shape and size and had a fondness for certain features that recurred again and again. M. Péricourt wondered whether this was what was called "an individual style." It had been the innocent face of a young man with fleshy lips, a strong nose, and a dimple that seemed to cleave the chin, but the most striking thing was the subject's strange gaze, squinting slightly, without a trace of a smile. This was all he could think to say, now that he had found the words . . . But who was there to say it to?

Madeleine pretended to be interested in another tomb and walked off a short distance, leaving him alone. He took out his handkerchief and dabbed his eyes. He read the name of his wife, Léopoldine Péricourt, *née* de Margis.

Édouard's name was not there.

Seeing this, he was distraught.

It made sense; his son was not supposed to be buried here, there could be no question of engraving his name, it was obvious, but to M. Péricourt it was as though fate had refused his son an official acknowledgment of death. There had been a document, a letter informing them he had died for France, but what kind of tomb was it where one did not even have the right to read his name? He turned this over in his mind, tried to persuade himself that it was not important, but what he felt was unanswerable. To see the name of his dead son, to read the name "Éduoard Péricourt" suddenly, inexplicably, seemed hugely important. He shook his head.

Madeleine had come back to join him, she squeezed his arm, and they walked back to the car.

He spent his Saturday taking telephone calls from people whose fate depended on his health. "Well, *monsieur*, are you feeling better today?" they said, or "You gave us quite a fright there, old man!" His answers were curt. To the world at large, this meant that everything was back to normal.

M. Péricourt spent Sunday resting, sipping tisanes, and swallowing the pills prescribed by Docteur Blanche. He filed some documents and, on a silver salver next to his letters, found the package wrapped in flowery paper that Madeleine had left, which contained a notebook and an old, handwritten letter that had already been opened.

He recognized it immediately. He sipped his tea, picked up the letter, read, and reread it. He lingered for a long time on the passage where Édouard's comrade talked about his death:

> *(. . .) occurred during an assault by our unit on a Boche advance post of crucial military importance to Victory. Your son, who was often in the front line, was struck in the heart by a bullet and died instantly. I can assure you that he did not suffer. Your son, who always spoke of the defense of his country as the greatest duty, knew the satisfaction of dying a hero.*

M. Péricourt was a man of affairs who controlled banks, colonial trading companies, and factories and was by nature deeply skeptical. He did not believe a word of this convenient fable crafted for the occasion like a chromolithograph intended to console grieving families. Édouard's comrade had an elegant hand, but the letter had been written in pencil, the paper was crumbling, all too soon it would fade, like an ineffectual lie no one would believe. He folded the letter, slipped it back into the envelope and put it in a desk drawer.

Then he opened the tattered notepad, the rubber band holding the covers in place was slack, as though it had sailed the world three times like an explorer's logbook. M. Péricourt knew at once it contained his son's drawings. Sketches of soldiers at the front. He knew that he would not be able to look through all these pages now, that it would take time before he could face the grim truth and his own devastating guilt. He stopped at a portrait of a soldier in full battle dress, helmet on, sitting on the ground, legs splayed in front of him, shoulders hunched, head slightly bowed, exhausted. But for the mustache, it could have been Édouard himself, he thought. Had he aged much during the years spent at war when M. Péricourt had not seen him? Had he grown a mustache as so many soldiers did? How many times did I write to him? he wondered. All these sketches in blue pencil, did he have nothing else to draw with? Surely Madeleine must have sent him packages? He felt suddenly sick as he remembered saying brusquely to one of his secretaries, "Remember to have a package sent to my son . . ." The woman's own son had fought at the front, had been lost there in the summer of 1914. M. Péricourt saw again the look of frozen horror on her face as she left his office. All through the war, she had sent packages to Édouard as she might have to her own son, she would simply say, "I've prepared a package," M. Péricourt would thank her and, taking a sheet of paper, would write "With all good wishes, my dear Édouard," then agonize over how to sign it: "Papa" seemed inappropriate, "M. Péricourt" ridiculous. He signed his initials.

He looked again at the slumped, exhausted solider. He would never truly know what his son had experienced, he would have to make do with the stories told by others, the stories of his son-in-law, for example, heroic anecdotes as dishonest as the letter from Édouard's comrade, these lies were all that he would ever have, he could never know the truth now. Everything was dead. He closed the notebook and slipped it into the inside pocket of his jacket.

Though she did not show it, Madeleine was surprised by her father's reaction. His impulsive visit to the cemetery, his tears, so unexpected . . . The gulf that had separated Édouard from his father had always seemed to her a geographical fact set down in the mists of time, as though the two men were separate continents on shifting tectonic plates that could not come together without creating a tidal wave. She had lived through it all, had witnessed it all. As Édouard grew up, she had seen her father's doubts and suspicions harden into withdrawal, rejection, hostility, anger, disavowal. Édouard's feelings had moved in the opposite direction: what at first had been a need for affection, for protection, gradually transformed into provocation and petulant outbursts.

Into a declaration of war.

Because the war in which Édouard met his death had been declared long before in his family between a father who was as harsh and inflexible as a German and this rakish, reckless, shallow, charming son. It had begun with discreet troop maneuvers—Édouard would have been eight or nine—signaling anxiety in both camps. The father had first been preoccupied, then fretful. Two years later, as his son grew, when there was no longer any doubt, he became cold, distant, contemptuous. Édouard, meanwhile, became rebellious and seditious.

The gap continued to widen until there was silence, a silence that Madeleine could not date precisely, when the warring factions ceased to communicate and, rejecting battle and confrontation, lapsed into wordless hostility and feigned indifference. It must have been a long time ago, because, try as she might, she could not remember the moment when pitched battle tipped into a dormant civil war, a series of skirmishes. Doubtless it had been triggered by a specific incident, but she had not noticed. One day, when Édouard was about twelve or thirteen, she realized that father and son now communicated only through her.

She spent her adolescence in the role of a diplomat who, being stationed between implacable enemies, is forced to make endless compromises, to listen to the grievances of both sides, to defuse hostilities, to allay the constant violent impulses. And spending so much time taking care of these two men, she did not realize that she was unattractive. Not ugly, but decidedly ordinary, at an age when being ordinary meant being less attractive than so many others. Then one day, tired of finding herself too often surrounded by dazzling young women—rich men marry pretty women who will give them beautiful children—Madeleine knew that she was not beautiful. She had been sixteen, perhaps seventeen. Her father kissed her on the forehead, but he did not even see her. There was no woman in the house to tell her what she should do, how she might make something of herself, she had to imagine, to observe other women, copy them, but never quite equal them. It was all the more difficult since she had little taste for such frivolities. She could see that her youth, which might have made her beautiful or at least striking, was melting away because no one thought to nurture it. She had money, true, of that there was no shortage in the Péricourt house, in fact it was all there was, and so she hired girls to do her make-up, manicurists, beauticians, dressmakers, more perhaps than she needed. Madeleine was not an ugly duckling, she was a lonely girl. The one man whose loving gaze might have given her the confidence to grow to be a happy woman was constantly occupied—a word that conjured a country under enemy control—by adversaries, by business, by rivals he needed to crush, by the fluctuations of the Bourse, by political connections, and, incidentally, by the son he ignored (a task that took considerable time). There were so many things that made him say, "Ah, Madeleine, there you are, I didn't see you, along to the salon, will you, I've work to do," failing to notice that she had changed her hair, that she was wearing a new dress.

And aside from an affectionate yet undemonstrative father, there was Édouard, at ten, at twelve, at fifteen, bursting with life, Édouard the apocalyptic, the performer, the actor, the fool, the outrageous, the glowing ember, the creative spark. It was Édouard who drew pictures three feet high on the walls that set servants howling and red-faced maids laughing and biting their fists, so lifelike was the caricature of M. Péricourt as a lecherous devil clutching his prick in both hands. Madeleine had wiped her eyes and quickly called the decorators. M. Péricourt would be surprised to find workmen in the house when he came home. Madeleine would explain, a little accident, nothing serious, Papa, she was sixteen and he would say, thank you, *chérie,* grateful that someone was taking care of the house, of the routine matters, he could not be everywhere at once. Because he had tried everything and nothing had worked, nannies, governesses, private tutors, au pairs, all of them left. There was something demonic about the boy, he's not normal, take my word for it. "Normal," the word that M. Péricourt clung to because it accurately described a father-son relationship that did not exist.

M. Péricourt's hostility to Édouard became visceral, for reasons Madeleine perfectly understood: Édouard behaved like a girl. How many times had she tried to teach him to laugh "normally," lessons that invariably ended in tears—M. Péricourt's hostility had become so ingrained that Madeleine was thankful these twin continents never collided; it was for the best.

When the family had learned of Édouard's death, she had accepted M. Péricourt's silent relief, in part because her father was all that she had left now (as you can see, there was a little of Princess Marya about her), in part because the war was over; though it had ended badly, it was over. She had thought long and hard before bringing home Édouard's body. She missed him terribly; just knowing he was so far away—almost in a foreign country—made her heartsick. But it was impossible, the government had forbidden it. She weighed this fact—in this, as in many things, she acted like her father—and when she had come to her decision, nothing could stand in her way. She made tactful inquiries and the necessary discreet contacts, found people willing to undertake the task, and—initially against her father's wishes and later without his consent—traveled to the place where her brother had died so she could bring him home and bury him in the vault where she too would one day be laid. Then she married the handsome Capitaine d'Aulnay-Pradelle, whom she had met there. We each settle down as best we can.

But, piecing together the fit of apoplexy at the Jockey Club, his unaccustomed weakness, and the sudden, shocking decision to go to a cemetery he seldom visited, and lastly his tears, Madeleine felt sorry for him. She felt devastated. The war was ended, the enemies might have been reconciled, but one of them was dead. It was a hollow peace. The family home in November 1919 was a desolate place.

In the late morning, Madeleine went upstairs, knocked at her father's study door, and found him standing pensively by the window. Outside, passers-by were carrying bouquets of chrysanthemums, and faint bursts of military music drifted up from the street. Seeing her father brooding, Madeleine suggested he might like to come downstairs and have lunch with her for a change and he agreed, though he did not seem hungry, and in fact he scarcely ate a thing, sending the plates back untouched, sipping at a glass of water.

"Tell me . . ."

Madeleine wiped her mouth and gave him a questioning look.

"This comrade of your brother . . ."

"Albert Maillard."

"If you say so . . . ," M. Péricourt said feigning absentmindedness, "Was he . . . ?"

Madeleine nodded and smiled encouragingly.

"Appropriately thanked? Yes, of course."

M. Péricourt bit his tongue. He found this habit in others of constantly anticipating how he felt and what he wanted to say so intensely irritating it almost made him want to rage like old Prince Bolkonsky.

"No," he corrected gently, "I was going to suggest that perhaps we might . . ."

"Invite him?" Madeleine said. "Yes, of course, that's a wonderful idea."

They sat in silence for a long moment.

"Obviously, there's no need to . . ."

Madeleine raised an amused eyebrow and waited for an end that did not come. Faced with boards of directors, M. Péricourt could cut someone short with a simple flicker of his eyes. With his daughter, he was incapable of finishing a sentence.

"Of course, Papa," she said, smiling again, "no need to shout it from the rooftops."

"It is no one's business," M. Péricourt concurred.

When he referred to "no one," he meant "your husband." Madeleine understood this and was not hurt.

He got to his feet, set down his napkin, smiled vaguely at his daughter, and made to leave.

"Oh, and, er . . . ," he said, stopping for a moment as though he had just remembered some trivial detail, ". . . could you call Labourdin? Ask him to come see me."

When he phrased things in this manner, it meant they were urgent.

* * *

Two hours later, M. Péricourt greeted Labourdin in the intimidating imperial *grand salon.* When the mayor arrived, he did not go to greet him, did not shake his hand. The two men remained standing. Labourdin was glistening. As always, he had rushed to get here, desperate to be of service, to prove himself useful, ever anxious to please—oh, how he would have loved to be a *fille de joie.*

"My dear friend . . ."

This was how their conversations invariably began. Labourdin was already aquiver with impatience. He was needed; he could be of service. M. Péricourt knew that his son-in-law exploited a number of his own connections and also knew that Labourdin had recently been appointed to the Adjudication Committee that had something to do with war graves—he had not followed the matter closely, but he was aware of the gist. Besides, if he needed to acquaint himself with the fine details, Labourdin would tell him. In fact, the mayor seemed about to do just that, convinced that this was the reason he had been summoned.

"The plans for a memorial in your *arrondissement,*" Péricourt said, "how far advanced are they?"

Labourdin, startled, clicked his tongue and stared wide eyed.

"*Mon cher président . . .*"

He addressed everyone as *président* because—like the ubiquitous *dottore* in Italy—these days, everyone was president of something and Labourdin preferred simple, pragmatic solutions.

"*Mon cher président,* the truth of the matter is . . ."

He felt mortified.

"Yes?" M. Péricourt said encouragingly. "It would be best to know the truth of the . . ."

"Well, we . . ."

Labourdin did not have the imagination to lie, even badly, so he blurted it out.

"We've got . . . nowhere."

There. It was done.

Almost a year he had been working on the proposal. Because everyone was agreed that an unknown soldier at the Arc de Triomphe next year was utterly inadequate, the people in his *arrondissement* and the veterans' associations wanted their own personal memorial. Everyone insisted; there had been a vote at the Conseil.

"We've appointed people!"

This was an indication of how seriously Labourdin had taken his task.

"But the obstacles, *mon cher président*, the obstacles! You cannot imagine . . ."

He was panting for breath at the mere thought of the obstacles. In addition to the technical difficulties, a public subscription needed to be organized, an open competition announced to solicit designs, a jury appointed, a site chosen, but there were no sites available, and most important, there were the financial obstacles.

"These things are ruinously expensive!"

There were constant arguments, and there was always some sort of delay, some insisted that their memorial be more impressive than the one planned in the neighboring *arrondissement*, there was talk of a commemorative plaque, of a fresco, everyone had an opinion, everyone knew best . . . Exhausted by the interminable squabbles, Labourdin had banged his fist on the table, then put his hat on and went to the nearest whorehouse to console himself.

"It's the money, you understand . . . the coffers are empty, as I'm sure you're aware. So the thing depends on the public subscription. But how will we raise it? Suppose we only raise enough to pay half the cost of the memorial, where would we find the rest? Because by then we would be committed."

He marked a pregnant pause so that M. Péricourt could appreciate the woeful consequences.

"We could hardly say 'Here, have your money back, we're not going ahead.' On the other hand, if we don't raise enough money and end up erecting a pitiful little monument, well, from an electoral point of view, that would be the worst possible result, I am sure you will agree."

M. Péricourt did agree.

"Honestly," Labourdin said, clearly overwhelmed by the enormity of the task, "it might seem straightforward, but in actual fact it's *sheer hell*!"

He had explained everything. He hiked up the front of his pants as if to say: I could do with a drink now. Péricourt heartily despised this little man, for all that he was capable of being surprisingly perceptive. As, for example, when he asked:

"But, *monsieur le président,* . . . why are you asking me about this?"

Fools can sometimes be surprising. The question was not a stupid one, M. Péricourt did not live in his *arrondissement,* so why should he be interested in someone else's war memorial? It was an extremely pertinent, insightful question and, in Labourdin's case, clearly a mental fluke. Even if he were dealing with an intelligent man—especially with an intelligent man—M. Péricourt would never stoop to sincerity, indeed he would be incapable, so he was hardly likely to do so when faced with this cretin . . . Besides, even had he wanted to, it was too convoluted to explain.

"I would like to make a gesture," he said. "I shall pay for your memorial. In full."

Labourdin's jaw dropped, he blinked rapidly, well, well, well . . .

"Find a location," Péricourt said. "Demolish something if need be. It's important that it be striking, don't you agree? It will cost whatever it costs. Announce a competition, appoint a jury for form's sake, but I shall decide because I am paying for everything. As to any publicity regarding this . . ."

M. Péricourt had had a long career as a banker; half his fortune had been made on the Bourse, the other half from sundry businesses. It would have been a simple matter for him to go into politics; many of his fellow businessmen had succumbed to this temptation but had little to show for it. His success was based on his knowledge and expertise; he was loath to risk it in circumstances as uncertain and often fatuous as elections. Moreover, he was not a political animal. For that, one required an inflated sense of ego. No, his thing was money. And money thrives in the shadows. For M. Péricourt, discretion was the paramount virtue.

"As to publicity, it goes without saying I do not wish my name to be mentioned. Set up a charitable organization, a benevolent association, whatever you like; I will make the necessary grant. I will give you one year. The inauguration will take place on November 11 next. One more thing: the memorial is to be engraved with the names of all the fallen heroes born in the *arrondissement*. Do you understand? Every last one."

This was a lot of information, and it took Labourdin a moment to digest it. By the time he had grasped what exactly it was he had to do and how swiftly the president wished to see it done, M. Péricourt was reaching a hand out toward him. Disconcerted, Labourdin mistakenly proffered his own hand and met only empty air as M. Péricourt simply patted him on the shoulder, then turned and retired to his apartment.

M. Péricourt stood by the window, stared unseeing at the street below, and brooded. Édouard's name could not be engraved on the family tomb, so be it. But he would erect a monument. One tailor made. Édouard's name would be carved there, surrounded by those of his comrades.

He pictured it in a beautiful little square.

In the heart of the *arrondissement* where he was born.

13

Stumbling through the driving rain, the shoebox tucked under one arm, his left hand swaddled in bandages, Albert pushed open the gate leading to a small courtyard heaped with door frames, wheels, tattered çarriage hoods, broken chairs, useless things, one could not help but wonder how they came to be there and what possible purpose they could serve. There was mud everywhere, but Albert did not even try to use the paving stones set out like checkers, because the recent floods had shifted them so much he would have had to leap like an acrobat to avoid getting his feet wet. The rubber on his soles had worn through, and besides, such gymnastics were ill advised for one carrying a shoebox full of glass vials . . . He crossed the yard on tiptoe and reached the tiny building whose second floor had been converted to be rented out for two hundred francs—a pittance compared with the usual rents in Paris.

They had moved in shortly after Édouard had been demobilized in June.

That day, Albert had gone to collect him from the hospital and, despite his meager resources, had shelled out for a taxi. Though, in the months since the war ended, people had become accustomed to the sight of cripples of all kinds—war had a baroque feel for mutilation—the sudden apparition of this golem, hobbling on his useless leg, with a gaping hole in the middle of his face, had still terrified the Russian taxi driver. Even Albert, who had visited his comrade every week, was shocked. Outside he seemed very different from how he had been indoors. It was like walking a wild animal from the zoo down the street. Not a word was spoken during the journey.

Édouard had nowhere to go. At the time, Albert was living in a drafty seventh-floor attic room with a toilet at the far end of the corridor, there was a cold tap and he washed himself using a basin and went to the public baths as often as he could. Stepping into the room, Édouard seemed to notice nothing, he sat in a chair by the window and looked out at the street, the sky, lit a cigarette, which he smoked through his right nostril. Albert immediately realized he would not move from that spot and the responsibility he had taken on would quickly become a real source of everyday strife.

From the first, living together proved difficult. Édouard's huge, scrawny carcass—only the gray cat that prowled on the rooftops outside was more emaciated—took up all the space. The room had been too small for one person. With two it seemed almost as crowded as the trenches. Not good for morale. Édouard slept on the bare floor without a blanket, spent his days with his crippled leg stretched out in front of him, smoking and staring out of the window. Before leaving in the morning, Albert would prepare something for Édouard to eat, but more often than not Édouard would ignore the food, the pipette, the rubber tube, and the funnel. He would spend the whole day sitting in the chair, a pillar of salt. He seemed to be letting life drain away like blood from an open wound. Living in close proximity to such suffering was so wearing that Albert would invent pretexts to go out. In fact, he would simply go and eat at a cheap café because trying to making conversation with Édouard left him almost as melancholy as his friend.

He got scared.

He tried to talk to Édouard about his future, about where he planned to live. But though he began the conversation a dozen times, Albert would trail off as soon as he saw that forlorn face, those glistening eyes—the only living thing that remained in this disturbing tableau—with their vacant stare of utter helplessness.

Albert was forced to accept that he was solely responsible for Édouard and would be for some time, until he recovered, until he began to enjoy life again, until he began to make plans for himself. Albert thought of this convalescence in terms of months, refusing to accept that months might not be the appropriate yardstick.

He brought paper and paints and Édouard thanked him but did not even open the package. He was not a scrounger nor an idler, he was simply an empty husk with no desires, no wishes, one might almost say no thoughts; had Albert left him tied up under a bridge like a stray dog and run away, Édouard would not have held it against him.

Albert had heard the word "neurasthenia," he made inquiries, he asked around, encountered others—"melancholia," "depression," "lassitude"—but words were of scant use, the truth was here before his eyes: Édouard was waiting for death—however long death took, it represented the only imaginable solution, not a change, merely a transition from one state to another, like those mute, impotent old men we cease to notice and are not surprised when finally they die.

Albert talked to Édouard all the time, which is to say he talked to himself, like an old tramp in his shack.

"I suppose I should consider myself lucky," he would say, whisking up an egg with meat bouillon for Édouard. "I could have ended up with some fathead contradicting everything I say."

He tried everything he could think of to cheer his comrade, hoping he might raise his spirits and finally unravel the mystery that had haunted him since the beginning: what would Édouard do if one day he wanted to laugh? At best, he produced a shrill, throaty noise, a sort of keening, that made you uncomfortable and desperate to help, the way you might say a word to help out a stutterer; it grated on his nerves. Thankfully, Édouard rarely made a sound; the mere effort seemed to tire him. But still Albert could not shake off the thought of Édouard laughing. In fact, since being buried alive, it was not the only thought that bordered on a fixation. Aside from the tension, the daylong worry, and the terror of all the things that might happen, he had troubling notions that haunted him, like his recent obsession with the head of the dead horse. He had had Édouard's sketch framed in spite of the expense. It was the only form of decoration in the room. To encourage his friend to start drawing again or at least to do something with his days, he would stand in front of the picture, hands in his pockets, admiring it and muttering about how Édouard had a real talent, and if he wanted . . . It was useless. Édouard would sit smoking a cigarette—sometimes the right nostril, sometimes the left—and gaze out at the chimneys and the corrugated iron roofs that were the only landscape. He was utterly impassive, had made no plan since his time in the hospital, where he had expended all his energy fighting doctors and surgeons, not because he refused to accept his condition, but because he could not imagine what would come next; could not imagine a future. When the shell had exploded, time had suddenly stood still. Édouard was worse than a broken clock, which at least gives the right time twice a day. He was twenty-four years old, and a year after being wounded, he had not managed to return to anything approaching his old self. To recover a shred of what he once had been.

He had spent a long time in shock, adopting a position of blind resistance, the way some soldiers, apparently, remained frozen in the position in which they were found—huddled, hunched, curled up on themselves; it was incredible the new horrors the war had dreamed up. The target of his resistance had been embodied by Professeur Maudret, a bastard in his opinion, less interested in his patients than he was in advancements in surgery—something that might be both true and false, but Édouard was not one for nuance, he had a gaping hole in the middle of his face and was in no mood to weigh pros and cons. He had clung to his morphine, expending all his energy trying to get larger doses, resorting to ruses unworthy of him—begging, cheating, pleading, shamming, pilfering—needing ever-larger doses, thinking perhaps that the morphine would finally kill him. After months of listening to his categorical refusals to accept grafts, prostheses, and surgical devices, Professeur Maudret finally threw him out on his ear—you break your back trying to help these people, offer them the latest surgical innovations, and still they'd rather stay the way they are, glaring at us as though we're the ones who fired the shell. His colleagues from the psychiatric unit (Soldat Larivière had been seen by several, but obstinately refused to speak to a single one of them) had various theories to explain the stubborn refusal of such men. Professeur Maudret, who had little interest in explanations, merely shrugged; he wanted to devote his time and his skills to men who were worthy of his efforts. He signed the discharge papers without a second's regret.

Édouard left the hospital with various prescriptions, a tiny dose of morphine, and a pile of papers in the name Eugène Larivière. A few hours later, sitting by the window in his friend's cramped apartment, he suddenly felt the weight of the world on his shoulders, as though he had just stepped into his cell, sentenced to life.

Édouard found it difficult to organize his thoughts, but he listened to Albert prattle on about his mundane worries, he tried hard to concentrate—of course they needed to think about money, it was obvious, and what was to become of him, what was to be done with his hulking frame, this was the harsh reality he could not get his head around; his concentration would trickle like water through a sieve, and by the time he found he could focus again, it was dark and Albert was coming home from work, or it was the middle of the day and his whole body was shrieking for his next injection. He made valiant efforts, he clenched his fists and vainly tried to picture the future, but it leached away through the tiniest of cracks, leaving him brooding about his past, which surged past like a river, a torrent of images with neither rhyme nor reason. The one that recurred most often was his mother. He had few memories of her now but clung desperately to those he had: faint sensations, a musky perfume he tried to summon up, the pink dressing table with its stool fringed with pompoms, her creams, her brushes, the soft feel of satin clutched one night as she bent over him, or the gold locket she would open for him, leaning down as though it were a secret. But of her voice, her words, her face, he could remember nothing. His mother had melted from his mind like all the other living creatures he had known. It was a devastating realization. Ever since his face had been obliterated, all other faces had faded. The faces of his mother, his father, his friends, his lovers, his teachers, even

Madeleine's . . . He thought about her a lot, too. Without a face, all that remained was her laugh. It tinkled and sparkled like no other. Édouard used to resort to all manner of foolishness to hear that laugh, though it had not been difficult: a drawing, a funny face, a caricature of one of the servants—they chuckled, too, since it was clear there was no malice in Édouard—but particularly his disguises, he had an inordinate fondness and an incomparable talent for dressing up, usually as a woman. Seeing him in makeup, Madeleine would be reduced to embarrassed giggles, not for her own sake but "because of Papa," she would say, "if he saw you dressed like that." She tried to anticipate everything down to the smallest detail. Sometimes, however, she could not control the situation, and there would be awkward, glacial dinners because Édouard had come downstairs having "forgotten" to take off his mascara. As soon as he noticed, M. Péricourt would get to his feet, set down his napkin, and demand that Édouard leave the table immediately. What? Édouard would yell, pretending to be offended, what did I do now? But no one would laugh.

All these faces, even his own, had disappeared; not a single one remained. In a faceless world, what was there to cling to, who was there to fight against? To Édouard the world now was a place of shadowy figures whose heads had been lopped off and whose bodies, as if to compensate, seemed ten times larger, like the hulking form of his father. Memories of his early childhood rose to the surface like bubbles, sometimes the delicious shudder of mingled fear and wonder at his father's touch, sometimes the way his father would smile conspiratorially during adult conversations about things Édouard barely understood and say: "Isn't that right, my son?" It felt as though his imagination had been reduced to clichés, and so sometimes his father's appearance was preceded by a dark, looming shadow like an ogre in a fairy tale. And his back! That vast, fearsome back that had seemed gigantic until he grew as tall as his father and later outstripped him; that back that seemed to express indifference, disdain, disgust.

There had been a time when Édouard hated his father, but that had passed: the two men had settled on mutual contempt. Édouard's life was crumbling because there was no longer even hatred to shore it up. Here was another war that he had lost.

And so the days passed turning over images and old hurts; Albert would leave and return. When it was time to talk (Albert always wanted to discuss things), Édouard would emerge from his daydream and find it was already 8:00 p.m. and he had not even thought to turn on the lights. Albert scurried around like an ant, chatted enthusiastically, but all that was apparent to Édouard was that they had money worries. Every day, Albert would mount an assault on the "*baraques* Vilgrain,"[5] the makeshift stores set up by the government to provide cheap necessities for those who were truly destitute, and every night he complained about how everything simply flew off the shelves. He never talked about the price of morphine; he tried to be tactful. He discussed money in general, but in an upbeat tone, as though this was a temporary setback they would look back on and laugh about in the way that men at the front had sometimes behaved as though the war were only an extended military service, a tiresome chore they would come away from with happy memories.

For Albert, their economic worries would be magically resolved, it was simply a matter of time. Édouard's disability pension would ease the pressure and provide support for his comrade. A soldier who had given his all for his country and would never be able to live a normal life, one of the heroes who had won the war and brought Germany to its knees: it was a topic of which Albert never tired. He sat, calculating Édouard's demobilization bonus, the *pécule*, the disability bonus, his pension as a *mutilé de guerre* . . .

Édouard shook his head.

"What do you mean, no?" Albert said. That's all I need, he thought. Édouard hasn't submitted the application, he hasn't sent back the forms.

"Don't worry," Albert said, "I'll deal with it."

Édouard shook his head again and seeing that Albert still did not understand, took the slate he used to communicate and scrawled in chalk: "Eugène Larivière."

Albert frowned. Édouard got to his feet and, from his knapsack, dug out a crumpled folder marked "Applying for Pensions and Disability

Benefits," containing a list of documents to be filed for review by the committee. Albert lingered over those Édouard had underlined in red: *Incident report relating to the illness or injury—Summary of the initial treatment at the admitting field hospital or infirmary—Evacuation papers—Medical files pertaining to initial hospitalization . . .*

The shock was terrible.

And yet it was obvious. No one named Eugène Larivière had been listed as wounded and transferred to a hospital during the assault on Hill 113. There would be records detailing how Édouard Péricourt was evacuated and later died of his wounds and others recording that Eugène Larivière had been transferred to Paris, but any official investigation would quickly reveal that the story simply did not add up, that the wounded soldier Édouard Péricourt could not be Eugène Larivière who had been demobilized two days later and transferred to the Hôpital Rollin on the avenue Trudaine. It would be impossible to provide the necessary documents.

Édouard had assumed a new identity; he could prove nothing, he would get nothing.

In fact, if the authorities were to dig a little deeper, examine the register, discover the deception, the false entries, he risked prison rather than a pension.

War had inured Albert to misfortune, but this time, he was devastated by what felt like a gross injustice. Worse, like a repudiation. What have I done, he thought, panic stricken; the anger that had been welling in him since he had been demobilized suddenly exploded, he slammed his head into the wall, sending the framed picture of the horse's head crashing down, the glass cracked down the middle. Albert found himself slumped, dazed, on the floor with a lump on his forehead that would not go down for weeks.

Édouard's eyes were glistening again. It was best not to cry in front of Albert, because these days his own situation was such that it took very little to bring him to tears . . . Édouard understood and simply laid a hand on Albert's shoulder. He felt utterly wretched.

They quickly needed to find a place that was big enough for two: one paranoid and a cripple. Albert's budget was pitiful. The newspapers still insisted that Germany would pay in full for everything it had destroyed during the war, which seemed like half the country. In the meantime, prices were rising, pensions and salaries went unpaid, transportation was chaotic, supplies erratic, and consequently there was a considerable amount of trafficking, meanwhile people were living by their wits, everyone knew someone who knew someone, contacts were made and addresses exchanged. This was how Albert came to be standing in front of number 9, impasse Pers, a middle-class house that had already taken in three lodgers. In the courtyard, there was a small two-story outbuilding, once a warehouse, now a storehouse, the upper floor of which was vacant. It was rickety but spacious, a coal-fired stove heated the low-ceilinged room and there was running water just below. There were two big windows and a large folding screen embroidered with pastoral scenes of a shepherdess and her sheep that had been ripped down the middle and crudely repaired.

Albert and Édouard used a handcart to move their belongings, since vans were expensive. It was early September.

Their new landlady, Mme Belmont, had lost her husband in 1916 and her brother a year later. She was still young, perhaps even pretty, though she was so haggard it was not possible to guess. She lived with her daughter, Louise, and insisted she felt reassured to have "two strapping young men" moving in because, living in this big house at the end of a cul-de-sac, she could not depend on her existing tenants—all of them old men—if there were any problems. She earned a modest living working as a cleaning woman here and there. The rest of the time, she spent standing at her window, staring out at the odds and ends her husband had had a habit of collecting that were now rusting away in the courtyard. Albert could see her when he leaned out his own window.

Her daughter, Louise, was smart and resourceful. She was eleven years old with eyes like a cat and too many freckles to count. She could be as lively as water rushing over rocks and a moment later thoughtful and still as an engraving. She spoke rarely—Albert had heard her speak on only three occasions—and she never smiled. But she was a very pretty child nonetheless; if she was half as pretty when she grew up, she would start wars. Albert never knew how she came to win over Édouard. Ordinarily, he refused to see anyone, but nothing would stop this girl. From the day they arrived, she had camped out at the foot of the stairs, watching. As everyone knows, children are by nature curious, girls especially. Her mother had probably said something about the new tenant.

"No oil painting, apparently. So badly scarred he never goes out, I heard from his friend who takes care of him."

Such a comment could hardly fail to rouse the curiosity of an eleven-year-old girl. She'll get bored soon enough, Albert had thought, but no . . . Seeing her every day, sitting on the top step by the door, anticipating any opportunity to get a glimpse inside, he had thrown open the door. The girl stood frozen on the threshold, her lips set in a perfect "O," her eyes wide, unable to utter a sound. Admittedly, with the gaping hole in the middle and those upper teeth that looked twice their actual size, Édouard's face was a spectacle, it was like nothing in this world. In fact, Albert had told him so in no uncertain terms: "With a face like that you could scare the crows out of the trees, old man, you could at least spare a thought for others." He had said it to encourage Édouard to have the graft, but it made no difference. Albert gestured to the door where the terrified girl had fled as soon as she saw him. Édouard sat, impassive, and puffed on his cigarette with one nostril while holding the other closed. He exhaled the smoke through his nose too, because through his throat . . . "You can't, Édouard," Albert had told him, "I can't stand it. It scares me if you want the truth, it looks like a volcano erupting, I swear, look at yourself in the mirror sometime, you'll see . . ." Albert had only been living with his friend since mid-June, and already they were like an old married couple. The day-to-day was difficult, they were always short of money, but as often happens, the problems had brought the two men closer, binding them together. Albert was truly touched by his friend's tragedy and could not seem to get past the idea that had Édouard not saved him, and only a few days before the end of the war . . . Édouard, for his part, being keenly aware that Albert was single-handedly responsible for both their lives, did his best to lighten the burden, doing small chores around the house—an old married couple, as I said.

A few days after running away, little Louise reappeared. Albert assumed that the sight of Édouard exerted a sort of fascination over her. She stood in the doorway of the living room for a moment, then without warning, she walked over to Édouard and brought her forefinger to his face. Édouard knelt down—Albert had seen him do some strange things—to allow the girl to trace the edge of the yawning chasm. She seemed engrossed, attentive, as though this were a piece of homework, like the maps of France she carefully traced in pencil.

It was at this moment that the two struck up a curious friendship. As soon as she came home from school, she would come up to see Édouard. She managed to find old newspapers for him to read, issues that were days or even weeks out of date. This was Édouard's sole occupation, reading newspapers, clipping out articles. Albert had glanced at the file in which he kept the cuttings, articles about those who had died in the war, about commemorations, lists of those missing in action; it was rather sad. Édouard did not read the Paris dailies, only the provincial papers. Louise always managed to find copies, no one knew how. Almost every day, she would bring Édouard a cache of old issues of *L'Ouest-Éclair*, the *Journal de Rouen* or *L'Est républicain*. She would sit at the kitchen table doing her homework while Édouard smoked his Caporals and cut out articles. Louise's mother made no comment.

One evening in mid-September, Albert had come home after a tiring shift as a sandwich man, having spent the afternoon trudging the Grands Boulevards between Bastille and République carrying a board (on one side extolling the virtues of "Pink" pills, *A jiffy is all it takes to cure all manner of ills*, on the other, those of Juvénil corsets, *Two hundred retailers in France!*). As he came in, he found Édouard lying on an ancient, battered couch Albert had found some weeks earlier and brought home using a handcart borrowed from an old comrade he had met during the Somme and whose only means of survival now was to drag a cart with what little strength he had left and his one remaining arm.

Édouard was smoking, as usual, and wearing a dark blue mask that extended from just below his nose, covering the lower part of his face, and jutted over his neck like the beard of an actor in a Greek tragedy. The dark, shimmering blue was speckled with gold, as though the paint had been sprinkled with sequins before it dried.

Albert signaled his surprise. Édouard gave a theatrical wave as if to say, “Well, how do I look?” It was odd. For the first time since they had met, Édouard’s expression seemed genuinely human. In fact, Albert had to admit it was very handsome.

There came a sudden, muffled sound from his left and, turning his head, Albert just caught sight of Louise scampering down the stairs. He had yet to hear her laugh.

Like Louise, the masks were now a permanent fixture.

Some days later, Édouard was wearing a white mask on which Louise had drawn a large smiling mouth. Édouard’s twinkling eyes made him look like an Italian actor, a sort of Sganarelle or Pagliaccio. Now when he had finished reading his newspapers, Édouard would turn them into papier-mâché in order to make chalk-white masks that Louise would later paint or decorate. What had started out as a game had become a full-time occupation. Louise was the high priestess and would scour the neighborhood and arrive with paste jewels, beads, fabric, colored felt, ostrich feathers, and imitation snakeskin. Since she also had to find the newspapers, it must have been a lot of work, running around trying to find these baubles and trinkets; Albert would not have known where to look.

Édouard and Louise spent their time making these masks. Édouard never wore the same one twice; the new one would replace the old, which was hung with the others on the walls of the apartment like hunting trophies or costumes in a fancy-dress shop.

It was almost 8:00 p.m. when Albert arrived at the foot of the stairs carrying his shoebox.

His left hand, the one that had been slashed by the Greek, was throbbing viciously despite Docteur Martineau’s bandage, and he was feeling unsettled. The shoebox, the spoils of a valiant struggle, offered him some relief; getting supplies of morphine had been time consuming and took its toll on a sensitive soul like Albert, who was so susceptible to emotions of all kinds . . . And yet he could not help but think that what he was carrying could kill his friend twenty times, a hundred times over.

He took three steps, lifted the dusty tarpaulin covering the remains of a broken-down cargo tricycle, pushed aside the hodgepodge in the bin, and carefully stowed his precious shoebox.

On his way home, he had done a quick calculation. If Édouard kept to his current—rather high—dose, they would not have to worry for almost six months.

14

Henri d'Aulnay-Pradelle found himself unthinkingly comparing the elegant stork mounted on the radiator cap in front of him and the lumbering corpulence of Dupré sitting next to him. Not that there was anything in common between the two; on the contrary, they could not have been more different, and in fact Henri was not comparing but rather contrasting. With its broad wings whose tapered points touched the hood or the slender, graceful neck that tapered to the willful beak, the stork in full flight looked a little like a wild duck, but it was more sturdy, more (Henri groped for the word) . . . more "ultimate," though God only knew what he meant by this word. And the grooves of the wings, he thought approvingly, like the folds of a drape . . . even the delicately curved legs . . . The bird seemed to cleave the air without even touching it, opening up a path like an outrider. Pradelle never tired of marveling at his stork.

Dupré, on the other hand, was a heavyset, bull-necked man. Not an outrider. A foot soldier. With that trait particular to the rank and file that they themselves call loyalty, fidelity, duty, or some such twaddle.

Henri believed the world was divided into two categories: those beasts of burden, doomed to work tirelessly, thoughtlessly to the end of their days, and the elite to whom everything was due. Because of their "personal coefficient." Henri was much taken with this phrase, which he had read in a military report and adopted as his own.

Dupré—Sergent-Chef Dupré—was a perfect example of the former category: hardworking, insignificant, stubborn, dull witted, biddable.

The stork chosen by Hispano-Suiza for the H6B (six-cylinder engine, 135 horsepower, 85 mph!) represented the celebrated fighter squadron commanded by Georges Guynemer, an exceptional individual. A man not unlike Henri, but for the fact that Guynemer was dead while Henri was still very much alive, giving him an indisputable advantage over the flying ace.

On one side, Dupré, his pants cut too short, his dossier in his lap, who had been silently gazing in wonder at the burl walnut dashboard ever since they left Paris, the one exception to Henri's resolve to invest the bulk of his profits in the restoration of la Sallevière. On the other, Henri d'Aulnay-Pradelle, the son-in-law of Marcel Péricourt, a hero of the Great War, a millionaire at thirty, a man destined for greatness, who was speeding though the Orléanais countryside at sixty-eight miles per hour and had already hit one dog and two chickens. Beasts of burden in their own way. It all came down to this: those who soared and those who succumbed.

Dupré had fought under the command of Capitaine Pradelle, who, when the man was demobilized, hired him for a song, a temporary salary that quickly became permanent. A man of peasant stock, destined to submit to extraordinary individuals, Dupré had welcomed his civilian subservience as a logical extension of the natural order of things.

They arrived in the late morning.

As some thirty workers looked on admiringly, Henri parked his magnificent automobile. Right in the middle of the courtyard. Just to show who was boss. The boss is the one who gives orders, otherwise known as the customer. Or the king . . . it amounts to the same thing.

Lavallée Timber Supplies and Cabinetry had languished for more than three generations until the war arrived, and with it, orders to supply the French army with hundreds of miles of railway sleepers, with beams and supporting braces for building, consolidating, and repairing trenches and passageways, which had led to an increase in the workforce from thirteen lumbermen to more than forty. Gaston Lavallée also owned a splendid automobile, but he brought it out only on special occasions—this was not Paris.

Henri and Lavallée shook hands in the courtyard; Henri did not introduce Dupré. Later, when he said, "You'll need to sort that out with Dupré," Lavallée would turn and give the menial walking behind them a curt nod by way of acknowledgment.

Before the tour, Lavallée suggested they have a small light meal and gestured to the steps leading to the house on the right of the vast workshops. Henri was raising a hand to dismiss the idea when he noticed the young woman in an apron on the steps, smoothing her hair as she waited for the guests. Lavallée added that his daughter Émilienne had prepared a little meal. In the end, Henri accepted the invitation.

"But we'll have to make it quick."

It was these workshops that had produced the magnificent sample coffin that had been sent to the War Graves Commission, a superb oak casket worth every centime of its sixty francs. Now that it had served its purpose in persuading the Adjudicating Committee, they could move on to more serious matters, to the coffins that would actually be delivered.

Pradelle and Lavallée strolled through the main workshop, followed by Dupré and a foreman who had dressed in his best overalls for the occasion. Stiff as dead soldiers, a phalanx of coffins, recognizably of decreasing quality, were lined up side by side.

"Our Fallen Heroes . . . ," Lavallée began grandiloquently, laying a hand on a chestnut wood coffin, a midrange model.

"Spare me the homilies." Pradelle cut him short. "What have you got for less than thirty francs?"

In the end the boss's daughter had proved rather unprepossessing (however much she smoothed her hair, she was dreadfully provincial), the white wine was too sweet and served lukewarm, and the food was inedible. Lavallée had orchestrated the occasion like a visit of a plenipotentiary from the tropics, the workers were forever winking and nudging each other, all of which was getting on Pradelle's nerves, he wanted to get down to business, and besides he wanted to get back to Paris for dinner, a friend had promised to introduce him to Léonie Flanchet, a vaudeville actress he had seen perform a week earlier, and who, everyone agreed, was a "stunner," something Henri was eager to confirm for himself.

"But . . . er . . . thirty francs is not what was agreed . . ."

"What we agreed and what will happen are two very different things," said Pradelle. "So let's start again from the beginning, but make it fast, I don't have all damn day."

"But Monsieur Pradelle . . ."

"D'Aulnay-Pradelle."

"Of course, if you . . ."

Henri glared at the man.

"Well, Monsieur d'Aulnay-Pradelle," Lavallée said in a conciliatory, almost pedantic tone, "we do have coffins in that price range, obviously . . ."

"Good, I'll take them."

". . . but I'm afraid it's impossible."

Pradelle gave him a look of profound stupefaction.

"The problem is transportation, *cher monsieur*," explained Lavallée. "If we were simply dealing with the local cemetery, they would be fit for purpose, but the coffins you require need to be able to travel. From here they have to be shipped to Compiègne, to Laon, where they will be unloaded, reloaded, and shipped on to wherever the bodies are being exhumed, then reshipped to the war graves—that's a lot of transportation involved . . ."

"I don't see the problem."

"The coffins we sell for thirty francs are made of poplar. Not very resilient. They'll warp, they'll crack, they may even fall apart, because they're not designed to be manhandled. At a bare minimum, you might get away with beech. Forty francs apiece. And that's only because of the quantity involved, otherwise they go for forty-five . . ."

Henri turned to his left.

"What's that one?"

They walked toward it. Lavallée laughed, a deep, forced, laugh.

"That's silver birch!"

"How much?"

"Thirty-six."

"And that one . . . ?" Henri pointed to the last one in the row, just before the coffins made from offcuts.

"That one's pine . . ."

"How much?"

"Er . . . thirty-three . . ."

Perfect. Henri laid a hand on the coffin, patting it almost admiringly as he might a racehorse, though it was impossible to tell whether he was admiring the quality of the workmanship, the modest price, or his own brilliance.

Lavallée felt he had to show some modicum of professionalism.

"If you'll allow me, this model is not really suited to your needs. You see . . ."

"My needs?" Henri interrupted. "What needs?"

"Transportation, *cher monsieur*! Once again the problem is the transportation . . ."

"You ship them flat, so there's no problem there . . ."

"Not at the start, no . . ."

"You assemble them when they arrive, so there's no problem there . . ."

"No, of course not. The problem, and forgive me for insisting on this point, is once they are handled: they have to be unloaded from the trucks, set down, moved, then the body is placed in the coffin . . ."

"I understand, but at that point, it is no longer your problem. All you need do is deliver them. Is that not so, Dupré?"

Henri had good reason to turn to his manager, since it would become his problem. He did not, however, wait for a response. Lavallée would have liked to set out his arguments, to talk about his company's reputation, to emphasize . . . Henri cut him dead.

"Thirty-three francs, you said?"

Lavallée quickly took out his notepad.

"Given the size of the order I'm making, let's say thirty francs."

In the time Lavallée took fumbling for a pencil, he had just lost three francs per unit.

"No, no, no," he protested. "It's thirty-three taking into account the quantity!"

On this occasion, on this particular point, Lavallée would stand firm. It was clear from his posture.

"I cannot accept thirty francs, it's out of the question!"

He seemed to have suddenly grown four inches, face flushed, pencil quivering, he was unyielding, as though prepared to die for the sake of three francs.

Henri nodded slowly and deliberately, I see, I see, I see . . .

"Very well," he said at length, "thirty-three francs it is."

Lavallée could not believe this sudden capitulation. He quickly scribbled the figure on his pad, this unexpected victory had left him trembling, exhausted, fearful.

"Remind me, Dupré . . . ," Henri said, sounding concerned.

Lavallée, Dupré, and the foreman all stiffened again.

"The coffins for Compiègne and Laon need to be five foot six, is that right?"

The Adjudicating Committee had set varying sizes for the coffins ranging from a handful measuring six foot two, a few hundred at five foot nine, with most measuring five foot six. There were a number of orders for even smaller coffins—five foot two and even four foot nine.

Dupré nodded.

"Thirty-three francs we agreed for five foot six," Pradelle turned back to Lavallée. "How much for four foot nine?"

Surprised by this change of tack, no one actually imagined what it meant in practice: shorter coffins. Lavallée had not considered the possibility, he needed to work out the figures; he reopened his pad and launched into calculations that took an age. Everyone waited. Henri was still standing next to the pine coffin; he had stopped stroking its hindquarters and now simply gazed at it longingly as though contemplating a night of pleasure with a new girl.

Finally, Lavallée looked up, and said in a dull voice, "Thirty francs . . ."

"Hmm, hmm," Pradelle murmured.

Everyone began to consider the practical implications of placing a five foot six soldier in a four-foot-nine coffin. The foreman imagined the soldier's head bowed, the chin pressed against the chest. Dupré saw the body laid on its side, the legs bent slightly. Gaston Lavallée could not picture anything, he had lost two nephews in a single day at the Somme, the family had claimed the bodies, he had personally made coffins of solid oak each with a large gilt cross and gilded handles, and he refused to imagine how one fitted a large body into a small coffin.

"Tell me, Lavallée," Pradelle said with the air of someone making a casual inquiry of no great importance, "roughly how much would a four foot three coffin sell for?"

An hour later, they had signed an agreement in principle. Two hundred coffins a day would be shipped to the Gare d'Orléans. The unit price had slipped to twenty-eight francs. Pradelle was extremely satisfied with the negotiations. He had just paid off his Hispano-Suiza.

15

The driver reappeared once again to inform Madame that Madame's car was waiting, if Madame would be so kind, and Madeleine gave a brief nod, thank you, Ernest, I'm coming, and said in a regretful tone:

"I'm afraid I really must go, Yvonne, I'm so sorry . . ."

Yvonne de Jardin-Beaulieu gave a little wave, very well, very well, but made no attempt to get up, she was enjoying herself too much, she could not bring herself to leave.

"What a husband you have, my dear," she said. "How fortunate you are."

Madeleine Péricourt smiled evenly, stared meekly at her nails thinking "whore" and said, "Come, come, you have your share of suitors . . ."

"Oh, me . . . ," said the young woman, affecting resignation.

Her brother, Léon, was too short for a man, but Yvonne was rather pretty. For those who like their women sluttish, Madeleine added mentally. She had a large, coarse, eager mouth that immediately evoked salacious images, something men were quick to notice; at twenty-five, Yvonne had already bedded half the Rotary Club. Half the Rotary Club was overstating the matter; Madeleine was being uncharitable.

In her defense, it was understandable that she should feel cruel—it had been scarcely two weeks since Yvonne first slept with Henri, and her haste in coming around to visit his wife so that she might enjoy the spectacle was indecent. More so than seducing her husband—no difficult feat. Henri's other mistresses had been more patient. They had waited for an opportunity to present itself, or contrived an accidental meeting in order to savor their victory. And afterward, as one, they would smile and simper, "Oh, what a wonderful husband you have, my dear, I do so envy you!" One of them, a month ago, had even dared to say, "Take good care of him, my dear, lest someone steal him away . . ."

In recent weeks Madeleine had barely seen Henri, so many trips, so many meetings, scarcely time to screw his wife's friends; this government order was taking up all his time and energy.

When he did come home, it was late, and she would mount him.

In the morning, he would get up early. But just before, she would mount him again.

The rest of the time, he spent mounting other women, went away on business, called, sent messages, sent lies. Everyone knew he was unfaithful to her (the rumors had first started in late May, when he was seen in the company of Lucienne d'Haurecourt).

M. Péricourt was distressed by the situation. "He will make you unhappy," he had warned his daughter when she first spoke of marrying Pradelle, but to no avail; she had simply laid her hand on his and that was that. He had given his consent; what else could he do?

"Very well," Yvonne said, "this time I really must go."

She had delivered her message; she had only to look at the frozen smile on Madeleine's face to know it had got through. Yvonne was exultant.

"It was so kind of you to visit," Madeleine said, getting to her feet.

Yvonne waved, it's nothing, nothing, the two women kissed, cheek pressed to cheek, lips in midair, must run, see you soon. There was no contest, she was the sluttiest of them all.

This unforeseen visit meant she was now running late. Madeleine looked up at the clock. Perhaps it was better this way, at 7.30 p.m. she was more likely to find him at home.

It was after eight o'clock when the car dropped her at the entrance to the impasse Pers. To go from the parc Monceau to the rue Marcadet did not simply mean crossing an *arrondissement*, it meant traversing a whole world, from the prosperous to the plebeian, from opulence to indigence. A Packard Twin-6 and a Cadillac Type 51 with a V8 engine were usually parked outside the Péricourts' elegant mansion. Here, through the holes in the worm-eaten wooden fence, Madeleine could see only a number of broken handcarts and old tires. She was unruffled. There had been limousines on her mother's side of the family, and handcarts on her father's, whose grandparents had been humble folk. Though it was now a distant memory, both sides of her family had known poverty and hardship, which, like puritanism or feudalism, never altogether fade but leave their mark on succeeding generations. Seeing his mistress wander off, Ernest, the chauffeur—the Péricourt family had called all their drivers Ernest ever since the first Ernest—eyed the courtyard in disgust, because his family had been chauffeurs for only two generations.

Madeleine walked past the wooden fence, rang the doorbell, and waited for a long while until a woman of indeterminate age finally appeared, then asked if she could speak to M. Albert Maillard. The woman took a moment to process this request, coming as it did from the well-heeled, sophisticated, elegantly made-up young woman whose powdery scent reached her like some ancient memory. "Monsieur Maillard," Madeleine said again. Without a word, the woman waved toward the far end of the courtyard. Madeleine nodded and, under the watchful eyes of the woman and of her chauffeur, she pushed open the worm-eaten gate and strode confidently through the muddy yard to the entrance to the little outbuilding, where she was lost from view, but here she stopped dead as the stairs above her head trembled under the weight of someone coming down. She looked up and recognized Soldat Maillard, he was carrying an empty coal scuttle; he, too, stopped dead, his foot hovering between stairs, mouthing, "Wh . . . ? What?" He looked utterly lost, just as he had in the cemetery on the day they had exhumed poor Édouard's body.

Albert froze, his mouth half open.

"Good day, Monsieur Maillard," Madeleine said.

She studied his moonlike face, his febrile body. A friend of hers had once had a dog that trembled continually; it was not an illness, the dog had always been like that, day and night it quivered from head to tail until one day its heart simply gave out. Albert reminded her of that dog. She spoke in a soft, gentle voice as though afraid that, faced with such a surprise, he might burst into tears or run off and hide in the cellar. Albert said nothing, shifting his weight from one foot to the other, swallowing hard. He glanced anxiously, almost fearfully, toward the top of the stairs . . . This was something Madeleine had noticed about the young man, this constant apprehension, this terror that something was about to happen just behind him; even in the cemetery, last year, he had seemed lost, helpless. With that gentle, naive expression of men who live in their own world.

Albert would have given ten years of his life not to be in this position, caught between Madeleine Péricourt at the foot of the stairs and her supposedly dead brother, who was upstairs, smoking through his nostril, wearing a green mask with blue feathers, looking like a budgerigar. Decidedly, Albert had been born to be a sandwich man. Realizing he had not greeted the woman, Albert tossed the coal bucket aside like a dishrag, extended a sooty hand only to quickly apologize and tuck it behind his back as he walked down the remaining steps.

"Your parents' address was on the letter you sent," said Madeleine gently, "I went there. Your mother said I would find you here." She gestured around her at the outbuilding, the courtyard, the stairs, with a smile as though it were a plush apartment. Albert nodded, unable to utter a single syllable. She might have arrived just as he was opening the shoebox, caught him fetching ampoules of morphine. Worse still, he imagined what would have happened if by some slim chance Édouard had come down to fetch the coal himself . . . It is in such details that it becomes apparent that fate is bunkum.

"Yes . . . ," Albert ventured, not knowing what question he was answering.

What he wanted to say was no, no I can't invite you upstairs, I can't offer you a drink, it's impossible. Madeleine Péricourt did not think him impolite, she attributed his awkwardness to surprise and embarrassment.

"The thing is," she began, "my father would like to make your acquaintance."

"Why me?"

The words came out as a heartfelt cry, his voice was strained, Madeleine shrugged, the answer was self-evident.

"Because you were there in the last moments of my brother's life."

She smiled as she said this, as she might to an elderly man whose confused eccentricities were understandable.

"Yes, of course . . ."

Now that he had managed to gather his wits, Albert wanted only one thing, he wanted her to leave before Édouard became worried and came downstairs. Or heard her voice and realized who it was below.

"All right . . . ," he said.

"Tomorrow, does that suit you?"

"Oh, no, not tomorrow, that's impossible."

Madeleine Péricourt was startled by the swiftness of this response.

"What I meant to say," Albert said apologetically, "was some other day, if you like, because tomorrow . . ."

He would have been incapable of explaining why tomorrow was the wrong day; he simply needed time to collect his wits. For a fleeting instant, he imagined what the conversation between his mother and Madeleine Péricourt had been like, and the color drained from his face. He felt ashamed.

"Very well, what day would suit you?" the young woman asked.

Albert turned again and glanced at the top of the stairs. Madeleine assumed he had a woman upstairs and her presence made him uncomfortable, she had no wish to embarrass him.

"How about Saturday?" she suggested. "You could come to dinner."

She said this in a cheery, almost impetuous tone as though the idea had only just occurred to her and she was sure they would have a rollicking good time.

"Well, um . . ."

"Excellent," she said. "Shall we say seven o'clock? Would that suit?"

"Well, um . . ."

She smiled.

"My father will be very happy."

The little social ritual now concluded, there was a brief silence, hesitant, almost contemplative, and this reminded them of their first meeting, reminded them that though they scarcely knew each other, they were bound by a terrible, furtive secret: the exhumation of a dead soldier whose remains they had smuggled away. What had they done with the body? Albert wondered and bit his lip.

"We're on the boulevard de Courcelles," Madeleine said, slipping on her glove, "at the corner of the rue de *Prony*, it's easy to find."

Albert nodded again, agreed, seven o'clock, rue de Prony, easy to find. Saturday. Silence.

"Well, then, I must go, Monsieur Maillard. And thank you again."

She half turned, then turned back and looked into his eyes. This solemn expression suited him, but made him look much older than his years.

"My father knows nothing of the details of . . . you understand . . . I should prefer that it remain so . . ."

"Yes, of course," Albert said quickly.

She smiled gratefully.

He was terrified that she would press money into his hand again. For his silence. Mortified at this thought, he turned away and went back up the stairs. Only when he got to the landing did he remember he had forgotten to get the coal and the ampoule of morphine. He trudged back down, feeling overwhelmed. He could not seem to think straight, to decide what it meant, being invited to dine with Édouard's family.

His chest tight with fear, he took the long-handled shovel and began to fill the coal scuttle, and from the street he heard the soft purr of the limousine pulling away.

16

Édouard closed his eyes and gave a long sigh of relief as his muscles slowly relaxed. He grasped the syringe that almost fell from his fingers and set it down next to him; his hands were trembling still, but already he felt his chest free of the vise-like grip. After his injections, he would stretch out for a long time, exhausted, though sleep rarely came. He felt himself drifting, his feverishness ebbing slowly, disappearing like a ship going out on the tide. He had never been interested in the sea, his imagination was not stirred by ocean liners; it must be something contained in these little vials of happiness, because for no reason he could understand, the images they evoked were often nautical. Perhaps, like oil lamps and potion bottles, they drew you into their world. While the syringe and the needle remained but surgical tools, a necessary evil, the ampoules were alive. He would peer into them, holding them up to the light, it was amazing what could be seen inside, a crystal ball had no more magical properties, no more fertile imagination. He drew much from these vials: rest, calm, consolation. The greater part of his day was spent in a hazy, indefinite state where time had no substance. Left to his own devices, he would have taken the injections one after another so he could stay like this, drifting, floating on his back in a sea of oil (more images of the sea, they seemed to come from long ago, perhaps from floating in the womb), but Albert was sensible, every morning he gave Édouard the minimum dose to get him through the day, he noted everything down, and when he came home in the evening, he would read aloud the list of days and dosages like a schoolmaster, turning the pages of his notepad, and Édouard would lie there and listen. Just as he did with Louise and the masks. Passively he allowed people to take care of him.

Though Édouard rarely thought of his family now, he thought of Madeleine more often than the others. He had so many memories of her, her stifled laughter, her conspiratorial smiles, her knuckles rubbing across his skull, that private understanding between them. He felt for her. Hearing that he was dead, she would have felt the terrible grief that women feel when they lose a loved one. But later, time, that great healer . . . Grief, too, is something we grow accustomed to in time.

It could not compare to the enduring horror of Édouard's face in the mirror.

For him, death was ever present, endlessly ripping open the wound.

Aside from Madeleine, who else was there? A few friends, but how many were still alive? Even Édouard, always the lucky one, had died in this war, so what chance did the others have . . . There was his father, of course, but what was there to say about him? He would go about his business, brusque and boring as ever, the news of his son's death had probably not set him back unduly, he would simply have climbed into his car and snapped at Ernest: "To the Bourse!" because there were decisions to be made, or "To the Jockey Club!" because there were elections to win.

Édouard never went out, he spent all his time in this apartment, in this hell. Then again, it was not even that—hell would surely be worse. No, what was disheartening was the persistent mediocrity, the poverty, the scrambling to make ends meet. People say you get used to anything, but it's not true. Édouard had not got used to it. When he could summon the energy, he would stand in front of the mirror and stare at his missing face; he could never find a flicker of humanity in this gaping throat, denuded of jaw and tongue. Those huge upper teeth. The swelling had subsided, the wounds had scarred, but the brute violence of this gaping void remained undimmed, this was the purpose of grafts, not to make you less ugly but to make you more resigned to your fate. With poverty, it was much the same. He had been born into a wealthy family, there was never any need to count the cost because money did not count. He had never been an extravagant boy, though among his classmates at school, he had known boys who liked to flash their money . . . He was not personally profligate, but the world in which he had grown up had been vast, luxurious, comfortable, the rooms always spacious, the seats plush, the meals lavish, the clothes costly; now he found himself living in this rickety apartment where the floors were warped, the windows grimy, the coal scarce, and the wine second rate . . . Everything about this life was ugly. Their finances depended entirely on Albert, it was impossible to find fault with him, he broke his back to make sure there was a supply of morphine, Édouard did not know how he did it, it must have cost a lot of money, Albert was a real friend. His devotion was enough to break your heart sometimes, he never complained, never criticized, always pretended to be cheerful though it was obvious that deep down, he was worried sick. There was no way of knowing what would become of them.

Édouard was a deadweight but had no fear of the future. His life had come crashing down in an instant, on a whim of fate, and it had swept everything away, even fear. The only truly overwhelming thing was the sadness.

And even that, over time, had become bearable.

Little Louise cheered him up with her masks, as tireless as Albert, she was a worker bee who brought him newspapers from the provinces. The improvement in his mood—something so fragile he did not confide it to anyone—owed everything to those newspapers and the ideas they had provided. As the days passed, he had sensed a feeling of excitement rising from deep within, and the more he thought about it, the more he experienced the heady euphoria he used to feel as a boy when dreaming up some prank, some caricature, some disguise, something that would shock. Now, nothing could ever be as ecstatic, as explosive as it had been in his adolescence, but deep in his gut he felt "something" seeping back. Even to himself he hardly dared pronounce the word: *joy*. A furtive, wary, intermittent joy. When he could manage to get his thoughts more or less in order, he occasionally—astonishingly—managed to forget the Édouard he was now, to become again the man he had been before the war . . .

At length, he got to his feet, caught his breath, steadied himself. Having sterilized the needle, he carefully put his syringe back in the small tin box, closed the lid, and set it on the shelf. He moved one of the chairs, carefully setting it down in the right place, and with some difficulty, given his stiff leg, he climbed onto it, gently pushed the trapdoor that led into an attic space too small for anyone to stand upright, a crawlspace filled with five generations of cobwebs and coal dust. With great care, he slid out the bag containing his greatest treasure: a large drawing pad that Louise claimed she had got as part of a swap—though what she had bartered was a mystery.

He clambered down and went back to the couch, sharpened a pencil, taking care that the shavings fell onto a scrap of paper, which he screwed up and placed inside the bag: a secret is a secret. As always, he began by leafing through the first drawings and felt a certain satisfaction and encouragement in observing how much he had accomplished. Twelve drawings so far, some soldiers, a few women, a child, but mostly soldiers, some wounded, some triumphant, others dying or kneeling or lying on the ground, here was an arm reaching out, he was proud of this outstretched arm, it was well drawn, had he been able to smile . . .

He set to work.

A woman this time, standing, one breast bared. Did the breast have to be bared? No. He began the sketch again, covering the breast. He sharpened his pencil again, he could have done with a finer point, paper that was not so coarse, he had to work on his knees because the table was the wrong height, what he really needed was a writing slope, but it was good that these things irritated him because it showed how much he wanted to work. He raised his head, held the page at arm's length to get an overview. It was a good start, the woman was standing, the folds were quite good, the drape of fabric was the hardest thing, everything depended on it: the drape of the fabric and the eyes, that was the secret. At moments like this, Édouard was almost his old self.

If he was not mistaken, he would make a fortune. Before the year was out. Albert would be surprised.

And he would not be the only one.

17

"A pathetic little ceremony at les Invalides, that's all . . . ?"

"Well, Maréchal Foch will be present . . ."

Henri whirled around, furious, indignant.

"Foch? So what?"

He was in his underpants and struggling with his tie. Madeleine started to laugh. Indignation is difficult for a man in his underpants to carry off . . . though he had fine, muscular legs. He turned back to the mirror to finish knotting his tie, his firm, powerful buttocks visible beneath his underwear. Madeleine wondered whether he was running late. Then decided it did not matter, she had time to spare, she had time enough for two, time was something she had in abundance, like patience and stubbornness. And besides, he spent enough of it on his mistresses . . . She came up behind him, he did not hear her, but he felt her cold hand inside his pants, her aim unerring, cajoling, languorous, insistent; her face pressed into his back as she said in a tender, deliciously sleazy voice:

"Darling, you don't really mean it! After all, Maréchal Foch is quite someone . . ."

Henri finished with his tie so he could think. In fact, he did not need to think, now was not the right time. They had done it last night . . . And now, again, this morning, honestly . . . Not that he did not have the stamina, that was not the issue, but there were times, like just now, when he felt a furious desire, when he had to fuck her at any opportunity. It won him a little respite. In exchange for his conjugal duty, he was free to take his pleasures elsewhere. It was a serviceable arrangement. It was tiresome. He had never been able to get used to her intimate private smell, something that was simply not talked about, though she might have understood, but sometimes she behaved like an empress and he a servant who knew his place. It was not unpleasant, strictly speaking, especially given how much time it took, but . . . he liked to be the one to decide, and with Madeleine it was always she who took the initiative. Over and over, Madeleine murmured "Maréchal Foch," she knew that Henri was not in the mood but she carried on, her hand became warmer, and she felt him uncoil like a fat, listless, yet powerful snake, he never refused her; he did not refuse her this time, it was over in a flash, he turned, lifted her bodily and laid her on the edge of the bed, he did not trouble to take off his tie or his socks. She clung to him, forcing him to stay inside her for a few seconds more. He stayed, then he got to his feet and it was over.

"July 14 was a different matter, that was all pomp and ceremony."

He had gone back over to the mirror, his tie needed readjusting.

"Celebrating our victory in the Great War on the revolutionary fourteenth! It's utterly preposterous . . . And for the anniversary of the armistice, they organize this intimate little ceremony at les Invalides! So intimate it might as well be a commemoration *in camera*!"

He was particularly proud of this expression. He had looked for the perfect turn of phrase, savored the words as though tasting a fine wine. A commemoration *in camera*. Very clever. He wanted to try it out, turned around, and in a bilious tone spat:

"A commemoration of the Great War *in camera*!"

Not bad. Madeleine had finally got up from the bed and put on a negligee. She would bathe after he left, there was no hurry. In the meantime, she tidied away the clothes. She put on a pair of slippers. Henri, by now, was in full flow.

"You have to admit, these commemorations have been taken over by the Bolsheviks."

"Please stop, Henri," Madeleine said as she opened the wardrobe, "you're beginning to annoy me."

"And the cripples are only too happy to go along with it! Well, if you want my opinion, the one day that should be reserved for honoring heroes is November 11! In fact, I'd go further than that . . ."

"Stop it, Henri," Madeleine interrupted angrily, "July 14, November 1, Christmas Day, or the twelfth of never, you don't really give a damn at all."

He turned and eyed her scornfully. Still in his underpants. But it did not make her smile now. She glared back at him.

"I know you need to rehearse these little outbursts before you perform them for your audience at the Veterans' Association, or your club or wherever," she said, "but I am not your coach! So you can save your tantrums and outbursts for anyone who cares to listen and leave me in peace!"

She went back to tidying, her hands were not trembling, her voice had not quavered. She would often say such things in a brusque, offhand manner, then forget about them. Like her father; they were two of a kind. Henri did not take offense. He pulled on his pants. Fundamentally, she was right, November 1 or November 11, what did it matter . . . ? But July 14 was different. He openly professed a visceral loathing for the *Quatorze Juillet*, the Enlightenment, the Revolution—not because he had given the matter much thought, but because he felt it was only right and fitting, given his standing as an aristocrat.

And because he lived with the Péricourts, who were *nouveaux riches*. The old man had married a de Margis, whose ancestors were little more than glorified wool merchants who had bought themselves a title, which—thankfully—could only be passed on to the men in the family; a Péricourt would never be anything more than a Péricourt. It would have taken five centuries before they could rank alongside the Aulnay-Pradelles. And even then . . . in five centuries, their fortune would have long since evaporated, while the Aulnay-Pradelles—Henri planned to revive the dynasty—would still be entertaining guests in the *grand salon* of the family home in la Sallevière. Speaking of which, he had to hurry, it was already nine o'clock. He would arrive late in the evening, and tomorrow morning would be spent giving the foremen their orders, checking the building work, you had to keep a close eye on these people, query the estimates, negotiate the prices. The restorations to the roof had just been finished, twenty-three hundred square feet of slate, a small fortune, now they were moving on to the ruined west wing, which would have to be rebuilt from the ground up, and that would mean scrambling around for suitable stone in a country that no longer seemed to have any trains or barges—he would have to exhume a lot of heroes to pay for that!

When he came to kiss her before he left (he planted a kiss on her forehead, he did not like kissing her on the mouth), Madeleine adjusted his tie, for form's sake. She stepped back to look at him. They were right, all those trollops of his, her husband was a very handsome man; he would make beautiful children.

18

The invitation to visit the Péricourts haunted Albert. He had never been entirely happy about Édouard's change of identity, he dreamed of the police coming to arrest him and throw him in prison. And what most saddened him about that was that there would be no one to take care of Édouard. And at the same time, he felt a surge of relief. Just as Édouard sometimes dimly resented him, so Albert felt bitter that Édouard had usurped his life. Since his comrade had got himself thrown out of hospital, and once they had recovered from the news that Édouard would not be able to draw a pension, Albert had had the impression that their life had settled into an orderly routine, an impression that was brutally contradicted by the arrival of Mlle Péricourt and by this invitation that preoccupied him day and night. After all, it meant sitting down to dinner with Édouard's father, perpetuating the travesty of his son's death, looking into the eyes of his sister, who seemed quite kind when she was not pressing money into your hand as though you were a delivery boy.

Albert spent all his time weighing up the possible consequences of this invitation. If he confessed to the Péricourts that Édouard was still alive (and how could he not?), what then? Forcibly drag him back to a family he wanted nothing to do with? That would mean betraying him. And why the hell was Édouard so determined not to go back to them, for Christ's sake? Albert would have been more than happy. He had never had a sister, so Édouard's family would have suited him perfectly. It had been a mistake to listen to his friend back in the hospital a year ago, he decided. Édouard had been suffering from profound depression; Albert should not have given in to him . . . but what was done was done.

On the other hand, if he did admit the truth, what would happen to the unknown soldier who, right now, was probably lying in the Péricourt family vault, an interloper whose presence they would be unlikely to tolerate for long. What would become of him?

The police would be called, Albert would be blamed. Or, worse, he would be forced to dig up the poor unfortunate soldier the Péricourts wanted to be rid of, and what would he do with the remains? They would trace it all back to the false entries he had made in the army ledgers!

Besides, the idea of going to visit the Péricourts, of meeting Édouard's father, his sister, maybe other members of the family, without telling his friend was disloyal. How would he react if he found out?

But surely telling him was also a kind of betrayal? Édouard would be here, alone, fretting, while his friend was spending the evening with the very people he had repudiated. Because in deciding never to see them again, he was effectively rejecting them, wasn't he?

He would write a letter, plead some unexpected emergency. But the Péricourts would only suggest another date. He would have to invent some other pretext. But they might send someone to look for him and find Édouard . . .

There seemed no way out. Everything was so confused, Albert was plagued by nightmares. In the early hours, Édouard, who scarcely slept, propped himself up on one elbow, gripped his friend's shoulder, and shook him awake, handed him the conversation pad with a questioning look. Albert shrugged that it was nothing, but still the nightmares continued; they seemed never ending, and he, unlike Édouard, needed sleep.

After much brooding and countless conflicting thoughts, he finally came to a decision. He would go to the Péricourts' house (otherwise they would come looking for him here), but he would hide the truth, it was the least dangerous solution. He would give them what they wanted, he would tell them how their son had died, that was what he would do. Then never see them again.

The problem was he did not really remember what he had written in his letter. He racked his brain. What had he said? A hero's death, a bullet straight to the heart, like something out of a novel, but in what circumstances? Then there was the fact that Mlle Péricourt had met him through that bastard Pradelle. What had he told her? He would have portrayed himself in a favorable light. What if Albert's version of events contradicted what Pradelle had told her? Who would she believe? They might think him an imposter.

The more he agonized, the more muddled his thoughts and memories became, and the nightmares returned, rearing out in the darkness like phantoms.

Then there was the awkward problem of what he should wear. He could not decently turn up at the Péricourts as he was; even in his best suit, he looked like a tramp.

Just in case he did finally decide to go to dinner at boulevard des Courcelles, he asked around to find a respectable suit. The only one he could find belonged to someone he worked with, a sandwich man rather shorter than he was who patrolled the Champs-Élysées. Albert had to tug the waist of the pants as low as possible so as not to look like a clown. He almost borrowed one of Édouard's shirts, since he had two, but changed his mind. What if the family recognized it? He borrowed one from the same colleague, which was too small, so the buttons gaped. There remained the delicate matter of shoes. He could not find any to fit him. He would have to make do with his own, a pair of battered clodhoppers he spent hours buffing in a vain attempt to make them look half-decent. Having mulled over his options, he concluded he would have to buy a new pair, which was now possible because the recent reduction in his morphine budget had given him some breathing space. A fine pair of shoes. Thirty-two francs from

Bata. Emerging from the shop with the package tucked under his arm, he realized that, ever since being demobilized, he had longed to buy himself a new pair of shoes, feeling that this, more than anything, determined a man's elegance. An old suit or an overcoat might be acceptable, but a man could be judged on the quality of his shoes. These were pale-brown leather; wearing them was the only pleasurable thing about this whole sorry affair.

Édouard and Louise looked up as Albert stepped out from behind the folding screen. They had just finished making a new mask: ivory colored with a pretty pink mouth set in a slightly condescending sneer, with two faded autumn leaves glued high up on the cheeks that looked like tears. And yet there was nothing sad about the overall effect; it was the contemplative expression of someone detached from the world.

But the mask was nothing compared to the spectacle of Albert as he emerged from behind the screen. A butcher's boy on his way to a wedding.

Édouard, assuming that his friend had an assignation, was touched.

Love was a subject they joked about, obviously, being young men . . . But it was a sore subject since both were young men without lovers. In the end, Albert had found that fucking Mme Monestier on the sly occasionally did him more harm than good, because it made him realize how much he missed love. He stopped screwing her, she persisted for a little while, then she stopped insisting. He saw pretty young girls here and there, in the shops, on the omnibus, many of them with no beau since so many men had been killed, girls who were waiting, watching, hoping, but Albert was no conquering hero, always glancing about him, skittish as a cat, with his battered shoes and a greatcoat that dribbled dye, he was not what anyone might call a catch.

And even if he did find himself a young lady who was not too disgusted by his appearance, what sort of future could he offer her? What was he supposed to say? "Come live with me, I share an apartment with a crippled ex-soldier who never leaves the house, shoots himself full of morphine, and wears carnival masks, but never fear, we have three francs a day to live on and a folding screen to protect your modesty"?

Besides, Albert was cripplingly shy; if things did not come to him . . .

And so he went back to Mme Monestier, but she had her self-respect, that woman, just because she was married to a cuckold didn't mean she had no pride. Her pride was in fact rather adaptable, since the actual reason she no longer needed Albert was because she was getting screwed by the new office clerk, a man who—to Albert's dim recollection—looked strangely like the young man who had been with Cécile in the elevator at La Samaritaine on the day Albert left his job and several days wages . . . If he had to do it over . . .

One night, he had talked to Édouard about this. He thought it would make him happy to confess that he, too, had decided he would have to give up on any idea of a normal relationship with a woman, but the situation was hardly comparable: Albert could begin again, Édouard could not. Albert might find himself a young woman—maybe a young widow, there were a lot of them about—as long as she was not too particular; he might have to search, to keep his eyes open, but what woman would have wanted Édouard, had he been attracted to women? The conversations had been painful for both of them.

But now, to suddenly see Albert in his Sunday best!

Louise gave a wolf whistle, walked over to him and waited for Albert to bend down so she could straighten his tie. They teased him, Édouard slapped his thighs and gave an enthusiastic thumbs-up, making a shrill tooting from the back of his throat. Not to be outdone, Louise tittered behind her hand and said, "Oh, Albert, you look so handsome . . . ," a woman's words, but how old was she, this child? He was rather wounded by their extravagant flattery; even good-natured mockery can be hurtful, especially in the circumstances.

Better to leave now, he thought, besides, he needed to think some more, and having done so, with little consideration for the relative merits of the arguments, he would make a spur-of-the-moment decision to go or not to go to dinner with the Péricourts.

He caught the métro and walked the last stretch of the way. The farther he traveled, the more ill at ease he felt. Emerging from his overcrowded *arrondissement* filled with Poles and Russians, he encountered tall, majestic buildings lining a boulevard that was three streets wide. As he approached the parc Monceau, he spotted the house—it would have been impossible to miss M. Péricourt's soaring mansion, outside which stood a gleaming automobile that a chauffeur in immaculate livery was rubbing down as though it were a thoroughbred racehorse. Albert was so awestruck he felt his heart stutter. Pretending to be in a hurry, he walked quickly past the house, tracing a wide circle through the adjoining streets, and came back through the park, where he found a bench from which he could just see the facade, and sat down. He felt flabbergasted. In fact, he found it difficult to believe that Édouard had been born here, had grown up in this house. In another world. And today, Albert had come bearing the most terrible lie imaginable. He was a reprobate.

Along the boulevard, bustling ladies stepped down from hackney carriages followed by maids weighed down with parcels. Delivery wagons pulled up outside tradesman's entrances, the drivers talking with supercilious footmen who, feeling it their duty to represent their masters, appraised the crates of vegetables, the baskets of bread with a critical eye while, some distance away, on the pavement next to the park railings, two elegant young women as slender as matchsticks walked arm in arm along the street, laughing. On the corner of the boulevard, two men were bidding each other farewell, a newspaper tucked under their arms, clutching their top hats—my dear fellow! see you soon!—looking for all the world like court judges. One of them stepped aside for a small boy in a sailor suit who hurtled past, bowling a hoop, a nanny ran after him, apologizing to the gentlemen; a florist's wagon appeared, delivering bouquets enough for a wedding, but there was no wedding, this was simply the weekly delivery, there are so many rooms, and one has to think about such things when entertaining guests, it costs a fortune I can tell you, but they laugh as they say this, it's amusing to buy so many flowers, we simply *love* to entertain. Albert stared at all these people in much the same way as once, through the glass walls of an aquarium, he had peered at tropical fish that scarcely looked like fish at all.

And he had almost two hours to kill.

He did not know whether to stay here on his bench or take the métro, but where would he go? Time was, he liked to stroll along the Grands Boulevards. But traipsing up and down them with a sandwich board had changed all that. He wandered around the park, and having arrived early, he completely lost track of time.

Seven fifteen p.m. When he realized he was late, his panic level soared; he broke out in a sweat, striding away from the house only to turn back again, staring at the pavement, twenty past and still he had not made up his mind. At about 7:30 p.m. he passed the house again, crossed to the opposite side of the street, decided to go home, but they would come fetch him, they would send a chauffeur who would not be as tactful as his mistress, the whys and wherefores rattled and ricocheted inside his head, and though he never understood how it came about, he climbed the six steps to the front door, rang the bell, furtively buffed his shoes, rubbing each against the back of the other calf, the door opened. Heart hammering wildly in his chest, he finds himself in a lobby that soars like a cathedral, there are mirrors everywhere, everything is beautiful, even the housemaid, a young woman with short dark hair, she is radiant, my God, those lips, those eyes; in the houses of the rich, Albert thinks, even the poor are beautiful.

On either side of the immense hallway tiled as a black-and-white checkerboard, five-globe lampposts flanked a monumental staircase of carved yellow sandstone, whose white marble banisters traced symmetrical spirals as they ascended to the upper landing. A warm yellow glow that seemed to come from heaven itself cascaded from an imposing art deco chandelier. The pretty housemaid looked Albert up and down and asked his name. Albert Maillard. He glanced around and felt a wave of relief. Despite making every possible effort, unless he had arrived in a tailor-made suit, a pair of overpriced shoes, a top-notch top hat, a dinner jacket or a tailcoat, whatever he wore was bound to make him look like a peasant, as indeed he did. The yawning gap between their world and his, the anxiety he had felt for days, the frustration of waiting . . . Albert suddenly started to giggle, naturally, spontaneously, his hand covering his mouth, and it was so obvious that he was laughing to himself, at himself, that the pretty housemaid began to laugh, too—her teeth, my

God, and that laugh, even her pink, pointed tongue was a vision. Had he seen her eyes as he arrived, or was he only now seeing them for the first time? Dark, shimmering. Neither of them knew what they were laughing at. Blushing furiously, and still laughing, she turned away; she had her duties to attend to. She opened the door on the left leading to a formal waiting room with a grand piano, tall Chinese vases, cherrywood bookcases filled with old books and leather armchairs; she gestured for him to sit wherever he liked, and could only manage to stammer "Sorry," since she still could not contain her giggles. Albert held up his hands, giggle away, it's all right.

Now he is alone in the room, the door has closed, the announcement is being made that M. Maillard has arrived, his laughing fit has subsided, overawed by this silence, this majesty, this opulence. He strokes the leaves of the potted plants, thinks about the little housemaid, if only he dared . . . He tries to read the titles of books, traces the intricate marquetry, his finger hovers hesitantly over the keyboard of the grand piano. He could wait for her until the end of her shift, who knows? But maybe she already has a young man? He tries one of the armchairs, sinks down, gets up again, tries the fine brushed-leather sofa, distractedly rearranges the English magazines on the low table, what should he do about the pretty little housemaid? Whisper something in her ear as he leaves? Or, better still, come back, pretend he has forgotten something, ring the doorbell, and press a bill into her hand with . . . what? His address? And besides, what could he have forgotten? He does not even have an umbrella. Still standing, he leafs through issues of *Harper's Bazaar*, the *Gazette des Beaux Arts* and *L'Officiel de la mode*. He sits on the sofa. Maybe waiting around until the end of her shift would be best, make her laugh the way he did earlier. On the edge of the coffee table, an album of photographs bound in silky, fine-grained calfskin. If he invited her for dinner, how much would it cost? And where would he take her? Another dilemma. He picks up the album, opens it, Duval's café is fine for him, but he could not possibly take a young woman there, not one who works in a great house, even in the kitchens they probably use silver cutlery, suddenly he feels a knot in his belly, his hands are sweaty, he swallows hard to stop himself from retching, he tastes bile in the back of his throat. In front of him is a wedding photograph: Madeleine Péricourt is standing next to Capitaine d'Aulnay-Pradelle.

It is him, there is no doubt, Albert would know him anywhere.

Still, he needs to check. He thumbs quickly through the book. Pradelle is on almost every page, the photographs as large as the pages of a magazine, there are crowds of people, mountains of flowers, Pradelle is smiling modestly, like a lottery winner who does not want to make a fuss but is happy to be gawked at; on his arm, a radiant Madeleine Péricourt is wearing the kind of dress no one wears in real life, bought to be worn just once, and there are morning suits, tailcoats, low-backed dresses the like of which he has never seen in life, brooches, necklaces, pale-yellow gloves, the happy couple are greeting their guests—it is him, it is Pradelle—sideboards groaning with gifts and next to the blushing bride, it must be her father, M. Péricourt, even smiling the man looks fearsome, and everywhere there are patent leather shoes, starched shirt-fronts, in the background, silk top hats hang from copper hooks, in the foreground, pyramids of champagne flutes, the liveried waiters wearing white gloves, the waltzes, the orchestra, the happy couple flanked by the guard of honor . . . Albert is turning the pages feverishly.

An article from *Le Gaulois*:

A Glorious Wedding

We held great expectations of this quintessentially Parisian event, and we were not disappointed by a wedding day on which grace and beauty were wedded to courage. To explain, for those few readers who do not already know, this was the wedding of Mlle Madeleine Péricourt, daughter of the celebrated industrialist Marcel Péricourt, to Henri d'Aulnay-Pradelle, patriot and hero.

The ceremony itself, at Notre-Dame d'Auteuil, was a simple, intimate affair, and scarcely two dozen friends and family members will have heard the stirring homily by Monsignor Coidet. The reception was held in the Bois de Boulogne, in the 18th-century Pavillon Armenonville, whose graceful Belle Époque architecture is matched only by the modernity of its fittings. The terraces, the gardens, and the salons of this royal hunting lodge teemed with the most elegant and eminent people in society. Some six hundred guests, we are told, greeted the young bride, whose dress (in tulle and duchesse satin) was personally designed as a gift by the celebrated couturière Jeanne Lanvin, a close friend of the family. The lucky man, the dapper Henri d'Aulnay-Pradelle, scion of one of France's oldest aristocratic families, is none other than the "*Capitaine Pradelle.*" whose numerous heroic feats include the capture of Hill 113 from the Boches on the eve of the armistice, and whose many acts of courage have seen him decorated four times.

The *président de la République*, M. Raymond Poincaré, a personal friend of M. Péricourt, made a brief, discreet appearance before leaving the distinguished guests—senior political figures, including M. Millerand[6] and M. Daudet,[7] and a number of great artists, including Jean Dagnan-Bouveret and Georges Rochegrosse,[8]—to enjoy a celebration that will, we have no doubt, long be remembered.

Albert closed the book.

The loathing he felt for Pradelle had become a form of self-loathing; he hated himself that he was still afraid of this man. The very name *Pradelle* made him quiver. How long would this carry on? It had been more than a year since he had heard the *capitaine* mentioned, but he still thought about him. He could not forget him. Albert had only to look around to see the damage that man had wrought in his life. And not only his own life. Édouard's face, his every gesture, everything about him bore the mark of that single moment when a man runs through an apocalyptic wasteland, eyes blazing, a man who sets little store by the deaths—or the lives—of others, summoning all his strength he crashes into a helpless Albert, and what follows, we already know: a miraculous rescue and the gaping void that cleaves Édouard's face. As though war were not misfortune enough.

Albert gazes blankly ahead. *So this is how the story ended. With this wedding.*

Though not a philosophical man, he thinks about the nature of his existence. And about Édouard, whose sister has unwittingly married the man who murdered them both.

He sees flickering images of the cemetery, the darkness. And images of the day before, when the young woman with an ermine muff appeared with the great Capitaine Pradelle by her side, her knight in shining armor. He remembers the journey to the cemetery, Albert sitting next to the sweaty driver who shifts his cigarette from one side of his mouth to the other with a flick of his tongue while Mlle Péricourt and Capitaine Pradelle follow in the limousine. He should have suspected something. "Albert never could see the nose in front of his face, if it was raining soup he'd be out there with a fork. Makes you wonder if that boy will ever grow up, he's come through a war and he's learned nothing, it's enough to drive you to distraction."

A moment ago, when he saw the first picture of the wedding, his heart was beating fit to burst, but now he can feel it slowing, dissolving, ready to stop.

Bile at the back of his throat . . . Again he feels an urge to retch that he manages to stifle only by getting up and rushing out of the room.

The penny has just dropped. Capitaine Pradelle is here.

With Mlle Péricourt.

He has been lured into a trap. A family dinner.

Albert will have to sit across the table, suffer the same withering stare he endured in Général Morieux's office when he almost ended up before a firing squad. There is nothing to be done. Will this war never be over?

He needs to leave now, to lay down his arms and surrender, otherwise he will die again, be killed again. He has to get away.

Albert leaps to his feet, rushes across the room, and just as he reaches the door, it opens.

Madeleine Péricourt is smiling at him.

"So you're here," she says. She sounds almost impressed, though why he cannot tell. That he found his way, that he found the courage?

Instinctively, she looks him over from head to foot. Albert too looks down, and now he sees it plainly: the shiny new shoes combined with the threadbare suit a size too small, it looks tawdry. He had been so proud of them, had wanted them so desperately . . . The shoes scream poverty.

All his absurdity is here, he despises them, he despises himself.

"Come," Madeleine says, "come with me."

She takes his arm, as though he were her friend.

"My father will be down in a moment, he's very eager to meet you . . ."

19

"Good evening, sir."

M. Péricourt was less tall than Albert had been expecting. We often expect the powerful to be tall and are surprised to find they are ordinary. Though they are anything but ordinary, as Albert could immediately see. M. Péricourt had a piercing gaze, his handshake lingered a fraction of a second too long, even his smile . . . There was nothing ordinary about him, he seemed to be made of steel, with exceptional self-assurance, it was from among such men that world leaders were chosen, it was because of such men that wars began. Albert felt afraid, he could not imagine being able to lie to such a man. And he kept glancing to the door, expecting Capitaine Pradelle to appear at any moment.

Very graciously, M. Péricourt waved toward an armchair, and they sat. In the blink of an eye, staff appeared wheeling a cart of drinks to them and then food. The pretty housemaid was among the servants, Albert tried not to look at her while M. Péricourt eyed him curiously.

Albert did not know why Édouard would not want to come back here, he must surely have good reason, and being in the presence of

M. Péricourt Albert could dimly sense why someone might feel the need to get away from such a person. He was a hard, unyielding man, forged from some new alloy, like a grenade, a shell, a bomb; who might kill you without realizing with a single shard of shrapnel. Albert's legs spoke for him, they itched to get up and leave.

"What will you drink, Monsieur Maillard?" Madeleine said, smiling.

He was rooted to the spot. What would he drink? He had no idea. On special occasions, and when he had the means, he drank calvados, a working-class drink he could not ask for here. He had not the first idea what he might have instead.

"What would you say to a glass of champagne," Madeleine said, to be helpful.

"Well . . ." Albert hesitated, he detested champagne

A nod, a long silence, then the butler appeared with an ice bucket, the cork was ceremoniously popped and caught. M. Péricourt gave an impatient wave, come on, come on, don't stand there all night.

"So did you know my son well . . . ?" he said, leaning toward Albert.

In that moment, Albert understood that this was how the evening would play out. M. Péricourt questioning him about his son's death under the watchful eye of his daughter. Pradelle would play no part in the proceedings. A family affair. He felt relieved. He looked at the table, at the bubbles in his glass of champagne. How to begin? What to say? He had been turning it over in his mind, but he could not find the words to begin.

M. Péricourt looked puzzled and felt it necessary to add:

"My son . . . Édouard . . ."

He was beginning to wonder whether this man had really known his son. Had he even written the letter, who knew how things were done in such circumstances, perhaps soldiers were randomly assigned the task of writing letters to the families of fallen comrades, each reciting the same phrases, or something very similar. But Albert's answer was immediate, sincere.

"Oh, yes, *monsieur*, I think I can say that I knew your son very well."

Very quickly, what M. Péricourt had wanted to know about the death of his son was of no importance. What this ex-soldier had to say was more important, because he talked about the living Édouard. Édouard in the muddy trenches, in the mess hall, waiting for cigarette rations, playing cards, Édouard sitting in the shadows, bent over this notepad, drawing . . . Albert was describing an imaginary Édouard rather than the man he had rubbed shoulders with in the trenches but scarcely knew.

For M. Péricourt it proved to be less painful than he had expected, indeed the stories, the images were almost pleasant. He found himself smiling; it had been a long time since Madeleine had seen her father genuinely smile.

"You'll forgive me for saying," Albert said, "but Édouard was always one for a joke . . ."

Emboldened, he told the story. And then there was the time that, and the day that he, and another thing I remember . . . It was not difficult, whatever stories he could remember about other comrades in the trenches, he attributed to Édouard as long as they flattered his memory.

M. Péricourt, for his part, was rediscovering his son, some of what he heard seemed astonishing (He really said that? His very words, *monsieur*!), yet none of it surprised him, since he was now convinced that he had never really known his son, he would have believed anything. Inane stories, mess hall anecdotes, infantile pranks, lewd jokes, but Albert, having finally found the right track, forged ahead determinedly, he even began to enjoy himself. He told stories about Édouard that had them in fits of laughter. M. Péricourt wiped tears from his eyes. Urged on by the champagne, Albert went on talking, not realizing that his tale was gradually shifting from barrack-room banter to frozen feet, from card games to rats the size of rabbits and the stench of the corpses on the battlefield that stretcher bearers could not recover. It was the first time Albert had talked about his war.

"And then there was the time, Édouard said out of the blue . . ."

Albert might have gone too far, been too earnest, too truthful, might have said more than he should and ruined the portrait of the composite comrade he called Édouard, but fortunately, he had M. Péricourt sitting directly opposite, and even when he smiled, even when he laughed, there was something of the wild cat about the man's gray eyes that was enough to curb any excesses.

"So how did he die?"

The question cut the air like the slice of the blade on the scaffold. Albert's lips hesitated to form the words. Madeleine was turned toward him, discreet, gracious.

"He was shot, *monsieur*, during the assault on Hill 113."

He stopped abruptly, feeling that the words "Hill 113" were sufficient. They had a particular resonance for everyone present. Madeleine remembered the explanation Capitaine Pradelle told her when she first met him at the Demobilization Center, clutching the letter informing her family of her brother's death. M. Péricourt could not help but think that it was the assault on Hill 113 that had cost his son his life and earned his future son-in-law the *Croix de Guerre*. For Albert, it evoked a slow procession of images, the shell crater, Pradelle bearing down on him . . .

"A bullet, *monsieur*," he said, with all the conviction he could muster, "we were charging the enemy position at Hill 113, your son, he was right at the front, he was a brave boy, you know . . . And . . ."

M. Péricourt leaned imperceptibly closer. Albert trailed off. Madeleine, too, leaned closer, questioning, considerate, as though trying to help him find some obscure word. In fact, until that moment, Albert had not really been looking, and now suddenly, with unerring exactness, he had seen Édouard's face in that of his father.

He fought it for a moment, then dissolved into tears.

He took his face in his hands and sobbed, stammering apologies, the pain was overwhelming, even when Cécile had left him he had not felt such anguish. The end of the war and the great weight of his loneliness came together in this pain.

Madeleine offered him a handkerchief, Albert went on sobbing, apologizing, all three fell silent, each immured in private grief.

After a moment, Albert noisily blew his nose . . .

"I'm so sorry . . ."

The evening, which had scarcely begun, had just ended with his moment of truth. What more could be expected of a simple meeting, a dinner? No matter what happened afterward, Albert, on behalf of all of them, had just said the only thing that mattered. M. Péricourt found it a little upsetting, because the question on the tip of his tongue had not been asked, and he knew he would not ask it now: did Édouard ever talk about his family? It did not matter; he knew the answer.

Drained, but dignified, he got to his feet.

"Come, my boy," he said holding out a hand to help Albert up, "Let's get you something to eat, it will do you good."

M. Péricourt watched Albert as he dug in. His moonlike face, his innocent eyes . . . How had they won the war with such men? Of all these stories he had told about Édouard, which were really true? He would have to decide for himself. The stories M. Maillard had told were less about the life of Édouard himself than about the world in which he had lived throughout the war. A world of young men risking their lives by day and joking at night, their feet half-frozen.

Albert ate slowly, greedily. He had earned his supper. He could not put a name to what he was eating; he would have liked to have had the menu to be able to follow the sinuous choreography of dishes: this was probably called a *mousse de crustacés*, this was a *gelée*, this must be a *chaud-froid,* and that had to be a *soufflé*; he was anxious not to make a show of himself, not to seem as destitute as he actually was. If he were Édouard—even with a gaping hole in his face—he would have rushed back here to gorge on the food, the décor, the opulence, without a moment's hesitation. Not to mention the pretty housemaid with the dark eyes. What made him uncomfortable, and made it impossible for him to appreciate what he was eating, was the fact that the door used by the waiters was directly behind him, and every time he heard it open, he stiffened and whirled around, which made him appear like a starving man greedily waiting for more food.

M. Péricourt would never know how much of what he had heard was true, or how much related to his son. It no longer really mattered. It is in the letting go that we begin to mourn, he thought. During the meal, he tried to remember how he had grieved for his wife, but that was long ago.

There came a moment when Albert, having stopped talking, now stopped eating; in the silences, the dining room was filled with a faint clatter of cutlery on china, like hail against a window pane. This was the awkward moment when it felt as though they were not making the most of the occasion. M. Péricourt was lost in his thoughts, so Madeleine returned to the fray.

"So, tell me, M. Maillard—I hope I'm not being indiscreet . . . what do you do for a living?"

Albert swallowed a mouthful of capon, picked up his glass of claret and murmured appreciatively, playing for time.

"Advertising," he said finally, "I'm in advertising."

"How fascinating," said Madeleine, "And . . . what exactly do you do?"

Albert set down his glass and cleared his throat.

"Well, strictly speaking, I don't work in advertising, I work as an accountant for an advertising company."

He could see from their faces that this was less impressive; it was not as modern, as exciting, and it deprived them of a potentially interesting topic of conversation.

"But I keep a keen eye on developments," Albert said, sensing the disappointment in his audience, "it is a . . . a sector that I find very . . . very . . . It's interesting."

This was all he could think to say. He prudently declined dessert, coffee, and liqueurs. His head tilted slightly, M. Péricourt was studying him while Madeleine, with a naturalness that attested to her experience of such situations, kept up a steady stream of small talk so there were no awkward pauses.

Albert stood in the hallway, waiting for his coat, expecting to see the pretty housemaid at any moment.

"Thank you so much, M. Maillard," Madeleine said, "for coming all this way."

It was not the pretty housemaid but an ugly one who appeared. She, too, was young, but ugly and obviously from the provinces. The pretty one must have finished her shift.

M. Péricourt suddenly remembered the shoes that had earlier caught his eye. He looked down as his guest slipped on his dyed greatcoat. Madeleine did not look, she had noticed the shoes when he first arrived: new, gaudy, obviously cheap. M. Péricourt was pensive.

"Tell me, M. Maillard, you say you're an accountant . . ."

"Yes."

This was something he should have noticed earlier: when the boy told the truth you could see it in his face . . . Too late now but it did not matter.

"Well," he said, "it so happens that we need an accountant. Credit is expanding as I'm sure you know, the country desperately needs to invest. There are a lot of exciting opportunities right now."

It was a bitter irony, Albert thought, that the manager of the *Banque de l'Union* had not said as much some months earlier when he refused to rehire him.

"Obviously I have no idea how much you earn," M. Péricourt went on, "but that is hardly important. Suffice it to say that if you are prepared to accept a position with us, it will be on the best possible terms, I will see to it personally."

Albert gritted his teeth. Overwhelmed by this information, he choked at the proposition. M. Péricourt looked at him benignly. Next to him, Madeleine smiled indulgently like a mother watching her child playing in the sandbox.

"The thing is . . . ," Albert stammered.

"We need young men who are talented and dynamic."

These words sent Albert into a panic. M. Péricourt was addressing him as though he had studied at *Les Hautes Études Commerciales de Paris.* M. Péricourt had clearly got the wrong man, and Albert was beginning to feel that simply getting out of the house alive was a miracle in itself. The idea of having any further dealing with the Péricourt family, even if it meant a job, with the shadow of Capitaine Pradelle prowling the hallways . . .

"I'm grateful, monsieur," Albert said, "but I'm very happy in my position."

M. Péricourt held up his hand, I understand, no problem. After the door had been closed, he stood for a moment in thought.

"Good night, my darling," he said finally.

"Good night, Papa."

He placed a kiss on his daughter's forehead. This was how all men treated her.

20

Édouard could tell immediately that Albert was upset. He had arrived back from his "assignation" looking miserable; the evening had obviously not gone as his friend had hoped in spite of his fine shoes. Or perhaps because of them, thought Édouard, who knew a thing or two about real elegance and had not thought much of Albert's chances when he saw his friend's new brogues.

As he came in, Albert had looked away, as though suddenly self-conscious, which was unusual. Generally when he came home he gave Édouard an insistent stare, designed to say he was not afraid to look at his friend's face even when, as tonight, he was not wearing a mask. Instead, Albert carefully put his shoes back in their box, as though hiding away a treasure, but he felt no joy, the treasure had been disappointing, he was angry at himself for giving in to temptation, it was such a lot of money and they had bills to pay, and all so that he could curry favor with the Péricourts. Even the little housemaid had laughed at him. He froze there, crouched on the floor, Édouard could see only his bowed back.

It was this that prompted him to speak, though he had vowed to keep mum until his plan was settled, and that was still some way off.

Moreover, he was not completely happy with what he had produced, and Albert was in no mood to deal with serious matters . . . all reasons for sticking to his original decision to wait until the last possible moment before saying anything.

He decided to come clean now only because his friend was so obviously upset. In fact, even that simply masked the real reason: he had been in a hurry since midafternoon when he had finished the drawing of a child in profile, he had been bursting to say something.

So much for good intentions.

"At least I had a good dinner," Albert said, without getting up.

He blew his nose, he did not want to turn around, to make an exhibition of himself.

Édouard was experiencing a moment of triumph. Not over Albert, assuredly, but for the first time since his life had crumbled, he felt strong, he could imagine a future where he was self-reliant.

As he got to his feet, Albert hid his face, kept his head bowed—I'm just going down for the coal—Édouard felt an urge to hug him, he would have kissed him if he still had lips.

Albert always wore his thick tartan slippers when he went downstairs. I'll be back, he said, as though this precision were necessary; such is the way of old married couples, they say things out of habit, not realizing their significance if anyone were paying attention.

As soon as he hears Albert on the stairs, Édouard hops on his chair, opens the trapdoor, takes down the bag, puts the chair back where it was, lies down on the couch, reaches down for his new mask, slips it on, and setting his sketchpad on his lap, he waits.

He is ready much too quickly, and time seems to crawl by while he waits for the sound of Albert's footsteps, which are particularly loud since he is carrying the large coal scuttle, which is heavy. At last, Albert pushes open the door. When, at last, he looks up, he is so shocked he lets fall the coal scuttle which lands with a clang. Albert stands, reeling, his hands clutching at the empty air for support, his mouth gapes as he pants for breath, finally his legs give out and he sinks to his knees, hysterical.

Édouard's mask—almost life size —is the dead horse's head.

He sculpted it from *papier-mâché*. Every detail is perfect, the mottled chestnut coloring, the horse's charred skin made from soft, dark suede, the gaunt jowls, the long angular muzzle, the nostrils flared like two dark pools . . . The mouth hangs open, the silken lips are plump, the resemblance is staggering.

When Édouard closes his eyes, it is as though the horse is closing its eyes, he is the horse. Albert had never made the connection between Édouard and the horse.

He is moved to tears, it is like rediscovering a childhood friend, a brother.

"Oh my God!"

He is laughing and crying, oh my God, oh my God, he says over and over, still on his knees, staring at the horse, making no attempt to get up, oh my God . . . It is foolish, he knows himself that it is foolish, he wants to kiss the horse's soft lips. Instead, he simply reaches out and traces them with his index finger. Édouard recognizes the gesture, it is the one Louise once made; he is overwhelmed. Everything they have to say is in this gesture. The two men sit in silence, each in his own world, Albert stroking the horse's head, Édouard accepting the caress.

"I'll never know what his name was . . . ," Albert said.

Even great joys are tinged with regret; there is a latent emptiness in everything we feel.

Then, as though it has just materialized on Édouard's lap, Albert notices the sketchpad.

"You . . . you've started drawing again?"

A cry from the heart.

"You don't know how happy that makes me . . ."

He laughs to himself, as though pleased to see his efforts rewarded. He nods to the mask.

"And this! Oh my God! What a night it's been."

"Can I . . . can I have a look?" He gestures eagerly toward the sketchpad.

He sits next to Édouard, who slowly, ceremoniously opens the book.

From the first page, Albert is disappointed. He cannot hide the fact. Oh yes, very good, very good, he mumbles to fill the silence because he does not know what to say without sounding insincere. What is there to say about this crude, ugly drawing of a soldier? Albert closes the pad.

"So tell me, then . . . ," he says, sounding impressed, "where did you get it?"

The diversion lasts as long as it lasts. From Louise, obviously. To her, finding a sketchpad would be child's play.

Then they go back to looking at the new drawings. What can he say? This time, Albert simply nods . . .

He pauses on the second page, two delicate pencil drawings of a statue on a plinth: the front view on the left, the side view on the right. The statue is of a soldier in full pack and helmet, his rifle slung over his shoulder, he is walking away, leaving, head held high, eyes fixed on some distant point, his hand trails behind him, the tips of his outstretched fingers touching those of a woman. She stands behind him wearing a pinafore, she is cradling a child and crying, they both seem so young. Above the drawing is a title: "The Leavetaking."

"It's amazingly well drawn."

This is all he can think to say.

Édouard is not offended, he leans back, takes off the mask, and sets it down so that the horse now seems to be rising out of the floor, turning its big soft lips toward Albert.

Édouard attracts Albert's attention, quietly turning to the next page, a drawing entitled "Charge!" This time, there are three soldiers, responding to the order in the title. They are moving forward as a group: one is brandishing his rifle; next to him, the second soldier has his arm outstretched about to toss a grenade; the third, some paces behind, has just been hit by a bullet or a piece of shrapnel, his body arched, his knees sagging, he is about to crumple . . .

Albert turns the pages: "The Dead Arise," then "*Poilu* Dying in Defense of the Flag" and "Brother in Arms" . . .

"Statues . . . ?"

It is a hesitant question. Because whatever Albert has been expecting, it was not this.

Édouard nods, staring at the drawings, yes, they're all statues. He looks pleased with himself. Fine, fine, fine, Albert is thinking, he is keeping everything else bottled up inside.

He thinks back to the sketchpad he found among Édouard's belongings full of spur-of-the-moment scenes sketched in blue pencil; he had sent it to the Péricourts with the letter informing them of Édouard's death. The subject was the same as in these new drawings, soldiers at war, but in the earlier pictures there was such truth, such honesty . . .

Albert knows nothing about art; something either moves him or it does not. The pictures he is looking at are well drawn, skillful, painstaking, but . . . he fumbles for the word . . . they're stilted. Finally, it comes to him: the pictures are not real. That's it! He was there, he was one of these soldiers, he knows that these are images made by those who did not go to war. They are noble, designed to move, but they are a little too effusive. Albert is a modest man, whereas here every line seems histrionic, as though sketched from high-flying adjectives. He carries on turning the pages: "France Mourns Her Heroes"—a weeping girl cradling the body of a dead soldier, next comes "An Orphan Contemplating Sacrifice"—a young boy sits, cupping his face in his hands, next to him—this must be what he is imagining—a soldier lies dying, he is reaching out his hand toward the child . . . Even to someone who knows nothing, it is obvious that this is hideous, it has to be seen to be believed. Here is a sketch titled "Le Coq Gaulois Trampling a Boche Helmet," my God, the cockerel is posed triumphantly, its beak thrust toward the heavens, and all those feathers . . .

Albert does not like what he sees. So much so that he finds himself speechless. He ventures a quick glance at Édouard, who is gazing tenderly at his work, like a father who is proud of his child and cannot see the child is ugly. Albert's bitterest regret, though he does not realize it in this moment, is the realization that Édouard lost everything to this war, even his talent.

"So . . . ," he begins.

Because he has to say something eventually.

"So, why statues?"

Édouard fumbles at the back of the book, pulls out a sheaf of newspaper clippings, and holds up one with a passage circled in thick pencil: ". . . here, as everywhere in France, towns, villages, schools, even railway stations, all want their own war memorial . . ."

The cutting is from *L'Est Républicain*. There are more, Albert has already seen the file, but he did not understand the logic behind it, the articles listing all those who died in a single village, a single corporation, the reports about commemorations, military reviews, public subscriptions, it all came back to the idea of war memorials.

"I see," he says, though he does not really see what this is about.

Édouard points to a scribbled calculation at the bottom of a page. "30,000 memorials × 10,000 francs = 300 million francs."

Now Albert begins to understand, because this is a lot of money. In fact, it is a fortune.

He cannot begin to conceive what one might buy with such a sum. His imagination batters itself against the number like a bee against a pane of glass.

Édouard takes the sketchpad and shows him the last page.

Patriotic Memories

Memorials, statues, stelae

in commemoration of our heroes

& in celebration of a victorious France

Catalog

"You want to sell war memorials?"

Yes. That's right. Édouard is thrilled with his scheme, he slaps his thighs, making that strange keening sound in his throat, Albert does not know where it comes from, only that he finds it grating.

Albert finds it difficult to understand why anyone would want to make war memorials, but the figure of 300,000,000 francs has managed to flutter into his imagination: it means "mansion," like the townhouse of M. Péricourt, it means "limousine," even "palace," it means . . . he blushes—"women" was what he thought—and for a fleeting second he pictures the little housemaid with the devastating smile. It is natural: when you have money, you want a woman to share it with.

He reads the lines that follow, an advertisement written in block capitals so neat it looks as though it has been printed:

". . . AND IN YOUR GRIEF YOU FEEL THE NEED TO KEEP ALIVE THE MEMORY OF THE CHILDREN FROM YOUR TOWN, YOUR VILLAGE, WHO WITH THEIR VERY BODIES MADE A LIVING RAMPART AGAINST THE INVADER."

"This is all very well," Albert says. "Actually, I think it's a good idea . . ."

Now he understands why he was so disappointed by the drawings; they are not meant to represent an artistic sensibility but to express a collective grief, to appeal to the wider public, who need sensation, who need heroism.

Later in the paragraph: ". . . TO ERECT A MONUMENT WORTHY OF YOUR COMMUNITY AND OF THOSE HEROES WHO YOU HAVE CHOSEN TO HOLD UP AS AN EXAMPLE TO FUTURE GENERATIONS. ACCORDING TO YOUR RESOURCES AND YOUR BUDGET, THE MEMORIALS DEPICTED IN THIS CATALOG CAN BE SUPPLIED IN MARBLE, GRANITE, BRONZE, CAST STONE. OR COPPER ELECTROTYPE . . ."

"But your plans sound a little complicated . . . ," Albert says. "First, because it's not enough to draw the memorials, you have to sell them; and second, once you've sold them, someone has to make them! You'd need money, employees, a factory, raw materials . . ."

He is staggered at just how just how difficult it would be to set up a foundry.

". . . and even if you can get them made, the memorials would have to be transported and erected on the site . . . You'd need lots of money!"

It always comes down to this. To money. Even the most industrious people cannot simply rely on energy. Albert smiles gently and pats his friend's knee.

"All right, listen, we'll think about it. I think it's great that you feel you want to work again, though I'm not sure this is the best way to go about it. Memorials are complicated. But let's not worry about that. The most important thing is that you've found your passion again, isn't it?"

No. Edward clenches his fist and saws at the air as though polishing a pair of shoes. The message is clear: No, we have to act now!

"Act now, act now . . . you've got some odd ideas."

On a blank page of the pad, Édouard starts to scribble numbers: 300 memorials—he crosses out 300 and writes 400. He's excited. 400 × 7,000 francs = 3 million!

He seems to have lost his mind. It is not enough that he wants to take on this impossible project, he wants to do it right now. In principle, Albert has nothing against three million francs. In fact, he would be all in favor. But Édouard has lost all perspective. He tosses off a few sketches, and already he is setting up a foundry. Albert takes a deep breath, steels himself, and tries to sound calm and reasonable.

"Listen, old man, it's just not practical. You don't seem to realize how much work it would take to create four hundred memorials . . ."

Huh! Huh! Huh! When Édouard makes this sound, it means something important, it is a sound he has made only once or twice since they met, it is peremptory but not angry, it means he needs to be heard. He grabs his pencil.

"We don't make them," he scribbles, "we just sell them."

"Yeah, yeah," Albert explodes, "but once we sell them, we'll have to fucking make them!"

Édouard leans closer, takes Albert's face in his hands as though he wants to kiss him on the lips. He shakes his head, a mischievous smile in his eyes, he picks up the pencil again.

"We just sell them . . ."

The things we long for most sometimes happen when we least expect them. This is what is about to happen to Albert. Delirious with joy, Édouard suddenly answers the question that has been nagging his friend since they met. He starts to laugh. He laughs for the first time.

The laugh sound almost normal, a throaty, high-pitched, slightly feminine laugh, a *bona fide* laugh of shifting vibratos and tremolos.

Albert's mouth drops open in astonishment.

He looks down at the page, at the last words Édouard has written.

We just sell them! We don't make them. We pocket the money.

"But . . . ," Albert says puzzled.

He is annoyed because Édouard has still not answered his question.

"And afterward?" he says, "What do we do?"

"Afterward?"

Édouard explodes with laughter again. Much louder this time.

"We take the money and fuck off!"

21

Not quite 7:00 a.m. and bitterly cold. It has not dropped below freezing since late January—which is fortunate because that would mean using a pickax, something strictly forbidden by the regulations—but the lashing wind is icy and wet, it seems hardly worth coming home from war to winters like this.

Having no desire to stand around uselessly, Henri stayed in the car, though it was not much better here: he could warm his face or his feet, but not both at once. Besides, everything seems to irritate Henri these days, nothing has been going right. Given the effort he invests into his business, he is entitled to a little peace, surely? But no, there was always some hitch, some snag, he needed to be everywhere at once. It was simple: he did everything himself. He had to be constantly on Dupré's back . . .

It was not entirely fair, Henri had to admit, Dupré was passionate, he was a hard worker, a grafter. I need to work out how much the guy brings in, set my mind at ease, Henri thought, but right now he was angry with the whole world.

In part, he was simply exhausted, he had had to leave in the early hours, and his little Jewish girl had been running him ragged . . . God knows, Henri had little time for Jews—the Aulnay-Pradelles had been anti-Dreyfusards since the Middle Ages—but Jewish girls could be hot-blooded little sluts when the mood took them!

Nervously, he buttoned his coat as he watched Dupré knock on the door of the Préfecture de Police.

The night watchman was pulling some clothes on. Dupré was explaining, pointing to the car; the concierge peered out, shielding his eyes as though staring into the sun. He already knew what was happening. It took less than an hour for news to travel from the war grave cemetery to the *préfecture*. One by one the lights in the office flickered on, and the door opened again, Pradelle finally got out of the Hispano and strode right past the concierge waiting to show him the way, indicating with a peremptory wave, don't bother, I know my way around, I feel right at home.

The chief of police did not see things the same way. At forty, Gaston Plerzec was still telling people that, despite the name, he was not Breton. He had not slept all night. As the hours passed, his addled brain began to confuse the bodies of the dead soldiers with the Chinamen, the coffins seemed to move about by themselves, some even sported a sardonic grin. He adopted a pose he felt reflected the seniority of his rank: standing in front of the fireplace, one hand on the mantelpiece, the other tucked into his vest, chin held high—the chin was very important for a *préfet*.

Pradelle did not give a tinker's damn about the *préfet*, his chin, or his fireplace, he swaggered in without noticing the pose, without so much as a by-your-leave, flopped into the armchair reserved for visitors, and snapped:

"What the hell is going on?"

This opening gambit left Plerzec at a loss.

The men had met twice before, at the technical meeting to inaugurate the government program, and at the groundbreaking ceremony for the cemetery—a speech by the mayor, a moment of silent prayer—Henri had spent the time stamping his foot impatiently, did these people think he had nothing better to do? The *préfet* was well aware—was there anyone who did not know?—that M. d'Aulnay-Pradelle was the son-in-law of Marcel Péricourt, a former classmate and personal friend of the Ministre de l'Intérieur. The Président de la République himself had attended his daughter's wedding. Plerzec hardly dared imagine the complex web of friends and acquaintance involved in this affair. This was what kept him awake; faced with the distinguished list of people behind these shenanigans and the power they represented, his career felt like a wisp of straw threatened by a flame. Only a few weeks earlier, coffins had begun to arrive at the future necropolis at Darmeville from all over the region, but seeing how the reburials were being carried out, Préfet Plerzec immediately became worried. When the first problems became apparent, he had instinctively tried to cover his back; a small voice now told him that he had probably acted out of panic.

They drove in silence.

Pradelle was beginning to wonder whether he had been too greedy. Fuck it.

The *préfet* coughed, the car drove over a pothole, he bumped his head, no one uttered a word of sympathy. In the backseat, Dupré, who had bumped his head many times before, now knew to sit with his knees splayed, with one hand gripping here, one hand there. The boss drove like a lunatic.

Having been alerted by the concierge, the mayor, with a ledger tucked under his arm, was waiting for them in front of the gates of the future Dampierre military cemetery. It would not be very large—nine hundred graves. It was impossible to work out how the ministry decided on the sites.

From a distance, Pradelle studied the mayor: he looked like a retired lawyer, maybe a schoolteacher—they were the worst. They tended to be nitpickers who took their responsibilities and their prerogatives very seriously. Pradelle settled on lawyer; teachers tended to be scrawny.

He parked the car and climbed out, the *préfet* trotting next to him, there were silent handshakes, this was a serious moment.

The temporary gate was pushed open. Before them was a vast, bared leveled field of stony soil over which, with string stretched taut, lines had been traced that were perfectly straight, perfectly parallel.

Military. Only the most distant rows had been finished as graves, and crosses were slowly covering the cemetery like a flag unfurling. Next to the gate stood a few workman's huts that served as offices, dozens of white crosses were stacked on palettes. Farther off, in a large barn, covered with army-surplus tarpaulins, perhaps a hundred coffins were piled up. Under normal circumstances, coffins were reburied as they arrived, so the surfeit of waiting caskets meant work had been delayed. Pradelle glanced around at Dupré, who gave a curt nod to confirm that they were running late. All the more reason to speed things up, Henri thought, quickening his pace.

It would be dawn soon. There was not a tree for miles around. The cemetery looked like a battlefield. The group followed the mayor, who was muttering "E13, let me see, E17 . . ." He knew precisely where grave E13 was—he had spent almost an hour there only yesterday—but to go straight there offended his scrupulous sensibilities.

Finally, they came to a freshly dug grave, where they saw a coffin, covered by a thin layer of dirt. One end had been cleared and raised slightly making it possible to read the inscription: "Ernest Blachet—Brigadier 133ème infanterie—Died in the service of his country, September 4, 1917."

"So?" Pradelle said.

The *préfet* nodded to the register the mayor was holding open in front of him, like a bible or a book of spells, and read aloud.

"Grave E13: Simon Perlatte—Soldat 2ème classe—VIème armée—Died for his country, June 16, 1917."

He snapped the register shut with a bang. Pradelle frowned. He felt tempted to repeat his question, "So?" But he allowed the information to percolate. And so the *préfet*—who, in the division of powers between the city and the *département*, was tasked with delivering the *coup de grâce*, spoke up.

"Your work crews have mixed up the coffins and the graves."

Pradelle turned to him, looking puzzled.

"The work is being done by your Chinamen," the *préfet* said. "They don't even bother to look for the right grave, they just bury the coffin in the first hole they find."

This time Henri turned to Dupré.

"Why the hell would the damn Chinamen do such a thing?"

It was the *préfet* who answered.

"Because they are illiterate, Monsieur d'Aulnay-Pradelle . . . To carry out this task, you have employed men who cannot read."

For an instant, Henri was unsettled, then he snapped back:

"What fucking difference does it make, for fuck's sake? When parents visit the grave, do they dig it up to check that it's their body, not someone else's?"

Everyone was shocked. Except Dupré, who knew his boss: in the four months since they started work, he had seen him plug a series of increasingly large gaps. The project was full of exemptions and exceptions, to keep an eye on everything would mean hiring someone, but the boss flatly refused; "we'll make do with what we have," he would say, "I've got too many men working on this thing already, and besides, there's you . . . I'm counting on you, all right, Dupré?" So the fact that there was a corpse where another corpse should be was unlikely to daunt him.

The mayor and the *préfet*, on the other hand, were outraged.

"Wait a minute, wait a minute, wait a minute . . . !"

This was the mayor.

"We have responsibilities, *monsieur*. This is a sacred duty!"

No preamble, straight in with the grandiloquent words. It was obvious what sort of man he was dealing with.

"Oh, I understand," Pradelle said in a more conciliating tone, "A sacred duty, of course. But, you know how it is . . ."

"Yes, *monsieur*, I know exactly how it is. It is an insult to the dead, that's what it is! So I am hereby suspending all work."

The *préfet* was relieved he had telegraphed the ministry in advance to warn him. He was covered. Phew.

Pradelle thought for a moment.

"Very well," he said at length.

The mayor heaved a sigh; he had not expected his victory to be so easy.

"I plan to have all these graves reopened," he said, his voice louder, more peremptory, "in order to check."

"As you wish," Pradelle said.

Préfet Plerzec allowed the mayor to do the talking, because the idea of an accommodating Aulnay-Pradelle left him perplexed. On their first two meetings, he had found the man brusque, arrogant, not at all the amenable man he seemed today.

"Very well," Pradelle said, pulling his coat tighter. He seemed visibly touched by the mayor's situation and prepared to make the best of a bad situation. "Have the graves reopened."

He made to leave, then turned back, as though to check on a minor detail.

"Obviously, you will let us know when we can start work again, won't you? In the meantime, Dupré, have the Chinamen transferred to Chazières-Malmont, we're running a little behind there. In fact, this whole thing could not have come at a better time."

"Wait a minute!" roared the mayor, "It's the job of your workmen to reopen these graves!"

"I fear not," Pradelle said. "My Chinamen are here to bury coffins. That's what they're paid for. Though, actually, I have no problem with them exhuming. I'll simply bill the government by the unit. Though it would mean three separate invoices—for burying the coffins, digging them up again and—when you've worked out who should go where—reinterring them."

"Absolutely not!" the *préfet* bellowed.

He was the one who signed off on invoices and expenses, he was the one responsible for the budget allocated by the state, and the one who, if there was any overspending, would get rapped across the knuckles. As it was, he had been transferred here because of an administrative error—a problem with the mistress of a minister who disliked Plerzec had escalated, and within the week he had been transferred to Dampierre—so there was no way he was about to risk spending the last years of his career in the colonies. He suffered from asthma.

"You cannot invoice three times, it is out of the question!"

"Sort it out between yourselves," Pradelle said. "I just need to know what to do with my Chinamen. Whether to keep them working here or send them elsewhere."

The mayor was distraught.

"Now, now, gentlemen!"

He made a sweeping gesture that encompassed the whole cemetery suffused by the dawn light. It was eerie, this vast expanse with no trees, no grass, no boundaries, beneath the cold milk-white sky, with these mounds of earth waiting to be tamped down by the rain, the discarded shovels, the wheelbarrows . . . It was a heart-wrenching spectacle.

The mayor reopened his register.

"Now, now, gentlemen," he said again, "we've already buried a hundred and fifteen soldiers."

He glanced up from his book, apparently dazed by this fact.

"And we have absolutely no idea who is who!"

The *préfet* thought that the mayor might be about to burst into tears. That was all they needed.

"These young men died for France," he said, "we owe them our respect!"

"Really," Henri said, "You owe them your respect?"

"Absolutely, and further . . ."

"Then perhaps you can explain to me why, in your cemetery, you have been allowing illiterate men to bury them any old way for the past two months?"

"I'm not the one who has been burying them indiscriminately! It is the fault of your Chi . . . your laborers!"

"But you have been appointed by the military authorities to maintain the registry, have you not?"

"A town hall clerk comes by twice a day! But he can hardly be expected to spend all day here!"

He gave the *préfet* the look of a drowning man.

Silence.

Everyone was abandoning everyone. The mayor, the *préfet*, the military authorities, the registrar, the Ministère des Pensions—there were so many middlemen in this process . . .

It was obvious that, if it came to apportioning blame, everyone would get their share. Except the Chinamen. Because they could not read.

"Listen," Pradelle suggested, "from now on, we'll see to it that our people are more careful, won't we, Dupré?"

Dupré nodded. The mayor was horrified. He would have to turn a blind eye, to knowingly leave crosses on these graves whose names bore no relation to those buried there and carry the secret with him. This cemetery would become his nightmare. Pradelle looked from the mayor to the *préfet* and back.

"I propose," he said in a confidential tone, "that we say nothing about this little incident . . ."

The *préfet* swallowed hard. By now his telegram would have landed on the minister's desk, like a request for a transfer to the colonies.

Pradelle put his arm around the shoulders of the bewildered mayor.

"What is important for the families, is that they have a place that they can visit. And after all their son is buried here, isn't he? That's what really matters, trust me."

The matter was settled. Pradelle climbed back into his car and furiously slammed the door, though he did not fly into a rage. He was quite calm as he pulled away.

For a long while, he and Dupré watched in silence as the landscape flashed past.

Once again they had come through by the skin of their teeth, but they were beginning to worry, more and more such incidents were being reported around the country.

Finally Pradelle said:

"We need to tighten up the operation, is that clear? I'm counting on you, all right, Dupré?"

22

No. A flick of his forefinger like a windshield wiper, only faster. A firm, definitive "no." Édouard closed his eyes; Albert's response had been entirely predictable. He was so timid, so fearful. Even when there was no risk, it could take him days to make even the most minor decision, so, obviously, selling war memorials and absconding with the cash . . . !

For Édouard, the only issue was knowing whether Albert would come around in time, because the best ideas are perishable goods. He could tell from the newspapers he was reading that soon the market would be flooded with offers of memorials, and when every artist, every foundry was rushing to meet demand, it would be too late.

It was now or never.

And for Albert, it was never. The flick of a forefinger. No.

But Édouard had stubbornly carried on with his work.

Page by page, his catalog of commemorative designs was taking shape. He had just turned out a very fine "Victory" inspired by the Nike of Samothrace—though in his version it had a soldier's head. And since he would be alone until Louise arrived in midafternoon, he had time to think, to attempt to find an answer to all the questions, to fine-tune his plan, which, even he was forced to admit, was not straightforward. Much less so than he had imagined; even as he dealt with problems, new ones were constantly turning up. But despite the problems, he believed wholeheartedly in the plan. As he saw it, it could not fail.

The real news was that he found himself working with unexpected, almost ferocious enthusiasm.

He threw himself into his work with relish, he was consumed, obsessed, his life depended on it. In rediscovering the old pleasures of troublemaking and his taste for provocation, he was becoming his old self.

Albert was delighted. He had never known this side of Édouard, except at a distance, in the trenches; seeing him come back to life was its own reward. As for his "plan," Albert considered it so unfeasible that he scarcely worried. To his eyes, it was fundamentally unrealistic.

The two men were locked in a trial of strength in which one pressed forward while the other resisted.

As so often, victory seemed assured, not to strength but to inertia. Albert had only to go on saying no in order to win. What he found most cruel was not refusing to be a part of this harebrained scheme, but the fact that he was disappointing Édouard, nipping his enthusiasm in the bud, consigning them both to a life of emptiness, to a future with no prospects.

He needed to come up with another plan . . . but what?

And so, every night, he would gently but halfheartedly admire the drawings Édouard had been working on, the new memorials, the new sculptures.

You get the idea? Édouard wrote on the conversation pad, People can design their own monument! Take a flag and a *poilu* and you have a monument. Raise the flag and you have a different model—call it "Victory." It's possible to be creative with no talent, no effort, and no ideas, the public will still lap it up.

Not quite . . . Albert thought, while Édouard could be accused of many things, he had a rare ability for coming up with ideas. Especially disastrous ones: changing his identity, being unable to collect his military pension, refusing to go home where he could have lived in comfort, refusing the grafts, becoming addicted to morphine, and now this war memorial scheme . . . Édouard's ideas were a pain in the backside.

"Do you really understand what it is you're suggesting?" Albert said. "This is . . . it's sacrilege! Stealing money intended for war memorials, it's like desecrating a cemetery, it's . . . it's an insult to patriotism! Granted, the government makes a small contribution, but most of the money for these memorial comes from the victims' families. From widows, parents, orphans, from friends who watched their fellow soldiers die! You make Landru[9] look like a choirboy. You would have the whole country up in arms, everyone will be against you. And when they catch you, you'll get a perfunctory trial, because they'll build the guillotine before it even starts. Now I know you don't much like your head anymore, but I'm rather attached to mine."

Muttering darkly, he went back to washing up—what a ludicrous plan. But a few minutes later, he was back, dishtowel in hand. The figure of Capitaine Pradelle, which had been haunting him since his visit to the Péricourts, had just appeared to him again. Suddenly, he realized that his brain had long been harboring thoughts of revenge.

The time had come.

It was blindingly obvious.

"You want to know what would be fair? Let me tell you what I think would be moral—putting a bullet in the back of that bastard Pradelle! That's what we should do! Because this life we're living, every miserable thing about it, is all his fault."

Édouard did not seem particularly enthused by this new plan. His hand hovered uncertainly over the sketchpad.

"Fine, fine!" Albert goaded him, "You seem to have forgotten all about Pradelle! But he's not in the same boat as we are, he came back from war a hero with his medals and his decorations, and he's collecting an officer's pension. I'm sure he's done well for himself out of the war . . ."

Could he go a step further? Albert wondered. The question was its own answer. Getting revenge on Pradelle suddenly seemed so urgent . . . He took the plunge.

"And with all his medals and his decorations, I'll bet he's made a good marriage . . . A hero like that would be a fine catch! Here we are slowly starving to death, while he's probably set himself up in business . . . Do you think that's moral?"

Astonishingly, the response to his plan was not what Albert had been expecting. His friend raised an eyebrow and bent over his pad.

"The war is to blame," he wrote, "No war, no Pradelle."

Albert almost choked. He was disappointed, but more than that, he was sad. He had to accept that poor Édouard no longer had his feet on the ground.

The two men returned to this conversation several times, but it invariably led to the same conclusion. In the name of morality, Albert longed for revenge.

"You're making this a personal crusade," Édouard wrote.

"Of course I am, I think what he's done to my life is personal, don't you?"

No, Édouard did not think so. Vengeance was not his idea of justice. Holding one man responsible was not enough. Though this was peacetime, Édouard had declared a war on war, something he intended to fight with the only means at his disposal, in other words, his talent. Morality was not his style.

It seemed each man was intent on writing his own story, but it was no longer clear if the narratives would be the same. They began to wonder whether they might not each have to write their own. Each in his own style. Separately.

Having come to this conclusion, Albert decided to think about something else. He could think about the housemaid at the Péricourts—my God, that sensual little tongue of hers—or about the new shoes he no longer dared to put on. Every evening, he would make Édouard's bouillon of meat and vegetables, and every evening Édouard would harp on about his plan—he was a pig-headed boy. Albert did not give an inch. Since morality had failed, he appealed to reason.

"For this plan of yours to work," he explained, "you'd need to set up a company, to fill in forms, provide documentation, have you thought about that? Once your catalog was out there, we wouldn't get far, I can tell you, we'd be arrested in a heartbeat. And between arrest and execution, you'd scarcely have time to draw breath."

Édouard seemed unshaken by these arguments.

"You'd need premises," Albert shouted, "You'd need offices! Don't tell me you're planning to meet clients in one of your carnival masks?"

Stretched out on the couch, Édouard continued to leaf through his monuments and sculptures. Stylistic exercises. Not everyone is gifted enough to turn out something ugly.

"And you would need a telephone! And someone to take calls, to write letters . . . and a bank account, if you're hoping to get any money."

Édouard could not help but smile inwardly. His friend's voice was tremulous with panic, as though they were planning to dismantle the Eiffel Tower and rebuild it a hundred yards away. He was scared to death.

"Everything's so simple for you," Albert said, "Hardly surprising, since you never set foot outside . . ."

He bit his lip; too late.

It was true, of course, but Édouard was hurt by these words. Mme Maillard often said: "My Albert's not a bad kid at heart, there's not many as kindhearted. But he never was one for tact. That's why he'll come to nothing in this life."

The only thing that might have shaken Albert from his obstinate refusal was money. The fortune Édouard held out for them. It was true that a vast fortune was being spent. The whole country was gripped by a frenzied desire to commemorate those who had died that was directly proportional to its revulsion for those who had survived. The financial argument swayed Albert, because he was the one who managed their money and he knew how difficult it was to earn any and how quickly it trickled away; he had to account for everything, the cigarettes, the métro tickets, the food. So all these things that Édouard's scheme lavishly promised, the millions, the cars, the hotels . . .

And the women . . .

On this last subject, Albert was beginning to feel anxious; it is possible to get by alone, but it is a loveless existence, and in time you become desperate to meet someone.

But his fear of getting involved in this lunatic scheme was stronger than his fierce need to find a woman. Surviving the war only to end up in prison, what woman deserved a man prepared to take such a risk? Although, looking at the women he found in magazines, he felt that many of them deserved the risk.

"Just think about it," he said to Édouard one night, "I flinch whenever I hear the door slam, can you really see me getting involved in something like this?"

At first, Édouard said nothing, he carried on drawing, allowed his plan slowly to mature, but he was beginning to realize that time was not on his side. In fact, the more they talked, the more reasons Albert found to oppose it.

"And let's say we did manage to sell some of these fictitious memorials of yours, and let's say the town councils are prepared to pay something in advance, how much would we actually make? A couple of hundred francs today, a couple of hundred francs tomorrow, we're not exactly talking big money! Taking a risk like this for a couple of *sous*, no thanks. The only way to make off with a fortune is if all the money comes in at once, and that's impossible, it would never work!"

Albert was right. Sooner or later buyers would realize that the company was phony. All they could do was pocket whatever monies had already been paid, which would be very little. But as he thought about this, Édouard came up with a solution. It was perfect.

On November 11 next, in Paris, the French government . . .

That night, Albert brought home a crate of fruit he had found on the pavement walking back from the Grands Boulevards. He cut away the rotten parts and pureed the rest to make juice. Having beef bouillon every night was dreary, and Albert did not have much imagination. Édouard ate whatever he was given; in this, at least, he was not difficult.

Albert wiped his hands on his apron and bent over the page—his eyesight had deteriorated since he came back from the war; if he had the money he would have bought glasses—he almost had to press his nose to the paper.

> *On November 11 next, in Paris, the French government will unveil the tomb of the "unknown soldier." You can join in this commemoration and transform this noble gesture into a vast, national tribute by unveiling a memorial in your own town on the same day!*

All the orders would come in by the end of the year, Édouard reasoned.

Albert nodded sadly. You're completely insane. He went back to his fruit juice.

Over the course of their interminable arguments on the subject, Édouard convinced Albert that with the money from the sales, they could both go and live in the colonies. Invest in some promising business ventures. Ensure they would forever be free of financial worries. He showed Albert cuttings he had clipped from newspapers and postcards Louise had brought him—views of lumber works in Cochinchine, potbellied colonists with pith helmets and smug smiles standing in front of Vietnamese natives carrying logs of timber. European automobiles with women in fluttering white scarves driving through the valleys of Guinea. Rivers in Cameroon and gardens in Tonkin where lush succulents spilled from ceramic pots, the shipping barges in Saigon flying the French ensign, the splendid palace of the governor, the square du Théâtre at twilight with gentlemen in smoking jackets and ladies in formal gowns carrying cigarette holders and iced cocktails, you could almost hear the orchestra playing . . . In these far-off places, life seemed easy, business straightforward, fortunes quickly made, the languorous climate tropical. Albert pretended to take only a passing interest, but he lingered longer than necessary on the photographs of Conakry market, in which tall, statuesque young black women, breasts bare, strolled around with a casualness that was deeply sensual, he wiped his hands on his apron again and went back to the kitchen.

Abruptly, he stopped.

"And another thing—how do you plan to print this catalog of yours and send it to hundreds of towns and villages? Where are you going to get the money, tell me that . . ."

Édouard had found answers to many of Albert's questions; but he had no response to this one.

To drive the point home, Albert went and fetched his wallet, spread its contents on the table, and counted.

"I've got 11 francs and 73 centimes. How much have you got?"

The question was cowardly, cruel, unnecessary, hurtful; Édouard had nothing. Albert did not press his advantage, he put away his wallet and went back to the food. They did not exchange another word all night.

The day came when Édouard had exhausted all his arguments without succeeding in convincing his friend.

The answer was no. Albert would not change his mind.

Time had passed, the catalog was almost finished; it needed only a few minor corrections before it could be printed and sent out. But everything else remained to be done, the organization would represent a vast amount of work, and there was no prospect of paying for it . . .

For his pains, Édouard had only a series of worthless sketches. He broke down. This time, there were no tears, no tantrums, no sulks; he felt insulted. He was being thwarted by a pissant little accountant in the name of inviolable pragmatism. The eternal struggle between the artist and the bourgeoisie was being played once more; though the details were slightly different, this was the war he had lost to his father. An artist is a dreamer, hence of no value. This was what Édouard thought he could hear behind Albert's pronouncements. With Albert, as with his father, he felt relegated to the role of scrounger, a ne'er-do-well interested only in vain pursuits. He had been patient, practical, persuasive, but he had failed. The rift between him and Albert was not a difference of opinion, but a difference of culture; Édouard found his friend petty, mean, with no drive, no ambition, no glint of madness.

Albert Maillard was simply a version of Marcel Péricourt. But for the wealth, they were identical. With their boorish certainties, both men swept aside the vital spark in Édouard; they killed it.

Édouard whined, Albert stood firm. They quarreled.

Édouard pounded his fist on the table, stared blackly at Albert and gave a hoarse, menacing growl.

Albert snapped that he had gone to war and was not about to go to prison.

Édouard overturned the couch, which did not survive the fall. Albert rushed over, he had been fond of the couch, it was the only stylish piece of furniture in this bleak hovel. Édouard went on howling, the noise was incredible, spittle sprayed from his exposed throat, it came from deep in his belly like an erupting volcano.

Albert picked up the pieces of the couch and said that Édouard could break every stick of furniture in the place, but it would not change anything, that neither of them was cut out for a career in crime.

Still Édouard howled, lumbering awkwardly around the room, breaking a window with his elbow, threatening to smash what little crockery they possessed. Albert rushed at him, grabbed him around the waist, and they tumbled on the floor.

They had begun to hate each other.

Albert was beside himself, he lashed out, hit Édouard on the side of the head, punched him in the chest, slammed him against the wall, all but knocking him unconscious. They both scrambled to their feet at the same time, Édouard cuffed Albert, who responded with a savage punch. Right in the face.

But Édouard had been standing right in front of him.

Albert's fist sank into the gaping void.

Almost up to the wrist.

And stuck there.

Horrified, Albert stared at his hand, buried in his friend's face as though it had split his head in two. And above his hand, Édouard's incredulous eyes.

The two men stood, frozen, for a second.

They heard a scream and both turned toward the door. Louise, her hand clapped over her mouth, was staring at them in tears; she raced out of the room.

They managed to extricate themselves, not knowing what to say. Awkwardly, they shook themselves. There was a guilty, self-conscious silence.

Their friendship could never survive this image of a fist lodged in a face as though splitting it in two. That gesture, that feeling, that hideous intimacy, it was all too shocking, too terrifying.

They did not share the same rage.

Or they expressed their anger very differently.

Édouard packed his bags the following morning. It was his haversack. He took his clothes, nothing else. Albert was leaving for work, he had thought of nothing to say. His last glimpse of Édouard was of his back as he sat, packing very slowly, like a man who cannot bring himself to leave.

All day, as he trudged the Grands Boulevards with his sandwich board, Albert brooded.

That evening, a simple note: "Thanks for everything."

The apartment seemed desolate, just like his life after Cécile left him. He knew it was possible to recover from anything, but every day since he had won the war, he had felt as though he was losing it.

23

Labourdin laid his hands on the desk with the same contented air as he might at a dinner table when seeing a baked Alaska arrive. Mlle Raymond looked nothing like an ice cream, yet the image of the delicate golden meringue was not entirely incongruous. She was a peroxide blonde with reddish highlights, a pallid complexion, and a rather pointed head. Whenever she came in and saw her boss in this pose, Mlle Raymond would give a disgusted, fatalistic pout. Because as soon as she stood next to him, he would slide his right hand up her skirt in a gesture that demonstrated a surprising agility for a man of his girth and a skill he conspicuously lacked in every other domain. She would swivel her hips, but in this Labourdin seemed to have intuition that verged on premonition. No matter which way she turned, he always hit his target. She had come to terms with it, she would wriggle quickly away, set down the file and, as she left, give a jaded sigh. Her piteous attempts to prevent this practice (tight-fitting skirts and dresses), served only to heighten Labourdin's pleasure. If she was a mediocre secretary when it came to shorthand and typing, her forbearance more than made up for her flaws.

Labourdin opened the file and clicked his tongue: M. Péricourt would be happy.

It was a fine set of regulations outlining "an open competition for designs from artists of French nationality for the construction of a memorial to those who died in the Great War of 1914–1918."

In this extensive document, Labourdin himself had written only a single sentence. He had insisted on drafting article 1, subsection (ii) all by himself. Each carefully weighed word was his own work, every capital letter. He was so proud of it that he insisted it be set in bold type: **"This Monument should evoke the painful and glorious Memory of our Victorious Dead."** Perfectly cadenced. He clicked his tongue again. Mentally, he patted himself on the back once more and then swiftly skimmed the rest of the document.

An excellent site had been found for the memorial, one previously occupied by a municipal garage—one hundred and thirty feet wide by one hundred feet deep—with the possibility of a garden surrounding the monument. The regulations required that the dimensions of the monument should "be in keeping with the chosen site." To inscribe all these names would require a large surface area. The operation was almost settled: a jury of fourteen people, among them eminent figures, local artists, serving officers, representatives of families' and veterans' associations, and so forth, handpicked from among the many people who owed Labourdin a favor (being president of the committee, he held the casting vote). This highly artistic and patriotic project was to be among the defining achievements of his mayoral term. His reelection was almost guaranteed. The schedule had been determined, the competition was about to be launched, work had already begun on leveling the site. The announcement would be published in the major newspapers of Paris and the provinces; it was a triumph, one he had skillfully managed . . .

Not a detail was missing.

Except for a blank space in article 4: "the allocated budget for the memorial is in the amount of . . ."

This gave M. Péricourt pause for thought. He wanted something striking but not grandiose and, from the information he had received, such memorials generally cost between 60,000 and 120,000 francs, with certain well-known artists commanding as much as 150,000 or even 180,000. Given such a broad range, where should he set the bar? It was not a matter of money, rather one of appropriateness. He needed to think. He looked up at his son. A month earlier Madeleine had discreetly placed a framed photograph of Édouard on the mantelpiece. She had several photographs but had chosen this one because it seemed to her a "middle-ground," neither too formal nor too provocative. Acceptable. Her father seemed strained by the changes in his life, and anxious not to overwhelm him, she moved tactfully, making small changes, a sketchpad one day, a photograph the next.

M. Péricourt had waited two days before moving the picture closer, setting it on the corner of his desk. He did not want to ask Madeleine when or where it had been taken; a father was supposed to know such things. To his eyes, Édouard looked about fourteen, meaning it would have been taken in 1909. He was leaning on a wooden railing. There was little background detail; it seemed to have been taken on the terrace of a chalet—Édouard had been sent skiing every winter. M. Péricourt could not remember where precisely, except that it was always the same ski resort, in the northern Alps, perhaps, or maybe the south. But somewhere in the Alps. His son was wearing a thick sweater and squinting into the sunlight with a broad grin, as though the person behind the camera was making faces. And this in turn amused M. Péricourt. He was a handsome boy, mischievous. Finding himself smiling now, so many years later, reminded him that he and his son had never laughed together. It broke his heart. Only then did he think to turn the frame around.

In the bottom corner, Madeleine had written: "1906, les Buttes-Chaumont."

M. Péricourt unscrewed the top of his fountain pen and wrote: 200,000 francs.

24

Since no one knew what Joseph Merlin looked like, the four men tasked with welcoming him had first considered having the station master make an announcement when the train arrived, then they thought of holding up a sign with his name on it . . . But none of their solutions seemed consistent with the dignity and solemnity required when greeting a representative of the ministry.

In the end, they decided to stand in a group near the end of the platform and keep an eye out since, after all, not many people alighted at Chazières-Malmont—about thirty, usually—and a civil servant from Paris would be easy to spot.

But they did not spot him.

In the end, those who got off the train numbered not thirty, but fewer than ten, and among them there was no ministerial representative. When the last traveler went out through the gate and the station was empty, they turned and looked at one another: Adjudant Tournier clicked his heels; Paul Cahbord, the registrar at Chazières-Malmont Town Hall blew his nose; Roland Schneider, of the Union National des Combattants, who was representing the families of the dead men took a long, deep breath intended to express the self-control he required not to explode. And they all left.

Dupré, for his part, was content simply to register the fact; he had wasted more time preparing for a meeting that would not now take place than he had spent managing the six other sites he was constantly shuttling between; it was disappointing. Once outside, the four men headed toward the car.

They were torn about how to feel. When they realized that the ministerial envoy had not arrived, each was disappointed . . . and relieved. Not that they were afraid, of course, they had carefully prepared for this visit, but an inspection is an inspection, such things can easily go awry, they all knew examples.

Since the problems with the Chinamen at the Dampierre cemetery, Henri d'Aulnay-Pradelle had been on edge. Like a bear with a sore head. He was breathing down Dupré's neck, issuing orders that invariably contradicted those he had given before. They needed to move faster, employ fewer people, cut corners wherever possible, as long as no one noticed. He had been promising Dupré a pay raise ever since he had hired him, although it never came. But: "I'm counting on you, Dupré, you know that?"

"The nerve!" Paul Chabord grumbled. "You'd think the ministry might have sent a telegram."

He nodded sagely: who did they take them for, they had sacrificed themselves for the Republic, the least they could expect was to be kept informed, etc.

As they were about to get into the car, a cavernous voice made them all turn suddenly.

"Are you the men from the cemetery?"

He was an elderly man with a very small head on a large body that looked hollow, like a chicken carcass after the meal. His limbs were too long, he had a red face and a forehead so narrow his close-cropped hair almost met his eyebrows. And a mournful expression. To make matters worse, he was dressed in a threadbare greatcoat of a prewar style that, despite the cold, hung open to reveal an ink-stained purple velvet jacket with several buttons missing, a pair of shapeless gray pants, and—this was the worst—a pair of huge, clodhopping shoes that looked positively biblical—a veritable scarecrow.

The four men were speechless.

Lucien Dupré was the first to react. Taking a step forward, he held out his hand.

"Monsieur Merlin?"

The ministerial representative made a sucking sound with his tongue against his gums as through removing a morsel of food. *Tssst.* It took a moment before anyone realized he was shifting his dentures, an irritating tic he continued to employ during the journey and made one want to find him a toothpick. As they pulled away from the station, what had been hinted at by his ragged clothes, his vast, filthy shoes, and his general appearance was confirmed: the man reeked.

As they drove, Roland Schneider launched into a sweeping strategic-military-geographic explanation of the region. Joseph Merlin, who seemed not to hear, interrupted him in midflow to say:

"For lunch . . . can we have chicken?"

His accent was nasal and grating.

In 1916, at the start of the battle of Verdun (ten months of sustained fighting, three hundred thousand dead), the region of Chazières-Malmont, which was not far from the front lines, accessible by road and close to the hospital that was the primary supplier of corpses, had come into its own as a practical place to bury soldiers. On numerous occasions, the shifting battle lines and strategic uncertainties had encroached upon the sprawling quadrilateral, which was now the resting place of more than two thousand corpses—no one knew the exact number, some said there were five thousand buried here, which was not impossible, this war had broken all records. These temporary graveyards generated registers, maps, and inventories, but when you have fifteen to twenty million shells falling on you in the space of three months—some days, a shell every three seconds—and you have to bury two hundred times more bodies than anyone could have expected in Dantesque conditions, these registers, maps, and inventories are of limited value.

The government had decided to create a huge war grave at Darmeville for all those buried in the makeshift cemeteries in the region, particularly the one at Chazières-Malmont. But, since no one knew how many bodies needed to be exhumed, transported, and reburied in the new necropolis, it was impossible to establish an overall price. The government was paying by the corpse.

This was one of the directly awarded contracts Pradelle had secured without having to bid. He had calculated that if they found two thousand bodies, he would make enough to be able to reroof half of the stables at la Sallevière.

Three thousand five hundred and he could reroof all the stables.

More than four thousand, and he would renovate the dovecote.

Dupré had brought some twenty Senegalese men to Chazières-Malmont and, to keep the authorities happy, Capitaine Pradelle (Dupré still referred to him thus out of habit), had agreed to employ a handful of local laborers.

The initial phase of the work entailed exhuming those soldiers whose relatives had been clamoring for their return and whose remains could easily be found.

Whole families had descended on Chazières-Malmont, an endless procession of tears and wails, of gaunt children, wizened parents tottering over precarious timber walkways so they did not have to wade through mud—as if to spite them, it had rained incessantly. The advantage of this was that, with the lashing rain, no one was keen to linger, so the exhumations were swift. Out of propriety, French laborers were hired because—for some inexplicable reason—some families had been shocked to see Senegalese laborers digging up the bodies; did the army think that exhuming their son's body was a menial task to be delegated to Negroes? When children arrived at the cemetery and saw these tall black men in the distance, soaked to the skin, unearthing and transporting coffins, they could not take their eyes off them.

The procession of families took forever.

Capitaine Pradelle was on the telephone every day.

"Is this bullshit nearly over, Dupré? When can we start the real work?"

The "real work" entailed the exhumation of all the other soldiers to be reburied at the Darmeville necropolis.

The task was far from easy. Some of the bodies could be cataloged because the crosses bearing the names were still in place, the balance remained to be identified.

Many soldiers had been buried with their broken identity disks, but not all of them—far from it; sometimes an investigation needed to be carried out based on objects found on the body or documents found in the pockets. These corpses had to be put to one side and listed while waiting for the results of the investigations, but all too often almost nothing was found, and such bodies were marked "unidentified soldier."

Work was now progressing well. Almost four hundred bodies had been exhumed. The coffins arrived in truckloads with a team of four men to assemble them, a second team to carry them to the gravesides and back to the wagons that would transport them to the necropolis at Darmeville, where another team of workers from Pradelle & Cie would rebury them. Two men were responsible for keeping the lists of names, epitaphs, and notes.

Joseph Merlin, emissary of the minister, strode into the cemetery like a saint at the head of a procession. His huge shoes tramped through every puddle, splattering all around. Only at this point did anyone notice he was carrying a battered leather briefcase. Though full to bursting with papers and documents, it seemed to flutter on the end of his arm like a sheet of paper.

He stopped. Behind him, the *cortège* froze, anxiously. Joseph Merlin slowly surveyed the scene.

The cemetery was pervaded by the acrid odor of putrefaction that could hit you in the face like a cloud moved by the wind, it mingled with the smoke rising from those caskets that, when disinterred, were damaged beyond repair and, according to regulations, had to be burned. The lowering sky was a grubby gray, and here and there were men carrying coffins or bent over the graves; two trucks stood with their engines idling while they were being loaded with coffins.

Merlin shifted his dentures, making the disagreeable sucking sound, and pursed his lips.

This was what he had been reduced to.

Almost forty years a civil servant and, just when he was about to retire, he had been detailed to inspect cemeteries.

Merlin had served variously at the Ministry of the Colonies, the Ministry of General Supplies, the Undersecretariat for Trade and Industry, the Ministry of Posts and Telegraphs, and the Ministry of Agriculture and Food Supply; thirty-seven years in the civil service, thirty-seven years of being pushed from pillar to post, of failing again and again, of being beaten down in every post he had ever held. He was not a likable man. Taciturn, prone to pedantry, conceited and cantankerous all year round, he was not a man to joke with . . . For decades, this disagreeable man, by his arrogant, bigoted behavior, had courted the contempt in his colleagues and the wrath of his superiors. He would arrive in a new post and be assigned a task, but his colleagues would quickly tire of him, and finding him ridiculous, truculent, old-fashioned, they would laugh at him behind his back, give him nicknames, play cruel pranks, he had seen it all. And yet he had never deserved this fall from grace. Indeed, he could provide chapter and verse on his heroic bureaucratic achievements, a list he kept constantly up to date so as not to have to reflect on a lugubrious career of overlooked probity that had merely succeeded in making him an object of derision. Sometimes his stint at one or other department had seemed like a daylong round of bullying; more than once he had had occasion to raise his walking stick, whirling it angrily about him, bellowing in his thunderous voice, ready to take on the whole world, he terrified people, especially women—it's got to the point where they don't dare go near him, they insist on having someone with them, we simply can't keep a fellow like this in the department, especially since—how do I put this delicately?—frankly, the man smells, and it's most off-putting. No one had kept him. In all his life, he had known only a single moment in the sun, which had lasted from the day he met Francine, one July 14, to the day Francine left him for an artillery captain the following November. Thirty-four years ago. That he should end his career inspecting cemeteries had scarcely come as a surprise.

It had been a year since Merlin arrived at the Ministry of Pensions, Bonuses, and War-Related Allowances. He had been moved from one division to another, and then one day the ministry had received troubling news about the condition of the war graves. Things were not going according to plan. A *préfet* had reported anomalies at Dampierre. He had retracted his statement the following day, but by then the bureaucratic wheels were turning. The ministry must ensure that it was spending the taxpayer's money appropriately so that those who had died for their country should have a dignified burial in accordance with the provisions set down in the relevant legislation . . .

"Ah, shit!" Merlin said, surveying the desolate scene.

Because he had been the one appointed to the task. He had seemed to be a perfect fit for this job that no one wanted. Managing the war graves.

Adjudant Tournier heard him

"Excuse me?"

Merlin turned, stared at him, sucked at his teeth. Ever since Francine had taken off with her capitaine, he loathed army officers. He turned back and surveyed the cemetery, as though only now realizing where he was and what he was supposed to do. The other members of the delegation were puzzled.

"Might I suggest we begin by . . . ," Dupré ventured.

But Merlin did not move, he stood rooted like a tree, gazing at this forlorn scene, which dimly echoed his sense of persecution.

He decided to speed things up, to get this chore over and done with.

"Fucking bastards."

This time, everyone distinctly heard what he said, but no one knew what to make of it.

The registers of births, marriages, and deaths drawn up in accordance with the prescriptions set out in the law of December 29, 1915; the establishment of written records as stipulated in the memorandum of February 16, 1916; the respect due to the deceased parties as laid out in article 106 of the annual budget; yes, yes . . . Merlin muttered, ticking here, signing here, the atmosphere was far from relaxed, but everything seemed to be going to plan. The man smelled like a skunk; standing next to him in the cramped shed that doubled as a civil registry was unbearable. In spite of the icy wind that gusted through the room, they decided to leave the window open.

Merlin had begun his inspection with a tour of the graves. At first, Paul Chabord had bustled after him with an umbrella, but the ministerial envoy's erratic peregrinations and his sudden changes of direction quickly eroded Chabord's goodwill, and after a while he simply used it to shelter himself. Merlin did not even notice. Rain coursed down his skull; he sucked on his dentures, he stared into the graves as though he did not know what he was supposed to be inspecting. *Tsst Tsst.*

They had moved on to inspect the coffins. As the procedure was explained to him, Merlin slipped on a pair of spectacles with lenses so gray and scratched they seemed fashioned from onion skin paper and studied the forms, the inventories, the plaques affixed to the caskets. Right, well, that's enough of that, he muttered, we're not going to spend all day. He took out a fat pocket watch and, without a word to anyone, strode off toward the administration hut.

At midday, he was busy filling out his inspection report. Watching him work, it was easy to understand why his jacket was spattered in ink stains.

Now all those present had to sign.

"Every man here does his duty," Adjudant Tournier said in a smug, military tone.

"I'm sure he does," Merlin said.

A formality. They were standing in the shed, passing around the pen and inkwell like an aspergillum at a funeral. Merlin jabbed a fat finger at the register.

"Here, whichever of you represents the families . . ."

The Union Nationale des Combattants did enough favors for the government to have a finger in every pie. Merlin grimly watched Roland Schneider sign and initial.

"Schneider," he said after a pause (he pronounced it "Ssshnay-dah" to emphasize his point), "sounds a little German, don't you think?"

The other man immediately bridled.

"Never mind," Merlin interrupted him and gestured again to the report. "Here, the municipal registrar . . ."

His comment had cast a pall over the proceedings. The rest of the signing was conducted in silence.

"*Monsieur*," Schneider began, when he had time to collect his thoughts, "your comment . . ."

But Merlin was already on his feet, two heads taller than Schneider, staring at him with his large gray eyes and asking, "Can we have chicken for lunch?"

Chicken was his only joy in life. He ate messily, adding grease marks to the pattern of ink stains; he never removed his jacket.

Over lunch everyone attempted to make conversation, everyone except Schneider, who was still racking his brain to come up with a rejoinder. Merlin, whose head was bent over his plate, responded with only the occasional grunt or a *tsst, tsst* as he sucked his dentures, thereby rapidly discouraging any fellow feeling. Even so, though the ministerial envoy had been unpleasant, the inspection had been passed, and the tense atmosphere shifted to one of relief verging on gaiety. The early work on the site had been difficult, and they had encountered a number of minor problems. In this sort of project, nothing ever goes exactly as expected, and regulations, however precise, never take account of those harsh realities that immediately become apparent once work begins. However conscientious and scrupulous the work, there are always unforeseen factors, problems to be resolved, decisions to be made, sometimes the best way forward is to go back . . .

Now, everyone was eager for the graveyard to be empty and the project to be over. The inspection had ended on a positive, reassuring note. In retrospect, all of them had been a little afraid. There was a lot of drinking—lunch was at the taxpayer's expense. Even Schneider forgot the slight, deciding that he felt nothing but scorn for this slovenly civil servant and poured himself some more Côtes-du-Rhône. Merlin had three helpings of chicken, wolfing his food as though he were starving. His stubby fingers were thick with grease. When he had finished, without a thought for the other guests, he tossed the napkin he had not used onto the table, got to his feet, and left the restaurant. The other men were taken aback, they scrambled to finish their meals, drain their glasses, ask for the bill, check the total, pay, then, knocking chairs over in their rush, they made for the door. When they emerged, they found Merlin pissing against the wheel of the car.

Before heading to the train station, they had to go back to the cemetery to collect Merlin's briefcase and his registers. His train was due to leave in forty minutes, there could be no question of hanging around any longer, especially since the rain—which had eased off while they were at lunch—was now pouring down. In the car, Merlin said nothing, not a word of thanks for their welcome or for the lunch, the man was a real asshole.

Back at the cemetery, Merlin walked quickly. The planks set over the puddles buckled dangerously under his weight. A scrawny dog trotted past and without warning, without even breaking stride, Merlin lashed out; balancing on his left foot he kicked the animal in the side, sending it howling a yard into the air and landing on its back. Before it could get up, Merlin had jumped down into a puddle that came up to his ankles and, to stop the dog from moving, planted a stout shoe on its chest. The poor animal, terrified of being drowned, barked all the louder, squirming in the muddy water, trying to bite; everyone was aghast.

Merlin bent down and grasped the dog's lower jaw with his right hand, the muzzle with his left. The dog struggled more fiercely. Merlin, who now had a tight grip, gave the animal another savage kick in the stomach, pulled its jaws apart as though it were a crocodile, then, suddenly, he let go, the dog flailed in the water, scrambled to its feet, and ran off.

The puddle was deep, Merlin's shoes had disappeared into the mud, but he did not care. He turned to the stupefied delegates who were lined precariously along the timber walkway. Then he held up a bone some eight inches long and waved it in their faces.

"I know a thing or two, *messieurs*, and let me tell you something, this is not a chicken bone!"

Joseph Merlin might be a disheveled and disagreeable civil servant, but he was also diligent, scrupulous and, truth be told, an honest man.

He did not show it, but he found visiting these graveyards heart wrenching. This was the third he had inspected since being appointed to the post no one wanted. For a man who had known nothing about war beyond food rationing and memoranda from the Ministère des Colonies, the first visit had been devastating. His deep-rooted misanthropy, so long fully armored, had been shaken. Not by the scale of the slaughter, that was something he could understand, since the beginning of time, the earth had been ravaged by disasters and epidemics, war being merely the fusion of the two. No, what he had found devastating was the age of the dead. Disasters kill everyone, epidemics decimate the children and the elderly; only wars massacre young men in such number. Merlin had not expected to be upset by this fact. But a certain part of him was still back in the time when he had known Francine, and in this huge, hollow, lumbering frame there was still the sliver of the soul of a young man, a man the age of these dead boys.

Much less stupid than most of his colleagues, from his first visit to a military cemetery, being a scrupulous civil servant, he had noticed irregularities. He had seen countless dubious details in registers, hastily covered-up discrepancies, but what did he expect? When he considered the scale of the task, when he saw those poor Senegalese laborers, soaked to the skin, when he thought about the terrible carnage, calculated the number of bodies that now needed to be exhumed, transported . . . could he really afford to be pernickety, uncompromising? You turned a blind eye, and that was that. Such tragic circumstances required a certain pragmatism and Merlin considered it fair to pass over such irregularities in silence, let it be over, good God, let the war finally be over.

But here in Chazières-Malmont, a terrible foreboding gripped at your chest. Piecing together the clues: the planks from old coffins tossed into pits, where they were buried rather than burned; the disparity between the number of coffins shipped and the number of graves dug; the vague figures entered for certain days . . . All these things left you puzzled. They undermined your sense of what was and was not fair. So, when you see a stray mutt trotting happily along with the ulna of a soldier between its teeth, your heart lurches in your chest. You need to investigate.

Joseph Merlin did not catch his train; instead he spent the day checking figures, demanding explanations. Schneider was sweating as though this were high summer, Paul Chabord blew his nose, only Adjudant Tournier continued to click his heels whenever the ministerial envoy addressed him, the gesture was meaningless, but by now it was instinctive.

Everyone kept staring at Lucien Dupré, who, for his part, could see his meager prospects of a pay raise evaporating.

In dealing with the registers, the reports, the inventories, Merlin needed no help. Several times, he checked the stock of coffins, he visited the warehouses and even the graves.

Then he went back again to check the stock.

From a distance, they watched as he came and went, scratched his head, glanced around him as though looking for the solution to some mathematical problem; it grated on their nerves, this ominous behavior, this man who did not say a single word.

Then, finally, he said it, that single word.

"Dupré!"

Everyone sensed that the moment of truth was at hand. Dupré closed his eyes. Capitaine Pradelle had been very clear: "He can look over the work, do his inspection, make his comments, we don't give a shit, all right? But I need you to keep him away from the stock . . . I'm counting on you, all right, Dupré?"

And this Dupré had done: he had had the stock moved to the municipal warehouse; it had taken two days' work, but the ministerial envoy, though he might not look up to much, knew how to count. He counted and recounted, he pieced together the information; it did not take long.

"There are coffins missing here," Merlin said, "and a lot of coffins at that, so I'd like to know what the hell you've done with them."

All this because the fucking stray dog that sometimes came looking for food had decided to show up today. For weeks, they had been throwing stones at it; they should have killed the wretched animal. This was what you got for being humane.

By the end of the day, when the workers began to file out of the already silent, tense graveyard, Merlin came back from the municipal warehouse and said simply that he still had work to do, that he was happy to bunk down in the administration shed. Then he strode off toward the rows of graves with the determination of a shambling, stubborn old man.

Before he hurried to telephone Capitaine Pradelle, Dupré looked around one last time.

There, in the distance, register in hand, Merlin had just come to a halt in front of a mound of earth to the north of the cemetery. For the first time, he took off his jacket, snapped shut his record book, wrapped it in the jacket, set it on the ground and grabbed a shovel, which, under the weight of his big muddy shoe, sank up to the hilt into the ground.

25

Where had he gone? Had he friends who would take him in, friends he had never mentioned? How would he survive without his morphine? Would he know how to get it? Perhaps he had decided at last to go back to his family, the most reasonable solution . . . But there was nothing about Édouard that was reasonable . . . Albert wondered what he had been like before the war. What sort of man had he been? And why had Albert not asked M. Péricourt more questions at the deplorable dinner? He had had as much right as they to ask questions, to find out what his comrade-in-arms had been like before they met.

But most important, where had he gone?

This was what had been troubling Albert's thoughts from morning to night since Édouard left four days earlier. He went over memories of their time together, brooding like a maudlin old man.

It was not exactly that he missed Édouard. In fact, his departure had brought a sense of relief; suddenly he was free of the host of responsibilities imposed on him by his friend's presence, he could breathe easily, he felt liberated. But he was worried. It's not like he's a child, Albert thought, though given his dependence, his immaturity, his tantrums, the comparison was perhaps appropriate. Why had he been so obsessed with this idiotic idea of designing war memorials? Albert thought the idea morbid. That he had come up with the idea in the first place was understandable in a way; like everyone, Édouard had dreams of revenge. But it was baffling how he had stubbornly refused to listen to Albert's perfectly sensible arguments. That he could not distinguish between a dream and a plan. In the end, the boy was simply a dreamer; it was probably common among the rich, who don't think that reality applies to them.

Paris was gripped by a damp, bitter cold. Albert had asked for new sandwich boards—the ones he had were heavy and buckled from the rain—but to no avail.

Sandwich boards were picked up every morning near the métro station and exchanged for new ones at lunchtime. There were about a dozen sandwich men working in the *arrondissement*—mostly demobilized soldiers who had not been able to find a proper job—and an inspector who lurked around corners and, the minute you took off the board to massage your shoulders, would leap out and threaten to have you dismissed if you did not get back to work right away.

It was Tuesday, the day he traipsed up and down the boulevard Haussmann between La Fayette and Saint-Augustin (on one side: *Raviba—fabric dye to revive your stockings*; on the other: *Lip, Lip . . . Hooray—the wristwatch of victory*). The rain, which had eased during the night, had started again at ten o'clock. Albert had just arrived at the corner of the rue Pasquier. To stop, even to get his cap out of his pocket, was forbidden; he had to carry on.

"That's what this job is about: walking," the inspector would say, "You used to be a foot soldier, well, this is just the same. Now, march!"

But in the lashing, freezing rain Albert did not care, he glanced around swiftly, then, sheltering next to a building, he bent his knees, resting the weight of the boards on the ground and was just about to unbuckle the leather straps when the whole building seemed to crumble and fall on top of him.

A vicious blow snapped his head back, sending his body sprawling. The back of his skull slammed against the stone wall, the sandwich boards fell, the straps snarled around his throat, choking him. He gasped for breath, flailing like a drowning man, unable to move with the heavy boards on top of him; and every time he tried to push them off, the straps around his neck tightened.

Suddenly, the thought hit him: this was like the shell crater. Trapped, paralyzed, suffocating; this was how he was fated to die.

Panic stricken, he thrashed wildly, he wanted to scream, but no sound came, everything was moving fast, too fast, he felt someone grab his ankles and drag him from beneath the debris, the straps tightened, he clawed at them with his fingers, desperate to ease the pressure so he could breathe, he felt a heavy blow land on one of the wooden boards and reverberate through his skull, then suddenly the daylight reappeared, the straps were untangled, Albert greedily gulped lungfuls of air, too much air, he started to cough and almost vomited. He tried to shield himself—but from what?—tried to struggle. He looked like a blind cat being attacked. Eventually, he opened his eyes and he understood: the building that had collapsed on top of him took on a human form, a furious face that loomed over his, the eyes starting from their sockets.

"Bastard!" Antonopoulos was roaring.

His heavy face, his sagging jowls were flushed with rage and his eyes bored savagely into Albert as though to split his skull. Having stunned his target, the Greek turned around and sat down heavily on the splintered timber, his huge ass pressing the board against Albert's chest while he grabbed his hair. Now that he had straddled his prey, he lashed out with his free hand, punching Albert in the face.

The first blow split Albert's brow, the second gashed his lips, he tasted blood in his mouth, he could not move for the weight of the Greek who went on roaring abuse, punctuating each word with another clout. One, two, three, four, Albert held his breath, he heard screams and tried to turn when his head exploded from a vicious blow to the temple. He blacked out.

Noises, voices, a commotion all around him . . .

Passers-by had intervened and managed to push the Greek off and roll him onto his back—something that took three men—and eventually to free Albert and lay him on the pavement. Someone talked of calling the police, and the Greek bridled, he did not want the police involved, what he wanted—as was obvious from the way he continued to shake his fist and scream "Bastard!"—was to beat the life out of the unconscious man lying in a pool of blood. There were appeals for calm, the women backed away, staring in horror at the bleeding unconscious man. Two men, heroes of the pavement, managed to keep the Greek on his back, like a tortoise unable to right itself. Orders were shouted, no one knew who was doing what, already some had started to chatter. I heard there's a woman involved, can you believe it? Keep hold of him! Keep hold of him? That's rich coming from you, why don't you come over here and help me! The problem was the Greek exerted a lot of strength as he tried to turn over, he was a whale of a man, but too flabby to pose any real danger. For Christ's sake, someone said, I wish the police would get here!

"No, not police!" the Greek roared, waving his arms.

The mere mention of "police" gave him the rage and the strength of ten. With a flick of his arm, he knocked one of the good Samaritans onto his back. As one, the assembled ladies gave a shriek of excitement and took a step back. Knowing nothing about the reason for the quarrel, distant voices began to speculate: "A Turk?"—"Don't be ridiculous, he's speaking Romanian!"—"No, no, no," interrupted an educated man. "Romanian sounds similar to French, that's definitely Turkish."—"Aha!" the first man said triumphantly, "A Turk, just like I said!" at which point two police officers arrived—what's going on here, then?—an idiotic question since it was patently clear they were trying to stop one man from beating the other to death. Well, well, well, said the policemen, we'll see about that. In fact, no one saw anything, because events took an abrupt turn. The passers-by who had been restraining the Greek relaxed their grip when they saw the officers. This was all it took for him to roll onto his belly, struggle to his knees, and get to his feet by which time there was nothing to be done, he gathered speed like a freight train, anyone trying to stop him risked being crushed, but no one tried, least of all the police. The Greek rushed at Albert who, though barely conscious, must have sensed the danger since, just as Antonopoulos reached him, Albert—or rather his body, since his eyes were closed and his head nodding gently like a sleepwalker—Albert also rolled onto his belly, scrambled to his feet and took off, zigzagging down the pavement, with the Greek hot on his heels.

The assembled crowd was disappointed.

Just as the action was about to start, the protagonists were disappearing. They had been cheated out of an arrest, an interrogation, after all they had played their part, the least they deserved was to know how the story ended. Only the policemen were not disappointed; helplessly, stoically they held up their hands,—what can you do?—hoping that the two men would keep running for a little while longer, since, once they crossed the rue Pasquier, it would not be their beat.

In fact, the chase came to nothing. Albert wiped his face with his sleeve so that he could see properly, he ran like a man possessed, he was much faster than the heavyset Greek, and before long he had outdistanced him by two, three, then four streets, he turned right, then took the next left, and short of doubling back and running into Antonopoulos, he managed to get off with no more than a fright, if one did not count the two smashed teeth, the cut above his eye, the bruises, the aching ribs, the abject terror, etc.

It would not be long before this stumbling, bleeding man attracted the attention of the police again. Already, pedestrians stepped aside, staring at him in alarm. Albert, confident that he had put enough distance between himself and his attacker, and knowing that he must look a sight, stopped at a fountain on the rue Scribe and splashed water on his face. Only then did he start to feel the pain from his injuries. Especially the wound over his eye. He could not stop the bleeding, even with his sleeve pressed against the gash, the blood kept streaming everywhere.

A young woman in a hat and elegant outfit was sitting alone, clutching her handbag tightly. She turned away as soon as Albert stepped into the waiting room, but it was difficult not to be seen since they were alone and the only two chairs faced each other. The woman fidgeted, looked out of the window though there was nothing to be seen, coughed so that she could bring her hand up to her face, more anxious at the thought of being noticed than of looking at this man who was bleeding profusely—he was already covered in blood—and whose face clearly indicated he had taken a beating. Seconds ticked past before, from the back of the apartment, they heard footsteps, then a voice, and Docteur Martineau finally appeared.

The young woman quickly got to her feet up, then immediately stopped. Seeing the state Albert was in, the doctor beckoned to him. Albert walked down the hallway, the young woman returned to her chair and sat down without a word, as though she had been scolded.

The doctor asked no questions, he inspected the damage and pressed his fingertips here and there before gravely offering his diagnosis. "Someone's obviously given you a good hiding . . ." He staunched the bleeding gums with cotton balls, recommended that Albert see a dentist, and stitched the gash above his eye.

"Ten francs."

Albert turned out his pockets, got down on all fours to pick up the coins that had rolled under the chair, the doctor grabbed the money; there was less than ten francs, much less, he shrugged wearily and showed Albert out.

Albert felt panic overtake him. He clung to the handle of the front door, the world started to spin, his heart was hammering, he felt the urge to vomit, felt as though he was melting or sinking into quicksand. A terrifying wave of dizziness. He stood, wide eyed, clutching at his chest like a man in the throes of a heart attack. The concierge appeared from nowhere.

"You're not going to throw up on my clean doorstep, are you, boy?"

Albert could not answer. The concierge looked at the freshly stitched eyebrow, she nodded and rolled her eyes to heaven; men never could stand pain.

The panic attack was short lived. Brutal but brief. He had suffered similar episodes in November and December 1918, in the weeks after he was buried alive. Sometimes at night he would wake up to find himself covered by earth, dead, suffocated.

As he walked on, the street seemed to dance, everything seemed new minted, realer than real, more hazy, dancing, shimmering. He staggered toward the métro station, every sound, every bang made him start; twenty times he whipped around, expecting the looming figure of Antonopoulos to appear. What rotten luck. In a city like Paris you could go twenty years without running into an old friend; he had run slap bang into the Greek.

His teeth began to ache.

He stopped at a café for a calvados but remembered, just as he ordered, that he had given his last centime to Docteur Martineau. He left the bar, tried to catch the métro, but the enclosed atmosphere felt suffocating, a new wave of panic rushed over him; he went back up to the street and set off walking. He arrived home exhausted and spent the rest of the day trembling with fear as he went over every detail of what had happened.

There were moments when he felt a terrible rage. He should have killed that fucking Greek bastard the first time! Most of the time he considered his life an unspeakable disaster, the sheer wretchedness was heart scalding, and he knew he might never escape it, something in his will to fight had been destroyed.

He looked at himself in the mirror, his face had swelled to impressive proportions, the bruises were turning blue, he looked like a convict. Once upon a time his friend had gazed into a mirror and contemplated his ruin. Albert calmly smashed the mirror on the floor, picked up the broken shards, and threw them into the trash.

The following day, he did not eat. He spent all afternoon going around and around the living room like a fairground pony. Every time he thought back to what had happened, he was gripped by fear. And by foolish notions: the Greek had found him, he could make inquiries, talk to Albert's employer, track him to his apartment, demand his money, kill him. Albert rushed to the window, but he could see only a street where at any moment Poulos *might* appear, only the owner's house, where, as always, Mme Belmont was at her window, staring into space, lost in her memories.

The future seemed black. No work, the Greek on his tail, he had to move, to find a new job. As though that would be easy.

Then he would reassure himself. It was ridiculous to think the Greek would come looking for him here, it was a fantasy. How would he even do it? He was hardly likely to rally his family and all his drug-dealing friends to track down a carton of morphine ampoules, the contents of which had long since been used. It was preposterous.

But if Albert's mind was capable of such thoughts, his body did not share them. He could not stop trembling, his fear was irrational and impervious to argument. The hours passed, night began to draw in and with it specters and terrors. Magnified by the darkness, his fears destroyed what little lucidity he could muster, and panic once more took hold.

Alone, Albert wept. There is a history to be written of the tears in Albert's life. These shifted from grief to dread according to whether he contemplated his present life or his future. He had cold sweats, bursts of depression, palpitations, black thoughts, a feeling of suffocation, of vertigo; never again, he thought, never again would he leave this apartment, and yet he could not stay here. He sobbed harder. Escape. The word rumbled suddenly in his mind. Escape. In the darkness, this notion swelled until it eclipsed all other thoughts. He could no longer imagine a future here, not simply in this room, but in this city, this country.

He ran to the dresser, took out the photographs and the postcards of the colonies. Start again from scratch. In the next flash, he saw Édouard. Albert rushed to the wardrobe and took out the horse's head mask. Carefully, as though handling a precious antique, he slipped it on. And immediately he felt safe, protected. He wanted to see himself; he rummaged in the trash for a shard of mirror large enough, but it was impossible. He looked for his reflection in the window, and seeing himself as a horse, his fears subsided, a gentle warmth washed over him, his muscles relaxed. As he adjusted the mask, he looked down into the courtyard at Mme Belmont's window. She was not there. He could see only a dim glow from some distant room in the house.

And suddenly everything was clear, it was obvious.

Albert took a deep breath before removing the mask. He felt an unpleasant coldness. In the way that a stove stores up heat and remains warm long after the fire has burned out, Albert had sufficient reserves of strength to open the door, his mask tucked under his arm, slowly go down the stairs, lift the tarpaulin, and see that the shoebox containing the ampoules was gone.

He crossed the courtyard, took a few steps out onto the pavement. It was pitch black, now; he hugged his horse head mask to him and rang the doorbell.

It was some time before Mme Belmont answered. When she recognized Albert, she did not say a word, but opened the door; Albert followed her down the hall to a room with its shutters closed. In a child's crib, too small for her, Louise was sound asleep, her legs drawn up. Albert bent over her. In sleep, the child was astonishingly beautiful. On the floor next to her, covered by a white sheet made ivory in the half-light, lay Édouard, his eyes open, staring up at Albert. Next to him, the box of morphine ampoules. With an expert eye, Albert immediately noticed that the stock had not been much depleted.

He smiled to free himself, slipped on the horse head mask and offered him his hand.

Toward midnight, Édouard was sitting by the window with Albert next to him, thoughtfully cradling the sketches for memorials in his lap. He had seen the state of his friend's face. A savage beating.

"Okay, try explaining it to me again, this thing with the memorials," Albert said. "How do you see it working?"

While Édouard wrote on a new conversation pad, Albert leafed through the designs. They studied the question. Most of the problems with the scheme were solvable. There was no need to set up a ghost company, only a bank account. No offices, just a post office box. The idea was to offer an attractive promotion for a limited time, to collect all the advance payments on the orders . . . and take off with the money.

There was, perhaps, one problem, but it was a big one: to set the scheme in motion, they needed money.

Édouard could not understand why this question of funds, which only recently had left Albert furious, was now seen as merely a minor obstacle. It obviously had something to do with his physical state, the bruises, the gash above his eye, the black eye . . .

Édouard thought back to Albert's "assignation" a few days earlier, his disappointment when he had come home; he had presumed there was a woman involved, a thwarted love affair. Perhaps Albert was making this decision in a fit of pique, he thought. Might he not change his mind tomorrow or the next day? But Édouard had little choice if he wanted to launch his scheme (and God knows he wanted it badly); he had to assume that his friend had come to a considered decision. And keep his fingers crossed.

All through their conversation, Albert seemed normal, rational, everything he said seemed sensible, but in midsentence he would suddenly be trembling from head to foot and begin to sweat despite the bitter cold. At such moments, he was like two distinct men: the ex-soldier, buried alive, quivering like a rabbit, and the former bank clerk, thinking, calculating.

So how were they to come up with the money to run this scheme?

Albert stared at the horse head mask, which calmly gazed back at him. It was encouraging, that gentle, placid gaze.

He got to his feet.

"I think I can find the money . . . ," he said.

He walked over to the table and slowly cleared away the clutter.

He sat down with a sheet of paper, an inkwell, and a nib, thought for a long time, then, having inscribed his name and address in the top right corner, he wrote:

Monsieur,

You were kind enough, when I came to visit you, to offer me a job as an accountant with one of your businesses.

If that offer still holds, you should know that . . .

MARCH
1920

26

Henri d'Aulnay-Pradelle, whose mind dealt only in black and white, acknowledging no shades of gray, often got the better of his interlocutors because his bluntness discouraged reasoned argument. For example, he could not but assume that Léon Jardin-Beaulieu, who was shorter than he, was also less intelligent. This was plainly absurd, but since Léon had a complex about his height that made him awkward, Pradelle invariably won the argument. In his sense of superiority, there was the matter of height, but there were two other factors named Yvonne and Denise, respectively Léon's sister and his wife, both Henri's mistresses. The former for more than a year, the latter since two days before her wedding. Henri would have found it even more piquant to have taken her on the eve of the ceremony, or better yet the morning it took place, but circumstances had not been propitious and two days before was still a fine result. Since that day, he would often say to intimate acquaintances, "In the Jardin-Beaulieu family, I am missing only the mother." The joke was particularly appreciated because Mme Jardin-Beaulieu was not one to excite the passions and was a woman of great modesty. Henri, with his customary boorishness, never failed to add that "she had much to be modest about."

In Ferdinand Morieux, a perfect fool, and Léon Jardin-Beaulieu, paralyzed by his inhibitions, Henri had recruited two business associates for whom he had nothing but contempt. Until now, he had had complete freedom to conduct his business in his own inimitable style—impetuous and expeditious, as we have seen—while his "associates" were content to collect their dividends. Henri did not keep them informed about anything; this was "his" business. Many obstacles had been overcome without his having to explain himself; he was not about to begin now.

"The problem is . . . ," said Léon Jardin-Beaulieu, "this time it is rather embarrassing."

Henri looked the man up and down. In their discussions, he always arranged matters so that he was standing, forcing Léon to tilt his head back as though staring at the ceiling.

Léon blinked rapidly. He had important things to say, but he was frightened of this man. And he despised him. It had grieved him to find that his sister was sleeping with Henri, but he had smiled wryly as though he had been complicit, perhaps even the instigator. When he heard the first rumors about Denise, his wife, it was a very different matter. He felt so humiliated he wanted to die. He had been able to marry a beautiful woman because of his fortune; he labored under no illusions as to her fidelity, present or future, but that confirmation had come from Aulnay-Pradelle was particularly painful. Denise herself had always treated Léon with disdain. She resented the fact that he had got what he wanted because he had the means. From the beginning of their marriage she had been condescending, and he could find nothing to oppose her decision to sleep in a separate room and lock her door every night. He did not marry me, she thought; he purchased me. She was not cruel by nature, but one must understand that this was a period when women were denigrated.

As for Léon, having to keep company with Henri because of their business affairs left his pride wounded. As though his calamitous conjugal relations were not bad enough! He bore Pradelle such a bitter grudge that, if their vast contracts with the government ended in disaster, he would not lift a finger—the financial losses involved would not bankrupt him—indeed, he would take great pleasure in watching his "associate" go under. But this was not simply about money. There was his reputation to consider. And the rumors he had heard here and there were very worrying. Abandoning Aulnay-Pradelle might mean being dragged down with him, and of that there could be no question. All this was talked about in veiled terms, no one really knew the details, but if there was mention of the law, then there must have been offense . . . Crimes! Léon knew a former classmate from his university days who, being obliged to work, had a senior position at the *préfecture*.

"My dear fellow," he had said in a concerned tone, "this whole affair stinks to high heaven . . ."

What exactly did it involve? Léon could not find out; even his friend at the Préfecture seemed not to know. Or worse, he did not want to talk about it. Léon imagined being summoned to a tribunal. A Jardin-Beaulieu in court! He was shaken at the very thought. Especially since he had done nothing wrong. But try proving that . . .

"Embarrassing." Henri calmly repeated the word. "And what exactly is so embarrassing?"

"Well, I don't know exactly . . . you tell me!"

Henri screwed up his mouth, I've no idea what you're talking about.

"There is talk of a report . . . ," Léon went on.

"Ah!," Henri said, "so that's what you meant? No, that's nothing, it has all been dealt with! A simple misunderstanding."

Léon was not to be fobbed off so easily.

"From what I know . . ."

"What?" Pradelle shouted. "What exactly do you know, huh? What *do* you know?"

Without warning, he had switched from apparent affability to venomous rage. It was something Léon had noticed often in recent weeks; he had agonized over the fact that Pradelle seemed permanently exhausted and could not help but wonder whether Denise had something to do with it. But Henri was clearly worried, because an exhausted lover is a happy lover, whereas Henri was tense, he was more brusque and belligerent than usual. Hence this sudden bilious outburst . . .

"If the problem has been dealt with, as you say," Léon ventured, "then why are you so angry?"

"Because, my dear little Léon, I am sick and tired of having to explain myself when I'm the one doing all the work. Because you and Ferdinand collect your dividends, but who does the organizing, who gives the orders, oversees the projects, handles the accounts . . . ? You? Ha! ha!"

The laugh was deliberately offensive, but remembering the consequences, Léon carried on as though he had not heard.

"I would be only too happy to help you. You're the one who is against the idea. You always say you don't need anyone."

Henri took a deep breath. What could he say? Ferdinand Morieux was a cretin and Léon an incompetent. In fact, aside from his name, his connections, his money, all things that were unrelated to him personally, after all, what was Léon? A cuckold, nothing more. Henri had left his wife's bed only two hours ago . . . It had been rather tiresome, in fact. He always had to pry her arms off him when he wanted to leave; it was an unending melodrama . . . Henri had had just about enough of this family.

"This is much too complicated for you, little Léon. Complicated, but not serious, so don't worry."

He was trying to sound reassuring, but his manner was anything but.

"Even so," Léon said, "at the Préfecture, I heard that . . ."

"What did you hear? What are they saying at the Préfecture?"

"That there have been worrying developments."

Léon was determined to find out what was going on, because this was not about his wife's frivolous affair or the prospect of his shares in Pradelle's business being worthless. He was terrified of being swept into a maelstrom that was all the more fearsome since politics was involved.

"These cemeteries are a very delicate matter . . ."

"Really? Well, well, 'a very delicate matter'!"

"Just so," Léon said, "a sensitive issue, in fact. The slightest blunder and it would cause a terrible scandal. With the new Chambre des Députés . . ."

Ah, the new government! In the parliamentary elections the previous November—the first since the armistice—the Bloc National[10] coalition had won a crushing majority made up almost entirely of war veterans. So patriotic, so nationalist, this coalition had been dubbed the "Blue Horizon Chamber" after the color of the French army uniform.

Though Léon might have his "nose glued to the road," as Henri liked to say, this point struck home.

It was the landslide majority that had allowed Henri to secure the lion's share of the government contracts and to get rich at lightning speed—more than a third of la Sallevière had been renovated in the space of four months; some days there were forty workmen on site . . . But the *députés* were also his biggest threat. A government of heroes tended to be fastidious on any subject that concerned their "dear departed." There would be much high-sounding rhetoric. The Chambre had been inept in paying demobilized soldiers their *pécule* or finding work for them, but they would be only too quick now to wallow in sanctimony.

This is what Henri had been led to understand at the Ministère des Pensions, where his presence had been requested. Not summoned, "requested."

"So, tell us, dear boy, is everything going as you might wish?"

Since he was the son-in-law of M. Péricourt, they handled him with kid gloves. Since his business associates included the son of a *général* and the son of a *député*, they used tweezers.

"This report by *préfet* . . . what was it? . . ."

A pretense of struggling to remember, and then, like a burst of laughter:

"Préfet Plerzec, ah yes, that's it. It's nothing, a trifling matter. You get these overzealous civil servants now and then, it was bound to happen. And in fact, the matter has been closed. The *préfet* all but apologized, if you can imagine that, my boy. It's ancient history now."

Then dropping to a confiding tone. Better yet, a shared secret:

"Though you might want to be a little more careful because a little pen pusher from the ministry is inspecting. He's a nitpicker, an obsessive."

No way of finding out anything more. "Be a little more careful."

Dupré had been blunt in his description of Merlin: a shit stirrer. A man of the old school. Filthy, apparently, quick to take offense. Pradelle found it difficult to imagine what he looked like, but assuredly like no one he had ever met. A third-rate bureaucrat with no career, no future—they were always the worst, always eager to avenge themselves. Ordinarily they have little say in matters; no one listens to them, they are scorned even within their own bureaucracies.

"That's true," he had been told at the ministry, "but that does not change the fact that . . . well, they can sometimes be somewhat of a nuisance . . ."

The silence that followed stretched out like an elastic about to snap.

"For the moment, my dear fellow, the best you can do is work quickly and work well. 'Quickly,' because the country needs to move on to other things and 'well' because the present Chambre is very touchy about anything to do with our Fallen Heroes, you understand."

A shot across his bows.

Henri had simply smiled and affected a knowing air, but he immediately summoned all his foremen, chief among them Dupré, to a meeting in Paris, where he threatened everyone, laid down strict instructions, issued warnings, promised bonuses . . . eventually. But there was no way to check the work being done: his company had to deal with more than fifteen temporary rural graveyards in the preliminary stage and seven, soon to be eight, huge war graves in the later stages.

Pradelle studied Léon. Looking down at him, he was suddenly reminded of Soldat Maillard, of looking down on him in the shell crater and seeing him in the very same position some months later, fumbling in the grave of some nameless soldier in order to please Madeleine.

That time, so distant now, seemed to him to have been marked by blessings from heaven: Général Morieux had sent him Madeleine Péricourt! A blessed miracle. Their meeting had been an incredible chance, the beginning of his success; knowing when to seize an opportunity, that was what mattered.

Henri crushed Léon beneath the weight of his stare. He looked so like Soldat Maillard sinking into the ground, he was just the type to get himself buried alive.

For the moment, however, he might still be useful. Henri laid a hand on his shoulder.

"There's no problem, Léon. And if there were, well, your father could have a quiet word with the minister . . ."

"B . . . but . . . ," Léon spluttered, "that's impossible! You know very well that my father was elected to parliament as a member of Action Libérale,[11] and the minister is Fédération Républicaine!"[12]

My God, thought Henri, other than lending me his wife, this idiot has been completely useless to me.

27

Four days he had been waiting with mingled apprehension and impatience, but finally his client, M. de Housseray, had come.

When you have never stolen more than a few francs here and there, going up to hundreds and then thousands in the space of two weeks can be nerve racking. This was the third time that Albert had defrauded his employer and his client in a month; he had hardly slept during that month and had shed eleven pounds. M. Péricourt, having run into Albert in the foyer of the bank two days earlier, had asked whether he was ill and suggested he take a few days off, despite the fact he had only just started working at the bank. Not exactly the sort of thing that endears you to colleagues and superiors. It was bad enough that he had been hired on the personal recommendation of M. Péricourt . . . Besides, there could be no question of his taking time off, Albert was here to work, which meant to dip into the till. And he had no time to waste.

At the Banque d'Escompte et de Crédit Industriel, Albert had a wide choice when it came to deciding who to fleece. He opted for the oldest and most reliable banking technique: if the face fits.

M. de Housseray had a face that fitted. With his top hat, his embossed visiting cards and his gold-handled walking stick, he exuded the delightful odor of war profiteer. Albert, worried as always, had naively thought he could make things easier by settling on a man he could revile. This sort of reasoning is typical of the rank amateur. In his defense, he had good reason to be worried. He was defrauding the bank in order to finance a subscription scam; in other words, he was stealing money in order to steal more money—it was enough to confuse any novice swindler.

First theft, five days after being hired, seven thousand francs.

A simple dummy entry.

You take a deposit of forty thousand francs, you credit it to his account. In the takings column, you register only thirty-three thousand francs, and that night you take the streetcar with a briefcase stuffed with bills. The advantage of working with a major bank is that no one would notice before the weekly audit which—since it involved stock portfolios, interest calculations, liquidations, loans, repayments, offsets, current account deposits, etc.—took almost three days. This time lag was crucial. You waited until the end of the first day of the inspection, debit the sum from an account that had just been audited and credit it to the defrauded account, due to be checked the following day. To the auditors, both accounts appear to be accurate. Then you repeat the operation the following week tapping a different account from a different sector: operating expenses, credit lines, investments, interest, shares, etc. It is a classic swindle known as the "Bridge of Sighs," simple to execute, hard on the nerves, and requiring considerable skill but little malice—perfect for a guy like Albert. The only serious problem is that it triggers an endless escalation, which, as the weeks pass, forces the swindler into an infernal race with the auditors. There are no records of the scheme being run for more than a few months before the perpetrator fled the country or ended up in prison, the latter being by far the more likely outcome.

Like many opportunistic thieves, Albert had convinced himself that it was only a loan: he would use the first money they received for the war memorials to pay off the bank before they scarpered. This naïive notion made it possible for him to put his plan into action, but it quickly faded when he was faced with other pressing concerns.

From the very first misappropriation, feelings of guilt rushed in to fill the gap opened up by chronic anxiety and emotion. His paranoia soon turned to pantophobia. Throughout the whole period Albert suffered an almost convulsive uneasiness, quaking at the slightest question, hugging the walls, his palms sweating so much he was constantly wiping his hands, making office work somewhat tricky; he was always on the lookout, always glancing at the door, even the position of his legs beneath the desk exposed a man ready to flee.

His coworkers found him bizarre; they thought him inoffensive—he seemed ill rather than dangerous. All the ex-soldiers they had hired showed pathological symptoms of some kind, so they were accustomed to such things. Besides, Albert had influential connections, so it was best to smile and carry on.

From the beginning, Albert had told Édouard that seven thousand francs would not be enough. There was the catalog to print, envelopes and stamps to buy, staff to pay for addressing the envelopes; they also needed a typewriter so they could respond to those asking for additional information; they would have to open a post office box—seven thousand francs was a derisory sum, Albert had said, I'm telling you as an accountant. Édouard had waved him off, maybe, we'll see. Albert recalculated. Twenty thousand francs minimum, he was sure. Édouard had been philosophical—let's go for twenty thousand then . . . You can tell he's not the one doing the stealing, Albert thought.

Having never admitted to his friend that he had been to dinner at his father's house, that he had sat opposite his sister, or that Madeleine had married that bastard Pradelle, the cause of all their problems, it was impossible for him to explain that he had accepted a job as a clerk in a bank whose founder and principal shareholder was M. Péricourt. Though he was no longer a sandwich man, Albert still felt caught in a vise between Péricourt *père*, the benefactor he was planning to defraud and Péricourt fils, with whom he would share the spoils of this embezzlement. To Édouard, he pretended it had been an extraordinary stroke of luck, running into an old colleague by chance, a vacancy at a bank, an interview that had gone better than expected . . . Édouard, for his part, accepted this suspicious, well-timed miracle without question. He had been born rich.

In fact, Albert would happily have kept this job at the bank. On his first day, when he was shown to his desk, saw the carefully filled ink-wells, the sharpened pencils, the neat columns of figures, the polished wooden hat stand with a hook of his own on which to hang his hat and coat, the pristine black oversleeves, it made him long for a peaceful existence. With a position as a bank clerk, he could have a comfortable life. Exactly the life he had imagined behind the lines. If he stayed on in this job, he might even try his luck with the Péricourts' pretty housemaid . . . Yes, a nice little life. Instead of which, this evening, feverish and queasy, Albert caught the métro with a briefcase containing five thousand francs in large denominations. The weather was still chilly; he was the only passenger sweating.

Albert had good reason to get home quickly: the one-armed ex-soldier with the handcart was supposed to collect the catalogs from the printers.

As soon as he stepped into the courtyard, he saw the bundles tied with string . . . They had arrived. This was disconcerting. The time had finally come. So far, everything had been preparation; now the real work would begin.

Feeling dizzy, Albert closed his eyes, opened them again, set down his briefcase, ran a hand over one of the packages, untied the string.

The "Patriotic Memory" catalog.

Anyone would have sworn it was real.

And it *was* real, printed by Rondot Frères, rue des Abbesses, as serious a printer as you could wish for. Ten thousand copies. Printing cost of eight thousand two hundred francs. He was about to pick up the top copy of the catalog and thumb through it, but his hand froze in midair at the sound of a horse-like whinny. Édouard's laugh, heard from the foot of the stairs. A high-pitched laugh trilling with vibrato, one of those laughs that hang in the air long after they fade. It sounded like a wild laugh, like that of a woman going mad. Albert grabbed his briefcase and rushed upstairs. Pushing open the door, he was greeted by a thunderous screech, a sort of *rrââhhhrr* expressing Édouard's impatience and relief that he was finally home.

The cry was no stranger than the atmosphere itself. Édouard, this evening, was wearing a mask in the shape of a bird's head with a long downward-curving beak, parted to reveal two unexpected rows of dazzling white teeth. This leering, carnivorous bird, painted in tones of red, had a savage, hostile look. The mask covered Édouard's forehead, leaving two holes for his swift, smiling eyes.

Albert, who had been feeling a somewhat confused delight at the prospect of showing off his wads of bills, had been upstaged by Édouard and Louise. The floor of the apartment was completely covered with pages from the catalog. Édouard was lying in a lascivious pose, his bare feet propped on one of the bundles while Louise, kneeling beside him, was painstakingly painting his toenails a vivid carmine. Engrossed in her task, she barely looked up to acknowledge Albert. Édouard began to laugh again, his booming, joyous *rrââhhhrr*, and gestured to the floor with a flourish, like a conjurer after a particularly impressive trick.

Albert could not help but smile; he set down his briefcase, took off his coat and hat. Here in their apartment was the only place he felt safe, where he found a little peace . . . Except at night. His restless nights were troubled, and would be for some time to come; he had to sleep with the horse head mask next to him in case of panic.

Édouard looked at him, one hand on the bundle of catalogs next to him, the other clenched in a victorious salute. Louise, who had said nothing, was now buffing the polish on his toenails with a chamois, so intent it seemed her life depended on it.

Albert sat next to Édouard and picked up a catalog. It was a slim brochure, sixteen pages, printed on lovely ivory paper, almost twice as tall as it was wide, the elegant text set in an elegant modern typeface of varying sizes. The cover read simply:

Catalog
The fine arts foundry

Patriotic Memory
Steles, memorials, & statues
To the glory of our Heroes
and of France Victorious

It opened onto a beautifully calligraphed page

Jules D'Épremont ✵✠
sculptor
Membre de l'institut

52 rue du Louvre
Boîte postale 52
Paris (Seine)

"Who exactly is Jules d'Épremont?" Albert had asked when the catalog was being designed.

Édouard had rolled his eyes, no idea. But he sounded distinguished: *Croix de Guerre, Palmes académiques,* address on the rue du Louvre.

"The thing is . . . ," Albert said, worried by the existence of this character, "it won't take long for people to realize he doesn't exist. 'Membre de l'Institut'—anyone can easily check with the Académie des Beaux-Arts!"

"But that's precisely why they won't check," Édouard scribbled. "It wouldn't occur to them to question a Membre de l'Institut."

Though still skeptical, Albert had to admit that, seeing the words in print, he felt no urge to question them.

There was a brief biographical note at the back of the catalog outlining his career as an *academic* sculptor, which was designed to reassure those unsettled by the notion of an artist.

The address, 52 rue du Louvre, was simply the post office where they had rented a P.O. box; by sheer chance, they had been assigned box number 52, so the overall effect was one of calm consideration rather than quirk of fate.

A line of small type at the bottom of the front cover read simply:

PRICE INCLUDES DELIVERY BY RAIL
WITHIN METROPOLITAN FRANCE.
ENGRAVED INSCRIPTIONS ARE
NOT INCLUDED IN THE PRICE.

The first page outlined the scheme:

Monsieur le Maire,

More than a year has passed since the end of the War, and towns and communities throughout France and the Colonies are rightly giving thought to honoring the memory of their children who fell on the field of battle.

If many of them have not yet done so, it is for want of means, not want of patriotism. This is why I believed it my duty, as an Artist and a War Veteran, to volunteer in such a noble cause. I have accordingly decided to put my talent and my experience at the service of those communities who wish to create a memorial by founding Patriotic Memory.

In the present, I humbly propose a series of figures and allegories created to perpetuate the memory of your dear departed.

On November 11 next in Paris, a tomb will be unveiled of the "Unknown Soldier," intended to represent the sacrifice of all. Such an exceptional event calls for exceptional measures: in order that you may add your own initiative to this great national commemoration, I am offering a concession of 32% on a range of works especially conceived for this momentous occasion, together with free delivery to the railway station closest to your town.

In order to take account of the time required for creation and transportation, and to ensure the highest quality of craftsmanship, I can only accept those orders that reach me before July 14, which orders will be delivered, at latest, by October 27, 1920, leaving ample time for the memorial to be raised on a preexisting pedestal. In the event that, on July 14, demand exceeds our capacity for production, which is sadly all too likely, we will be able to honor only a limited number of orders strictly according to date received.

I fondly hope that this **never to be repeated** *offer will afford your patriotism the opportunity to honor your Glorious Dead, so that their heroism may forever be seen by their sons and daughters as the exemplar of all sacrifice.*

I remain, Monsieur le Maire, yours faithfully,

JULES D'ÉPREMONT
Sculptor ✵✠
Membre de l'Institut
Alumnus of the École Nationale des Beaux-Arts

"This discount . . . why 32 percent?" Albert said.

Ever the accountant.

"To give the impression that it has been painstakingly calculated," Édouard wrote, "It's an incentive! This way, all the money will arrive by July 14. The next day we do a bunk."

On the following page, elegantly framed, was a brief clarification.

All of our designs can be supplied
in chased and patinated bronze or
in chased, bronzed cast iron.
These noble raw materials impart a classic,
sophisticated character to the memorials,
one that perfectly epitomizes
the incomparable French soldier
or any of the other motifs
extolling the courage of our fallen heroes.

The workmanship is guaranteed of impeccable quality
and will last indefinitely subject to routine
maintenance every five or six years.

Only the plinth,
easily fashioned by a reputable stonemason,
remains at the expense of the buyer.

The catalog of designs followed, seen in front elevation, in profile or in perspective, with details in the margins of the dimensions and the various possible heights and widths: "The Leavetaking," "Charge!," "The Dead Arise," "A *Poilu* Dies in Defense of the Flag," "Brothers in Arms," "France Mourns Her Heroes," "Le Coq Gaulois Trampling a Boche Helmet," "Victory!," etc.

Aside from three pinchbeck pieces for those with very limited budgets (*Croix de Guerre*, 930 francs, "Funerary Torch," 840 francs, and "Bust of a *Poilu*," 1,500 francs), the memorials ranged in price from 6,000 to 33,000 francs.

At the end of the catalog, there was a further explanation.

Patriotic Memory is unable to accept inquiries by telephone, however
all written inquires will receive a prompt and timely response.
In view of the significant discount offered, all orders
should be accompanied by a down payment in the amount
of 50% of the total, payable to *Patriotic Memory*.

Allowing for the discount of32 percent, each order should, in theory, bring in between 3,000 and 11,000 francs. In theory. Unlike Albert, Édouard had no doubts about the matter and was slapping his thighs in glee. The jubilation of the one was proportionate to the apprehension of the other.

With his injured leg, Édouard had not been able to carry the bundles of catalog upstairs. Assuming the thought had even occurred to him . . . This was the result of his upbringing, he had always had someone to fetch and carry for him. In this regard, the war had merely been a brief parenthesis. He gave an apologetic wave, his eyes twinkling, as though he could not be of help because of his nails, fluttering his hands as if to say, the polish . . . it's not dry . . .

"Fine," Albert said, "I'll deal with it."

He was not really angry, manual work and menial tasks gave him time to think. He made a series of trips up and down the stairs, conscientiously stacking the bundles at the far end of the room.

Two weeks earlier, he had inserted a newspaper advertisement looking for staff. There were ten thousand envelopes to be addressed, all following the same formula:

Hôtel de Ville
name of town
name of département

They had drawn up the list using the *Dictionnaire des communes*, careful to exclude Paris and the immediately surrounding areas as being too close to the notional headquarters of the company. Better to target middling sized towns in the provinces. They offered fifteen centimes per address. With so much unemployment, it had not been difficult to recruit five people with elegant handwriting. Five women—Albert had thought this best, he felt they were less likely to ask questions. Or perhaps he was looking for an opportunity to meet women. They believed they were working for a master printer. Everything had to be done within ten days. A week earlier, he had visited them to deliver blank envelopes, ink, and nibpens and the very next day, having finished his shift at the bank, he set about collecting them; he had dug out his duffel bag from the war—it had seen some things, that bag.

They would spend the evenings stuffing envelopes; Louise would help. The little girl had no idea what was going on but was eager to help. She was delighted by this new venture because it made her friend Édouard happy, that was clear from the increasingly colorful and outrageous masks, in a month or two they would be living in a fantasy world, Louise was enchanted

Albert had noticed that she looked less and less like her mother, not physically—Albert had a poor eye for faces, he scarcely noticed whether people looked alike—but the sadness etched into Mme Belmont's face as she gazed out of her window was no longer mirrored in Louise's. She was like an insect emerging from a chrysalis, growing prettier and prettier. Albert would sometimes secretly watch her, there was a grace about her that almost moved him to tears. Mme Maillard had always said, "If you left him to his own devices, Albert would spend his whole life crying; I might as well have had a daughter for all the difference it makes."

Albert took the envelopes to the post office on the rue du Louvre to ensure the frank mark corresponded to their official address. It required a number of trips over several days.

Then the wait began.

Albert was eager for the first payments to arrive. He sounded almost prepared to grab the first few hundred francs and abscond. Édouard had a rather different opinion on the matter. As far as he was concerned, there would be no absconding before they had a million.

"A million?" Albert had shrieked, "You're completely insane!"

They began to argue over what constituted a sufficient profit, as though neither now doubted that the plan would succeed—something that was far from certain. Édouard believed success was guaranteed. Inevitable, he had written in big letters. Albert, having taken on a cripple outlawed from society, stolen twelve thousand francs from his employer, and set up a scheme that could warrant him a death sentence or life in prison, had no choice but to pretend he believed in success. He was already preparing to leave, he spent whole evenings poring over timetables for trains to Le Havre, Bordeaux, Nantes, or Marseille, depending on whether he was planning to take a boat to Tunis, Algiers, Saigon, or Casablanca.

Édouard carried on working.

Having created the Patriotic Memory catalog, he had been wondering what a real Jules d'Épremont would do while waiting for responses to his commercial proposition.

The answer had come to him out of the blue: he would submit bids.

Several large towns with the financial means to avoid buying mass-produced monuments were inviting bids from artists for original memorials. The newspapers had published several such invitations for works with budgets ranging from eighty to a hundred and even a hundred and fifty thousand francs, but the juiciest and, to Édouard, the most tempting proposition was from the very *arrondissement* where he had been born, which was offering the winning artist a budget of some two hundred thousand francs. So he had decided to kill time by working on the proposal that Jules d'Épremont would send to the selection committee, a large triptych entitled *Gratitude*: on one side, "France Leading Her Troops to War," on the other "Valliant Soldiers Attacking the Enemy," these scenes flanking a central panel depicting "Victory Crowning the Children Who Died for their Country," a vast allegorical frieze in which a woman in long, flowing robes stretched out her right hand to crown a triumphant poilu while looking upon a lifeless soldier with the tragic, inconsolable gaze of a *mater dolorosa*.

As he put the finishing touches on the principal design, paying particular attention to the perspective since it would form the cover of his application, Édouard chuckled.

"A turkey!" Albert laughed as he watched his friend work, "I swear, you cluck like a turkey."

Édouard laughed all the more and bent eagerly over his sketch.

28

Général Morieux looked two hundred years older. Take from a military man the war that gives him a reason to live and the vigor of a man half his age and you are left with an aging fossil. Physically, all that remained was a paunch and a pair of whiskers, a flabby, unfeeling mass that slept most of the time. The only problem was, he snored. He would flop into the nearest armchair with a sigh that sounded like a death rattle and five minute later his belly was rising and falling like a Graf Zeppelin, his mustache quivering when he inhaled, his jowls shuddering when he exhaled; it could go on for hours. There was something primordial, something daunting, about this listless magma of flesh, and indeed no one dared to wake him. Some were reluctant even to come near.

Since his demobilization, he had been appointed to countless commissions, subcommittees, committees. He was always first to arrive, panting and perspiring if the meeting was being held upstairs, then he would slump in a chair, responding to greetings with a churlish grunt or a nod, then doze off and begin to snort. Someone would shake him gently when it came time to vote, what do you think, *général*, m'yess, yes, of course, of course, I agree, rheumy eyes watering, of course, of course, face flushed scarlet, lips trembling, eyes wild, just getting him to sign something was an ordeal. Attempts were made to get rid of him, but the minister insisted on keeping Général Morieux. Sometimes the irritating, ineffectual old fogey had inadvertent flashes of insight. One such time occurred when he heard—it was early April and the *général* was suffering from hay fever, something that provoked stentorian sneezes, he even managed to sneeze while asleep, like a dormant volcano—when he heard, between two snores, that his grandson Ferdinand Morieux had run into some worrying problems. Général Morieux had no respect for anyone below his rank. Although he considered his grandson, who had failed to pursue a glorious career in the army, an inferior, depraved creature, the young man still bore the name Morieux, something about which the *général* cared, being greatly concerned with posterity. His fondest wish? His photograph in the *Petit Larousse illustré,* a dream that would not survive the slightest blot upon the family name.

"What? What? What?" He roused himself with a start.

It had to repeated loudly so he could hear. Something to do with Pradelle & Cie, a company in which Ferdinand was a shareholder. I'm sure you remember, they explained, the company the government entrusted with transporting the bodies of dead soldiers to the new war graves.

"What are you . . . ? Bodies? Dead soldiers?"

He tried desperately to focus his attention on this information for the sake of Ferdinand; with some difficulty his brain managed to create a mental map of the problem into which he slotted the words *Ferdinand, dead soldiers, corpses, graves, anomalies, affair*; for him, this was a considerable effort. In peacetime, he struggled to understand things. His aide-de-camp, a second lieutenant as frisky as a thoroughbred, looked at him and sighed like an irritated and impatient nurse. Then he took it upon himself to explain. Your grandson Ferdinand is a shareholder in Pradelle & Cie. Granted, all he does is collect his dividends, but if the company were to be caught up in a scandal, your name would be mentioned, your grandson would be vulnerable, your name would be tarnished. The *général*'s eyes grew wide like a startled bird's, hell, shit, the prospects of appearing in the *Petit Larousse* looked grim. The *général* seethed with indignation; he even decided to get up from his chair.

He gripped the arms of the chair and sat up, angry and exasperated. He had won the war, for Christ's sake; surely he was entitled to a bit of damn peace!

M. Péricourt woke up exhausted and went to bed exhausted. I'm flagging, he thought. He continued to work, to arrive promptly at his meetings, to give orders, but he was only going through the motions. Before going to join his daughter, he took Édouard's sketchpad from his pocket and slipped it into his desk drawer. He often carried it with him, though he never opened it in front of others. He knew every page by heart. Carrying it around like this, the book was bound to get damaged; he needed to do something to protect it, perhaps have it properly bound; having never had to deal with practical matters, he felt utterly at a loss. There was Madeleine, of course, but her mind was on other things . . . M. Péricourt felt terribly alone. He closed the drawer, left the study and went to join his daughter. What had he done that his life had come to this? He was a man who had inspired nothing but fear and as a result, he had no friends; he had only acquaintances. And Madeleine. But that was not the same; a man cannot speak candidly to his daughter. Besides, now that she was . . . in a delicate condition. More than once, he had tried to recall the time when he had been an expectant father, but in vain. He was astonished at how few memories he was able to recollect. At work, his memory was legendary, he could quote every word of a board meeting at some company he had taken over fifteen years ago, but about his family he could remember nothing, or almost nothing. Though God knew how much family mattered to him. And not just now that his son was dead. His family was the very reason he worked so hard, took so much trouble. So they would be safe. So they would have . . . all these things. And yet his memories of family occasions were so faint that they all seemed the same. The Christmas dinners, the Easter celebrations, the birthdays seemed like a single event repeated over and over; some minor details changed;

there were the Christmases before his wife had died and those after, Sundays before the war and Sundays now. But all things considered, the differences were slight. And so he had no memory of his wife's confinements. Four, he seemed to remember, though here again they all merged into one, but whether it was one of those that had gone to term or one that had come to nothing, he would have been unable to say. Now and then, by chance coincidence, a random image flickered in his mind. As when Madeleine sat with her hands clasped over her now swollen belly, and he remembered seeing his wife in that selfsame pose. He felt happy, almost proud; it did not occur to him that all pregnant women look a little alike and so he decided to consider this fleeting recollection a victory, proof that he had a heart, that he had family feelings. And because he had a heart, he was loath to burden his daughter with his worries. In her condition. He would have liked to do as he always did, to take it all upon himself, but that was no longer possible; in fact he had already waited too long.

"I'm not disturbing you?" he said.

They looked at each other. The situation was awkward for them both. For her, because ever since he had begun grieving for Édouard's death, M. Péricourt had suddenly, drastically aged. For him, because pregnancy did not flatter his daughter; Madeleine did not have that glow, that ripeness M. Péricourt had observed in some women, the serene, confident air of accomplishment some shared with brooding hens. Madeleine looked simply fat. Her whole body had ballooned, even her face, and it upset M. Péricourt to see her look so much like her mother, another woman who had not been beautiful, not even when pregnant. He did not believe that his daughter was happy; she seemed only satisfied.

No, he was not disturbing her (Madeleine smiled), I was just day-dreaming, she said, but none of this was true: he was disturbing her and she had not been daydreaming. The fact that he was taking such precautions meant that he had something to say to her, and since she already knew, or feared she knew what that was, she forced a smile, patting a seat next to her. Her father sat and, as so often, such was their relationship, nothing needed to be said. In fact, had it concerned only the two of them, they would simply have exchanged pleasantries, each knowing what lay behind these trite remarks, then M. Péricourt would have got to his feet, planted a kiss on his daughter's forehead and left, satisfied—and rightly so—that he had made himself understood. But today, words were necessary because it did not concern only them. And both of them were frustrated that this private moment was brought about by circumstances beyond their control.

Madeleine would often lay her hand on her father's, but today, she just sighed softly; they were bound to clash, perhaps even to argue, something she had no wish to do.

"I had a telephone call from Général Morieux," M. Péricourt began.

"Did you now . . . ?" Madeleine smiled.

M. Péricourt hesitated over how best to approach the matter and settled on what, he felt, best suited him: fatherly firmness and authority.

"Your husband . . ."

"You mean your son-in-law . . ."

"If you prefer . . ."

"I do prefer . . ."

Back when he had longed for a son, M. Péricourt had hoped that the boy would take after him; in a girl, such similarities upset him because women do things very differently from men; they do things in a roundabout manner. This insidious way of saying things, for example, of implying that they were talking, not about the blunders of her husband, but those of his son-in-law. He pursed his lips. He had to be careful, to remember "her condition."

"Be that as it may, things have not improved . . . ," he said.

"What things?"

"The manner in which he conducts his business affairs."

As soon as he uttered this word, M. Péricourt ceased to be a father. Suddenly, the problem seemed resolvable; because he knew everything there was to know about business, there were few problems that he could not resolve given time. He had always considered the head of the family to be like the head of a company. Now, faced with this woman, so grown up, so strange, so little like his daughter, he was stricken with doubt.

He shook his head irritably, and in the grip of this mute anger, he remembered everything he had wanted to say before now, everything she had refused to let him say, what he thought about her marriage, about that man.

Madeleine, sensing that he was about to be cruel, deliberately clasped her hands over her belly and crossed her fingers. M. Péricourt observed this and fell silent.

"I've spoken to Henri, Papa," she said at length, "He has had a number of temporary difficulties. That was his word, 'temporary,' nothing serious. He has promised me . . ."

"What he has promised is of little consequence and less value, Madeleine. He tells you whatever suits him, because he wishes to protect you."

"That is as it should be, he is my husband . . ."

"My point exactly. He is your husband; he should be keeping you safe, not putting you in danger!"

"In danger!" Madeleine shrieked with laughter. "Good heavens, so I'm in danger now, am I?"

She laughed long and loudly. And he was too little of a father not to be annoyed.

"I will not support you, Madeleine," he snapped.

"But, Papa, no one has asked for your support? Support for what? Against what?"

In their refusal to face facts, they were alike.

Though she gave a very different impression, Madeleine knew things. This business with the war graves had not been as straightforward as it had seemed. Henri was increasingly irritable, distracted, short- tempered, nervous; it was just as well she had no need of his conjugal services; indeed, even his mistresses seemed to be complaining about him of late. Yvonne, only the other day: "I ran into your husband, *chérie*, and he is positively unapproachable these days. Perhaps he never did have the temperament to be a man of means . . ."

In his work for the government, there had been problems, complications, it was all *sotto voce*, but she gleaned snatches here and there; the ministry had been telephoning. Henri would adopt his bluff, magisterial tone—no, no, my dear fellow, ha! ha! that was all dealt with ages ago, don't worry—and hang up with a deep furrow on his brow. A squall, nothing more, Madeleine had been accustomed to such things, she had spent her life watching her father weather such storms, to say nothing of the war; she would not panic because of two telephone calls from the *préfecture* or the ministry. Her father did not like Henri, that was all. Nothing he did would please M. Péricourt. Male rivalry. Sparring cocks. She hugged her belly more tightly. Message received. Reluctantly, M. Péricourt got to his feet and made for the door, then he turned back; he could not help himself.

"I don't like your husband."

There, he had said it. In the end, it had not proved terribly difficult.

"I know, Papa," Madeleine smiled. "It doesn't matter. He's my husband."

She patted her belly.

"And this is your grandson. I'm sure of it."

M. Péricourt opened his mouth to speak, but decided it was better to leave the room.

A grandson . . .

He had been avoiding this thought from the first, because it had not come at the right time, he could not bring himself to make a connection between the death of his son and the birth of a grandson. He almost hoped it was a girl so that he would not have to think about it. There would perhaps be a second child, but by then time would have passed, the memorial would be built. He clung to the notion that erecting the monument would signal the end of his grief and his remorse. For weeks now he had not slept properly. With the passage of time, Édouard's death had taken on a colossal importance, it had even begun to affect his professional activities. Only recently, during a board meeting of one of his companies, "la Française des Colonies," his eye had been caught by a shaft of sunlight cutting obliquely across the hall and illuminating the top of the conference table. A ray of sunlight is a commonplace thing, yet its effect on him was almost hypnotic. Everyone has moments when they become dissociated from reality, but the expression on M. Péricourt's face was not blank, it was a look of fascination. Everyone saw it. They carried on with the meeting, but without the chairman's powerful gaze, his keen, radiographic attention, the discussion slowed, jolting and juddering like a car running out of fuel, before eventually trailing off into silence. In fact, M. Péricourt was not gazing at this beam of sunlight, but at the motes of dust, a nebula of dancing particles, and it took him back—how many years? Ten, fifteen? How tiresome it was to have no memory for such things! Édouard had just painted a picture, he would have been sixteen, no, younger, fifteen, a painting that was simply a mass of tiny points of color, no brushstrokes, only dots, it had a name, this technique. It was on the tip of his tongue, but the word would not come. It was a painting of young girls in a meadow, he seemed to remember. He had found the technique so absurd that he had scarcely notice the subject of the picture. How foolish he had been. His little Édouard had stood, waiting diffidently while his father held up this picture he had come upon by chance, this preposterous, trivial object . . .

What had he said all those years ago? Disgusted with himself, M. Péricourt sat in the hushed boardroom shaking his head. He stood up and left without a word, without so much as a glance, and went home.

Now, as he left Madeleine, he was again shaking his head. But the thought was not the same, indeed it was almost the reverse, he felt angry: coming to his daughter's aid amounted to helping her husband. In the end, these things make you ill. Morieux might have become a doddering old fool (perhaps he had always been one), but the rumors he had passed on about Pradelle's business affairs were disturbing.

The name of Péricourt would be mentioned. There was talk of a report. Scandalous, it was whispered. Where the devil was it, this report? Who had read it? And who had written it?

I'm taking this too much to heart, he thought. After all, it's not as though it concerns my companies, the man does not even bear my name. As for my daughter, she is protected by her marriage contract. Besides, I don't give a curse about what happens to Aulnay-Pradelle (even when he mentally pronounced the name, he uttered the four syllables with unalloyed contempt); there is a whole world between him and us. If Madeleine should have a child (this time or another, with women it was impossible to know how these things will turn out), surely Péricourt was capable of providing for their future?

This last idea, objective and rational, convinced him. His son-in-law could sink or swim, he, Péricourt, would be standing on the bank with lifelines to save his daughter and his grandchildren.

And if that meant pushing Pradelle under, so be it.

M. Péricourt had killed many men in the course of his long career, but never had the notion seemed as consoling as it did now.

He smiled, recognizing that very particular shudder he felt when, from among many possible candidates, he had chosen the most effective solution.

29

Joseph Merlin had never slept well. Unlike some insomniacs who spend their whole lives not knowing the cause of this misfortune, he knew precisely: his life had been a constant hail of disappointments to which he had never grown accustomed. Every night he brooded over the disagreements in which he had not prevailed, replaying them to change the outcome to his advantage; he remembered every professional slight, fretted over problems and setbacks: there were more than enough to keep him awake. There was something profoundly egocentric about the man; the epicenter of Joseph Merlin's universe was Joseph Merlin. Having no one and nothing in his life—not even a cat—everything was about him, his existence had curled in on itself like a dry leaf around an empty space. For example, in the course of these long, sleepless nights, he had never once thought about the war. For four years, he had thought of it only as a tiresome inconvenience, an assortment of tribulations, chief among them food rationing, that served only to aggravate his crabby temperament. His colleagues at the ministry, especially those who had someone they loved fighting on the front lines, had been shocked to see this embittered man worrying only about the price of public transport and the shortage of chicken.

"For God's sake" they would say indignantly, "don't you realize, there's a war on?"

"A war? Which war?" Merlin would say, "There have always been wars. Why should I take any more interest in this war than in the last one? Or the next?"

He was considered a defeatist, almost a traitor. On the front lines, he would quickly have found himself facing a firing squad; on the home front, such an attitude was less dangerous, though his indifference led to further snubs: people called him "the Boche," and the name stuck.

At the end of the war, when he was transferred to the war grave inspectorate, "the Boche" became "the Vulture," "the Carrion Bird," "the Raptor," according to the circumstances. Again, he suffered sleepless nights.

The inspection of Chazières-Malmont was his first visit to one of the military cemeteries managed by Pradelle & Cie.

When they read his report, his superiors found the situation alarming. No one was clamoring to take responsibility, and so the document quickly rose to dizzy heights until eventually it landed on the desk of the director general, who, like his colleagues in other ministries, was an expert in hushing up such dossiers.

Meanwhile, Merlin spent every night in bed, honing the words he would say to his superiors when he was summoned to appear, all of which amounted to a simple, brutal fact, one that would have serious consequences: thousands of French soldiers were being buried in coffins that were too small. Regardless of a soldier's height—whether five foot two or more than five foot nine (from the military records available, Merlin had compiled a detailed list of the heights of the soldiers concerned), he was buried in a coffin measuring four foot three. To make the bodies fit, it was necessary to break the necks, saw off the feet, break the ankles; in short, the bodies of these fallen soldiers were being treated like lumber to be hacked and sawed. The report went into macabre detail about the process, explaining that "having no knowledge of anatomy nor any appropriate tools, laborers are reduced to breaking bones with the blades of their shovels, sometimes with the heels of their boots against flat stones, sometimes with pickaxes; despite such measures, it is often impossible to fit the remains of taller soldiers into such small caskets, forcing workers to pack in as much as possible with any surplus being tossed into a coffin serving as a trash can which, once full, is sealed and marked 'Unidentified Soldier,' consequently making it impossible to assure families that the bodies of the loved ones they have come to mourn are intact, something further exacerbated by the scant time allotted for exhumations by the company that secured the contract, leading workers to place only those parts of a corpse that are immediately apparent into coffins with no attempt made to comb the grave for bones, documents, or objects that might help confirm or determine the identity of the deceased as required by regulations, with the inevitable consequence that it is not uncommon to encounter scattered bones that cannot confidently be identified as belonging to any particular corpse; hence, in addition to its serious, its systematic failure to provide instructions concerning the respectful exhumation of bodies, and its use of coffins that fail to meet the stipulated requirements, the aforementioned company . . ." As is apparent, Merlin could compose sentences running to more than two hundred words; in this, he was considered an artist by his colleagues at the ministry.

The report was a bombshell.

It was deeply worrying for Pradelle & Cie, but also for the Péricourt family, who were very much in the public eye, and for the government, which had felt it sufficient to inspect work only after the event, by which time it was too late. If word got out, there would be a scandal. It was decided that, henceforth, all information relating the affair was to be sent directly and without delay to the office of the director general. And, in order to silence Merlin, a message had been sent through the appropriate channels informing him that his report was being studied attentively, that it was much appreciated, and that he would be advised of any further action in the fullness of time. Merlin, with almost forty years' experience in the civil service, immediately knew that his report had been buried, something that did not particularly surprise him. There were doubtless murky areas in the process by which contacts had been awarded. It was a sensitive subject; anything that might embarrass the government was bound to be brushed aside. Merlin knew that it was not in his interests to be difficult; if he were, he would once again find himself moved around like a pawn. No, thank you. A man of duty, he had done his duty. In his own estimation, he was beyond reproach.

Besides, he was nearing retirement; there was nothing to be done but wait to draw his pension. All that was expected of him was to carry out perfunctory inspections, sign his name, rubber-stamp the registers, and wait until rationing ended and chickens were once more available in markets and on restaurant menus.

Realizing this, he went home and slept soundly for the first time in his life, as though his brain, like sediment in fine wine, required an exceptionally long time to settle.

His sleep was troubled by sad dreams in which rotting soldiers sat up in their graves and wept; they tried to cry for help, but no sound came; their only comfort came from lanky Senegalese laborers, naked as the day they were born, chilled to the marrow, throwing shovelfuls of earth over them as one might throw a coat over a drowned man dragged from the water.

When he awoke, Merlin found himself gripped by a profound emotion that, for the first time, did not concern him alone. The war, long since over, had finally intruded upon his life.

What followed was the result of a curious alchemy influenced by the bleak atmosphere of those cemeteries, which reminded Merlin of the bleakness of his own life; the oppressive nature of the bureaucratic obstacles being placed in his path; and his instinctive intransigence: a public servant of his integrity could not turn a blind eye. Though he had nothing in common with them, these young men were victims of an injustice that he alone could set right. Within days, it had become an obsession. The thought of these dead soldiers preyed on his mind, like love, like jealousy, like a cancer. He shifted from grief to indignation. He became angry.

Since he had received no orders telling him to curtail his assignment, he sent a message to his superiors informing them that he intended to inspect the cemetery at Dargonne-le-Grand and immediately took the train heading in the opposite direction to Pontaville-sur-Meuse.

From the station, he walked almost four miles through the driving rain to the military cemetery. He walked in the middle of the road, his oversized shoes tramping through the puddles, refusing to step aside for the cars that sounded their horns as though he did not hear them. To pass him, they had to mount the grass shoulder of the road.

The strange apparition that materialized outside the cemetery gates was a hulking figure with a menacing air, his fists deep in the pockets of a coat that, though the rain had now stopped, was wringing wet. But there was no one there to see; the midday bell had sounded, the site was closed. On the railing was a list of all the objects found on unidentified bodies, which families could inspect at the town hall: the photograph of a young girl, a pipe, a check stub, initials found on underclothes, a leather tobacco pouch, a lighter, a pair of round spectacles, a letter that began "My Darling" but was unsigned—a piteous, tragic litany. Merlin was struck by the humble nature of these relics. So many penniless soldiers. It was unbelievable.

He looked down at the lock and chain, raised a foot and gave the small padlock a kick that would have felled a bullock, strode into the cemetery, and kicked open the wooden door to the administration shed. The only people on site were a dozen Arabs, eating lunch beneath a tarpaulin ballooned by the wind. From a distance, they watched as Merlin kicked open the gates and the office door, but, daunted by the physical prowess and obvious self-assurance of the man, they made no move to get up, to intervene; they went on chewing their bread.

What was known locally as "Pontaville Square" was a field that was anything but square, bordered by woodlands, where an estimated six hundred soldiers had been buried.

Merlin rummaged through the cabinets looking for the registers in which every operation was supposed to be detailed. Now and then, as he scanned the daily reports, he glanced out of the window. The exhumations had begun two months earlier; looking out he could see a field littered with graves, mounds of earth, tarpaulins, planks, wheelbarrows, and makeshift storage sheds.

From an organizational standpoint, everything seemed in order. He would not find here the same sickening carelessness he had witnessed at Chazières-Malmont, the caskets of human detritus like something from a slaughterhouse, which he had discovered hidden behind stacks of new unused coffins.

Generally, having checked that registers were being kept, Merlin began his inspections by making a tour of the site; he trusted to his instincts, lifting a cover here, checking an identity disk there. Only then did the real investigation begin. His work involved going endlessly back and forth between the rows of graves and the archived ledgers, but he had quickly acquired a sixth sense, an unerring ability to sniff out the slightest sign of duplicity, a minor irregularity, a detail indicating some anomaly.

This was certainly the only ministerial assignment that required a civil servant to dig up bodies, but there was no other way to check. However, Merlin's colossal frame was well suited to the task; his hefty shoes could drive a shovel a foot into the ground, his huge paws could wield a pickax as though it were a fork.

Having completed an initial tour of the site, Merlin began his detailed cross-referencing. It was twelve-thirty.

At 2:00 p.m. he was standing in front of a pile of sealed coffins to the north of the cemetery when the site manager, a certain Sauveur Bénichou—a puce-faced alcoholic of about fifty, scrawny as a weed—showed up with two others, probably foremen. This little group was in a state of high indignation, chins jutting, voices loud and booming, this site was strictly off limits to the public, they could not have people wandering in off the road, he must leave immediately. And since Merlin did not even acknowledge their presence, they raised the tone to the next level: if he refused to comply, they would be forced to contact the *gendarmerie* because this site was under the auspices of the government . . .

"That's me," Merlin interrupted, turning toward the three men.

He broke the ensuing silence.

"I *am* the government here."

He plunged his hand into his pocket and took out a crumpled sheet of paper that did not look much like an official pass, but given that he did not look much like a ministerial envoy, the men did not know what to think. Everything about him seemed suspicious: his colossal frame, his stained threadbare clothes, his huge shoes; even so, no one dared challenge him.

Merlin looked the three men up and down: Sauveur, who smelled of plum brandy, and his two acolytes. The first, a hatchet-faced man with an oversized mustache stained yellow with tobacco, patted his breast pocket to hide his lack of composure; the second, an Arab still wearing the cap, pants, and boots of a *caporal d'infanterie*, stood stiffly to attention as though to prove the importance of his position.

Tsst, tsst. Merlin sucked at his denture as he stuffed the paper back into his pocket. Then he nodded to the pile of coffins.

"And, as you can imagine, the government has a few minor questions."

The Arab foreman stiffened a little more. His mustachioed companion took out a cigarette (he did not take out the pack, only a single cigarette, like a man reluctant to share, a man sick and tired of scroungers). Everything marked him out as a mean, tightfisted man.

"For example," Merlin said, suddenly waving three identity cards, "the government is wondering which coffins correspond to these three men."

In Merlin's huge fists, the papers looked no bigger than postage stamps. The question made the three men distinctly uneasy.

When a row of graves was exhumed, the result was a row of coffins on the one hand, a series of identity cards on the other.

Ideally in the same order.

But one ID card misfiled or missing was enough to throw everything into disarray so that the ID cards were unrelated to the contents of the coffins.

And if Merlin was brandishing three cards that did not correspond to any coffin . . . it meant the whole sequence was wrong.

He shook his head and surveyed the area of the cemetery that had already been unearthed. Two hundred and thirty-seven soldiers had been exhumed and transported a distance of fifty miles.

Paul was in Jules's coffin, Félicien in Isidore's, and so on.

All the way up to number 237.

And it was now impossible to determine who was who.

"Who do the ID cards belong to?" Sauveur Bénichou stammered, glancing around as though suddenly disoriented, "Let me think . . ."

An idea occurred to him.

"You see," he said, "we were just about to deal with this."

He turned to his men, who seemed suddenly much smaller.

"Isn't that right, boys?"

Neither knew what he was talking about, but they did not have time to think.

"HA!" Merlin roared, "Do you think they're complete idiots?"

"Who?" Bénichou said.

"The government!"

He seemed like a lunatic; Bénichou considered asking to see his official pass again.

"So, where are they, these three little rascals? And what about the three men you'll have left over when you're finished, what are you planning to call them?"

Bénichou launched into a tedious technical explanation about how they had thought it "more reliable" to leave writing up the identity cards until *after* they have a whole row of coffins, so they could be simultaneously noted in the register because if the ID cards were drafted . . .

"Bullshit!" Merlin cut him short.

Bénichou, who was having trouble believing it himself, lowered his head. His assistant patted his breast pocket.

In the silence that followed, Merlin had a strange, fleeting vision of a vast war grave, dotted here and there with families at prayer, and—as though by some second sight—he alone could peer through the earth itself, see the quivering corpses, hear the harrowing cries as they called out their names . . .

The damage already done was irreparable, those soldiers were lost, anonymous bodies sleeping beneath carefully marked crosses. The only thing to do now was to make the best of what was yet to be done.

Merlin reorganized the work, wrote instructions in large letters, issued orders in a curt, peremptory tone—You, over here! Now listen carefully—threatening formal proceedings, fines, dismissals if the work was badly done; whenever he walked away they could distinctly hear him say "fucking morons."

As soon as his back was turned, it began again, it was never ending. This fact, far from discouraging him, served only to fuel his rage.

"You, over here, now! Move it!"

He was speaking to the man with the mustache; he was maybe fifty and his face so thin his eyes looked as though they were perched on either side, like a fish's. Standing about a yard away from Merlin, he resisted the urge to pat his breast pocket again and instead took out a cigarette.

Merlin, who had been just about to speak, paused for a long moment. He looked like someone struggling desperately to remember a word that is on the tip of his tongue.

The mustachioed foreman opened his mouth, but before he had time to utter a sound, Merlin had dealt him a resounding slap. Against his flat cheek it sounded like a bell. The man stepped back. All eyes turned to stare. Bénichou, emerging from the shed where he kept his pick-me-up (a bottle of *marc de Bourgogne*) gave a hoarse roar, but all the workmen were already moving. The dumbfounded mustached man was clutching his cheek. Merlin quickly found himself surrounded by a baying pack, and had it not been for his age, his colossal build, the authority he had displayed since the start of the inspection, his huge hands and his monstrous feet, he might have worried; instead of which, he calmly pushed past everyone, took a step toward his victim, thrust a hand into the man's breast pocket and bellowed "Aha!," when it reemerged as a fist. His other hand held the man by the throat; he looked about to strangle him.

"Oh my God!" Bénichou shouted as he finally staggered up.

Without releasing his grip on the throat of the man who, by now, was starting to change color, Merlin held his closed fist toward the site manager, then opened it.

A solid-gold identity bracelet appeared, turned the wrong way up. Merlin released his prey, who immediately started coughing his lungs out and turned to Bénichou.

"What's his name, your boy?" Merlin asked, "His first name?"

"Er . . ."

Sauveur Bénichou, beaten and helpless, shot his foreman an apologetic glance.

"Alcide," he muttered grudgingly.

It was barely audible, but that did not matter.

Merlin turned over the bracelet as though it were a coin and they were playing heads or tails.

There, engraved on the nameplate: Roger.

30

My God, what a morning! If only he could wake up to such a morning every day! Everything seemed to be going perfectly.

First, the designs. Five had been chosen by the selection committee, each more magnificent than the last. A distillation of patriotism. They brought tears to your eyes. Labourdin had been carefully preparing for his moment of triumph: presenting the designs to Président Péricourt. For this, he had contacted the municipal works department and ordered a large wrought iron display stand to be made and assembled in his office, on which the designs could be hung to their best advantage—an idea he had got from his one and only visit to the Grand Palais. He could imagine M. Péricourt, hands clasped behind his back, strolling in a leisurely fashion between the sketches, going into raptures over one ("France, Sorrowful Yet Victorious," Labourdin's own favorite)—studying another ("The Triumphant Dead"), pausing, hesitating. He could already picture the chairman turning to him, awestruck and embarrassed, unsure which to choose . . . At that point, Labourdin would utter a perfectly cadenced sentence that he had been honing, weighing, polishing, one that communicated both his aesthetic taste and his sense of duty:

"Monsieur le président, if I may be so bold . . ."

He would then move toward "France, Sorrowful" as though to slip an arm around her shoulder.

". . . I feel that this Magisterial Opus perfectly encapsulates everything our Compatriots wish for, to express all their Anguish and their Pride."

The capital letters came instinctively. Flawless. First, "Magisterial Opus," a stroke of inspiration, next "Compatriots" which sounded rather better than "constituents"; finally, "Anguish" and "Pride." Labourdin was in awe of his own genius.

At around ten o'clock, with the wrought iron display set up in his office, the hanging had begun. A stepladder was needed to hang the sketches: Mlle Raymond was called.

The moment she stepped into the room, she realized what was being asked of her and clenched her knees instinctively. Labourdin, standing at the foot of the stepladder, a smile playing on his lips, was rubbing his hands like a horse trader.

Mlle Raymond scaled the four steps with a sigh, and began to squirm. Oh, what a glorious morning! As soon as the designs had been hung, the secretary clambered down, clutching her skirt. Labourdin stepped back to admire the result, the right side, he felt, looked a little lower than the left—don't you think? Mlle Raymond closed her eyes, climbed again, Labourdin rushed to the stepladder; never had he spent so much time under her skirts. By the time everything was in peace, the district mayor was in a priapic frenzy approaching apoplexy.

But bang, just when everything was ready, Président Péricourt canceled his visit and sent a courier to fetch the designs and bring them to him. All that work for nothing, Labourdin thought. He followed in a hackney cab, but despite his expectations, he was not admitted to the deliberations. Marcel Péricourt wished to be alone. It was almost noon.

"See to it a light lunch is brought for *monsieur le maire*," M. Péricourt sent word.

Labourdin rushed over to the young housemaid, a ravishing little brunette with doe eyes and a firm bust, and asked if he might have a glass of port wine, cupping her left breast as he did so. The young girl merely blushed; she was new to her job and the position was well paid. When she brought the port, he launched an attack on her right breast.

My God, what a morning!

Madeleine came upon the mayor snoring like a furnace bellows. His sprawling frame, together with the remnants of the chicken in aspic that he had devoured and the empty bottle of Château Margaux on the low table next to him, lent the scene a pathetic, almost obscene licentiousness.

She knocked discreetly on the door to her father's study.

"Come!" he said immediately, recognizing her knock.

M. Péricourt had propped the drawings up against the bookcase and cleared a space so that, sitting in his armchair, he could see them all at once. He had barely stirred for more than an hour, engrossed in his thoughts, his eyes moving from one to the other. From time to time he got up, went over to study some detail, then returned to his chair.

At first, he had been disappointed. Was this all there was? They looked just like the other memorials he had seen, but larger. He could not help but check the prices, mentally calculating the tariff and the volume. He needed to concentrate. Then choose. But, yes; disappointing. He had had great hopes for the project. But now that he saw the proposals . . . So what had he expected? This would be a memorial like any other, not something to appease the seething emotions he found so overwhelming.

Madeleine, though not surprised, shared the same impression. All wars are alike; all war memorials, too.

"What do you think?" he said.

"They're all a bit . . . bombastic, don't you think?"

"They're lyrical."

They fell silent.

M. Péricourt sat in his armchair, like a king enthroned facing a row of dead courtiers. Madeleine studied the proposals. They agreed that the best of them was Adrien Malendrey's "Victory of the Martyrs," which alone encompassed all the victims: the widows (a woman in a mourning veil), the orphans, (a little boy, hands pressed together, praying as he gazed toward a soldier), and the soldiers themselves. The sculptor's chisel had fashioned the whole nation into a martyred country.

"A hundred and thirty thousand francs," M. Péricourt says.

He cannot stop himself.

But his daughter does not hear, she is studying a detail in a different portfolio. She picks up the drawing, holds it to the light; her father gets up and comes over, he does not like this submission, "Gratitude"; nor does Madeleine, she finds it overstated; no, it's not that, there is something about it, some trifling detail . . . what is it? In the panel of the triptych entitled "Valiant Soldiers Attacking the Enemy," almost hidden in the background, a soldier lies dying, he has an innocent face, full lips, a strong nose . . .

"Wait," M. Péricourt said, "Let me see." He bends and pores over the drawing. "You're right, you're absolutely right."

The soldier looks vaguely like the young men in Édouard's sketches. He is not exactly the same: this man stares out of the picture, while Édouard's models tended to have a slight squint. And a dimple that seemed to cleave the chin. But the similarities remain.

M. Péricourt puts away his spectacles.

"In art, one often comes across the same figures . . ."

He was speaking like a connoisseur. Madeleine, who knew much more about art, decided not to contradict him. After all, it was only a detail, it was not important. What her father needed was to build his monument and begin to take an interest in other things. His daughter's pregnancy, for example.

"That idiot of yours, Labourdin, is sleeping out in the hall," she said with a smile.

He had forgotten Labourdin.

"Let him sleep," he said. "It's what he does best."

He kissed her on the forehead. She moved toward the door. From a distance, the submissions looked impressive, she had a sense of the size and scale, she had noticed the dimensions: forty feet, fifty feet, and the height . . .

But that face . . .

Only once did M. Péricourt look at it again. And he tried to find the same face in Édouard's sketchpad, but the men his son had drawn were not figures, they were real men he had met in the trenches, while the young soldier with the full lips was an idealized model. M. Péricourt had always refrained from any precise image concerning what he referred to as his son's "affective sympathies." Even in private, he never thought in terms of "sexual preference" or anything of that sort; he found such terms too precise, too shocking. But, as with those thoughts that surprise you, though you realize that they have long been dormant before they surfaced, he wondered whether the young man with the squint and the cleft chin had been one of Édouard's "friends." One of Édouard's lovers, he mentally corrected himself. And the idea no longer seemed as shocking as before, merely troubling; he did not want to imagine . . . Did not want it to become too real . . . His son was "different," that was all. All around him he saw men who were not different—his employees, his colleagues, his clients, their sons, brothers—but he no longer envied them as once he had. He could not even remember what virtues he had hitherto seen in them, what qualities had once led him to think them better than Édouard. He despised himself for his past foolishness.

M. Péricourt sat down again and stared at the gallery of pictures. His perspective was slightly altered. Not that he had noticed some new merit in the pictures, no, he still found all of them embarrassingly fulsome. What had changed was his way of seeing, much as our perception of a face changes the longer we observe it: the woman we thought quite pretty a moment earlier comes to seem banal, the ugly man in whom we discover a charm we are surprised to have overlooked. Now that he had grown used to them, the submissions calmed him. It had to do with their substance: some were in stone, others in bronze, weighty materials that seem indestructible. This was precisely what had been missing at the family vault where Édouard's name was missing, this illusion of eternity. It was important to M. Péricourt that this project, this memorial he was commissioning, transcend him, that it eclipse his life in time, in weight, in mass, in volume, that it be stronger than he was, that it restore his grief to a natural scale.

Each submission was accompanied by a dossier detailing the previous works of the artist, the price, the time it would take to create. M. Péricourt read the letter that had come with the proposal by Jules d'Épremont, but he learned nothing from it, he leafed through the other sketches showing the memorial in profile, in rear elevation, in perspective, in an urban environment . . . From each, the young soldier stared out with that serious face . . . It was enough. He opened the door and called, but to no avail.

"Labourdin, for Christ's sake!" he bellowed, shaking the mayor awake.

"Huh . . . Wh . . . ? Who?"

Eyes thick with sleep, he looked as though he did not know where he was or why he was there.

"Come with me!"

"Me? Where?"

Labourdin stumbled into the study, rubbing his face to wake himself, stuttering excuses that M. Péricourt did not even hear.

"This one."

Labourdin, beginning to come around, realized that the chosen submission was not the one he would have recommended but decided that his little speech was perfectly suited to any memorial. He cleared his throat.

"*Monsieur le président*, if I may be so bold . . ."

"What?" Péricourt snapped without looking up.

He had put on his glasses again and was standing, bent over his desk, writing, satisfied with his decision, confident that he was doing something of which he could be proud, something that would be salutary for him.

Labourdin took a deep breath, puffed out his chest.

"This work, *monsieur le président*, I feel that this Magisterial Opus . . ."

"Here," Péricourt interrupted, "here is a check to cover the submission and the initial work. Make all necessary inquiries about the artist, obviously! And the company responsible for building it. And submit the dossier to the *préfet*. If there is the slightest problem, call me and I will deal with it. Anything else?"

Labourdin grabbed the check. No, there was nothing else.

"Ah, yes," M. Péricourt said, "I'd like to meet the artist, this . . ." (he cast about for the name) "Jules d'Épremont. Have him come here."

31

The atmosphere in the house was not, one might say, euphoric. Except for Édouard, but he never behaved as others did; for months now, he had been laughing all the time, it was impossible to make him see sense. It was as though he did not understand the gravity of what was happening. Albert tried not to think about his morphine intake, which was more serious than ever; he could not keep an eye on everything, besides he had his own problems. On his first day at the bank, he had opened a company account for Patriotic Memory to bank monies as they arrived . . .

Sixty-eight thousand, two hundred twenty francs. That was it. The sum total . . .

Thirty-four thousand each.

Albert had never had so much money in his life, but the benefits had to be set against the risks. He had risked thirty years in prison for embezzling less than five times a laborer's annual salary. It was ridiculous. It was June 15. The War Memorial Sale would be over in less than a month, and they had nothing, Or next to nothing.

"What do you mean, nothing?" Édouard wrote.

Today, in spite of the heat, he was wearing a tall African mask that covered his whole face. A pair of horns rose above his head, curled about themselves like a ram's horns, while, from the corners of the eyes, two dotted lines of phosphorescent blue trickled like tears of joy down to a multicolored beard that opened out like a fan. The whole thing was painted in tones of ochre, yellow, and vivid red; there was even a twisting velvety band between forehead and the horns, a dark-green snake so lifelike one would have sworn it had coiled around Édouard's head and was eating its own tail. The brash, vivid, lively colors of the mask clashed with Albert's mood, which these days came only in black and white—more often black.

"What I said! Nothing!" he yelled waving the account book.

"Be patient," Édouard said, as he always did.

Louise simply lowered her head a little. She was busy kneading *papier-mâché* for the new masks. Dreamily, she stared down at the enamel basin, deaf to the raised voices; she had already heard everything they had to say . . .

Albert's accounts were punctilious: 17 crosses, 24 torches, 14 busts—items that brought in nothing—there were only nine orders for memorials. And even then, two town councils had sent down payments of twenty-five rather than fifty percent, and had asked for some leeway in settling the balance. Of the three thousand acknowledgment slips printed in anticipation of the orders, only sixty had been needed . . .

Édouard was refusing to leave the country until he had made a million; so far, they had not received so much as a tenth of that.

And every day was one day closer to the scheme being discovered. The police might already have begun an investigation. Just going to the post office on the rue du Louvre sent cold shivers down Albert's spine; a hundred times he thought he would piss his pants as he stood in front of the open box and saw someone walking toward him.

"I don't know why I bother to say anything," he said to Édouard. "You don't believe anything unless it suits you."

He tossed the account book on the floor and put on his coat, Louise went on kneading the *papier-mâché*, Édouard tilted his head to one side. Albert often flew into a rage, and, unable to express the suffocating feelings, he would storm out and not reappear until the early hours.

These last months had proved a terrible strain for him. At the bank, everyone thought he was sick. No one was surprised, ex-soldiers all had their battle-scars, but Albert seemed more shell shocked than the others—the persistent anxiety, the fearful twitches . . . But since he was kindly and well liked, everyone was quick to offer their advice: have your feet massaged, eat more red meat, have you tried linden blossom tea? Albert, for his part, would look at himself in the mirror as he shaved in the morning and think he looked like death warmed up.

By that time, Édouard would already be tapping away at the typewriter and clucking with delight.

The two men experienced things very differently. The long-awaited moment when they would know whether their madcap scheme had succeeded should have been a moment of joy, of shared triumph; instead it had driven a wedge between them.

Édouard, ever in the clouds, heedless of consequences, gloated as he answered the inquiries they received, never doubting their success. He took great delight in composing his replies in the bureaucratic bohemian style he imagined Jules d'Épremont would use. Albert, meanwhile, consumed with fear, with regret and even resentment, was visibly wasting away.

More than ever he hugged the walls; he barely slept, one hand always on the horse head that he now carried around the apartment with him. If he could, he would have taken it to work, because the very thought of going to the bank every morning made him sick and the horse head was his sole protection, it was his guardian angel. He had embezzled some twenty-five thousand francs and, from the down payments they had received—as he had vowed and despite Édouard's protestations—he had repaid his employer in full. Even so, he still had to run the gauntlet of inspectors and auditors because the dummy entries were still there, proving there had been a fraud. He was continually compelled to create new entries to hide the old ones. If he were caught, there would be an investigation, they would find out everything . . . They had to get away. With what little was left after the bank had been paid back: twenty thousand francs each. A terrified Albert now realized just how easily he had given in to the wave of panic that had followed his encounter with the Greek. "Typical Albert, that is!" Mme Maillard would have said, had she known, "Always did take the coward's way out. That's probably how he came back from the war without a scratch on him. Even in peacetime he's a coward. If ever he does find himself a woman, I hope the poor thing has nerves of steel . . ."

"If ever he does find himself a woman . . ." When he thought about Pauline, he felt a desperate urge to run off by himself, never to see another living soul. When he imagined his future if they were caught, he felt a strange, unhealthy nostalgia. In hindsight, the years he had spent in the trenches seemed to him an easy, almost happy time and when he looked at his horse head, the shell crater seemed like a haven.

What a waste this whole scheme had been . . .

It had started out well enough. No sooner did the catalog drop onto the desks of town halls through the provinces than requests for information flooded in. Twelve, twenty, some days twenty-five letters. Édouard spent his whole time writing responses, he was indefatigable.

When the mail arrived, he would give a joyous yelp, thread a sheet of Patriotic Memory–headed writing paper into the typewriter, put the "Triumphal March" from *Aïda* on the gramophone, turn up the sound, stick a finger in the air as though to find out which way the wind was blowing, then swoop down on the keys like a pianist. It was not for the money that he had dreamed up this scheme, but for the feeling of euphoria, the extraordinary thrill of provocation. Here he was, a faceless man thumbing his nose at the whole world, and this made him deliriously happy, it reminded him of who he truly was and what he had almost lost.

Most of the customer inquiries concerned practical considerations: installation methods, warranties, packing, technical specifications for the pedestals . . . As typed by Édouard, Jules d'Épremont had an answer for everything. He wrote fantastically informative letters that were reassuring and personalized. Letters that inspired confidence. The councilors and town clerks would often offer detailed descriptions of their projects, unwittingly drawing attention to the sordidness of the scam, since the government made only a symbolic contribution "in proportion to the efforts and the sacrifices made by the community to glorify, etc . . ." The town councils raised what they could—all too often very little—and so the bulk of the money came from public subscription. From individuals, schools, parishes, whole families scraped together a pittance so that the name of a brother, a son, a father, a cousin, might be engraved on a monument that would stand in the center of the village or by the church for all time, or so they thought. Given the difficulty of raising funds quickly enough to take advantage of the discount offered by "Patriotic Memory," many of the letters asked if they might come to some arrangement, some agreement about a schedule of payment. Was it possible "to reserve a bronze model with only 660 francs down payment"? After all, they implored, though not quite the fifty percent requested, it amounted to forty-four percent. "The thing is, the money's been coming in rather slowly. There's no doubt we'll meet our financial obligations, we make a firm undertaking." "We've organized the children at the local school to go door to door making a collection," someone else explained. Or: "Madame de Marsantes has willed a part of her estate to the town. Heaven forbid that she should pass away, but perhaps the bequest might stand as surety so that a fitting memorial might be bought for Chaville-sur-Saône, where we lost almost fifty of our young men and now find ourselves providing for eighty orphans?"

The closing date of July 14, fast approaching, panicked more than one letter writer. They had scarcely had time to convene a meeting of the council. But the offer was so tempting.

Édouard-Jules d'Épremont, a noble gentleman, granted all requests, offered special discounts, deferred payments, there was never any problem.

He usually began by complimenting his correspondent on the excellent choice. Whether he wished to purchase "Charge!," a simple torch, or "Le Coq Gaulois Trampling a Boche Helmet," M. d'Épremont confided that he had a particular soft spot for that very model. Édouard loved this moment of pompous confession and drew his inspiration from the preposterousness he had witnessed from the stuffy, self-satisfied professors at the École de Beaux-Arts.

Whenever a composite project was suggested (when, for example, someone contemplated pairing "Victory" with "*Poilu* Dying in Defense of the Flag"), Jules d'Épremont was always enthusiastic, lavishing praise on his correspondent's artistic sensibility, confessing himself surprised at the originality and elegance of the combination. He was understanding about financial matters, compassionate in all things, an expert technician, impeccably well informed, and a master of his craft. No, he assured people, there was no problem with using cement, and, yes the stele could be built in the French style using brick, or granite, too, yes, absolutely, and obviously all Patriotic Memory designs were approved and came with an official certificate from the Ministère de l'Intérieur. There was no problem to which, under Édouard's light touch, a simple, practical, reassuring solution could not be found. He helpfully reminded his correspondents of the criteria necessary to obtain the meager state subsidy (minutes of the council meeting, sketch of the monument, an artistic appraisal by the steering committee, an estimate of the cost of the memorial, a statement of ways and means), offered some advice on the process, and supplied a superb receipt that alone was worth the down payment.

This final flourish was worthy of being ranked in the annals of classic swindles. At the end of the letter: "Please allow me to congratulate you on the discrimination and the captivating vision of your choice" Then, with circumlocutions to convey his hesitancies and his qualms, Édouard would add a further sentence, adapting it according to the correspondent: "The plans you have submitted marry a delicate artistic sensibility to profound patriotic feeling, in recognition of which I would like to offer you a reduction of15 percent, over and above the existing discount. In view of this exceptional offer (which I would request you to reveal to no one), I would ask that you pay the initial down payment in full."

Édouard would sometimes admire his work, holding a letter at arm's length and clucking contentedly. He felt that the sheer volume of inquiries, which took up much of his time, was a clear sign the scheme would be a success. Letters flooded in, Édouard's in-tray was filled to overflowing.

Albert simply snorted.

"Don't you think you're laying it on a little thick?" he said.

He had little trouble imagining that these kindhearted letters would only add to the charges leveled against them when they were arrested.

Édouard, with a regal wave, played the grand gentleman.

"Why not be generous, my friend?" he scrawled on his conversation pad, "It costs nothing, and these people need reassurance. They are contributing to a glorious project. In a sense, they're heroes, wouldn't you say?"

Albert was a little shocked: this mocking use of "heroes" to refer to people raising money for a war memorial . . .

Abruptly Édouard ripped off his mask to reveal his face, that monstrous gaping crater and, from above the void, his eyes—the only living, human trace—stared intently.

Albert rarely saw the horror of that ruined face now, since Édouard traded one mask for another. Sometimes, even when he slept, he was an Indian warrior, a mythical bird, a savage joyful beast. Albert, who never slept for longer than an hour, would go over, and with the gentleness of a new father, carefully remove the mask. In the half-light, he would gaze at his sleeping friend, struck by how closely his ruined face—but for the crimson color—resembled the maw of certain cephalopods.

In spite of the energy Édouard expended in replying to the torrent of inquiries, firm orders were slow to arrive.

"Why?" Albert said tonelessly, "What's wrong? It's as if they're not convinced by the responses . . ."

Édouard mimed a sort of Indian war dance, Louise burst out laughing. Albert, sick with worry, picked up his accounts and read through them again.

Though he scarcely remembered it now, since fear had engulfed everything, he had experienced a kind of elation at the end of May, when the first payments arrived. Albert had insisted the monies be used to repay the bank; Édouard, unsurprisingly, had protested.

"What's the point of reimbursing the bank?" he wrote on his pad, "We're running away with stolen money anyway! At least stealing from a bank is less immoral."

Albert refused to budge. Once, he had almost given himself away by mentioning the Banque d'Escompte et de Crédit Industriel, but Édouard did not recognize the name, he had never known anything about his father's business affairs. He could hardly justify himself to his friend by saying that it had been kind of M. Péricourt to offer him the job, and he did not want to go on cheating him. This, obviously, was an rather elastic approach to morality, since he was happy to cheat perfect strangers, many of them from modest backgrounds, who were scrimping and saving to erect a memorial to their loved ones, but it was not the same, he knew M. Péricourt personally, and besides, ever since he had met Pauline . . . When all was said and done, he thought of M. Péricourt as a kind of benefactor.

Though not persuaded by Albert's reasoning, Édouard had finally given in and the first down payments had been used to pay off the bank. Once that was done, each of them had spent a symbolic sum on some little luxury, a foretaste of the opulent future that lay in store.

Édouard had bought a top-notch gramophone and several records. There were military marches—despite his leg, Édouard liked to parade around the apartment, Louise by his side, in a mask that was a preposterous caricature of a soldier; a selection of operas, about which Albert knew nothing, and Mozart's Clarinet Concerto, which on certain some days was played over and over as though the gramophone were broken. Édouard still wore the same clothes he always had, the two pairs of pants, two pullovers, and two thick sweaters that, once a fortnight, Albert took to the laundry.

Albert had bought a pair of shoes. And a suit. And two shirts. Top quality. Nothing but the best this time. He had been particularly inspired, because it was around this time that he had met Pauline. Since then, everything had become much more complicated. With Pauline, as with the bank, one little lie had been enough to leave him endlessly scrambling to cover his tracks. What had he ever done to the Good Lord that he spent his days running from a hungry beast about to devour him? This was why he had said to Édouard that, although the lion mask was beautiful (actually it was a mythical beast, but on this point Édouard did not correct him), magnificent even, it gave him nightmares and he would be grateful it could be put away once and for all. Édouard did as he was asked.

And so to Pauline.

They had met because of a board meeting at the bank.

It was common knowledge that for some time now M. Péricourt was no longer as diligent in his work. He was less in evidence at the bank, and those who did see him said he had aged terribly. Was his daughter's marriage the cause? Or the weight of worries and responsibilities? No one even considered that it might be his son's death since, the day after he learned of the death, M. Péricourt had presided over the shareholders' Annual General Meeting with his customary aplomb; everyone had thought it brave of him to carry on despite his misfortune.

Whatever the cause, M. Péricourt was no longer the man he had been. Only a week ago, he had suddenly walked out of a meeting, "carry on without me," granted there were no critical decisions to make, but it was unlike the president to abdicate responsibility, he was more inclined to insist on personally making every decision, inviting opinions only on minor points that he had already settled. But at 3:00 p.m., he had got to his feet and walked out. Later, when it was discovered he had not gone home, there was some talk of a doctor's appointment, while others insisted there must be a woman involved. Only the guard at the cemetery gates, who had not been invited to join these conversations, could have told them where he really was.

At four o'clock, needing to get M. Péricourt to sign the minutes so the directives could be approved and implemented quickly (M. Péricourt did not like delays), it was decided to send the papers to his house. This was when they remembered Albert Maillard. No one at the bank knew how the boss and the clerk were connected, they knew only that the latter owed his job to the former. On this subject, too, there had been wild rumors, but Albert, with his blushes, his irrational fears, his nervousness, his way of flinching at the slightest sound, had discouraged all speculation. The managing director would gladly have delivered the documents to M. Péricourt's home in person, but, feeling that the role of errand boy was unbecoming to a man of his standing, he sent Albert.

No sooner had he received the order than Albert started to tremble. The boy was a conundrum. He had to be chivvied along, handed his coat, pushed out of the door; he seemed so disturbed, they were concerned that he might lose the papers along the way. A taxi was called, the return journey paid in advance, and the driver advised to keep an eye on Albert.

"Stop!" Albert shouted as soon as they reached the parc Monceau.

"But we're not there yet . . . ," the driver said hesitantly. He had been entrusted with a delicate mission and already there were problems.

"I don't care," Albert said. "Stop the car!"

When a customer gets angry, the best thing to do is get him out of the cab (Albert got out); wait until he is some distance away (the driver watched Albert falteringly head away from the address where he was supposed to be going); then, if you've been paid in advance, stamp on the accelerator and drive away, justifiable self-defense.

Albert did not even notice, so preoccupied had he been since leaving the bank at the thought of finding himself face-to-face with Pradelle. He had already imagined the scene, the *capitaine* gripping his shoulder, bending close.

"Well, well, Soldat Maillard, come to pay Capitaine d'Aulnay-Pradelle a little visit, have we? That's very kind of you . . . Come this way . . ."

Leading him down a corridor that turns into a cellar, they need to have a little chat, Pradelle beating him, trussing him up, torturing him, and, when Albert is finally forced to confess that he is sharing an apartment with Édouard Péricourt, that he has stolen money from the bank, that they are involved in an unspeakable swindle, Pradelle roaring with laughter as he looks up to heaven, invoking the wrath of the gods who rain down on him a quantity of earth equal to that displaced by a 95mm shell when you are at the bottom of a crater clutching the horse head mask you intend to wear when you arrive at the gates of a heaven reserved for fools.

As he did the first time, Albert turns, hesitates, retraces his steps, petrified at the thought of bumping into Pradelle, of having to see M. Péricourt, whose money he has embezzled, of seeing Édouard's sister and suddenly blurting out that her brother is still alive. Clutching the papers to him like a soul condemned, he racks his brain for some way he might deliver them to M. Péricourt without going into the house.

He needed someone to do it for him, that was it.

He was disappointed that the cab driver had taken off, he could have parked two streets away, delivered the message, and come back, Albert would have kept an eye on the taxi . . .

It was at that moment Pauline appeared.

Albert was standing on the other side of the street, one shoulder pressed against the wall; he saw her, but before he realized that this young woman was the answer to his prayers, he saw her as the embodiment of another fear. He had often thought about her, the pretty little housemaid who had laughed at his ridiculous shoes.

He walked straight into the lion's den.

She was hurrying along the street, probably late for her shift. As she walked, she had half-unbuttoned her coat to reveal a pale-blue calf-length dress cinched with a low-waisted belt. She was wearing a matching scarf. She skipped lightly up the steps to the front door and disappeared.

A few minutes later, Albert was ringing the bell, she opened the door, recognized him, he puffed out his chest because, since their last meeting, he had bought new shoes, and being a perceptive young woman, she noticed; she also noticed that he had a new coat, a fine shirt, a handsome tie, and still that curious, embarrassed expression as though he had just wet himself.

Who knows what was going through her mind, she started to laugh. The scene played out again, almost exactly as it had six months before. But things could not be exactly the same. They stood staring at each other as though he had come to see her, which, in a sense, was almost true.

There was a silence. God, but Pauline was pretty—the air of Love itself. Twenty-two, perhaps twenty-three, a smile that made your hair stand on end, velvet lips parted to reveal two perfect rows of dazzling teeth, and those eyes, that hair, cut short as was fashionable these days, flattering the nape of her neck, the curve of her throat, and, on the subject of curves, her sheer dress and white apron made it easy to imagine her breasts. Brunette. Ever since Cécile, he had hardly looked at a brunette, he had never looked at anyone.

Pauline glanced at the file crumpled in Albert's hands, reminding him of the reason for his visit, but also his dread of unpleasant encounters. He has already stepped inside; the most pressing thing now is to get out, quickly.

"I'm from the bank," he said foolishly.

Her lips formed a little circle. Without meaning to, he had made his impression: the bank, imagine that.

"This is for Monsieur Péricourt," he said and, realizing that he suddenly seemed more important, he could not help but add, "I have to give it to him in person . . ."

M. Péricourt was not at home; the young woman suggested that he wait and opened the drawing room door, bringing Albert crashing back to earth: it was madness to think of waiting, just coming here had been . . .

"No, no, thank you."

He held out the file. They both noticed it was damp with sweat, Albert tried to dry it on his sleeve, dropped the file, pages fluttering everywhere, and suddenly they were both on all fours, you can picture the scene . . .

This was how he had come into Pauline's life. Twenty-five? She did not look it. Not virginal, but virtuous. Her fiancé had been killed in 1917, there had been no one since, she assured him. Pauline made a pretty liar. It was not long before she and Albert were canoodling, but she did not want to go further since, for her, it was serious. She was drawn to Albert, to his innocent, heartbreaking face. He stirred motherly feelings in her, besides he had a good position as a bank clerk. Since he knew the owners, he probably had a great career ahead.

She did not know how much he earned, but it was obviously quite a bit since he invited her to nice restaurants, not swanky, but places with fine food and a middle-class clientele. He took taxis, at least when dropping her home. He invited her to the theater, not troubling to confess that it would be the first time he had set foot inside such a place, suggested the Opéra on Édouard's advice, but she preferred music hall.

Albert's money trickled through his fingers, his salary was not enough, and he had already drawn heavily on his share of the meager spoils from their scheme.

And now that it seemed clear that very little money was likely to come in, he wondered how to dig himself out of a hole that, for once, he had jumped into with no help from anyone.

If he were to go on courting Pauline, he wondered whether he might not have to "borrow" some more money from M. Péricourt's bank.

32

Henri had been born to a crumbling family and had spent his childhood watching the rot worsen, the catastrophes proliferate. Now that he was about to snatch a definitive victory from Fate, he was not going to let some insignificant civil servant stand in his way. Because that was what it amounted to. He would send the little inspector scurrying back under his rock. Who the hell did he think he was?

There was a considerable dose of self-deception behind this swaggering braggadocio. Henri needed to believe in his success; he could not bring himself to believe even for a second that in an era so propitious to the making of fortunes, he would not make his mark. The war had proved it: he had no fear of adversity.

Although it had to be admitted that, this time, the mood was rather different . . .

It was not the nature of the problems that worried him, but the sheer number of them.

The government had thus far not been too intrusive when it came to the reputations of Péricourt and Aulnay-Pradelle. Now, suddenly, this nonentity from the ministry had delivered a new report after an unscheduled visit to Pontaville-sur Meuse, peddling tales of theft and trafficking . . .

And, anyway, did this fellow even have the right to inspect sites without authorization?

Whatever the case, this time the government was proving more intractable. Henri had immediately requested an audience. But this had proved impossible.

"We can't cover up . . . all this stuff," he had been told on the telephone. "Until now, we were dealing with minor technical difficulties. But even then . . ."

The voice on the other end of the line became more muted, more embarrassed, as though confessing a secret and worried about being overheard.

". . . those coffins that did not meet the standards laid down in the contract . . ."

"I've explained all that!" roared Henri.

"Yes, I know. A manufacturing error . . . But this thing at Pontaville-sur Meuse, it's not the same. Dozens of soldiers buried under the wrong names is embarrassing enough, but the theft of personal belongings . . ."

"Oh, please . . ." Henri gave a blustering laugh. "Are you accusing me of grave robbing now?"

The silence that followed startled him.

The matter was serious, because it was no longer a question of one item, or even of two . . .

"There is talk that it was an arrangement . . . a systematic practice throughout the cemetery. The report is damning. This all happened behind your back, of course, you are not personally implicated."

"Ha! Ha! I'm happy to hear it."

But his heart was not in it. Personal or not, the criticism weighed heavily. If Dupré were here, he would have given him a hard time, but right now there was nothing to be lost by waiting.

At this point, Henri recalled that changes in strategy had proved very successful during the Napoleonic wars.

"Do you really think that the budget allocated by the government is enough to hire workers of unimpeachable competence and integrity?

Do they really think that at those prices we can afford be discriminating, to handpick our workers?"

Deep down, Henri knew he had been somewhat lax in his approach to hiring, opting always for the cheapest labor, but Dupré had assured him that the foremen were experienced, for Christ's sake! And that the laborers would be properly trained!

The minion on the telephone suddenly sounded harried, and the conversation ended on a note as black as a gathering storm cloud:

"The Central Services Department is not in a position to deal with the matter alone, Monsieur d'Aulnay-Pradelle. It will be have to be referred to the office of the minister himself."

A cowardly retreat!

In a black rage, Henri slammed down the phone, picked up a piece of Chinese porcelain, and shattered it against the inlaid table. The ingratitude! He had greased enough palms in that department, the least he could expect was a little protection! With the back of his hand, he dashed a crystal vase against the wall. What if he were to tell the minister just how his high-ranking civil servants had profited from his generosity?

Henri took a deep breath. His fury was directly proportionate to the gravity of the situation, since even he did not believe in this threat. Oh, there had been the occasional gift, a plush hotel room, a girl he had paid, a lavish meal, a box of cigars, a few bills picked up here and there, but to acknowledge even the most trivial corruption would be tantamount to admitting to bribery, he would be shooting himself in the foot.

Madeleine, alerted by the commotion, came in without bothering to knock.

"What's going on?"

Henri turned and saw her standing in the doorway. Though only six months pregnant, she looked full term. He found her ugly, though that was nothing new, it had been a long time since she had stirred in him even a flicker of desire. The reverse was also true, of course, he could scarcely remember Madeleine's passions. There had been a time when she behaved more like a mistress than a wife, when she hungered for him, craved him! All that was long ago, and yet Henri felt more attached to her now than he had then. Not to her, strictly speaking, but to the mother of his future son. An Aulnay-Pradelle heir who could take pride in his name, his fortune, his family home, a son who would not have to struggle as he had but who would build upon what his father hoped would be a sizable inheritance.

Madeleine tilted her head and frowned.

The ability to make swift decisions in difficult circumstances was one of Henri's talents. In a flash, he reviewed all the possible solutions to his troubles and realized that his wife was his last hope. He adopted the expression he most despised, the one that least suited him, that of a man overcome by events, he heaved a despondent sigh and slumped into a chair.

Madeleine immediately felt torn. She knew her husband better than anyone, and his affected helplessness left her unmoved. But there were ties between them; he was the father of her child. With only weeks to go before her confinement, she did not want to have to face new problems; she wanted peace. She had no need of Henri, but, just now, having a husband was useful.

She asked what was wrong.

"Business," he said cagily.

It was the sort of thing M. Péricourt said. When he did not wish to explain something, he would say, "It's just business." It was a man's expression. Eminently practical.

Henri looked at her and pursed his lips, Madeleine still found him handsome. Seeing he was waiting, she persisted.

"Well?" she moved toward him, "what is it?"

He was forced to make a painful confession, but the ends justified the means.

"I may need your father's help . . ."

"Why?"

Henri gave a dismissive wave, it was all too complicated . . .

"I see," she smiled, "Too complicated to explain to me, but straightforward enough to ask me to intercede . . ."

Henri, playing the broken man to the hilt, gave her a poignant smile, one he often used to seduce. It had served him well, that smile . . .

If she pressed him, Henri would simply lie to her, he always lied, even when it was pointless, it was in his nature. She laid a hand against his cheek. Duplicitous he might be, but he was handsome; this pretense of helplessness made him look younger, emphasized the delicacy of his features.

Madeleine reflected for a moment. Even in the first flush of their relationship, she had paid little heed to what her husband said; she had not married him for his conversation. Since she became pregnant, his pronouncements had drifted past like an insubstantial haze. And so, while he did his best to look stricken and overwhelmed—she trusted he was more convincing with his mistresses—she gazed at him with that nebulous tenderness one reserves for other people's children. He was beautiful. She would like to have a son like him. A little less mendacious, but just as handsome.

Then she left the room without a word, smiling softly as she always did when she felt the baby kick. She went straight to her father's study.

It was 10:00 a.m.

Recognizing his daughter's knock, M. Péricourt got up and went over, kissed her forehead, nodded at her belly, smiling, is everything all right? Madeleine made a face: so-so.

"I'd like you to speak to Henri, Papa," she said, "He has been having problems."

M. Péricourt stiffened imperceptibly at the mention of his son-in-law.

"Can't he deal with his problems by himself? And what exactly are these problems?"

Madeleine knew more than Henri believed she did, but not enough to enlighten her father.

"His contract with the government . . ."

"What about it?"

M. Péricourt said this in the steely tone he adopted when preparing to stand on principle; at such times he was difficult to manipulate. Intractable.

"I know that you don't like him, Papa, you've said as much before."

There was no anger in her voice, in fact she smiled gently, and since she seldom asked for anything, she calmly played her trump card.

"I'm asking you to see him, Papa."

She did not need to lay her hands on her belly. Her father had already nodded: very well, send him up.

M. Péricourt did not even pretend to be working when Pradelle knocked at the door. As he stepped into the room, Henri saw his father-in-law enthroned behind his desk at the far end, like God the Father. The distance between the desk and the chair reserved for visitors was boundless. In moments of adversity, Henri preferred to steel himself and attack head-on. The more daunting the problem, the more savage he became, he would not hesitate to kill. But today, the man he wanted to kill was the man whose help he needed; he loathed this position of subservience.

Since they met, the two men had been waging a war of contempt. M. Péricourt would greet his son-in-law with a curt nod, Henri responded in kind. From the instant of their first meeting, each had bided his time, waiting for an advantage, watching as the balance of power shifted: Henri had seduced his daughter, M. Péricourt had prevailed on the marriage contract . . . When Madeleine told her father she was pregnant, she had done so in private, Henri had been deprived of his victory, but it had been a decisive point. The balance of power was reversed: Henri's problems were temporary, Madeleine's child was not. And, as he saw it, this meant M. Péricourt was in duty bound to help him.

Marcel Péricourt smiled elusively, as though he could read Pradelle's mind.

"Yes . . . ?" he said gravely

"Could you have a word with the Ministre des Pensions?" Henri said in a clear voice.

"Of course, he is a dear friend." M. Péricourt hesitated for a moment. "He owes me a great deal. A personal debt, you might say. Ancient history now, of course, but the sort of affair that can make or break a man's reputation. In short, the minister is at my disposal, if I might put it so."

Henri had not anticipated such an easy victory. His assessment of the situation had proved more accurate than he had imagined. This was further confirmed when M. Péricourt looked away, staring down at his desk blotter.

"What does it concern . . . ?"

"A trifle . . . It's . . ."

"If it is a trifle," M. Péricourt said, looking up, "why trouble the minister? Why trouble me?"

Henri relished this moment. His adversary would put up a fight, try to put him in a difficult position, but sooner or later he would be forced to capitulate. Had he time, he would have enjoyed drawing out the delectable conversation, but it was urgent.

"There is a report that needs to be buried. It concerns my businesses, it is a tissue of lies and . . ."

"If it is lies, what have you to fear?"

Henri could not help himself, he smiled. Was the old man planning to carry on this fight for long? Did he feel the need to land a blow before he would shut up and do as he was bid?

"It's complicated . . ."

"And so?"

"And so I would be grateful if you could intercede with the minister and have the matter buried. For my part, I can assure you that there will be no recurrence of the incidents in question. They were the result of an oversight, nothing more."

M. Péricourt paused for a long moment, staring hard into Pradelle's eyes as if to say, "Is that all?"

"That's all," Henri assured him. "You have my word."

"Your word . . ."

Henri felt his smile wither, the old man was beginning to irritate him with these remarks. What choice did he have? His daughter was heavily pregnant, was he threatening to bankrupt his own grandson? It was a joke! Pradelle made a final concession.

"I'm asking this not only for myself, but for your daughter . . ."

"I'll thank you not to bring my daughter into this!"

This time, Henri could take no more.

"But that's exactly what's at stake here! My reputation, my businesses, so for the sake of your daughter and the future of your unborn . . ."

M. Péricourt could have raised his voice, but instead he tapped the desk blotter with his forefinger. A sharp rap like a teacher calling an unruly pupil to order. M. Péricourt remained calm, his voice was serene, he did not smile.

"This matter concerns you and only you, *monsieur*," he said.

Henri felt a creeping panic, but, though he racked his brain, he could not see how his father-in-law could avoid intervening on his behalf. Was he prepared to turn his back on his own daughter?

"I have been informed of your problems. Perhaps before you were."

This sounded promising, Henri thought, if Péricourt was trying to humiliate him, it meant he was prepared to give in.

"Not that I was surprised, I always knew you for a crook. One with an aristocratic name, but a crook nonetheless. You are an utterly unscrupulous man, driven by greed alone, and I confidently predict you will come to a very bad end."

Henri made to get up and leave.

"No, no, *monsieur*, you will stay and listen to what I have to say. I have been expecting your request, I have given the matter a great deal of thought, and I will tell you how I see things. In a few days, the dossier on you will be referred to the minister, and having been made aware of the various reports concerning your activities, he will set about revoking all the contracts you signed with the government."

Henri's earlier arrogance had drained from his face, he stared straight ahead with a look of horror, like a man watching a house being swept away by floodwaters. His house, his life.

"You have defaulted on contracts entered into with the nation; an inquiry will be launched to determine the exact nature of the material damage to the state, which you will have to pay from your personal fortune. If, as I have calculated, you do not have the necessary funds to meet the debt, you will be forced to request help from your wife, a request I will strongly oppose, as is my legal right. At that point, you will have to sell your family estate. Not that you will have any further need of it, since the government will haul you before the courts and, in order to exonerate itself, will have to join with the public prosecutor in the civil action brought by families and the war veterans associations. And you will end up in prison."

Henri had resigned himself to appealing to the old man because he knew he was in a delicate position, but what he was hearing was infinitely worse than anything he had imagined. The problems had escalated so quickly, he had not had time to react. Suddenly, a thought came to him.

"So, you are the one who . . . ?"

If he had had a gun, he would not have waited for an answer.

"No, no, why would I bother? You needed no help from anyone in getting into this mess. Madeleine asked me to speak to you, so I am speaking to you, and it is to say this: neither she nor I will be caught up in your business affairs. She wished to marry you, so be it, but you will not drag her down with you, I shall see to that. As far as I am concerned, you can sink without a trace; I will not lift a finger to help."

"You want a war?" Henri thundered.

"Do not ever raise your voice to me, *monsieur* . . ."

Henri did not wait to hear the rest of this sentence to get to his feet and stalk out of the room, jerking the door viciously behind him. The ripples from the bang would set the whole house quaking. But the door, fitted with a pneumatic damper, swung slowly to, *pff* . . . *pff* . . . *pff* . . . , with a soft, rhythmic hiss.

Henri had reached the ground floor by the time it finally closed with a muffled thud.

Still at his desk, M. Péricourt had not moved.

33

"It's nice here . . . ," Pauline said, looking around.

Albert wanted to say something, but the words stuck in his throat. He spread his hands wide, dancing from one foot to the other.

Since they had known each other, they had always met outside. She had a small attic room in the servants' quarters of the Péricourts' mansion, and the agency had been clear: "Visitors are strictly forbidden, *mademoiselle*," the accepted way of telling one's domestics that if they wished to fuck, they should do so elsewhere, we'll have none of that here, this is a god-fearing house, and so on . . .

Meanwhile, Albert could hardly bring Pauline back to his apartment. Édouard never went out—where could he go? And besides, even if he had agreed to let Albert have the apartment to himself for the night, it would be no use. Albert had been lying to Pauline from the start, what could he do now? I live in lodgings, he had told her, the landlady who runs the place is very strict, very suspicious, visitors strictly forbidden, just like yours, but I'm looking to find somewhere else.

Pauline had been neither shocked nor impatient. In fact she seemed reassured. She said it was all right, that she was "not that kind of girl" (implication: she did not sleep around), that she wanted a "serious relationship" (implication: marriage). Albert found it impossible to sort the truth from the lies. She did not want to "do it," he accepted that, but every time he took her home and they were about to go their separate ways, there were wild, passionate kisses; they would huddle in doorways, legs entwined, rubbing against each other frantically. Pauline would inevitably push Albert's hand away, but she did so later and later; in fact the other night she had gripped him harder, let out a long hoarse cry, and sunk her teeth into his shoulder. He had climbed back into the taxi gingerly, like a man carrying explosives.

This was how things stood on June 22, when the Patriotic Memory scheme eventually took off.

All of a sudden, money began to pour in.

Torrents of it.

Within a week, their tidy little sum quadrupled. More than 300,000 francs. Five days later, they had banked 570,000 francs; by June 30, they had 627,000 . . . there was no end to it. They had orders for 100 crosses, 120 torches, 182 busts, and 111 memorials of various designs; Jules d'Épremont had even won the contract for the memorial to be built in the *arrondissement* where Édouard was born, a down payment of 100,000 francs had been paid by the council.

Fresh orders came in every day, and with them more payments. Édouard spent his mornings making out receipts.

This manna from heaven had a curious effect; only now did they begin to realize what they had set in motion. They were already rich, and Édouard's hypothetical million francs no longer seemed a pipe dream. July 14 was still some way off and the bank account of Patriotic Memory was swelling daily . . . Each day, 10,000; 20,000; 50,000; 80,000 francs . . . it was incredible. One morning, there had been a draft for 117,000 francs.

At first, Édouard was delirious with joy. When Albert had come home with a briefcase filled with bills, he had tossed them in the air and watched them fall like life-giving rain. He asked whether he might take some of his share right now, and Albert, laughing, had said of course, no problem. The following day, Édouard created an extraordinary mask, a swirling spiral made entirely of two-hundred franc bills. The effect was superb, a seething mass of bills that seemed to be ablaze, wreathing his face in a halo of smoke. Albert was amazed, but he was also shocked, one did not do such things with money. He might be swindling hundreds of people, but he had not abandoned all moral sense.

Édouard, for his part, was stamping his feet with glee. He never counted the money, but the orders he carefully preserved like trophies, rereading them at night, sipping a drink using his pipette; this file was his Book of Hours.

When the wonder of being rich began to fade, Albert began to comprehend the magnitude of the risk. The more the money poured in, the more he felt the noose tighten around his neck. Ever since the total had reached 300,000 francs, he had thought only of getting away. Édouard demurred; his target of 1 million was not negotiable.

And there was Pauline to think of. What could he do?

Albert, besotted, longed for her with a passion magnified a hundredfold by the self-restraint she imposed on him. The problem was, he had started out on the wrong footing; one lie had led inevitably to another. Could he really tell her the truth now, without losing her? "Pauline, I need to tell you something, the truth is I work as a clerk in a bank, but only so I can get my fingers in the till because a friend (a crippled war vet with a hole for a face and a loose grip on reality) and I have set up a deeply immoral scheme to swindle half the country, and two weeks from now, on July 14, we plan to run off to the far side of the world, do you want to come with me?"

Did he love her? He was crazy about her. But with Albert, it was impossible to know what would prevail: the fierce desire he felt for her or the mounting dread of being arrested, tried, and sentenced. He had not dreamed of the firing squad since those long nights back in 1918 after he had been interrogated by Général Morieux under the stern eye of Capitaine Pradelle. Now he had those dreams every night. When he was not making love to Pauline, he was being gunned down by twelve identical facsimiles of Capitaine Pradelle. Whether it ended with him dying the little death or the actual one, the effect was the same, he would wake with a start, bathed in sweat, haggard and howling. He would grope for his horse head mask, the only thing that could calm his fears.

The first feverish joy of realizing that their plan had succeeded mutated quickly, in both men and for different reasons, into an strange coolness, the calm one feels after completing an important task that has required a great deal of time and that, in hindsight, no longer seems as necessary as one had supposed.

With or without Pauline, all Albert could talk of was leaving. Now that the money was rolling in, Édouard could think of little reason to demur. Reluctantly, he accepted.

It was agreed that, since the Patriotic Memory promotion was to come to an end on July 14, they would leave on the fifteenth.

"Why wait until the day after?" Albert said, flustered.

"Alright, the fourteenth," Édouard wrote.

Albert threw himself on the shipping company maps, tracing a line from Paris—a night train that would arrive in Marseille in the early hours—then the route of the first ship leaving for Tripoli. He was thankful he had kept the military record belonging to poor Louis Évrard, which he had stolen a few days after the armistice. The next day, he would buy the tickets.

Three tickets.

One for Eugène Larivière, two in the names of M. and Mme Louis Évrard.

He had no idea how to go about things with Pauline. Was it possible, in two weeks, to persuade a girl to leave everything and flee eighteen hundred miles with you? He was beginning to have his doubts.

This particular June seemed to have been made for lovers, a blissful balminess and, when Pauline was not on shift, for long endless evenings, hours and hours spent caressing, talking, sitting on park benches. Pauline told him about her girlish dreams, about the apartment, the children she wanted one day, talked about a future husband, her description gradually coming to sound more like the Albert she knew and less like the real Albert, who was nothing but a small-time crook about to flee the country.

In the meantime, he had money. Albert looked around for lodgings where he could bring Pauline, if she agreed to join him. He dismissed the idea of a hotel, deciding that, in the circumstances, it would be in poor taste.

Two days later, he found a clean, tidy lodging house near Saint-Lazare run by two sisters, broad-minded widows who rented two apartments to straitlaced civil servants, but reserved a small second-floor bedroom for clandestine couples whom they welcomed, day or night, with a complicit smile, having had holes drilled in the partition wall at bed level: each sister had her own.

Pauline had been hesitant. The same old refrain, "I'm not that kind of girl," but then she agreed. They took a taxi. Albert opened the door to a room that was furnished in just the style Pauline dreamed of, heavy curtains that looked swanky, wallpaper on the walls. A small pedestal table and a squat armchair made it seem as though it were more than just a bedroom.

"It's nice . . . ," she said.

"Yes, it's not bad," Albert said.

Was he a complete idiot? Whatever the case, he certainly did not see what was coming. Allow three minutes for going in, looking around, taking off her coat, add another minute for boots because of the laces, and you had Pauline, naked, standing in the middle of the room, smiling, accessible, confident, breasts so white you could weep, deliciously curving hips, a perfectly trimmed delta . . . All this to say that this was not her first time, and that, having spent weeks protesting about the kind of girl she was not, having paid lip service to respectability, she was keen to get started. Albert was completely out of his depth. Add another four minutes and you have Albert howling with pleasure. Pauline looked at him, puzzled and concerned, but quickly closed her eyes again because Albert still had reserves. He had not experienced anything like this since Cécile, the night before he was called up, some centuries ago, he had so much catching up to do that eventually Pauline had to say, it's two in the morning, darling, maybe we should get a little sleep, all right? They snuggled like spoons. Pauline was already asleep when Albert started crying—quietly so as not to wake her.

He would come home late at night after leaving Pauline. From the day she first lay on top of him in the little furnished room, Édouard saw less and less of him. Before picking her up on the nights when she was not working, Albert would go back to the apartment with his briefcase crammed with bills. Tens, hundreds of thousands of francs were stuffed into a suitcase and slipped under the bed he no longer slept in. He would check that Édouard had eaten and, before going out, he would say goodnight to Louise, bent over tomorrow's mask, and she would answer distractedly with a sulky stare as though he were abandoning them.

One evening when Albert came home—it would have been July 2, a Friday—with a briefcase containing 73,000 francs, he found the apartment empty.

With a multitude of masks of every shape and color hanging on the wall, the huge room looked like the reserve collection of a museum. A caribou with outsized antlers fashioned from tiny slivers of wood glowered down at Albert. Everywhere he looked—from the richly bejeweled Indian with lips like snakes, to the strange, tortured individual with the enormous nose, like a liar caught in the act, who made you want to absolve him of his sins—creatures gazed at him kindly as he stood in the doorway with his briefcase.

You can imagine his panic: Édouard had left the apartment only once since they had moved in. There was no sign of Louise. No note on the table. Albert dived under the bed, the suitcase was still there, and if there was any money missing, it was not obvious—there was so much cash, someone could take fifty thousand and it would be impossible to tell. It was 7:00 p.m. Albert dropped his briefcase and rushed down to Mme Belmont.

"He asked if he could take Louise away for the weekend. I said yes . . ."

It was expressed in her usual tone, clipped, impassive, factual, like a headline in a newspaper. The woman was utterly disembodied.

Albert worried because Édouard was capable of anything. Imagining him at large in the city was enough to panic anyone . . . Albert had explained a thousand times that the situation was dangerous, that they had to leave as soon as possible. And that if they really had to wait (Édouard was deeply attached to the idea of his million) they had to be vigilant, and, above all, to not attract attention.

"When people realize what we've done," he said, "it won't take them long to track us down. There's evidence I was at the bank, people saw me every day at the post office on the rue du Louvre, the mailman has been delivering cartloads of mail here, we hired a printer who will turn us in the moment he realizes the mess we have got him caught up in. It will take the police a couple of days to find us. A couple of hours, maybe . . ."

Édouard assented. A couple of days. Be vigilant. And now, two weeks before they were due to disappear, he had walked out of the apartment and gone wandering around Paris with a little girl, or elsewhere, as though he were no more hideous or identifiable than any other war veteran you might see on the street . . .

Where in hell could he have gone?

34

"I have had a letter to say the artist is in the Americas . . ."

Labourdin always used the plural when talking about America, believing that an expression that encompassed the whole continent thereby enhanced his own importance. M. Péricourt was irked.

"He will be back in mid-July," the mayor reassured.

"That seems rather late . . ."

Labourdin, who had anticipated this reaction, gave a smile.

"Not at all, not at all, *monsieur le président*! He is so excited about the project that he has set to work already. And he is making great strides. Just think, our memorial will have been conceived in New York (Labourdin pronounced it *Nooyeurk*) and constructed in Paris, what a powerful symbol . . ."

With a relish he normally reserved for richly sauced meats and his secretary's *derrière*, he took a large envelope from his inside pocket.

"I have here some new sketches sent by the artist."

M. Péricourt held out his hand, but Labourdin could not resist holding the envelope a fraction of a second longer.

"Beyond magnificent, *monsieur le président*, consummate!"

What did it mean, this prolixity? It was impossible to tell. Labourdin constructed sentences from sounds rather than ideas. M. Péricourt wasted no time thinking about it, Labourdin was a perfectly spherical imbecile—turn him any which way and he was equally stupid: there was nothing to be understood, nothing to be gleaned.

M. Péricourt dismissed the man before opening the envelope, he wanted to be alone.

Jules d'Épremont had enclosed eight drawings. Two elevations sketched from an unusual angle, as though the viewer were beside the memorial and looking up from below, it was very striking. The first was of the right-hand panel "France Leading Her Troops to War"; the second, the left: "Valiant Soldiers Attacking the Enemy."

M. Péricourt was thunderstruck. The memorial, previously inert, had taken on a very different quality. Was it the unusual perspective? The fact that it seemed to loom over you, dwarfing you, crushing you . . . ?

He tried to articulate his impression. The word came to him, straightforward, almost senseless, yet it meant everything: "alive." It was an absurd choice of word, the sort of thing Labourdin might use, but there was a truthfulness in these two scenes, a realism that surpassed the newspaper photographs he had seen of soldiers dying on the battlefield.

The six other sketches were details from the whole: the face of the woman in flowing robes, the profile of one of the soldiers; the face that had persuaded M. Péricourt to settle on this design was not there . . . Exasperating.

He leafed through the pictures, set them against the shelves, and spent a long moment trying to imagine walking around the actual memorial, even projecting himself inside it. There is no other way to express it: M. Péricourt began to live *inside* his memorial, as though he had a double life, a mistress holed up in his rooms, and spent hours there unbeknownst to everyone. After several days, he knew the project so intimately that he could imagine it from perspectives the artist had not drawn.

He made no attempt to hide anything from Madeleine, it was futile. Had there been a woman in his life, she would have guessed it in a heartbeat. When she came into the study, she would find her father standing in the middle of the room with the drawings spread out on the floor, or sitting in his armchair with a magnifying glass considering some detail. He handled the drawings so much that he was afraid he might crease them.

A picture framer was summoned to take measurements (M. Péricourt refused to be parted from the drawings) and two days later returned with the glass frames; by evening, the work had been completed. In the meantime, two laborers had come to dismantle various sections of the bookcases to create space where they would hang. The study went from being a framing workshop to a gallery devoted to a single work: his memorial.

M. Péricourt continued to work, attending conferences, chairing board meetings, meeting with stockbrokers and branch managers in his office, but more than ever, he could not wait to come home, to shut himself away. As a rule, he dined alone, having his meals brought to him.

A gradual maturation had taken place in him. He finally began to understand certain things, to rediscover old sorrows such as he had felt at the death of his wife, the impressions of emptiness, of resignation he had experienced then. He no longer reproached himself about Édouard; in making peace with his son, he had made peace with himself, with the man he had been.

This consolation was accompanied by another discovery. From the sketches Édouard had made in the trenches and these new drawings of the memorial, M. Péricourt began to have an almost physical sense of something he would never truly know: war. He who had always had little imagination suddenly felt his emotions stirred by the simple contemplation of the sketched face of a solider, the tumult of a frieze . . . And he experienced a sort of transference. Now that he no longer rebuked himself for having been a thoughtless, insensitive father, now that he accepted his son, his son's life, he suffered all the more greatly from his death. A few days before the armistice!—as though the injustice of Édouard dying when others had come back alive were not enough. Had he died instantly, as M. Maillard had said? Sometimes,

M. Péricourt had to restrain himself from summoning the *poilu* who now worked somewhere in his bank and wringing the truth from him. But, in the end, how much could his comrade really know about what Édouard had felt at the moment he died?

The more he studied this work in progress, the more M. Péricourt felt himself drawn, not to the strangely familiar face that Madeleine had pointed out and he himself had remembered, but to the dead soldier in the right-hand panel and the inconsolable gaze turned on him by "Victory." The artist had managed to capture something uncomplicated and profound. M. Péricourt felt tears start as he realized that his emotion came from the fact their roles had been reversed: he was now the dead soldier. His son was "Victory," gazing down upon his father with a look that was sorrowful, desolate, heartrending.

It was past 5:30 p.m., but the afternoon heat showed no sign of abating. Inside the rented car it was sweltering; even rolling down the window offered no relief, nothing but a warm, muggy breeze. Henri nervously tapped his knee. He could think of nothing but M. Péricourt's remark about selling la Sallevière. If it came to that, he would kill the old bastard with his bare hands! What part had Péricourt really played in his predicament, he wondered. Had he stirred things up? Why had this government minion suddenly turned up, why had he been so dogged, so relentless? Was his father-in-law not behind it? Henri was lost in conjecture.

His gloomy thoughts and his suppressed fury did not stop him from keeping a close eye on Dupré, some distance away, anxiously pacing like a man in a quandary.

Henri rolled up the window so that he would not be seen, recognized, there was little point in hiring a car only to be spotted on a street corner . . . He had a lump in his throat. During the war, at least he knew his enemy! Though he tried to focus on the trials he had to face, his thoughts drifted back to la Sallevière. He would never give it up. He had been there only last week; the restoration work was faultless, the estate and the grounds looked magnificent. One could easily imagine the majestic facade as horses and hounds set off on a hunt, or the bridal party returning from his son's wedding . . . He refused to give up on such dreams; nothing, and no one, would take them from him.

After his meeting with Péricourt, he had one round left, just one.

And I am an excellent marksman, he reassured himself.

He had had only three hours in which to organize a counteroffensive, his shock troops amounted to Dupré. Too bad, he would fight to the death. If he won this battle—it would be difficult, but he could pull it off—his sole target would become that old bastard Péricourt. However long it takes, he thought, I will destroy him. Just the sort of pledge to rally his spirits.

Dupré suddenly looked up, crossed the street, strode quickly past the entrance to the ministry, and grabbed the arm of a man who turned in surprise. Watching from a distance, Henri sized up the individual. Had he been the sort of man who took pride in his appearance, anything was possible, but the man looked like a tramp. This would be a delicate negotiation.

Standing in the middle of the pavement looking bewildered, he towered head and shoulders above Dupré. Dubiously, he followed Dupré's signal and glanced toward the car in which Henri was sitting. Henri noticed the man's filthy, decrepit clodhoppers; it was the first time he had seen a man who resembled his shoes. Eventually, the two men turned began to walk slowly toward the car. A first-round victory, Henri decided, though no guarantee of a victory.

This became clear as soon as Merlin got into the car. He was surly and smelled foul. He had had to bend low in order to get in and now sat with his head drawn in as though expecting a hail of missiles. He set down between his feet a fat leather briefcase that had seen better days. He was long past his prime, and surely close to retirement. Wild eyed, ill mannered, and unkempt, everything about the man was shabby and ugly, it was surprising he still had a position.

Henri proffered his hand, but Merlin did not react, he merely stared. Best to get to the heart of the matter.

Henri spoke with an affected familiarity, as though they had known each other for a long time and were discussing some trivial matter.

"You wrote two reports, I believe . . . concerning the cemeteries in Chazières-Malmont and Pontaville?"

Merlin responded with a grunt. He did not like this man who reeked of money and looked like a crook. The very fact that he had ambushed him here so that they could meet surreptitiously in a car . . .

"Three," he said.

"I beg your pardon?"

"Three reports, not two. I'm about to file one about the cemetery at Dargonne-le-Grand."

From the way he said it, Pradelle realized that the screw was about to tighten.

"Whe . . . when did you visit the site?"

"Last week. Not a pretty sight."

"In what sense?"

Pradelle, who had been preparing to defend himself on two fronts, now found he would have to deal with a third.

"You know . . . ," said Merlin.

He had bad breath and a grating, nasal voice. Henri had hoped to be smiling, genial, the sort of man who inspires confidence, but Dargonne . . . it was more than he could bear. Dargonne was a small cemetery, no more than two or three hundred graves; the bodies were being brought from Verdun. What the hell had his men done this time? He had heard of nothing untoward. Instinctively, he looked across the street to where Dupré was standing, smoking, peering into windows, plainly as nervous as Henri. Merlin was the only one who seemed calm.

"You need to keep an eye on your workforce . . ."

"Of course! That's precisely the problem, *monsieur*. But it's almost impossible given the number of sites we have to oversee."

Merlin was not going to offer a crumb of sympathy. He held his tongue. For Henri, it was essential to get the man to talk, there is nothing to be had from a man who says nothing. He adopted the tone of a man intrigued by a story that does not concern him personally, something frivolous but fascinating . . .

"So . . . Dargonne . . . what exactly has been happening there?"

Merlin said nothing for a long moment. Henri wondered whether he had heard the question. When at length he spoke, his face was utterly impassive, only his lips moved; it was impossible to gauge his mood.

"You're paid by the unit, yes?"

Henri held out his hands, palms upward.

"Of course. That's standard practice, we're paid based on the amount of work involved."

"And your laborers are paid by the unit . . . ?"

Henri made a face: obviously, so what? What was he getting at?

"That would explain why you have coffins filled with dirt," Merlin said.

Henri's his eyes widened; what the hell was the man talking about?

"There are coffins with no bodies in them," Merlin went on, "To pad out their pay packets, your men are transporting and interring coffins that contain no remains. Just soil to make up the weight . . ."

Pradelle's instinctive reflex was surprising. He thought: the fucking idiots, I've had just about enough of them! He casually lumped Dupré together with all the cretins hoping to make a little extra cash with this nonsense. For a brief moment, the whole affair no longer concerned him, let them sort it out, he was sick and tired of the whole thing!

Merlin's voice jolted him back to reality and the fact that, as director of the company, he was the one in the firing line; the minions would be dealt with later.

"And then . . . and then there's the Boches," Merlin said.

Still only his lips moved.

"The Boches?"

Henri sat up in his seat. This was the first glimmer of hope. Because when it came to the Boches, he could hold his own against anyone. Merlin shook his head—no—a movement so slight that at first Henri did not notice. Then doubts began to set in: the Boches? What did he mean, the Boches? What the hell had they to do with anything? His bafflement was could be read in his face, and Merlin responded as though he had voiced his confusion.

"If you go there, to Dargonne . . . ," he said.

Then stopped. Henri jerked his chin, go on, spit it out, let's get this over with.

". . . there are French graves with Boche soldiers in them."

Henri was aghast, his mouth opened and closed like a fish. This was a disaster. A corpse is a corpse when you come down to it, and as far as Pradelle was concerned, once a man was dead, he didn't give a tinker's curse whether he was French or German or Senegalese. In the makeshift graveyards, it was not uncommon to come across the body of a foreign soldier, or even several, who had strayed between the scouts and the shock troops; soldiers were forever moving back and forth across the lines . . . Draconian instructions had been set down on the subject: the bodies of German soldiers were to be strictly separated from those of the victorious heroes; special sections had been set aside for them in the government war graves. Although the German government and the German War Graves Commission were in discussion with French authorities about the eventual fate of the tens of thousands of "foreign bodies," in the meantime deliberately burying a Boche—they were plainly identifiable by their uniforms—in the grave of a French soldier was tantamount to sacrilege.

The very idea of a Boche soldier in a French tomb, of families kneeling in prayer over the mortal remains of enemy soldiers, over the bodies of the men who had killed their children, was unthinkable, it verged on desecration.

Outrage guaranteed.

"I'll take care of it . . . ," Pradelle muttered, though he had no idea of the scale of the catastrophe, or how to rectify it.

How many were there? How long had they been putting Boche corpses in French coffins? How could they be tracked down?

It was more important than ever that this report be hushed up.

It was imperative.

Henri studied Merlin more carefully and realized he was even older than he had appeared . . . those deep wrinkles, that glassy film over the eyes that indicates cataracts. He had a disproportionately small head, like certain insects.

"How long have you been a civil servant?"

Pradelle's questions was curt, peremptory, his tone almost military. To Merlin, it sounded like an accusation. He did not like Aulnay-Pradelle, the man was exactly as he had pictured him, he was a loudmouth, a chancer, a rich bastard, a cynic—a word much in vogue sprang to mind: "profiteer." Merlin had got into the car because he had had no choice, but he felt as uncomfortable there as in a coffin.

"A civil servant? All my life."

It was said without pride, without bitterness, the simple factual statement of a man who had never imagined being anything else.

"And what is your grade, Monsieur Merlin?"

He had hit the nail on the head, but it was a crass remark, because for Merlin, who was only a few months from retirement, being at the bottom of the heap was a raw wound, a humiliation. His only promotions had been awarded for length of service, and he found himself in the position of a rank-and-file soldier about to finish his career as a private.

"Your work on these inspections has been extraordinary," Pradelle went on ingratiatingly. If Merlin had been a woman, he would have grasped his hand.

"Thanks to your efforts, your diligence, we will be able to deal with these improprieties. Any corrupt workers will be immediately dismissed. Your reports will be invaluable, we will use them to sort this out once and for all."

Merlin wondered for a moment who exactly Pradelle meant when he said "we." Then the answer came to him, "we" was a euphemism for Pradelle's supremacy, his friends, his family, his connections . . .

"I'm sure the minister himself will be impressed," Henri said, "I'd even venture to say grateful! Yes, grateful for your diligence and your discretion. Because it goes without saying that, though your reports will be invaluable to us, I'm sure you agree that no one would benefit from this news becoming public . . ."

"Us" stood for a whole world of power and influence, of friends in high places, decision makers, the cream of the crop, everything, in fact, that Merlin despised.

And yet, and yet . . . Sad though it was, in spite of himself Merlin felt something swelling inside him, like an unbidden erection. After the years of humiliation, the thought of a promotion, of silencing the wagging tongues, perhaps even being in charge of those who had humiliated him . . . For a few seconds he was swept along.

Pradelle could see from this pathetic man's face that he could be bought by any prospect of advancement, for a string of glass beads like the Negroes in the colonies.

". . . and I shall personally see to it that your talents and your efficiency are not forgotten, on the contrary, they will be amply rewarded!"

Merlin nodded.

"Here, while I think of it . . . ," he said in a dull voice, bending over his bulging briefcase and rummaging inside. Henri could breathe easily now, he had found the key. Now all he needed to do was persuade the man to withdraw his reports, retract everything, write new positive reports in exchange for some award, some promotion, some bonus: with such mediocrities anything would do.

Merlin continued rummaging in his case, then he sat up again, clutching a crumpled piece of paper.

". . . while I think of it," he said again, "here's something else you might like to sort out."

Henri took the piece of paper and read it. It was an advertisement. Blood drained from his face. A company called Frépaz was offering to pay "a fair price for any and all dentures, even if cracked or broken."

The inspection report was dynamite.

"Works pretty well, apparently," Merlin said, "turns a little profit for the workers on the ground, only a couple of centimes per denture, but, you know, mighty oaks from little acorns grow."

He nodded to the pamphlet.

"You can keep that, I put a copy in with my report."

He bent down to pick up his briefcase, his tone now that of a man no longer interested in the conversation. And this was so, because the vision he had glimpsed had come too late. The burning desire for promotion, for status, had guttered out. He was on the brink of retiring from the Civil Service, he had long since given up all thought of preferment. Nothing could wipe out the forty years he had endured. Besides, what would he do sitting in a manager's chair giving orders to people he despised? He tapped his bag—right, well, it's not that I'm bored or anything, but . . .

Pradelle suddenly gripped his arm. Beneath the coat he felt how thin the man was, felt the bone, it was a disagreeable feeling. Merlin flinched, though he was not easily intimidated. Pradelle's whole body exuded violence, he was gripping Merlin's forearm with cruel force.

"How much do you earn?"

Merlin pretended to think. Of course he knew the figure by heart, 1,044 francs a month, 12,000 francs a year, a pittance on which he had eked out a living all his life. He owned nothing, he would die nameless and destitute, would leave nothing to anyone, but it hardly mattered, there was no one to leave it to. The shame he felt about his salary was a more sensitive subject than his status, which mattered only within the ministry. Financial hardship is something you take with you everywhere, it shapes your life, rules it entirely, it oozes from every pore. Privation is worse than utter destitution, it is possible to be destitute but noble, but hardship fosters meanness, it turns a man into a skinflint, debases him, makes him less than whole, it robs him of his pride, his dignity.

This was how Merlin felt, his eyes grew dim, and when he came to his senses again, he was dazzled.

Pradelle was holding out a large envelope stuffed with bills big as banana leaves. There was no more attempt at subtlety. The former *capitaine* had not needed to read Kant to know that every man has his price.

"Let's not beat around the bush," Pradelle said. "There is fifty thousand francs in this envelope . . ."

Now Merlin truly was out of his depth. Five years' salary for a man at the end of his career. Faced with such a sum, no one can be unmoved, you cannot help yourself, before you know it images flash before your eyes, mentally you begin to calculate, how much does it cost to buy a home, an automobile . . . ?

"And in this one" (Pradelle took a second envelope from his inside pocket), "there is precisely the same sum."

A hundred thousand francs. Ten years' salary. The proposition had an immediate effect, Merlin seemed twenty years younger. He did not hesitate, in a flash he ripped the envelopes from Pradelle's hands.

He hunched over, snuffling loudly, he looked like he was sobbing as he bent down and began stuffing the envelopes into his briefcase as though there was a hole in the bottom he was trying to plug.

Even Pradelle was surprised at the swiftness of his reaction, but a hundred thousand francs was a lot of cash, he wanted to ensure he got value for money. He gripped Merlin's arm so hard he almost snapped the bone.

"I want you to flush those reports down the toilet," he said through gritted teeth. "Write to your superiors, tell them you made a mistake, tell them what you like, I don't give a damn, just make sure you take the blame. Is that clear?"

It was crystal clear. Yes, yes, yes, Merlin spluttered, sniffling, tears in his eyes; he scrambled out of the car. Dupré saw the towering figure suddenly pop out onto the pavement like a champagne cork.

Pradelle gave a satisfied smile.

He thought about his father-in-law. Now that the horizon seemed clearer, he could devote his energies to the vital question: how could he crush the old bastard completely?

Dupré crouched and, peering through the windshield, gave his boss a questioning look.

And as for you, Pradelle was thinking, I'll take you in hand . . .

35

The chambermaid had the disagreeable feeling of being a trainee acrobat. The large lemon, an exemplary yellow, kept wobbling around on the silver tray, threatening at any moment to fall and roll down the stairs; with her luck, it would probably roll like this all the way to the manager's office. Just the ticket to get herself an earful, she thought. There was no one about to see, she stuffed the lemon in her pocket, flipped the tray under her arm, and carried on up the stairs. (At the Lutetia, staff were not allowed to use the elevator. It was preposterous!)

If any other guest had requested a lemon be brought up to the sixth floor, she would have been brusque. But not with Monsieur Eugène. Monsieur Eugène was different. He never spoke. When he wanted something, he left a message written in large letters for the bellboy outside the door of his suite. He was very polite, very correct.

But mad as a hatter.

In the household (for which read "at the Lutetia"), it had taken only two or three days before everyone knew about Monsieur Eugène. He paid for his suite in cash several days in advance; as soon as he received the bill it was paid. A real character: no one had ever seen his face, and as for his voice, he would only grunt or give a shrill laugh that either made you titter or chilled your blood. No one knew what he did precisely, he wore huge masks, never the same one twice, and he had strange whims: he did Indian war dances in the corridors that had the chambermaids giggling, he ordered extravagant quantities of flowers . . . And that was not all. A week ago, he had requested a string octet and, when advised they were about to arrive, had gone downstairs to the lobby, stood on the top step, and conducted the ensemble as they played Lully's *Marche pour la Cérémonie des Turcs*, then went back to his room. Monsieur Eugène had given all the staff fifty francs for their trouble. The manager himself had visited him to say that, while his generosity was much appreciated, these little whims . . . This is a grand hotel, Monsieur Eugène, we have to think of the other guests, and of our reputation. Monsieur Eugène had nodded, he was not a difficult guest.

The masks particularly intrigued the staff. When he first arrived he had been wearing a mask that looked almost normal; it looked so real anyone would have sworn it was a man suffering from paralysis. The features were frozen, but so lifelike . . . Much more so than the waxworks at the Musée Grévin. This was the mask he wore when he went out, which was very rarely. He had set foot outside only once or twice, always late at night, it was obvious he did not want to run into anyone. Some said he frequented places of dubious repute—at that time of night, he was hardly going to church!

Gossip was rife. Anyone who had been up to his room was immediately interrogated—what had they seen this time? When he ordered the lemon, there had been much talk about who would take it up. When she went back downstairs, the chambermaid knew she would be bombarded with questions, since the other maids had all reported the most amazing scenes, arriving to find Monsieur Eugène dressed in an African bird mask and squawking wildly, or performing to an audience of empty chairs draped with empty suits, a one-man show where the actor seemed to be on stilts and babbling unintelligible words . . . This, then, was the question: no one doubted that Monsieur Eugène was an eccentric, but who was he really?

Some said he was mute since he made only gurgling sounds and wrote his requests on loose sheets of papers; others said he was a *gueule cassée,* his face blown off in the war, who knows why, the *gueules cassées* we know are ordinary folk, not rich men like him, yes, yes, you're right, that's strange, I never noticed . . . Nonsense, snapped the linen maid, speaking from her thirty years' experience in the hotel business, I'm telling you, that whole thing is a trick. She was convinced he was a criminal on the run, a rich escaped convict. The chambermaids laughed; they were convinced Monsieur Eugène was a great actor, an American star who was staying in Paris incognito.

He had shown his military record when he first checked in, he was obliged to provide some form of identification, although the police rarely inspected hotels of this standing. Eugène Larivière. The name did not ring a bell with anyone. In fact, it sounded slightly fake . . . No one could quite believe it. Besides, the linen maid said with authority, there's nothing easier to fake than a military record.

Aside from his rare, intriguing nocturnal sorties, Monsieur Eugène spent most of this time in his large sixth-floor suite, and his only visitor was the little girl with whom he had first arrived, a strange, silent child with the solemn air of a governess. He could have communicated through her, but no, she, too, was mute. About twelve, judging by her appearance, she would arrive in the late afternoon and dash through the lobby without a word to anyone, though they had noticed how pretty she was, a triangular face with high cheekbones and dark, sparkling eyes. She dressed modestly and correctly, and it was clear she had a modicum of education. His daughter, some claimed. Adopted, others suggested, but on this subject, too, no one knew anything for sure. Every evening, he would call room service and order all manner of exotic dishes, but always accompanied by beef bouillon, fruit juices, compotes, sorbets, and sundry liquid provisions.

Then, at about 10:00 p.m., the girl would come downstairs, solemn and self-composed, she would take a taxi on the corner of the boulevard Raspail and always asked the fare before getting in. If it seemed excessive, she would haggle, only for the driver to realize when they had reached their destination that with that wad of bills in her pocket she could pay his fare thirty times over . . .

At the door to Monsieur Eugène's suite, the chambermaid took the lemon from her pocket and balanced it carefully on the silver tray, rang the bell, and patted down her uniform, anxious to make a good impression; she waited. Nothing. She knocked again, more discreetly this time; she was happy to serve, but reluctant to disturb. Still nothing. And then something. A slip of paper slid under the door: "Leave the lemon outside, thank you." She was disappointed, though not for long because, just as she bent to set down the tray and the lemon, a fifty-franc bill appeared under the door. She pocketed the money and bolted, like a cat afraid of having a fishbone snatched away.

Édouard opened the door a crack, stretched his arm out and pulled the tray inside, closed the door, went to the table, set down the lemon and, taking a knife, cut it in half.

His suite was the largest in the hotel; the vast windows facing the Bon Marché overlooked the whole of Paris. It required a lot of money to stay here. Sunlight streamed through the trickle of lemon juice Édouard delicately squeezed into the soup spoon, where he had already placed the correct dose of heroin, the color was beautiful, an iridescent, almost bluish yellow. It had required two nighttime excursions to find the heroin. And the price . . . The fact that Édouard had registered the price meant it had to be extremely expensive. But it did not matter. Under the bed, his demobilization haversack was stuffed with the handfuls of bills stolen from the suitcase of the prudent ant, Albert, packed ready for their departure. If the housekeeping staff had helped themselves, Édouard would not even have noticed, and, besides, everyone had to live.

Four days until their escape.

Édouard carefully mixed the brownish powder into the lemon juice, making sure there were no crystals that had not dissolved.

Four days.

In his heart, he had never believed that they would leave, not really. This glorious war memorial scam, a masterly hoax, a joyous, life-affirming prank, had been a means to pass the time, to prepare himself for death, but nothing more. He did not feel bad about dragging Albert into his crazy scheme, convinced that, sooner or later, something good would come of it for everyone.

Having stirred the powder, he set the spoon down on the table, anxious not to spill the contents despite his trembling hands. He picked up the lighter, pulled at the oakum, and began rolling the flint wheel with his thumb to produce the sparks that would eventually light the wick. Meanwhile, since he needed to be patient, he surveyed the vast suite. He felt at home here. He had always lived in cavernous rooms; this was a world made to his size. A pity his father could not see him in this opulent setting, because, when all was said and done, Édouard had made his fortune much more quickly and by means that were probably no more dishonest. He did not know exactly how his father had made his money, but he felt sure that wealth inevitably obscured countless crimes. He at least had killed no one, merely assisted at the death of various illusions, the inevitable effect of time, nothing more.

At last, the wick began to burn and give off heat. Édouard balanced the spoon, and the liquid began to bubble, sizzling faintly; he had to be careful, this was the most important part. Once the mixture was ready, Édouard had to wait for it to cool. He got up and walked over to the windows. A beautiful glow enfolded Paris. He did not wear a mask when he was alone and so caught his reflection in the glass, just as he had in 1918, in the window of his hospital room, when Albert had thought he just wanted some fresh air. What a shock.

Édouard studied himself. He no longer felt distraught, one becomes accustomed to anything, but the sadness was the same; as time passed, the flaw that had opened up in him had grown and still it continued to grow. He had loved life too much, that was the problem. For those who did not care so deeply, things must appear much simpler, but for him . . .

The mixture had now reached the perfect temperature. Why was he still haunted by the image of his father?

Because the story between them was unfinished.

The thought stopped Édouard short. Like a revelation.

Every story must have an ending, it is in the nature of things. Be it tragic, unbearable, even ridiculous, there should be an end to everything, and with his father there had been none, they had parted as sworn enemies, had never seen each other again, one was dead, the other still alive, but no one had had the last word.

Édouard tied the tourniquet around his arm. As he pushed the liquid into his vein, he could not help but gaze upon this city, marvel at the light. The flash took his breath away, light exploded behind his eyes, never had he dreamed of light so sublime.

36

Lucien Dupré arrived just before dinner; Madeleine had already come downstairs and had settled herself at the table. Henri was away, so she was dining alone, her father had asked that his meal be brought up to his rooms.

"Monsieur Dupré . . ."

Madeleine was so terribly civilized one might have thought she was genuinely pleased to see him. They were standing in the spacious hallway, and Dupré, standing stiffly in his coat, hat in hand, looked like a pawn on the chessboard of the black-and-white tiled floor, which indeed is what he was.

He had never known what to think of this calm, determined woman, he knew only that she scared him.

"Excuse me for disturbing you," he said, "I was hoping to speak to *monsieur*."

Madeleine smiled, not at the request but at the formulation. This man was her husband's closest collaborator, but he spoke like a manservant. She smiled helplessly and was about to say something, but just at that moment the baby gave a kick that left her winded, and her knees gave way under her. Dupré rushed forward and awkwardly cradled her, not knowing where to put his hands. In the arms of this squat but powerful man, she felt safe.

"Would you like me to call for help?" he said, helping her to one of the chairs that lined the hallway.

She laughed frankly

"My poor Monsieur Dupré, I could be constantly calling for help! This baby is the very devil, he loves gymnastics, especially in the evening."

Settled in the chair, she caught her breath and clasped her hands over her belly. Dupré was still bent over her.

"Thank you, Monsieur Dupré . . ."

She hardly knew the man, good day, good night, how are you, but she never listened to the answer. Now she suddenly realized that, though he was very discreet and very submissive, he probably knew a great deal about Henri's life and therefore about her marriage. The idea irked her. To be humiliated, not by this man, but by circumstance. She pursed her lips.

"You are looking for my husband?" she said.

Dupré straightened up, instinct told him not to persist, to leave as quickly as possible, but already it was too late, as though he had lit a fuse and now found the emergency exit double-locked.

"The fact is," Madeleine said, "I have no idea where he is either. Have you made a tour of his mistresses?"

The question was voiced in the kindly tone of one who genuinely wishes to help. Dupré fastened the last button of his coat.

"I can make you a list, if you wish, though it might take a little time. If you do not find him with any of them, might I suggest you try the brothels he sometimes frequents? Start with the one on the rue Notre-Dame-de-Lorette, Henri is very fond of it. If he's not there, you could try the one on the rue Saint-Placide, and there is another one near les Ursulines—I can never remember the name of the street."

She paused for a moment and then went on.

"I don't know why bordellos are so often located on streets with ecclesiastical names . . . The homage of vice to virtue, no doubt."

The word *brothel* from the lips of this blue-blooded, pregnant woman alone in this great house was not so much shocking as terribly sad. The pain that it implied . . . In this, Dupré was mistaken, Madeleine felt no pain, it was not her heart that had been wounded (love had long since faded), merely her pride.

Dupré, at heart a soldier, remained stone faced. Madeleine, angry at herself for taking on this ludicrous role, made a little gesture—only for him to stop her: please . . . don't apologize. This was the unkindest cut: he understood her. She quickly left the hallway with a murmured, barely audible good-bye.

Henri laid his cards on the table with a desultory flourish—four of a kind—as if to say, what can you do, some days things just go right. Everyone around the table laughed, none more than Léon Jardin-Beaulieu, who had lost more than anyone, he laughed to let people know he was a good sport, and that he did not care—fifty thousand francs in an evening, so what? And it was true. Losing money hurt him less than Henri's insolent success. The man had taken everything from him. Both men were thinking the same thing. Fifty thousand francs, Henri thought, another hour like this and I'll have won back the money I gave that ministerial mediocrity, though at least the old tramp can buy himself some new shoes . . .

"Henri . . . !"

He looked up. Someone nodded to him, it was his turn to call. Pass. He felt angry at how he had handled the affair. Why had he given the man a hundred thousand? He could have achieved the same result for half as much, less perhaps. But he had been flustered, he had been hasty, he had failed to keep his head. He might have got away with thirty thousand . . . Luckily, Léon the cuckold was on hand. Henri smiled at him over his cards. Léon would reimburse him, if not the full amount, then most of it, and thinking about it, about Léon's wife and his fine Cuban cigars, more than made up the difference. It had been a splendid idea to have him as an associate . . . though not the golden goose, there was great sport in the plucking.

A few hands later, forty thousand francs, his winnings were dwindling slightly. His instinct told him it was best to stop now, he stretched languorously, everyone got the message, someone claimed to be tired, people called for their coats. It was 1:00 a.m. as Henri and Léon strolled back to their cars.

"Honestly," Henri said, "I'm shattered."

"It is late . . ."

"The reason, my dear man, has more to do with the ravishing mistress I've been seeing (a married woman, I shall say no more). So young, so shameless, you cannot imagine. Insatiable!"

Léon slowed his pace, he felt himself choking.

"If it were left to me," Henri said, "I would award a medal to cuckolds—they deserve one, don't you think?"

"B . . . but . . . your wife . . . ," Léon stammered.

"Oh, Madeleine is a different matter, she is a mother now. As you'll realize when your time comes, it is something rather different from being a wife."

He lit a last cigarette.

"And you, dear fellow, happily married?"

At that moment, Henri thought, his pleasure would be complete if Denise had made some excuse about visiting one of her girlfriends and was somewhere where he could go to her right now. Failing which, he decided that a detour via the rue Notre-Dame-de-Lorette would not take too long.

As it turned out, it took an hour and a half . . . It's always the same, you tell yourself you'll just drop in for a minute, you have the choice between the two girls free and you take them both, one after the other . . .

He was still smiling when he arrived back at the boulevard de Courcelles, but the smile froze when he saw Dupré. At this time of night, his being there could not be a good sign; how long had he been waiting?

"Dargonne is closed," Dupré announced without the courtesy of a greeting, as though these three words were enough to explain the situation.

"What do you mean, closed?"

"And Dampierre. And Pontaville-sur-Meuse. I've telephoned the others, but I haven't managed to get through. I think all our sites have been shut down."

"Shut down by whom?"

"By the *préfecture*, though they say the order came from higher up. There is a *gendarme* outside every cemetery . . ."

Henry was in shock.

"A *gendarme*? What the devil is going on?"

"Apparently they are sending in inspectors. In the meantime, all work has been suspended."

What was happening? Had that ministerial mediocrity reneged on the promise to withdraw his report?

"All the sites?"

There was no need to repeat himself, his boss had understood perfectly. But what still seemed to escape him was the scale of the problem. Dupré cleared his throat.

"There's something else I wanted to say, sir . . . I need to go away for few days."

"Not now you don't, my friend. I need you here."

Henri's voice conveyed his usual brusque arrogance, but Dupré's silence lacked the usual meek deference. In the confident tone he used when giving orders to his foremen, a tone less timorous and submissive, Dupré said:

"I have family matters to attend to. I don't know how long I will be, you know what it's like . . ."

Henri shot him a look, the harsh glare of a captain of industry, and was alarmed by Dupré's reaction. The situation was more serious than he had supposed, because Dupré merely nodded, turned on his heel, and left. He had delivered his message, his work was done. Once and for all. Another man would have hurled abuse, Pradelle simply clenched his teeth. Henri thought, as he had many times before, that it had been a mistake to have underpaid him. Dupré's loyalty should have been rewarded. Too late now.

Henri checked his watch: 2:30 a.m.

As he climbed the steps, he noticed there was a lamp still lit in the hall. He was about to push the front door when it was opened by the maid, the brunette, what was her name? Pauline, that was it, a pretty little thing, why had he not screwed her already? But he did not have time to think about such things.

"Monsieur Jardin-Beaulieu telephoned several times . . ." she said.

Henri intimidated her, her chest heaved.

". . . but the telephone kept waking Madame, so she took the phone off the hook and asked me to wait up and give you the message: you are to telephone Monsieur Jardin-Beaulieu as soon as you arrive."

First Dupré, now Léon, whom he had seen less than two hours ago. Henri instinctively eyed the breasts of the young maid, but he was beginning to lose his footing. Could there be some connection between Léon's telephone call and the cemeteries being shut down?

"Very well," he said, "very well."

The sound of his own voice reassured him. He had panicked needlessly. He needed to check. It was possible that one or two cemeteries had been temporarily closed, but it was hardly likely they would close all of them, since to do so would magnify a minor problem into a major scandal.

Pauline had obviously been dozing on one of the hall chairs because her eyes were puffy. Henri continued to stare at her as he thought about other things, but the look was the one he always used with women, it made them uncomfortable. Pauline took a step back.

"If you have no further need of me, *monsieur*?"

He shook his head, and the girl immediately fled.

He took off his jacket. Telephone Léon. At this hour. As though he did not already have enough on his plate, he had to take responsibility for that midget!

He went into his study, reconnected the telephone, asked the operator to put him through, and as soon as the call was answered, said:

"What the hell is it now? Still on about that damn report?"

"Not that one," said Léon. "Another one . . ."

Léon did not sound panicked, indeed he sounded calm and controlled, which was surprising in the circumstances.

"It's about . . . um . . . Gardonne."

"No, no," Henri interrupted irritably, "Not Gardonne, Dargonne! And anyway . . ."

Suddenly Henri realized, and he fell silent, dumbstruck by the news.

This was the report he had paid a hundred thousand francs to bury.

"Three inches thick," Léon said.

Henri frowned. What could he possibly have written, the fucking pen pusher who had taken his money, to make the file so thick?

"They've never seen anything like it at the ministry," Léon said. "There was a hundred thousand francs with the report, in large bills, all carefully clipped to the pages. There is even an appendix listing the serial numbers."

He had handed in the money. It was unbelievable.

Henri, shaken by this piece of information, could not manage to piece together the puzzle: the report, the ministry, the money, the closed sites . . .

Léon filled in the blanks.

"The inspector details serious lapses at the cemetery and further alleges attempted suborning of a duly sworn civil servant, claiming the hundred thousand francs as proof. They constitute an admission of guilt. Which means that the allegations in the report are founded, because you don't try to bribe an official for no reason. Especially not with that much money."

Calamity.

Léon said nothing for a moment, to allow time for this revelation to sink in. His voice was so calm that Henri had the unsettling impression of listening to a perfect stranger.

"My father was apprised of the situation this evening," said Léon. "As you can imagine, the minister did not hesitate for a second, he has to cover his own back, so he ordered that all the sites be shut down. Logically, he'll take some time to gather evidence to corroborate the complaint, have inspections conducted of some of the cemeteries, and then—in about ten days—he will probably issue a writ against your company."

"You mean *our* company."

Léon did not respond immediately. Evidently this was an evening for pregnant pauses. What with Dupré and now this midget . . . At length, Léon spoke, his voice soft, measured, as though vouchsafing a secret.

"No, Henri, my mistake, I forgot to tell you . . . I sold all my shares last month. To small shareholders who are counting on your success, I do hope you won't disappoint them. This affair no longer concerns me personally. I am calling to warn you simply because you are a friend . . ."

Another loaded silence.

Henri would kill the midget, rip him apart with his bare hands.

"Ferdinand Morieux sold his shares too," Léon said.

Henri said nothing, he slowly replaced the receiver, utterly drained by this news. Had he wanted to stab Jardin-Beaulieu, he no longer had the strength to hold the knife.

The minister, the shutdown of the cemeteries, the bribery charge, it was all too much. The situation was spinning out of control.

He did not take a moment to think, did not check the time. It was almost three o'clock when he burst into Madeleine's bedroom. She was wide awake, sitting up in bed—with all the commotion going on in this house, it's impossible to get a wink of sleep. Léon was calling every five minutes, you really need to talk to him . . . I disconnected the telephone. Did you call him back . . . ? Madeleine trailed off, startled by the look of sheer panic on Henri's face. She had seen him anxious sometimes, angry, shamefaced, worried, she had even seen him distraught—only last month, for example, when he put on that little show of a man in desperate straits, but the following morning there had been no trace of concern, he had settled the problem. Tonight his face was ashen, he was agitated, his voice quavered, and most worryingly, there were no lies. His face betrayed not a vestige of his customary cunning, his guile; she could tell at a glance when he was shamming, but tonight he seemed so perfectly sincere . . .

It is simple, Madeleine had never seen him in such a state.

Her husband did not apologize for bursting into her room in the middle of the night, he sat on the edge of the bed and he talked. He resolved to say only as much as he could without permanently besmirching his image. But even an account of the bare facts meant saying things that were disagreeable to him. The undersized coffins, the greedy, feckless laborers, foreigners who hardly spoke a word of French . . . And the enormity of the task. It was unimaginable! Even so, he had to admit: the German bodies in French graves, the coffins filled with dirt, the pilfering at the sites, there were official reports, he had thought he was doing the right thing by offering a little money to the investigator, a foolish blunder, but it was done . . .

Madeleine nodded, intent on what he was saying. She felt it could not all be his fault.

"But why should you have to take all the blame in this affair? That seems very unjust . . ."

Henri was amazed—at himself for being able to say these things, to admit to mismanaging the situation; amazed at Madeleine, for calmly hearing him out and, if not defending him, at least understanding; amazed at the bond between them, because this was the first time they had treated each other as adults. They spoke without anger, without irritation, as though chatting about renovations on the house, as though discussing a vacation or a domestic problem, in fact this was the first time that they had truly understood each other.

Henri found himself looking at her differently. What first struck him was the staggering size of her breasts. Through the sheer negligee, he could see her huge, dark nipples, the curve of her shoulders . . . Henri took a moment to contemplate her, Madeleine smiled, it was a moment of intense intimacy, he felt a fierce desire for her, and this wave of passion did him good. The fierceness of the desire also had something to do with the motherly, protective air that Madeleine radiated, one that that made one want take refuge in her arms, to melt away. The subject of their conversation was grave, yet there was a lightness about the way she listened, something simple and reassuring. Gradually, Henri relaxed, his voice became softer, the torrent of words slowed. Looking at her, he thought: this woman is mine, and felt a sudden, unexpected pride. He reached out a hand and touched her breast, she smiled gently, the hand glided over her belly, Madeleine's breath became heavy, almost labored. There was a measure of calculation in Henri's gesture, he had always had a way with Madeleine—but it was not just that. It felt like being reunited with someone he had never really met. Madeleine spread her legs, then quickly gripped his wrist.

"Now is hardly the moment," she whispered, though the tone of her voice said otherwise.

Henri nodded slowly, he felt strong again, he felt confident.

Madeleine plumped the pillows behind her, took a deep breath, settled back with a sigh, and stroked the prominent blue veins on the back of his hand as she listened, he had such beautiful hands.

Henri gathered his thoughts, he needed to get back to the point.

"Léon has walked away. I can expect no support from his father."

Madeleine was indignant, she was shocked at the idea that Léon would not help, surely it was his business too?

"No, that's the problem," Henri said, "He has no stake in the business anymore. Neither has Ferdinand."

Madeleine's lips formed a silent *ah*.

"It would take too long to explain," he said sharply.

She smiled; her husband was back. In one piece. She stroked his cheek.

"My poor darling . . ."

Her voice was tender, affectionate.

"It's really serious this time?"

He squeezed his eyes shut—yes—then opened them, and then took the plunge.

"Your father has always refused to help me, but . . ."

"Yes, and if I ask again, he will refuse again."

Henri was still holding Madeleine's hand in his, but now their arms were resting on their knees. He had to persuade her. The idea that she might refuse was impossible, unthinkable. Old man Péricourt had wanted to humiliate him, well, now that he had succeeded, he had (Henri fumbled for the word) a duty—that was it—he had a duty to be reasonable. After all, what did he stand to gain by seeing his name dragged through the mud in the event of a scandal? Well, not a scandal exactly, there were hardly grounds for that, let's say an unpleasant incident. Granted he might not be well disposed to help his son-in-law, but surely he could do this small favor to make his daughter happy? He spent his life intervening on behalf of other people, often on matters that did not even concern him personally! Madeleine agreed.

"That's true."

But still Henri sensed a reluctance. He bent over her.

"You don't want to ask him . . . because you're afraid he will refuse, is that it?"

"No, no," Madeleine said quickly. "It's not that at all."

She withdrew her hand from his and laid it on her belly, the fingers slightly splayed.

"I won't ask him because I *don't want to* ask. The fact is, Henri, I'm happy to listen, but I have no real interest in this business."

"I understand," Henri conceded, "and I'm not asking you to take an interest, all I'm asking . . ."

"No, Henri, you don't understand. It is not your business that does not interest me, it is you."

She had said it with no change of tone, her manner was still casual, smiling, affectionate, terribly intimate. It was such a shock that at first Henri thought he had misheard.

"I don't understand . . ."

"Of course you do, my darling, you understand me perfectly. It is not what you do that leaves me cold, but what you are."

He should have got to his feet and left, but Madeleine's eyes held him there. He did not want to hear any more, but he was a prisoner of circumstance, like a defendant forced to listen to the judge pass sentence.

"I never had any illusions about what you were," Madeleine told him. "Nor what our marriage would be like. I admit I was in love for a time, but I soon realized how things would end. If I stayed with you, it was because I needed you. I married you because I was the right age, because you asked me, and because Aulnay-Pradelle has a nice ring to it. Had it not been so mortifying being your wife, being constantly humiliated by your affairs, I would have liked to keep the name. But, no matter."

Henri got to his feet. This time, he made no spurious appeals to honor, he did not argue, did not mire himself in more lies: Madeleine's tone was calm, deliberate, what she was saying was final.

"What saved you until now, my love, was the fact that you are handsome."

Lying back in bed, hands cupping her belly, she watched as her husband made to leave, she spoke tenderly, intimately, as though bidding him goodnight.

"I'm sure you've given me a beautiful child. I never expected anything more of you. Now that he's almost here" (she patted her belly gently), "you can do as you please, you can do nothing at all, I really do not care. It is a shame, but I've got over it because I have my consolation. As for you, judging by what little I know, it sounds as though you are facing a catastrophe from which you will never recover. But it no longer concerns me."

All too often in such circumstances Henri smashed something—a vase, a figurine, a window, an ornament. Tonight, however, he simply walked out and slowly closed the door to his wife's bedroom.

As he shambled down the corridor, he thought about la Sallevière as he had seen it only days ago, its majestic facade impeccably restored, gardeners had set about redesigning the gardens in the French style, painters were about to begin work on the ceilings of the salons and the bedrooms, restorers were working on the cherubs and the paneling . . .

Stunned by the series of betrayals he had suffered in a few short hours, Henri desperately tried to give substance to this cataclysm, but he could not, it was all words, images, there was nothing real.

To lose everything like this, as swiftly as he had gained it, was something he was incapable of grasping. If, eventually, he succeeded, it was thanks to something he said aloud as he stood alone in the corridor:

"I am dead."

37

The last deposits brought the balance of the Patriotic Memory account to 166,000 francs. Albert did a quick calculation, he needed to be clever, not to make conspicuous withdrawals, though the bank was large enough to trade 7 or 8 million francs in a day, and the steady flow of cash from businesses and department stores meant the cashiers' desks could take in 400,00 or 500,000, sometimes more.

Since the end of June, Albert could hardly bear to go on living in his own skin.

In the morning, between fits of nausea, and as dog tired as if he had led an assault on a German position, he would go to work in a state close to implosion. He would not have been surprised to find that a scaffold had been erected outside the bank during the night so he could be summarily guillotined in front of the assembled staff, led by M. Péricourt.

He spent his days moving through a thick haze, voices reached him only after a long delay. Speaking to him meant breaching this wall of dread. Albert would look as though he had been drenched by a jet from a fire hose. "Huh, what?" were always his first words, but no one paid any attention, they were used to him now.

He spent his mornings lodging the previous day's payments received in the Patriotic Memory account and trying to extract from the seething turmoil in his brain the precise amount he would withdraw in cash. At noon as, one by one, the tellers took their lunch, Albert would make the rounds of the vacated cash desks and make his withdrawals, nervously signing Jules d'Épremont, as though the customer always visited at lunchtime. As he went, he stuffed the money into a briefcase, which, by afternoon, would have swelled to four times its usual size.

Twice before, heading toward the revolving door in the evening, and hearing a colleague call his name, or thinking a customer was eyeing him suspiciously, he had pissed himself and had been forced to take a taxi home. On other nights, he poked his head out of the door before leaving in case the guillotine that was not there in the morning had been erected during the day in front of the métro—you never knew.

In his briefcase—which most clerks used to carry their lunch—Albert took home 99,000 francs in large denominations. Why not a hundred thousand? Superstition, you might think, but it was not that, it was about style. A matter of elegance—mathematical elegance in this case, but even so—because in doing so, Patriotic Memory had now swindled 1,111,000 francs. To Albert, there was beauty in that neat row of ones. The minimum Édouard had stipulated had been successfully exceeded, and for Albert, today was a personal victory. It was Saturday, July 10, and he had asked his manager for four days' vacation in honor of July 14, and since, by opening time on the fifteenth, he planned to be on a ship bound for Tripoli, today was his last day at the bank. As with the armistice in 1918, he was just astonished to have come through alive. Anyone else might have thought himself immortal. But Albert could not imagine that he would survive a second time; even as the hour of his departure for the colonies approached, he did not truly believe it.

"See you next week, Monsieur Maillard!"

"Huh? What? Eh . . . yes, yes, goodnight."

Seeing that he *was* still alive, and that the totemic total of one million had been reached, Albert began to wonder whether it might not be wise to change the tickets for the train and the boat and leave earlier. But on this point, more than any other, he was torn.

He would be happy to leave soon, right now if that were possible . . . but what about Pauline?

A hundred times he had tried to talk to her, a hundred times he had lost his nerve, Pauline was wonderful, silk outside and velvet within, and so clever. But she was the kind of working-class girl who had middle-class dreams. A white wedding, an apartment, three kids, maybe four, that was what lay ahead for her. Had it been up to him, Albert would happily settle down, Pauline, four children, why not? He would have been glad to keep his job at the bank. But now that he was a notorious swindler—soon, God willing, an international fugitive—that future was fast disappearing and with it Pauline, their marriage, their children, their home, and his career at the bank. There was only one hope: confess everything, persuade her to leave with him three days from now, with a suitcase stuffed with a million francs in large bills, a friend with a face that looked like a split watermelon, and half the French police force on their heels.

In other words, there was no hope.

Or he could go alone.

Asking Édouard for advice would be like talking to a wall. Though he loved the man for all sorts of reasons, in the end Albert thought Édouard rather selfish.

He visited him every other evening, after he had stashed the loot in a safe place and before meeting up with Pauline. Now that there was no one in the apartment on the impasse Pers, Albert had decided that it was not a safe place to keep the money on which their futures depended. He considered various solutions, he could have rented a safe deposit box at the bank, but in the end settled on a left-luggage office at the Gare Saint-Lazare.

Every evening, he checked the suitcase out, went into the station café toilets where he added the day's takings, then returned it to the baggage clerk. They thought he was a traveling salesman. Girdles and corsets, Albert had said, it was all he could think of. The counter clerk would wink at him, and Albert would give a discreet shrug that only further enhanced his reputation. Just in case they needed to leave in a hurry, Albert had also left a hatbox in which he had packed the framed sketch of the horse's head—he had never had the glass replaced—and, carefully wrapped in tissue paper, his horse head mask. Albert knew that if even he had to make a run for it, he would abandon the suitcase rather than that hatbox.

After he had been to the train station and before meeting Pauline, Albert would pay a visit to the Lutetia, working himself up into a terrible state. A luxury Parisian hotel was hardly ideal for someone trying not to attract attention . . .

"Don't worry," Édouard wrote, "The more visible you are, the less people see you. This is about Jules d'Épremont—not a living soul has ever seen him, but everyone trusts him." And he gave one of the braying laughs that made your hackles rise.

Albert had counted off the weeks, then the days, and now that Édouard, under his assumed identity of Eugène Larivière, had taken to committing his quirks and caprices at a grand hotel, he was counting down the hours and even the minutes to their departure, set for July 14, taking the 1:00 p.m. Paris-to-Marseille train so they would be in time to catch the Messageries Maritimes steamship *S.S. D'Artagnan* for Tripoli the next day.

Three tickets.

Those last minutes as he prepared to leave the bowels of the bank that afternoon had been as agonizing—he supposed—as childbirth, every step was painful but, finally, he emerged onto the pavement. He could hardly believe it. The sun was shining, his briefcase was heavy, to his right, no sign of a scaffold, to his left, no waiting *gendarmes* . . .

Nothing but the slim figure of Louise standing on the pavement opposite.

He was disconcerted by the sight of her, a bit like when you bump into a shopkeeper you have only ever seen behind the counter, though you recognize him, you dimly feel that this is not the natural order of things. Louise had never come to meet him. As he scurried across the road, he wondered how she had found the address of the bank, but the girl spent her time listening, she probably knew a lot about their scheme.

"It's Édouard," she said, "You have to come right now."

"What about Édouard, what's the matter?"

But Louise did not answer, she had already hailed a taxi.

"The Hôtel Lutetia."

In the car, Albert set his briefcase at his feet. Louise stared straight ahead, as though she were driving. Fortunately for Albert, Pauline was working this evening, and since she would finish late and had an early start tomorrow, she intended to sleep "at home." Which, for a servant, means someone else's home.

"For God's sake . . . !" Albert blurted after a minute, "What's happened to Éd . . ."

Noticing the driver's sidelong glance, he quickly corrected himself.

"What's happened to Eugène?"

Louise's face was contorted, like a worried mother or a wife. She turned to Albert, spread her arms. Her eyes were filled with tears.

"I think he's dead."

Albert and Louise crossed the lobby of the Lutetia at a pace they hoped looked normal. They could not have been more noticeable. The elevator attendant pretended not to notice their nervousness, he was young, but very professional.

They found Édouard on the floor, his legs splayed, his back propped against the bed. In a sorry state, certainly, but not dead. Louise reacted with her usual calm. The room stank of vomit, she opened all the windows and mopped up the vomit with towels from the bathroom.

Albert knelt and bent over his friend.

"What's up, old man? Not feeling well?"

Édouard's head nodded gently, his eyes fitfully opening and closing, he was not wearing a mask and the stench from the gaping wound in his face was so strong that Albert had to draw back. He took a deep breath and, grabbing his friend under the armpits, dragged him onto the bed. When a man has no mouth, no jaw, nothing but a cavernous hole and a set of top teeth, it's difficult to pat his cheeks. Albert forced Édouard to open his eyes.

"Can you hear me?" he said over and over, "Can you hear me?"

Since he got no reaction, he decided to use strong-arm tactics. He got up, ran into the bathroom and filled a glass with water. Turning back to the bedroom, he got such a shock that he dropped the glass and felt so dizzy he slumped to the floor.

From the back of the bathroom door, like a bathrobe on a peg, hung a mask.

The face of a man. The face of Édouard Péricourt. The real Édouard, as he had been before. Only the eyes were missing.

Albert lost all sense of where he was and found himself in the trenches, a few feet from the ladder, the other guys are all there, some in front, some behind him, tense as drawn bows, ready for the assault on Hill 113. Over there, Lieutenant Pradelle is scanning the enemy lines through binoculars. Berry is standing in front of him, and in front of Berry, a guy he hardly knows turns around, Péricourt gives him a smile, a beaming smile. Albert thinks he looks like a boy about to do something naughty; before he has time to respond, Péricourt has turned away.

This is the face he saw that night, without the smile. Albert is stunned, he never again saw that face, except in his dreams, now here it is, emerging from the door, as though Édouard himself is about to appear like a ghost. It triggers a sequence of images, the two soldiers shot in the back, the assault on Hill 113, Lieutenant Pradelle slamming into him, the shell crater, the wave of earth crashing over him.

Albert screamed.

Louise appeared in the bathroom door, alarmed.

Albert shook himself, ran the tap, splashed water on his face, filled the glass again and, without looking at the mask, marched back into the bedroom and tipped the whole glass down his friend's throat. Édouard immediately hauled himself onto his elbows, coughing uncontrollably, as Albert himself had probably coughed when he returned from the dead.

Albert helped him to sit up, leaning him forward in case he vomited again, but no. It took some time for the coughing fit to ease. Édouard was awake, but so exhausted, to judge from the dark circles around his eyes and his general state of neglect, that he immediately slipped into a kind of trance. Albert checked his breathing and decided it was normal. With no thought for Louise, he stripped his comrade and got him under the covers. The bed was so big that he was able to perch next to him, with Louise on the other side.

They sat like bookends, each holding one of Édouard's hands while he slept, a worrying gurgle coming from his throat. On the large circular table in the middle of the room, they could see the long, slender syringe, the lemon cut in two, traces of a brownish powder that looked like clay on a scrap of paper, the flint lighter, the twisted wick curved so that it looked like a comma.

Next to the table, the rubber tourniquet.

They did not speak, lost in their thoughts. Albert was no expert in such matters, but the powder looked like something he had been offered when he was looking for morphine. It was the next stage: heroin. Édouard had not even needed a middleman to get it . . .

Curiously, Albert's first thought was: what use am I, then? As though, on top of all his other worries, he had not been asked to deal with this one.

How long had Édouard been taking heroin? Albert found himself like those parents who fail to notice the signs and now find it is too late.

Four days before they were due to leave . . .

But what did it matter, four days before, four days after . . . ?

"So you're leaving?"

Louise's thoughts had taken the same path, her voice was thoughtful, distant.

Albert responded with silence. Which meant "yes."

"When?" she said, not looking at him.

Albert said nothing. Which meant "soon."

Louise turned to Édouard and, reaching out her forefinger, as she had that first day, she meditatively traced the edge of the gaping wound, the red, inflamed flesh like an exposed mucous membrane . . . Then she got up, put on her coat and, coming to the other side of the bed where Albert sat, she bent and planted a lingering kiss on his cheek.

"You will come say good-bye?"

Albert nodded. "Yes, of course."

Which meant "no."

Louise nodded; she understood.

She kissed him again and left the room.

Her absence created an air pocket of the sort people apparently experience in airplanes.

38

It was so unprecedented that Mlle Raymond was in shock. In fact, in all the years she had worked for the mayor, it had never happened. That she had walked across the room three times without his ogling her was one thing, but that three times she had been behind his desk, three times without him pushing his hand, middle finger erect, up her skirt . . .

For several days now, Labourdin had not been himself, glassy eyed, slack jawed, Mlle Raymond could have performed the dance of the seven veils and he would not have noticed. His face was ashen, he trudged heavily like a man expecting to have a heart attack at any moment. Good, she thought. Die, you bastard. Her boss's decline offered the first reprieve she had had since joining the corporation. It was a godsend.

Labourdin got to his feet, wearily pulled on his jacket, picked up his hat, and left his office without a word. One of his shirttails was hanging out of his pants, the sort of detail that can make any man look like a tramp. In his plodding tread there was something of a cow heading to the slaughter.

At the Péricourt residence, he was informed that *monsieur* was not at home.

"I'll wait," he said.

He pushed open the door to the drawing room, slumped onto the nearest sofa, and stared vacantly into space, and it was in this position that M. Péricourt found him three hours later.

"What in damnation are you doing here?"

M. Péricourt's arrival plunged Labourdin into confusion.

"Ah, *monsieur le président, monsieur le président* . . . ," he said, struggling to get up from the sofa.

This was all he could think of, as though somehow the word *président* said all that needed to be said.

Despite his exasperation, M. Péricourt had a farmer's fondness for the bovine Labourdin. "Explain it to me" he would often say, with that infinite patience reserved for cattle and imbeciles.

But today, he remained glacial, forcing Labourdin to redouble his efforts to extricate himself from the sofa and explain, "Obviously, *monsieur le président*, no one could have foreseen, not even you, I fear, *monsieur le président*, everyone believed, how could anyone anticipate such a thing," and so forth.

M. Péricourt allowed this torrent of futile words to wash over him. In fact he was not listening. There was no point in going on. But still Labourdin persisted in his lamentations.

"And this Jules d'Épremont, *monsieur le président*, he does not exist, can you imagine it?"

He sounded almost impressed.

"I mean, how can a member of the Institut de France working in the Americas, not exist! Those sketches, those magnificent drawings, that magisterial project, it all had to be created by someone, after all!"

Having reached this point, Labourdin desperately needed a response, otherwise his brain would go around in circles for hours.

"So, the man does not exist," M. Péricourt summed up.

"Precisely so!" Labourdin said, genuinely relieved to have been so comprehensively understood. And just imagine, the address at 52, rue du Louvre does not exist either! Can you guess what it is?

Silence. Regardless of the circumstances, Labourdin liked guessing games; idiots love to make an effect.

"A post office!" he said. "The address is nothing but a post office box."

He was dazzled by the ingenuity of this stratagem.

"And this is something you have only just noticed now . . . ?"

Labourdin interpreted this reproach as an encouragement.

"Exactly, *monsieur le président*! Although . . ." (he raised a finger to emphasize the finesse of his approach) "I had my doubts. Obviously, we received a receipt, a typewritten letter explaining that the artist was in the Americas, and the various drawings that you've seen, but, for my part, I . . ."

He affected a doubtful expression gave a little shake of his head to express what words could not convey: his acute perspicacity.

"But you paid him?" M. Péricourt said icily.

"But, but, but, but, but . . . what choice was there? Of course we paid, *monsieur le président*."

He was categorical.

"No payment, no commission, and no commission would mean no memorial. What could we do? We made a down payment to Patriotic Memory, we had no choice."

As he spoke, he took some sort of pamphlet from his pocket. M. Péricourt snatched it from him and nervously leafed through it. Labourdin did not even wait for him to ask his next question.

"The company doesn't even exist!" he yelped, "It's a . . . it's a . . ."

He stopped in his tracks. He had been mulling over the word for days. and now he had forgotten it.

"It's a . . ." He carried on because he had noticed that his brain was like an automobile engine, a few turns of the crank and sometimes it would start up again. "Front. That's it. It's a front organization!"

He gave a beaming smile, proud to have overcome this linguistic hurdle.

M. Péricourt continued to flick through the slim catalog.

"But . . . these designs are for mass production," he said.

"Um . . . yes," Labourdin said, who did not see what the *président* was getting at.

"We commissioned an original work, did we not?"

"Aaaah," Labourdin said, having briefly forgotten this question might arise, though he recalled preparing an answer. "Quite right, my dear *président*, indeed, most original. The thing is that Monsieur d'Épremont, *membre de l'Institut*, has designed mass-produced sculptures, but he also creates works that are 'tailor made,' as you might say. The man can turn his hand to anything!"

And then he remembered the individual he was describing was purely fictitious.

"I mean he could . . . turn his hand to anything." His voice dropped to a whisper, as though the artist had recently passed away and on that account was unable to complete a commission.

As he turned the pages and studied the various memorials, M. Péricourt came to appreciate that the swindle had been on a national scale.

There would be a colossal scandal.

Without regard for Labourdin, who was hiking up his pants with both hands, M. Péricourt turned on his heel, went back to his study, and contemplated the scale of the setback.

All around, the sketches, the framed drawings, the models of "his memorial" magnified his humiliation.

It was not about the money he had lost, not even the fact that he had been swindled. No, what wounded him was that they had made a mockery of his grief. He cared little about money and reputation, he had a surfeit of both, and the business world had long since taught him that anger is a bad counselor. But mocking his grief amounted to denigrating his son's death. As he had done himself, once. Far from making amends for the wrongs he had done his son, this war memorial had compounded them. What he had hoped might be an atonement had become a farce.

The Patriotic Memory catalog offered a range of mass-produced memorials at an attractive discount. How many of these nonexistent memorials had been sold? How many families had poured their money into these pipe dreams? How many towns and villages had been fleeced, victims of their trusting innocence. That anyone could have the effrontery, that anyone could have the temerity to contemplate swindling grieving people was literally unbelievable.

M. Péricourt was not sufficiently great hearted to feel a kinship with the possibly countless victims of this scheme, nor to think of coming to their aid. He thought only of himself, of his pain, his son, *his* story. He was sorry that, having failed to be a good father, he would never become one now. But, more egoistically, he felt furious, as though personally targeted: those who had paid for mass-produced models were gullible victims of a huge hoax, while he, in commissioning a unique monument, felt like a victim of extortion.

His pride was sorely wounded.

Sickened and appalled, he sat at his desk and reopened the catalog, which he had unthinkingly been twisting in his hands. He read the long letter the charlatan had written to the mayors of towns and villages. It was clever, reassuring, it sounded so official. M. Péricourt paused for a moment at the line that probably, more than anything, guaranteed the scheme's success, the "exceptional offer" that, to those with modest budgets, must have seemed like a godsend . . . Even the symbolism of the date July 14 . . .

He looked up at his desk calendar.

Swindlers rarely give their victims time to react or to verify who they were dealing with. Since they had received a formal acknowledgment of their order and a receipt in due form, they had no reason to worry before July 14, the date when the supposed promotion ended. Today was July 12. A matter of days. Since there had been no mention of the scheme in the newspapers, the swindlers would doubtless wait around to collect the last down payments before they fled. As for their customers, the more shrewd—and the more suspicious—would soon want to confirm that their trust had been well placed.

What would happen then?

The scandal would break. In a day or two, perhaps three. Perhaps it was only a matter of hours.

And then?

The newspapers would vie with each other in jingoistic emotion, the police would come under considerable pressure, outraged on behalf of the nation, members of parliaments would cloak themselves in patriotic virtue . . .

"Bullshit," M. Péricourt muttered.

And when these louts were eventually tracked down and arrested, it would be three, perhaps four years before they came to trial, by which time tempers would have cooled.

Even mine, he thought.

This notion did not console him; tomorrow was of no consequence, right now he was suffering.

He closed the catalog and smoothed it with the flat of his hand.

When Jules d'Épremont and his cohorts were arrested (if indeed they were caught), they would cease to be individuals. They would become freaks, newsworthy curiosities, as Raoul Villain[13] had been, as Landru was becoming.

Delivered up to an enraged public, the guilty men would cease to belong to their victims. And who would there be for him to despise once these bandits became public property?

Worse still, his name would be dragged through the trial. And if, by some misfortune, he was the only person to have commissioned a custom-made memorial, then he above all would be ridiculed: See him? Poured a hundred thousand into their scheme for all he ever saw for his money. The idea was odious, people would think him a gullible dupe, a sucker. This prosperous industrialist, this formidable banker had been well and truly fleeced by a bunch of second-rate crooks.

Words failed him.

His wounded pride blinded him.

Something mysterious and critical was happening to him: he wanted to get his hands on the men who had committed this crime as much as he had ever wanted anything, wanted it with a passion. He did not know what he would do with them; he knew only that he wanted them.

Riffraff. A gang of thugs. Had they already fled the country? Perhaps not.

Could he get to them before the police?

It was midday.

He jerked the bell pull and ordered that his son-in-law be summoned. Have him brought here.

Forthwith.

39

Henri d'Aulnay-Pradelle strode into the vast post office on the rue du Louvre in midafternoon and chose a bench from which he could keep an eye on the rows of post office boxes lining the wall next to the monumental staircase that led up to the first floor.

Box 52 was no more than fifty feet away. Henri feigned interest in his newspaper but soon realized that he could not keep up such a pretense for long. Before they checked their box, these crooks would surely keep watch for a while to make sure there was nothing untoward, and they probably checked in the morning rather than the afternoon. And now that he was here, his worst fear was that he would be trapped indefinitely: at this late stage, as far as the crooks were concerned, there were more risks involved in coming to pick up the last few payments than in catching a train to some far-flung corner of Europe or a steamship to Africa.

They would not come.

And his time was precious.

This thought depressed him.

Abandoned by his workers, deserted by his business associates, disowned by his father-in-law, forsaken by his wife, with no prospect of help against the impending debacle . . . Henri d'Aulnay-Pradelle had been suffering the worst three days of his life until that last-minute summons, the messenger who came to find him urgently with a scribbled note on Marcel Péricourt's visiting card:

"Come see me immediately."

He had leapt in a taxi, raced to the boulevard de Courcelles, in the house he encountered Madeleine on the stairs . . . She had that same vacant grin on her face, as always, like a goose laying an egg. She gave not the slightest sign that she remembered how coldly she had dispatched him only two days ago.

"Ah, so they managed to find you, *chéri*?"

She sounded relieved. The bitch. She had told the messenger he would find him in Mathilde de Beausergent's bed; Henri could not help wondering how she knew.

"I do hope you weren't interrupted before your climax," she said, and since Henri did not respond, added, "But of course, you're on your way to see Papa . . . All this men's business is so tiresome . . ."

Then she cupped her hands over her belly and returned to her favorite pastime, trying to guess whether the baby was kicking with his feet, his heels, or his elbows, he thrashed about like a fish, the little beast; she loved to talk to him.

As time dragged on and countless people came and went, opening every box except the one he had been watching, Henri shifted his position to a different bench, a different floor, he went up to the smoking area, from where could peer down at the ground floor. This idleness was death by a thousand cuts, but what could he do? He cursed Péricourt, it was his fault he was forced to hang around here uselessly. At their meeting he had been shocked by the old man's appearance. He looked dead on his feet, his face was haggard, his shoulders hunched, his eyes ringed with dark circles . . . He had been showing signs of frailty for some time, but his condition seemed to have suddenly deteriorated. At the Jockey Club, it was whispered that he had never quite been the same since his fit of apoplexy the previous November. When speaking of Marcel Péricourt, Docteur Blanche, the epitome of discretion, lowered his eyes; that said it all. An unmistakable sign had been a fall in the share price of some of his companies. They had rallied since, but even so . . .

The very idea that he might be ruined only for the old goat to kick the bucket afterward—too late—was unbearable. If only the bastard could die now rather than in six months or a year . . . True, his will was categorical, as was the marriage contract, but Henri still had an unshakeable confidence in his ability to get what he wanted from any woman, a talent that had only ever failed him with his wife (the irony!). But if need be, he would muster all his powers and make short work of Madeleine; he would have his share of the old man's fortune, he'd see to that. What a mess. He had wanted too much, or too fast . . . No point raking over the past, what was done was done; Henri was a man of action, not one to feel sorry for himself.

"You are facing very serious problems," the old man said as Henri sat down opposite him, still clutching the visiting card bearing his summons.

Henri had said nothing, because it was true. A problem that might have been fixed—that little business with the war graves—seemed almost insurmountable, now that he stood accused of bribing an official.

Almost. But not utterly impossible.

Because, the fact that Péricourt had sent for him, had stooped so low as to ask for his help, had sent a messenger to his mistress's bed to fetch him, must surely mean he needed him desperately.

What could have happened that the old man had been reduced to calling upon Henri d'Aulnay-Pradelle, whose very name he could not mention without contempt? Henri had not the slightest idea. But here he was, in the old man's study, no longer standing, but sitting, and it was not he who was asking for help. A ray of hope began to glimmer. He asked no questions.

"Without my help, your problems are insoluble."

Here, Henri's pride led him to make his first mistake: he pursed his lips dubiously. M. Péricourt reacted with a fury of which his son-in-law had not thought him capable.

"You are dead!" he roared. "Dead, do you understand? Given the business you are mixed up in, the government will take everything from you, everything! Your wealth, your property, your reputation . . . you will never recover! And you will end up in prison."

Henri was of that breed of men who, having made a tactical blunder, are capable of excellent intuition. He got up and made to leave.

"Stop right there!" M. Péricourt said.

Without a moment's hesitation, Henri turned, strutted across the room, leaned over his father-in-law's desk, and said:

"Well, stop wasting my time, then. You need me—I don't know why, but let me be very clear, regardless of what you ask, my conditions will be the same. You have the minister in your pocket? Very well then, you will personally intercede on my behalf, you'll have every scrap of evidence against me buried, I want no charges brought against me."

Henri settled himself once more in the armchair and crossed his legs, looking for all the world as though he were at the Jockey Club waiting for the steward to bring his brandy. Another man in this situation might have trembled, worried about what would be asked in return; not Henri d'Aulnay-Pradelle. Having spent three days brooding over his impending downfall, he was prepared for anything. Just tell me who to kill.

M. Péricourt was forced to explain everything: how he had come to commission a war memorial, the extent and scale of this swindle of which he was perhaps the most important, the most prominent victim. Henri had the good sense not to smirk. And he began to sense what it was his father-in-law was going to ask.

"The scandal is about to break," Marcel Péricourt said. "If the police manage to arrest these men before they get away, everyone will want a piece of them—the government, the courts, the newspapers, the veterans' organizations, the victims . . . I don't want that. I need you to find them."

"What do you plan to do with them?"

"That's not your concern."

"Why me?" he said.

He quickly bit his tongue, but it was too late.

"To find scum takes someone well acquainted with the gutter."

Henri took this on the chin. M. Péricourt immediately regretted the insult, not because he felt he had gone too far, but because it might be counterproductive.

"Furthermore, time is of the essence," he said in a more conciliatory tone. "It could be a matter of hours. And you are the only man I have at hand."

Toward six o'clock, having moved perhaps a dozen times, Henri was forced to face the fact that his surveillance mission would not produce results. Not today, at least. And no one could say whether there would be a tomorrow.

What alternative did he have but to wait around on the off chance that the men who had rented Box 52 would make an appearance? The printworks that had produced the catalog?

"No," Péricourt had been adamant. "If you go, you would have to ask questions, and if word gets out that there are concerns about the printer, it will be traced to their clients, to this company, to the swindle, and there will be a scandal."

If he could not go to the printer, that left only the bank.

To find out where Patriotic Memory had deposited the down payments received from its clients would take time, and approval, all things that Henri did not have.

It was the post office or nothing.

True to his nature, he decided to disobey. Despite M. Péricourt's injunction, he took a taxi to Rondot Frères, printer, rue des Abbesses.

On the way, he again flicked through the Patriotic Memory catalog his father-in-law had given him . . . M. Péricourt's reaction was not simply that of a seasoned businessman who has been cheated; he had taken it personally. So what was it really about?

The taxi was held up for some time on the rue de Clignancourt. Henri closed the catalog, vaguely impressed. The men he was looking for were clearly experienced criminals, a highly organized gang he had little chance of finding since he had few resources and even less time. He could not help feeling a sneaking admiration for the sheer ingenuity of the scam. The catalog was a masterpiece. Had it not been for the fact that his life depended on catching these men, he would have smiled. Instead, he vowed that if it came to his life or theirs, he would bombard this gang with everything he had: with grenades, with mustard gas, with a machine gun if he had one. Give him a breach the size of a mouse hole, he would wreak carnage. He felt the muscles in his stomach and his chest tense, his lips tighten . . .

That's all I ask, he thought, just give me one chance in ten thousand, and you are all dead.

40

"He's been a little unwell," Albert told the staff at the Lutetia, who were worried that they had had no news of Monsieur Eugène. No one had seen him in two days, he no longer made calls to room service; they had grown accustomed to his extravagant tips, and this sudden dearth provoked much disappointment.

Albert refused to let them call the hotel doctor. He came all the same, Albert opened the door a crack—he's feeling much better, thank you, he's resting—and shut the door again.

Édouard was not feeling better, he was not resting, he could keep nothing down, his throat wheezed like a blacksmith's bellows, and he still had a raging fever. It was taking a long time for his temperature to come down. Albert wondered whether he would be fit to travel. How the hell had he got hold of heroin? Albert had no idea whether it was a large quantity of heroin, he knew nothing about such matters. And if not, if Édouard needed more during the crossing—which would take several days—what then? Having never been aboard a ship, Albert was terrified at the thought of being seasick. If he could not look after his sick friend, who would?

When not sleeping or violently throwing up what little food Albert could get him to swallow, Édouard lay motionless, staring at the ceiling; he left his bed only to go to the toilet. Even then Albert hovered. "Don't lock the door," he said, "in case something happens and I need to help." Even when he was on the toilet . . .

He did not know which way to turn.

He spent all day Sunday taking care of his friend. Édouard spent most of the time in bed, bathed with sweat, racked by convulsions followed by terrible groans. Albert shuttled between the bedroom and bathroom with fresh towels, he called room service and ordered eggnog, beef bouillon, fruit juice. Toward the end of the day, Édouard asked for a dose of heroin.

"Just to get me through," he wrote feverishly.

In a moment of weakness, alarmed by his friend's condition and panicked at the thought of their imminent departure, Albert agreed, though he regretted it at once: he had not the slightest idea how to do it yet here he was, yet again, coming to the rescue . . .

Though Édouard's movements were hesitant—due partly to agitation and partly to exhaustion—it was obvious he had done this many times before; to Albert this was a new betrayal, and he felt hurt. Yet still he played the role of assistant: holding the syringe, flicking the flint wheel over the tinder . . .

It felt a lot like their early days together. The opulent suite at the Lutetia had little in common with the military hospital where, two years earlier, Édouard had almost died of septicemia waiting for a transfer to Paris, but the closeness between them, the fatherly care of the one for the other, Édouard's addiction, his deep unhappiness, the black despair that Albert generously, guiltily, clumsily tried to keep at bay, brought back memories, though it was impossible to say whether they were comforting or troubling. It was like a wheel coming full circle, a return to the beginning.

As the injection went in, Édouard's whole body jolted, as though someone had kicked him viciously in the back and tugged his head by the hair . . . It lasted only a moment or two, then he lay on his side, his face serene, and he slipped into salutary listlessness. Albert sat helplessly, watching him sleep, and his pessimism once again took the upper hand. In his heart, he had never quite believed they would succeed in pulling off their scheme, or, if they did, that they would manage to get away; now, with his friend in such a sorry state, he did not see how they could possibly take a train to Marseille and then a steamship crossing lasting several days without being spotted. To say nothing of his worries about what to do about Pauline—confess all? run away? lose her? War had been a lonely business, but it was nothing compared to the period since demobilization that was beginning to seem a veritable descent into hell; there were times when he felt ready to turn himself in, to get it over once and for all.

But, since he had to do something, sometime in the late afternoon Albert went down to the lobby while Édouard was asleep to confirm that M. Larivière would be checking out at noon on July 14.

"What do you mean, 'confirm'?" the manager said.

A tall, grim-faced man, he had fought in the war and had come close enough to a sliver of flying shrapnel to lose an ear. A few inches closer and he would have ended up with a face like Édouard's, but he had been lucky: he could hold his glasses in place with a piece of sticky tape that neatly matched his epaulets, which hid the ugly scar where the shrapnel had grazed his skull. Albert remembered stories he had heard of soldiers who lived with pieces of shrapnel in their brain because they could not be removed, but no one he knew had ever met one. Maybe the manager was one of these living dead. If so, he did not seem much affected; he still had an unerring ability to tell the gentry from the masses. He pursed his lips faintly. Regardless of what he said, and despite his neatly pressed suit and his polished shoes, Albert was obviously a commoner, perhaps it was something about his gestures, or maybe his accent, or that deference he could not but adopt before a man in uniform—even a hotel manager.

"So, Monsieur Eugène is leaving us?"

Albert nodded. Obviously Édouard had made no mention of his departure. Had he ever really planned to leave?

"Of course!" Édouard wrote in answer to Albert's question when he woke. His handwriting was shaky but still legible.

"Of course, we leave on the fourteenth!"

"But you haven't got anything ready . . . ," Albert insisted. "I mean, no suitcase, no clothes . . ."

Édouard slapped his forehead, what an idiot I am . . .

He scarcely ever wore the mask with Albert, and the sour stench from his exposed throat was sometimes hard to bear.

As the hours passed, Édouard's mood improved. He was eating again, and though still unsteady on his feet, by Monday his recovery seemed significant, and reassuring. When he left the suite, Albert considered taking the stuff with him—the heroin, the few remaining ampoules of morphine—but abandoned the idea as too tricky; Édouard would not let him, and besides he did not have the courage—what little strength he had was entirely focused on anticipating their departure, on counting the hours.

Since Édouard had made no preparations, Albert went next door and bought him clothes at the Bon Marché. To ensure that he was not let down by his taste, he quizzed a sales clerk, a man of about thirty who eyed him contemptuously. Albert said he wanted something "very *chic*."

"And what particular sort of 'chic' are we looking for?"

The clerk, seemingly eager for his response, loomed over Albert, staring at him.

"Well," Albert stammered, "it's . . . I suppose what I mean is . . ."

"Yes?"

Albert racked his brain . . . He had never thought "chic" could mean anything other than "chic." He waved toward a shop dummy on his right, a wave that encompassed everything: the hat, the shoes, the coat.

"I think that's chic . . ."

"Ah . . . that gives me a better idea," the clerk said.

He carefully removed the outfit, laid it on counter, and stepped back to admire the ensemble, as though contemplating a painting by an old master.

"Monsieur has excellent taste."

He recommended an assortment of matching ties and shirts, Albert made much of seeming hesitant, but agreed to everything, then watched with relief as the clerk packed it all up.

"We will need . . . a second outfit," Albert said. "For over there."

"I see . . . for over there," the clerk echoed as he finished tying the parcel. "And where precisely is 'over there'?"

Albert had no intention of mentioning their precise destination, absolutely not, on the contrary, he had to be cunning.

"The colonies," he said.

"I see . . ."

The clerk suddenly seemed intrigued. Perhaps he, too, had once had dreams and plans.

"What kind of outfit did you have in mind?"

Albert's sense of the colonies was a hodgepodge of picture postcards, stories he had heard, photographs he had seen in magazines.

"Something that would be appropriate in a place like that . . ."

The clerk pursed his lips and gave a knowing look—I think we have just the thing—this time there was no dummy for him to get a sense of the overall effect, what about this jacket, feel that fabric, and these pants, the height of elegance and yet extremely practical, and, of course, this hat.

"Are you sure?" Albert ventured.

The clerk was positive: the hat makes the man. Albert, who believed that shoes made the man, bought everything he suggested. The clerk gave a broad grin—perhaps at the mention of the colonies, or perhaps the fact he had just sold two outfits—but it gave him a curiously predatory air Albert had previously seen in bank managers, an expression he did not like at all, but he could ill afford to make a scene here, right next door to the hotel, they would be leaving in two days, there was no point making a mistake that would ruin all their efforts.

Albert also bought a fawn leather trunk, two new suitcases—one to carry the money—and a new hat box for the horse head mask, and had everything delivered to the Lutetia.

Last, he chose a pretty, very feminine box, into which he put forty thousand francs. Before going back to wake his comrade, he went into the post office on the rue de Sèvres and mailed it to Mme Belmont with a little note saying the money was for Louise, "when she grows up," that he and Édouard were counting on her "to invest it wisely until Louise is old enough to make use of it."

When the clothes were delivered, Édouard looked at them and nodded in satisfaction, he even gave a thumbs up—bravo, perfect. He doesn't give a damn, Albert thought. And he went to find Pauline.

In the taxi, he rehearsed his little speech and arrived filled with the best of intentions: this time he would tell her the whole truth, there was no alternative, today was July 12, two days from now—if he were still alive—he would be leaving, it was now or never. But his resolve was more like a prayer because, in his heart, he knew he could not bring himself to make such a confession.

He thought about the reasons he had not told her before now. It all came down to a moral issue he suspected was insurmountable.

Pauline had come from a humble background, a good Catholic family, her father was a laborer, her mother a factory worker, no one is more particular about decency and honesty than humble working-class folk.

To Albert's eyes, she looked more dazzling than ever. He had bought her a hat that brought out all the grace of her perfectly triangular face, of her radiant, disarming smile.

Sensing Albert's awkwardness—he was even quieter than usual and seemed perpetually on the brink of saying something, but no words came—Pauline tingled at the most thrilling moment of their relationship. She was convinced he intended to propose but could not bring himself to take the plunge. Albert was not just shy, she thought, he was a little self-conscious. He was adorable, really sweet, but unless you wormed the words out of him, you could be waiting around forever.

At the moment, she was enjoying this dithering, she felt desired, she did not regret giving in to his advances, to her own passions. She pretended to be amused, but she was convinced that this was the moment. For days now, she had taken a certain pleasure in watching as Albert tied himself in knots.

And tonight (they were having dinner in a little restaurant on the rue du Commerce), the way he had said:

"The thing is, Pauline, I am not enjoying my job at the bank, I've been wondering whether I should try my hand at something else . . ."

He's right, she thought, these are not the kinds of decisions to make when you have three or four children, you need to be a young man to strike out on your own.

"Really?" she answered casually, one eye on the waiter bringing their entrées. "Like what?"

"Well . . . I don't really know . . ."

It sounded as though he had spent much time thinking about the question but never about the answer.

"My own little business, maybe," he said.

Pauline flushed. A little shop . . . The pinnacle of success. Just think . . . Pauline Maillard, Fancy Goods, Paris.

"So . . . ," she said, "what sort of shop?"

Or maybe just: Maison Maillard. Groceries, Haberdashery, Wines & Spirits.

"Well, er . . ."

Typical, Pauline thought, Albert does things his own way, but his own way doesn't get him far.

". . . maybe not a shop as such . . . More a trading company."

To Pauline, who found it difficult to grasp what she could not see, the concept of a "trading company" sounded very vague.

"Trading in what?"

"I thought maybe tropical hardwoods."

Pauline froze, a forkful of leek vinaigrette hovering a few inches from her lips.

"What?"

Albert immediately started to backtrack:

"Or vanilla, or coffee, or cocoa perhaps, that sort of thing . . ."

Pauline nodded gravely, as she always did when she did not understand. Pauline Maillard, Vanilla & Cocoa, she did not much care for the sound of it. Nor could she imagine who might be interested.

Albert realized he had taken the wrong tack.

"It was just a thought . . ."

And so, one thing leading to another, tripping over his own arguments, he gradually trailed off, he gave up; he could sense Pauline slipping away from him, he hated himself, he felt a desperate urge to get up, to leave, to bury himself somewhere.

Dear God, he wanted the ground to open up and swallow him . . .

It always came back to that.

41

The chain of events that began on July 13 could feature on the syllabus of fireworks manufacturers or bomb disposal experts as the perfect example of an explosive situation that starts with a slow burn.

When the morning edition of *Le Petit Journal* appeared at about 6:30 a.m., it was merely a single guarded paragraph, albeit on the front page. The headline was merely conjecture, but it was tantalizing:

War Memorial Fraud . . .
An Impending National Scandal?

Though it was a brief paragraph, the article nonetheless attracted attention, sandwiched as it was between damps squibs such as Spa Conference Shows No Sign Of Reaching Agreement, an account of the death toll of the war: Europe Has Lost 35 Million Men, and the meager Schedule of July 14 Celebrations, which made much of the fact that obviously this year's celebrations could not possibly rival those of July 14 last year.

What did the article actually say? Nothing. That was its strength: it left ample room to the collective imagination to fill the gaps. There were no facts, but there were rumors that "maybe" some towns and villages "might have" commissioned war memorials from a company "some feared" might be a "straw" company. It could not have been more guarded.

Henri d'Aulnay-Pradelle was among the first to read it. Emerging from his taxi, he bought *Le Petit Journal* and while waiting for the print-works to open (it was not yet seven o'clock), stumbled on the article, nearly threw the paper into the gutter in a rage, but calmed himself. He read and reread it, weighing every word. He still had a little time, and that reassured him. But very little, which made him angrier still.

A man in overalls came and opened up with Henri already on his heels, good morning—he fluttered the Patriotic Memory catalog—you printed this, I need some information about the clients. The man explained that he was not the manager.

"Look, here he comes now."

The manager—a man about Henri's age carrying a lunch bucket and looking like a foreman who had married the owner—held in his hand a rolled-up copy of *Le Petit Journal* but, mercifully, had not yet read it. Men like this were always impressed by Henri since everything about him said "gentleman," the sort of rich, fastidious client who never asks the price. And so, when Henri asked if he might have a quiet word, the old hand said by all means, and as the typographers, printers and compositors began their day, he gestured to the glass door of the office where he received clients.

The shop floor workers were eyeing him surreptitiously; Henri turned his back so he could not be seen and immediately laid a two-hundred-franc bill on the desk.

The staff could see very little—the customer's back, his unruffled manner—and he left quickly, the meeting was cut short, a bad sign, since it meant he had not placed an order. But when he came to join them, the boss had a smug smile, which was surprising since it galled him not to close a deal. He had just earned four hundred francs—he could hardly believe it—simply for telling this gentleman that he had no name for the client, a man of average height, nervous, worried even, who had paid fifty percent up front in hard cash and the balance the day before delivery; had no delivery address for the catalogs since a messenger had come to fetch them, a man with a hand cart, only one arm, but a strapping man.

"I've seen him around here."

This was all Henri had managed to discover. No one knew him personally, the man with the cart, but he had been seen around. A one-armed man was hardly unusual these days, but one who pulled a handcart was rare enough.

"Maybe not from around here exactly," the printer had said. "I mean, not from the *quartier*, but he must live somewhere nearby . . ."

It was 7:30 a.m.

In the lobby, breathless, ashen, on the verge of apoplexy, Labourdin rushed up to M. Péricourt.

"*Monsieur le président, monsieur le président*" (not even a "good morning"), "I swear on my life that this has nothing to do with me!"

He held out *Le Petit Journal* gingerly as though it were ablaze.

"It's a disaster, *monsieur le président*! But upon my word . . ."

As if Labourdin's word had ever counted for anything.

He was close to tears.

M. Péricourt snatched the newspaper from his hands and shut himself away in his office. Unsure what to do next, Labourdin loitered in the hall—should he leave? was there something he could do to help? Then he remembered that the *président* had always told him, "Never take any personal initiative, Labourdin, always wait to be told what to do . . ."

He decided to await orders and settled himself in the drawing room. The housemaid appeared, the coquettish little brunette whose tits he had squeezed a few weeks ago. She kept her distance as she inquired whether there was anything he would like.

"Some coffee," he said, with weary resignation.

Labourdin did not have the stomach for anything more.

M. Péricourt read the article again. The scandal would break tonight, at latest tomorrow. He left the paper on his desk, without anger, too late. With each new piece of bad news, he seemed to shrink, his shoulders sagged, his backbone bowed, he grew physically smaller.

As he sat down at his desk, he glanced at the upside-down newspaper. This article was spark enough to light the fuse, he thought.

And he was right: no sooner had they read the article in *Le Petit Journal* than reporters from *Le Gaulois*, *L'Intransigent*, *Le Temps,* and *L'Écho de Paris* leapt into action, summoning taxis, calling informants. The government refused to comment, which proved there was something going on. Every reporter in the city waited, poised for action, convinced that when the story exploded, the spoils would go to those on the front lines.

The night before, as he had opened the lavish box from Le Bon Marché, unwrapped the tissue paper, and saw the ludicrous outfit Albert had bought for him, Édouard had let out a cry of joy. It was love at first sight: knee-length shorts in khaki twill, a beige shirt, a belt with the sort of fringes one saw on the jackets of cowboys in illustrations, ivory-colored knee-length socks, a pale-brown jacket, safari boots, and a hat with a preposterously large brim intended to protect the wearer from a sun, from which there was much to fear. A safari costume for a masked ball. All he needed was a cartridge belt and a hunting rifle, and he could be Tartarin de Tarascon. He had put it on right away and roared with laughter as he admired himself in the mirror.

It was in this bizarre getup that the bellboy from the Lutetia saw him when he came with room service: a lemon, a bottle of champagne and some vegetable bouillon.

He was still wearing it as he injected the morphine. He knew nothing of the effects of taking morphine, then heroin, then morphine—catastrophic perhaps, but just now, he felt calm, serene, relaxed.

He turned toward the steamer trunk—the globe-trotter model—then threw the window wide. He had a particular love of the skies over the Île-de-France, which, he felt, could surely have few equals. He had always loved Paris, had left it only to go to war, and had never thought of living elsewhere. Even today, it was strange. The effect of the drugs, probably: nothing was entirely real, nothing was entirely certain. What you see is not exactly reality, your thoughts are ever shifting, your plans are like illusions, you live in a dream, in a story that is never quite your own.

And there is no tomorrow.

Albert, whose mind of late had been preoccupied with other things, was utterly enraptured. Imagine: Pauline sitting on the bed, a taut stomach leading upward to a flawlessly defined navel, perfectly rounded breasts, pale as snow, nipples of a pink so delicate it could make you weep, and, between them, the little gold crucifix, swinging, swaying, never at rest . . . The sight was all the more moving since she herself was completely oblivious, distracted, her hair still tousled, because a moment earlier she had jumped on Albert in the bed. "This is war!" she shouted, laughing, and had launched a full frontal attack, bold and fearless, she had quickly outflanked him, and before long he surrendered, beaten, happy in defeat.

They had not had many days like this, when they could afford to lounge in bed. Twice, three times, perhaps. Pauline often worked impossible hours at the Péricourt residence, but not today. Albert was officially "on leave." "The bank gives all the staff a day off to celebrate July 14," he had explained. Had Pauline not spent her whole life as a maid of all work, she might have been shocked to hear of a bank giving its staff anything, instead she supposed it was a manager's chivalrous gesture.

Albert had gone down to get some *pains au lait* and the newspaper; the landlady permitted tenants to have a gas ring "strictly for the making of hot beverages," they could make coffee.

Pauline, naked as the day she was born, glistening from the exertions of battle, sipped her coffee and read out the celebrations that were to take place the following day. She had folded the newspaper to read the list.

"'Monuments and public buildings will be hung with bunting and illumination.' That will be pretty . . ."

Albert was finishing shaving; Pauline liked a man with a mustache—in those days, there was no other kind—but hated stubble on his cheeks. It scratches, she said.

"We'll need to set off early," she said, hunched over the newspaper. "The parade starts at eight o'clock, and Vincennes, and that's not exactly around the corner . . ."

In the mirror, Albert observed Pauline, devastatingly beautiful, shamelessly youthful. We'll go to the parade, he thought, then she'll go off to work, and I'll leave her forever.

"At les Invalides and Mont Valérien, cannons will be fired!" she said, taking a gulp of coffee.

She would search for him, would come here, ask for Albert, no, no one has seen M. Maillard; she would never understand, she would suffer the most terrible grief, invent all manner of reasons for his sudden disappearance, unable to bring herself to believe that Albert had lied to her, no, impossible, there must be a more romantic explanation, he had probably been kidnapped, perhaps even killed somewhere, his body, never found, had been dumped in the Seine; Pauline would be inconsolable.

"Oh," she said, "Just my luck: 'The following theaters are offering free admission to *matinée* performances: the Opéra, the Comédie-Française, the Opéra-Comique, the Odéon, the Porte-Saint-Martin . . .' I start my shift at one o'clock."

Albert liked this fiction in which he mysteriously disappeared, Pauline would give him a romantic nonspeaking role rather than the venal reality.

"And there's a ball being held at the place de la Nation! I don't finish work until ten-thirty, so by the time we got there it would be almost over . . ."

She said it without regret. Seeing her sit on the bed, devouring the sweet buns, Albert wondered: is this really a woman who would be inconsolable? No, you only had to look at her magnificent breasts, her voluptuous mouth, she was temptation incarnate . . . It reassured him to think that, though she would be hurt by his going, it would not be for long; he took a moment to consider the idea that he was the sort of man a woman would get over.

"Oh, my God," Pauline said suddenly, "How awful! How wicked!"

Albert whipped his head around, cutting his chin.

"What?" he said.

He was fumbling for a washcloth, a nick like that could bleed badly. Did he have an styptic pencil somewhere?

"Listen to this," Pauline said. "There are these people who have been selling war memorials . . ." (She looked up from the paper, she could hardly believe it.) "*Fake* memorials!"

"What? What?" Albert said, coming back to the bed.

"They've been selling memorials that don't even exist!" Pauline expanded, poring over her paper. "Careful, darling, you've cut yourself, you'll get blood everywhere!"

"Let me see! Let me see!" Albert howled.

"But *chéri* . . ."

She set down the paper, moved by Albert's reaction. She understood. He had been to war, he had lost friends, comrades, of course he would be sickened at the idea that people might stoop to such a cruel scheme, but even so . . . She dabbed his bleeding chin while he read and reread the brief article.

"Come on, *chéri*, pull yourself together! It's not good for you, getting yourself into a state!"

Henri spent the day wandering the *arrondissement*. Someone had mentioned a messenger who lived at 16—or perhaps it was 13—rue Lamarck, but there was no one of that name at either house. Henri took taxis everywhere. Someone else thought they knew someone with a handcart who ran errands from a shop at the far end of the rue de Caulincourt, but the place had long since been shut down.

Henri went into a café on the corner of the street. It was 10:00 a.m. A one-armed fellow who pulls a handcart? No, the description rang no bells with anyone. He walked down the even-numbered side of the street, then he would walk back on the odd-numbered side and comb every street and back alley in the *arrondissement* if he had to, but he would find the man.

"A one-armed man? Really? Can't be easy lugging a handcart, are you sure?"

Shortly before eleven o'clock, Henri turned into the rue Damrémont, having been assured that the coalman on the corner of the rue

Ordener had a handcart. As to the number of his arms, no one could say. It took Henri more than an hour to scour the length of the street, but finally, as he came to the junction with Montmartre Cemetery, he happened upon a laborer who said cheerily: "'Course I know him! A real character, that one! Lives on the rue Duhesme, number 44. I know on account of he's neighbor to a cousin of mine."

But there was no longer a 44, rue Duhesme, the place was now a building site and no one could say where the coalman lived now, though they seemed certain he had both his arms.

Albert rushed into Édouard's suite like a flurry of wind.

"Look, look, read this!" he yelled, brandishing the crumpled newspaper under Édouard's nose as he struggled awake.

At eleven o'clock in the morning! Albert thought, then, seeing the syringe and the empty morphine vial on the table, realized time had little to do with Édouard's tiredness. Having spent two years studying his friend, Albert had enough experience to be able to tell at a glance the difference between a mild dose and one likely to do damage. From the way Édouard was shaking himself awake, he could tell that this one had been calmative, to alleviate the worst of the withdrawal symptoms. But how many shots had there been, since the massive dose that had so terrified him and Louise?

"Are you all right?" he asked worriedly.

Why was Édouard wearing the colonial outfit from le Bon Marché? It was not at all appropriate to Paris, in fact it looked faintly ridiculous.

Albert did not ask any questions. All that mattered was the newspaper.

"Read it!"

Édouard sat up, read the article and, now completely awake, tossed the paper aside and let out a hoarse *rrââââhhh*, which in his language, was a sign of jubilation.

"B . . . but you don't seem to realize," Albert stammered. "They know everything, they'll track us down."

Édouard leapt out of bed, grabbed the bottle of champagne from the ice bucket on the table and poured a prodigious quantity into his throat—the noise it made . . . He started to cough violently, clutching his stomach, but still he danced about, howling *rrâââhhh!*

As in many couples, sometimes roles are reversed. Seeing his friend's distress, Édouard picked up the conversation pad and wrote:

"Don't worry, WE'RE LEAVING!"

He truly has no sense of responsibility, Albert thought. He waved the newspaper.

"Read it! Good God Almighty!"

At these words Édouard feverishly made the sign of the cross several times; it was one of his favorite jokes. Then he picked up the pencil again.

"They know NOTHING!"

Albert hesitated, but he was forced to acknowledge that the article was vague in the extreme.

"Maybe," he conceded, "but time is not on our side."

This was something he had witnessed at La Cipale before the war: cyclists racing after one another, impossible to tell who was chasing who, it electrified the spectators. Now he and Édouard had to run as fast as possible before the wolf's jaws snapped their spines.

"We have to go now! What are we waiting for?"

Weeks he had been saying the same thing. Why wait? Édouard had reached his million, so why?

"We're waiting for the boat," Édouard wrote.

It was obvious, though it had not occurred to Albert: even if they left for Marseille immediately, the steamship would not weigh anchor two days early.

"Then we'll change the tickets," Albert said, "We'll go somewhere else."

"Draw attention . . ." Édouard scrawled.

It was cryptic, but clear. With the police searching for them and the papers filled with stories about this affair, could Albert really afford to say to the clerk at Messageries Maritimes: "I was supposed to be going to Tripoli, but if you've got something leaving for Conakry earlier, I'll take it, I can pay the difference in cash"?

To say nothing of Pauline . . .

Blood drained from his face.

What if he confessed the truth and she was so shocked she turned him in to the police? "How awful!" she had said, "How wicked!"

The suite at the Hôtel Lutetia was suddenly silent. Whichever way he turned, Albert was trapped.

Édouard laid a hand on his friend's shoulder, he hugged him.

Poor Albert, he seemed to say.

Only when he broke for lunch did the manager of the printworks on the rue des Abbesses have time to open his newspaper. As he was smoking his first cigarette and waiting for his lunch bucket to warm up on the gas stove, he read the short article. And he panicked.

First that gentleman who had shown up at the crack of dawn and now this article in the newspaper, Jesus Christ, he stood to lose everything, his company had printed the catalog . . . He would be lumped in with these villains, he would be charged as an accomplice. He stubbed out his cigarette, turned off the gas ring, pulled on his jacket, called in his senior clerk, he would be out all day, and tomorrow being a holiday, he would not be back until Thursday.

Henri was still bounding from one taxi to another, indefatigable, increasingly short tempered, irritable, his curt questions soliciting ever fewer responses. And so, making a great effort, he forced himself to be more ingratiating. At two o'clock in the afternoon he made his way along the rue Poteau and came back via the rue Lamarck before tackling the rue d'Orsel and the rue Letort, handing out money—ten francs, twenty francs—rue du Mont-Cenis, thirty francs to an overbearing woman who insisted the man he was looking for was a Monsieur Pajol who lived on the rue Coysevox. Again Henri drew a blank; it was now 3:30.

Meanwhile, the article in the *Petit Journal* had begun its work. People telephoned one another—have you seen the paper? By early afternoon, a few readers from the provinces began to call the newspaper's offices to say that they had contributed to a public subscription for a memorial and were wondering whether they might be among the "victims" mentioned.

At the offices of *le Petit Journal*, a map of France was pinned up with colored tacks marking the location of the callers in towns and villages in Alsace, Bourgogne, Bretagne, Franche-Comté, Saint-Vizier-de-Pierlat, Villefranche, Poitiers-sur-Garonne, there had even been one from a school in Orléans . . .

At five o'clock, they finally managed to obtain the name and address of Patriotic Memory and those of the printers from one of the town halls (until then, their calls had gone unanswered; like Labourdin, most councilors were quaking in their boots).

Reporters visited 52 rue du Louvre and were shocked to discover there was no company; they raced to the rue des Abbesses. At six-thirty, the first journalist to arrive found the printworks closed.

When the afternoon editions appeared, they still had little additional evidence, but what they had seemed sufficient to take a more confident tone than they had that morning.

The printed certainties:

PROFITEERS SELL PHONY WAR MEMORIALS
Scale of Fraud Not Yet Known

A few more hours of investigating, making calls, answering telephones, asking questions, and the late editions were categorical:

WAR MEMORIALS: OUR VALIANT HEROES' MEMORY MOCKED
Thousands cheated by unscrupulous profiteers

UNSPEAKABLE "SALE" OF PHONY WAR MEMORIALS
How many victims?

MEMORY THIEVES
Organized criminals sell hundreds of nonexistent war memorials

WAR MEMORIAL SCANDAL:
STILL NO GOVERNMENT STATEMENT

The bellboy who brought up the newspapers Monsieur Eugène had sent down for found him in a mask and full colonial regalia. With feathers.

"What do you mean, with feathers?" he was asked as soon as he stepped out of the elevator.

"Exactly as I said," the young man said, prolonging the suspense. "With feathers."

In his hand, he held the fifty francs he had been given for his trouble, all eyes were on the money, but still, this business about the feathers, they were anxious to know more.

"Like angel's wings on his back. Green feathers. Huge, they were!"

Hard as they tried, it was difficult to imagine.

"They looked to me like dusters that had been pulled apart and the feathers glued together."

If they envied the young man, it was not simply because of this business with the feathers, but because he had earned his fifty francs just as rumors that Monsieur Eugène was leaving tomorrow morning were spreading like wildfire; all the staff could think about was what they stood to lose, Monsieur Eugène was the sort of guest you encounter once in your career, and perhaps not even then. Everyone present was mentally calculating how much this or that colleague had had from Monsieur Eugène, some complained they should have set up a kitty. Their eyes flashed with regret and resentment . . . How many more times would Monsieur Eugène need errands before he left for who knew where? And who would get to attend him?

Édouard read the papers eagerly. We're heroes again! he was thinking.

Albert was probably reading the papers, too, though his thoughts would have been very different.

The newspapers now knew about Patriotic Memory. However much they protested, they were clearly impressed by the audacity, the cunning ("these dazzlingly ingenious swindlers"), though the flattery was expressed in shocked outrage. All that remained was to find out the scale of the fraud. To do that, they needed access to the bank records, but who could they find on July 14 to open up the offices and show them the records? No one. The police were ready to pounce at the crack of dawn on July 15. By then, he and Albert would be far away.

Far away, Édouard thought again. And in the time it takes the papers and the police to track down Eugène Larivière and Louis Évrard, two soldiers reported missing in action in 1918 . . . we have time for a whirlwind tour of the Middle East.

The floor was carpeted with newspapers as once it had been strewn with pages from the freshly printed catalog of "Patriotic Memory."

Édouard suddenly felt weary. He was feverish. He frequently had hot flushes after an injection, just as he came back to earth.

He took off his safari jacket. The angel's wings slipped away and fell to the floor.

The man with the handcart went by the name of Coco. To compensate for his missing arm—lost at Verdun—he had fashioned a harness that fastened over his chest, wrapped around his shoulders, and hooked onto a wooden shaft screwed to the handcart. A lot of war veterans—especially those with nothing but a state pension—had become extraordinarily inventive; there were clever little carts for legless cripples, homemade gadgets of wood, metal, or leather to replace missing hands, feet, legs; the country had a host of resourceful demobilized soldiers, it was a shame that most of them were unemployed.

It was on the corner of the rue Carpeaux and the rue Marcadet that Henri finally tracked down Coco, whose harness meant he was forced to pull the cart with his head bowed and his body at a slight angle, which further accentuated his resemblance to a workhorse or an ox. Exhausted by a day spent combing the streets, scouring the *arrondissement*, Pradelle had spent a fortune in tips for worthless information.

The moment he found Coco, he knew he was saved; rarely had he felt more invincible.

The baying pack (Henri had read the late editions of the papers) was already onto this war memorial scandal old Péricourt seemed to care so much about, but he had a head start that would allow him to get the better of them all and bring enough information back to the old bastard for him to make the promised telephone call to the minister, who, in a few scant minutes, would wipe his slate clean.

Henri would once again be as white as snow, his reputation restored, he would be able to start over again and keep what he already had, besides, the refurbishment of his estate at la Sallevière was almost complete, and his bank account continued to siphon exorbitant sums from state coffers. He had become embroiled in this mess through no fault of his own, but now that the worst was past, people would see who Henri d'Aulnay-Pradelle truly was.

Henri brought a hand to the pocket stuffed with fifty-franc bills but, when Coco looked up, he changed his mind and went for the other pocket, the one where he kept twenty-franc bills and coins, sensing that he could get the result he wanted cheaply. He thrust his right hand into the pocket and jingled the loose change. He asked his question, those catalogs you picked up from the printworks on the rue des Abbesses, ah, yes, said Coco, where did you drop them off? Four francs. Henri dropped four francs into the remaining hand of the barrow boy, who thanked him profusely.

Don't mention it, Henry thought, already in a taxi on his way to the impasse Pers.

The large house with the wooden fence that Coco had described came into view. He had had to wheel the handcart all the way to the bottom of the stairs, you bet I remember the place, had to deliver a bench there once, one of them sofa things, what are they called . . . Anyway a bench, but that was a while back, months and months ago, but that day at least there was someone to give me a hand, but with them there catalogs for . . . whatever it was. Coco could not read very well; this was why he pulled a handcart.

Henri asks the taxi to wait, hands over a ten-franc bill, the driver is delighted, take all the time you need, your lordship.

He opens the gate, crosses the courtyard, and stands at the foot of the steps; he peers up, there is no one around, he takes the risk, climbs the stairs warily, ready for anything, oh, how he wishes he had a grenade at this very moment, but it doesn't matter; he pushes open the door, the apartment is empty. Deserted, to be more precise. That much is obvious from the dust, the dishes, the place is not particularly untidy, but it has that empty quality of uninhabited rooms.

Suddenly, a noise behind him, he turns, runs to the door. A dull clatter of footsteps, *clack clack clack,* a little girl scurrying down the stairs and running off, he can only see her back, how old is she? Henri has no idea when it comes to children . . .

He searches the apartment from top to bottom, tossing everything on the floor, nothing, not a single document, but wait—a copy of the Patriotic Memory catalog propping up the wardrobe!

Henri smiles. His amnesty is fast approaching.

He takes the stairs four at a time, races out of the gate, walks up to the front door of the house, and rings the doorbell, once, twice, crumpling the catalog between his hands, he is getting nervous, very nervous, but finally the door is opened by a woman of uncertain age, a face as long as a ship canal, mute. Henri waves the catalog, gestures to the outbuilding at the far end of the courtyard, I'm looking for the people who were living here, he says. He reaches for his money. He is not dealing with Coco now, instinctively he flourishes a fifty-franc bill. The woman stares at the money, but she makes no move to take it, she stares blankly, but Henri is convinced that she understands. He repeats the question.

Then he hears it again, *clack clack clack.* He glances to his right, the little girl, at the far end of the street, running.

Henri smiles at this ageless, voiceless, sightless woman, this ectoplasm, thanks, it's all right, stuffs the money back in his pocket, he has already spent enough for today, gets back in the taxi, where to now, your lordship?

A hundred yards away, on the rue Ramey, there are hansom cabs and taxis. The little girl is clearly experienced, she has a word with the driver, shows him her money, a child like that taking a taxi, a driver can't help but be suspicious, but not for long, she has money, a fare is a fare, go on, get in child, she gets in, the taxi drives off.

Rue Caulaincourt, place de Clichy, past the Gare Saint-Lazare, around the Madeleine. Everywhere is decked out for the July 14 celebrations. As a national hero himself, Henri approves. Crossing the bridge at la Concorde, he thinks of les Invalides nearby, where tomorrow the gun salute would be fired. But at no point does he take his eye off the little girl's taxi, which is now crossing the boulevard Saint-Germain and heading up the rue des Saints-Pères. Henri mentally congratulates himself, he would be prepared to bet his life that the girl is headed—where else?—for the Hôtel Lutetia.

Thank you, your lordship. Henri tips the taxi twice as much as he gave Coco, when you're happy you don't count the cost.

The little girl clearly knows her way around, she does not hesitate for an instant, she pays the taxi driver, leaps out onto the pavement, and the doorman nods to her, Henri thinks for a brief second.

Two possible solutions.

Wait for the girl, grab her as she comes out, stuff her in his pocket, rip her limb from limb in the nearest doorway, extract the information he needs and dump her remains into the Seine. Fresh meat, the fish will love her.

Option two: go in, find out more.

He goes in.

"Monsieur . . . ?" the receptionist asks.

"D'Aulnay-Pradelle . . ." (Henri proffers a visiting card.) "I don't have a reservation . . ."

The receptionist takes the card. Henri spreads his hands in a gesture that is at once helpless, rueful, but also conspiratorial, the gesture of a man in a difficult position whose manner makes it clear that he is prepared to show his gratitude to anyone prepared to help. A delicate manner the receptionist associates with only the best clients . . . meaning, the richest clients. This is the Lutetia.

"I don't think that will be a problem, *monsieur* . . ." (He checks the card.) "Monsieur d'Aulnay-Pradelle. Let me see . . . would you prefer a room or a suite?"

Between aristocrat and flunky there is always common ground.

"A suite," Henri says.

Obvious, really. The receptionist purrs—but soundlessly, he is a professional—and pockets the fifty francs.

42

By 7:00 a.m. the following morning, crowds were thronging the métro, the tramways, and the buses heading toward the Bois de Vincennes. All along the avenue Daumesnil, vehicles were nose to tail, taxis, carriages, hansom cabs, cyclists weaved through the traffic, pedestrians quickened their pace. Though they did not know it, Albert and Pauline presented a curious sight. He trudged along, eyes glued to the pavement, looking like a miserable or anxious malcontent while she gazed up at the heavens, skipping along and commenting on the airship that hovered over the parade ground.

"Hurry up, *chéri*," she said, "We'll miss the start."

But it was idle chatter, said simply for the sake of saying something. The stands by now were full to bursting.

"My God, what time did they get here, I wonder?" Pauline said.

Up ahead, lined up in marching order, ramrod straight and quivering with impatience, the Special Forces, the troops from the Military Academies, and from l'Armée Coloniale, and behind them, the artillery and the cavalry. Since the only seats remaining were so far back, shrewd street hawkers were offering wooden boxes on which latecomers could perch for one or two francs. Pauline managed to get two for one franc fifty.

The sun was beating down on the Bois de Vincennes. The colorful outfits of the women and the garish uniforms contrasted with the officials' black frock coats and top hats. Though it may simply have been the jaundiced view of the common masses, the *beau monde* seemed preoccupied. And perhaps they were, or some of them at least, everyone had read the morning edition of *Le Gaulois* or *Le Petit Journal*, this business of the war memorials was on everyone's mind. That the scandal had broken on a national holiday seemed not coincidence, but symbolic, almost an act of defiance. "A Nation Outraged" ran one headline, "Our Glorious Dead Insulted" others trumpeted in outsize type. It had now been confirmed: a company, disgracefully calling itself "Patriotic Memory," had sold hundreds of nonexistent memorials and made off with the takings; there was talk of a million francs, maybe two, no one seemed to know the extent of the damage. Rumor trumped scandal, and while they waited for the parade to start, people swapped information gleaned from who knew where: some said this was "another dirty trick by the Boches!" Nonsense, insisted others with no more facts to back up their claim, though one thing was certain, the crooks had escaped with ten million francs.

"Ten million francs," Pauline said to Albert, "Can you imagine?"

"That sounds like an exaggeration to me," he said in a voice so low she scarcely heard.

People were already insisting heads should roll—as usual, this being France—particularly because the government was "in it up to its neck." *L'Humanité* had explained it best: "Given that the commissioning of these war memorials must have required government involvement, if only in terms of subsidies—which, it must be said were appallingly inadequate—who is going to believe that prominent individuals were unaware of what was happening?"

"Whatever happened," said a man standing behind Pauline, "they must have been real professionals to pull off a scam like this."

Everyone felt that the swindle was utterly disgraceful, but they could not help but admire the sheer audacity of the scheme.

"It's true," Pauline said. "You have to admit, they're clever."

Albert was feeling a little off color.

"What's the matter, *chéri*?" Pauline said, pressing a hand to his cheek. "Are you not feeling well? Maybe watching the troops march past brings back terrible memories?"

"Yes," Albert said, "That's what it is."

And as the first notes of *Sambre-et-Meuse* were sounded by the Garde Républicaine and Général Berdoulat raised his sword in salute to Maréchal Pétain, flanked by various senior officers, Albert was thinking, ten million clear profit—any man here would cut my throat for a tenth of that.

It was now eight o'clock, his meeting with Édouard at the Gare de Lyon was set for 12:30 p.m. ("Not a minute later," he had insisted, "otherwise I'll just worry . . .") The train for Marseille left at 1:00 p.m. Pauline would be left alone. Albert would be left without Pauline. Where was the profit?

The crowds applauded as cadets from the École Polytechnique[14] marched past, followed by officers from Saint-Cyr with their tricolor shako plumes, the Republican Guard, the Fire Services, then came the rank-and-file soldiers in their pale-blue uniforms, the crowd leapt to their feet. There were cries of "Vive la France!"

Édouard was standing in front of a mirror when he heard the cannons being fired at les Invalides. For some time now, he had been worried to notice that his exposed throat was flushing a vivid crimson. He felt weary. The morning newspapers had not brought him the same joyous thrill as those the day before. How quickly emotions aged, and how badly his throat had aged!

What would he look like when he was old? The cleft in his face would leave little room for wrinkles, other than on his forehead. It amused Édouard to imagine that the folds and furrows that could find no space on his missing cheeks, his missing lips would all flow to his forehead, as diverted rivers carve out new channels, following the path of least resistance. As an old man, he would be no more than a forehead as rutted as a parade ground above a gaping crimson void.

He checked the time. Nine o'clock. He was so tired. On the bed, the chambermaid had set out his full colonial regalia. It lay there like a corpse emptied of all substance.

"Is this how you wanted it, *monsieur*?" she had said hesitantly.

The hotel staff were no longer surprised by Monsieur Eugene's notions, but even so, that safari jacket with the huge green feathers stitched to the back . . .

"You're planning to wear this . . . out?" she had said, surprised.

In answer, he simply pressed a crumpled bill into her hand.

"So . . . should I ask the bellboy to come get your trunk?" she said.

His luggage was to be collected at eleven and go on ahead of him to be loaded onto the train.

He would keep only the ancient, battered haversack into which he had packed his few personal belongings. Albert was the one who carried the important things, I'm always afraid you'll lose them, he would say.

It did him good to think about his friend, in fact he felt an inexplicable pride as though, for the first time since they had met, he was the parent and Albert the child. Because at heart, Albert, with his terrors and his nightmares, was just a kid. Like Louise, who had unexpectedly reappeared last night—what a pleasure to see her again.

She had rushed in, panting for breath.

A man had been at the impasse Pers. Édouard had bent forward, tell me all about it.

He's looking for you, he ransacked the apartment, asked all sorts of questions, we didn't say anything, obviously. A lone man. Yes, in a taxi. Édouard had stroked Louise's cheek, traced the curve of her lips with his forefinger, thank you, that's very sweet, you did the right thing, now go, it's getting late. He would have liked to kiss her forehead. She would have liked this, too. She shrugged, hesitant, then decided to go.

A lone man in a taxi, clearly not the police. A particularly shrewd reporter. He had tracked down their address, so what? Without their names, what could he do? And even if he had their names, how would he track Albert to his lodging house or Édouard to the Lutetia? Especially as the train was leaving in a few hours.

Just a little, he thought. No heroin this morning, just a drop of morphine. He needed to stay lucid, thank the hotel staff, say his good-byes to the manager, get into the taxi, go to the station, find the train, meet up with Albert. And then . . . then would come the surprise that thrilled him. Albert had shown him only his own ticket, but Édouard had rummaged around and found the others, in the names of M. and Mme Louis Évrard.

So there was a woman. Édouard had long suspected it, but why the hell did Albert have to be so mysterious? He was like a child.

Édouard took his injection. The relief was instantaneous, he felt calm, weightless, he had been very careful with the dose. He went and lay down on the bed, he ran his finger around the edge of cleft in his face. My safari suit and I are like two dead men side by side, he thought, one empty, the other hollow.

Except for checking stock market prices, which he did unfailingly morning and evening, and a few financial magazines, M. Péricourt did not read the newspapers. Others read for him, wrote up brief digests, advised him of any pressing matters. He was loath to depart from this rule.

On a sideboard in the hallway, he glimpsed the front page of *Le Gaulois*. Damn. He had expected the scandal would break at any moment; he had no need to read the papers to know what they were saying.

His son-in-law's hunt had been tardy and futile. Or perhaps not, for here they were sitting face to face. M. Péricourt said nothing, merely folded his arms. He would wait as long as he needed, but he would ask no questions. He could, however, offer a little motivation . . .

"I had the Ministre des Pensions on the telephone discussing your situation."

This was not how Henri had envisaged this interview, but so be it. All that mattered was that his slate be wiped clean.

"He told me it is serious," M. Péricourt said, "He went into some detail. Very serious indeed"

Henri was baffled. Was the man trying to raise the stakes, to bargain over what he, Henri, had to report?

"I found your man," he said bluntly.

"Who is he?"

Péricourt blurted the question. A good sign.

"And what does the minister have to say on the subject of my 'serious' situation?"

Both men marked a silence

"That it will be almost impossible to resolve. What do you expect? The reports have already been circulated, the matter is no longer a secret . . ."

For Henri, there could be no question of giving up now; he would sell his skin whatever the price.

"'Almost impossible' is not 'impossible.'"

"Where is he, this man?" M. Péricourt asked.

"In Paris. For the moment."

Pradelle fell silent, he studied his fingernails.

"You're certain it's him?"

"Absolutely."

Henri had spent the previous evening in the bar of the Lutetia, he had even considered telephoning Madeleine, but there was no point now.

The first nuggets of information had come from the barman, everyone was talking about him, about this Monsieur Eugène who had checked in two weeks ago. His presence had eclipsed everything else, the daily news, the July 14 festivities, he monopolized all attention. And made the barman's resentment bitter: "He only tips the people he sees, so whenever he orders a bottle of champagne, the money goes to whoever delivers it, not a centime for the barman who prepared it, the man's a boor, if you want my opinion. I hope he's not a friend of yours? Oh, the little girl, yes, there's been a lot of talk about her, but she hasn't been in here, a bar is no place for children."

This morning, he had got up at 7:00 a.m. and talked to the staff, the bellboy who brought his breakfast, the chambermaid, he had even sent down for newspapers just for the opportunity to talk to someone else. It all tallied. This Monsieur Eugène was anything but discreet. He clearly believed he had complete impunity.

According to the barman, the girl Henri had followed had only ever visited one guest at the hotel.

"He's leaving Paris," Henri said.

"Destination?" M. Péricourt asked.

"I suspect he's fleeing the country. He leaves at noon."

He let this information percolate, then added:

"I reckon once he leaves, he will be almost impossible to find . . ."

"I reckon." Only a boor would use such a phrase. Oddly, since he was not really a pedant in linguistic matters, M. Péricourt was shocked to hear such an uncouth expression from the lips of the man to whom he had given his daughter's hand.

A military band passed beneath the windows of the study, forcing the two men to pause a moment. From the sound of firecrackers and children wailing, it was obvious a large crowd had gathered to watch the parade.

Once calm was restored, M. Péricourt decided to cut to the chase.

"I shall intercede with the minister and . . ."

"When?"

"As soon as you have told me what I wish to know."

"His name—or at least the one he is going by—is Eugène Larivière. He's staying at the Lutetia."

It seemed important to pad out the information, to give the old man value for his money. Henri explained about Monsieur Eugène's whims, his extravagant tastes, the chamber orchestras, the elaborate masks so that no one ever saw his face, the exorbitant tips, the rumors that he took drugs. Last night, the chambermaid had seen a safari suit, and of course there was the steamer trunk . . .

"What do you mean, feathers?" M. Péricourt interrupted.

"Feathers. Green feathers. Arranged like angel's wings."

M. Péricourt had formed his own picture of the swindler, made up of what little he knew about such criminals, and it was nothing like his son-in-law's description. Henri realized old Péricourt did not believe him.

"He lives expensively, he squanders money, he's lavish in his generosity."

Good. The mention of money refocused the old man's concentration, forget the talk of string quartets and angel's wings, let's talk about money. A man who steals and spends, this was something his father-in-law could understand.

"Did you see him?"

Ah, this was a problem. What should he say? Henri had been in the hotel, he knew the man was staying in suite number 40, at first he had wanted to see the man's face and maybe grab him, since he was alone it would not be difficult: he would simply knock on the door and when the man opened, knock him to the ground, truss his wrists with a belt . . . then what?

What exactly did M. Péricourt want? Did he want the man handed over to the police? Since the old man had said nothing of his intentions, Henri had thought it better to double back to the boulevard des Courcelles.

"He checks out of the Lutetia at noon," he said, "You have enough time to have him arrested."

The thought had not occurred to M. Péricourt. He had wanted to find the man for himself. In fact, he would rather suppress the news of his escape than be forced to share the information; he pictured the melodramatic arrest, the interminable investigation, the trial . . .

"Very well."

As far as he was concerned, the interview was at an end, but Henri did not move. On the contrary, he uncrossed and recrossed his legs to make it clear that he was staying, that he expected the reward he had earned and had no intention of leaving before he got it.

M. Péricourt lifted the telephone receiver and asked the operator to get the Ministre des Pensions on the line, at home, at the ministry, wherever he happened to be, it was urgent, he needed to speak to him immediately.

He hung up, and the two men waited in a ponderous silence.

Finally, the telephone rang.

"I see," said M. Péricourt slowly, "Have him call me immediately he returns. Yes. Extremely urgent."

Then, to Henri: "The minister is attending the military parade in the Bois de Vincennes. He is expected home in an hour."

Henri could not bear the thought of having to sit here for an hour or more. He got to his feet. The two men were not in the habit of shaking hands, and so they merely sized each other up and Henri left the study.

M. Péricourt listened as Pradelle's footsteps faded, then sat down again and turned to stare out of the window: the sky was a perfect blue.

Henri wondered whether he should call on Madeleine.

Why not? Just once would not hurt.

There were trumpets, the cavalry raised clouds of dust, next came the heavy artillery, huge field guns towed by tractors, then the gun carriers, the armored cars, and last the tanks, ten o'clock sounded, it was over. The parade left a curious impression, a fulfillment, and an emptiness. The crowds began to drift away, silent but for the children, who were excited that they could finally run and play.

Pauline held Albert's arm as they walked.

"Where are we going to find a taxi?" he wondered aloud, his voice expressionless.

They had to call at his lodging house so Pauline could change her clothes before starting her shift.

"We've spent enough money already," she said. "Let's take the métro, we have time, don't we?"

M. Péricourt waited for the minister's call. It was almost eleven o'clock when the telephone rang.

"Ah, my dear fellow, I do regret . . ."

But the minister did not sound as though he regretted anything. He had been expecting this call for days, indeed he was surprised it had not come before now: sooner or later, M. Péricourt was bound to intercede on behalf of his son-in-law.

And it would be an awkward conversation: the minister owed much to Péricourt, but this time he could do nothing, the cemetery scandal was out of his hands, the prime minister himself was incensed, nothing could be done now . . .

"It's about my son-in-law," M. Péricourt said.

"Ah, my dear fellow, a deplorable affair . . ."

"Serious?"

"Extremely serious. There is talk of . . . criminal charges."

"Really? That bad?"

"I'm afraid so. Fraudulently securing government contracts, hushing up malfeasance, theft, trafficking, attempted bribery, it could hardly be more serious."

"Good."

"What do you mean, good?"

The minister was puzzled.

"I simply wanted to inquire about the extent of the damage."

"Colossal, my dear Péricourt, there is bound to be a scandal. Especially in the current circumstances, what with this business of the war memorials, the government is in a terrible situation . . . Obviously I had contemplated intervening on behalf of your son-in-law, but . . ."

"Don't!"

The minister could not believe his ears . . . Don't?

"I wished to be kept informed, nothing more," M. Péricourt said, "There are arrangements I need to make for my daughter. As for Monsieur d'Aulnay-Pradelle, let justice take its course. That would be best."

Tellingly, he added: "Best for all concerned."

To the minister, getting off so lightly seemed a miracle.

M. Péricourt replaced the receiver telephone. His son-in-law's disgrace, which he had just pronounced without a second's hesitation, prompted only one thought: should he tell Madeleine right away?

He looked at his watch. He would do it later.

He asked for the car to be brought around.

"No chauffeur, I shall drive myself."

At 11:30 a.m., Pauline was still basking in the excitement of the parade, the music, the cannon fire, the roar of the engines. They had just arrived back at Albert's lodging house.

"I mean, really," she said, taking off her hat. "Charging a whole franc for a measly wooden box."

Albert stood, frozen, in the middle of the room.

"What's the matter, darling, are you feeling all right? You're very pale . . ."

"It was me," he said.

Then he sat stiffly on the bed, staring at Pauline, it was done, he had confessed, he did not know what to make of this unexpected decision, nor what else he might say. The words had tumbled from his lips without his conscious intention. As though they were someone else's.

Pauline looked at him, still clutching her hat.

"What does that mean, 'it was me'?"

Albert looked in a sorry state, she hung up her coat and went to sit next to him. White as a sheet. He was definitely sickening for something. She pressed a hand to his forehead, no doubt about it, he was running a temperature.

"Did you catch cold?" she said.

"I'm going away, Pauline, I'm leaving."

His sounded overwrought. The misunderstanding over his health lasted barely a second.

"Going away . . . ," she echoed, on the brink of tears. "What do you mean going away? You're leaving me?"

Albert bent and picked up the newspaper, which was still folded open at the article about the war memorials, he handed it to her.

"It was me," he said again.

It took several seconds for the information to filter through. She bit her fist.

"My God . . ."

Albert got up, opened the dresser drawer, took out the Messageries Maritime tickets, and handed her hers.

"Will you come with me?"

Pauline was staring vacantly, her eyes glassy as a waxwork dummy's, her mouth half-open. She looked at the tickets, then at the newspaper, but could not shake off her astonishment.

"My God . . . ," she said again.

Albert did the only thing he could. He got up and, bending down, dragged the suitcase from under the bed, set it on the comforter, and opened it to reveal a staggering amount of paper money in neat packets.

Pauline gave a little cry.

"The train leaves for Marseille in an hour," Albert said.

She had three seconds in which to decide whether to be rich or spend the rest of her life as a housemaid.

She only needed one.

The suitcase full of money was obviously a factor, but what had swayed her were the steamship tickets marked "First Class Cabin." Everything those words represented.

In a flash, she snapped the suitcase shut and ran to put on her coat.

As far as M. Péricourt was concerned, the matter of the war memorial was closed. He did not know why he was driving to the Lutetia, he had no intention of going in, of meeting this man, of speaking to him. Any more than he intended to turn him in to the police or prevent him from fleeing. No. For the first time in his life, he accepted defeat.

He had been categorically beaten.

Strangely, he felt almost a sense of relief. To lose was to be human.

He was going to the Lutetia in much the way a man signs an acknowledgment of debt, because it was a necessary act, because he can do no other.

It was not a guard of honor—such things are not done in grand hotels—but it looked very much like one: all those who had served Monsieur Eugène were standing to attention in the lobby. He stepped out of the elevator, shrieking like a madman, decked out in his safari suit, the feathery angel's wings now clearly visible.

He was not wearing one of the outrageous creations with which he had entertained the staff, but his "normal man" mask, the face that was frozen yet so lifelike. The one he had worn when he first arrived.

It was something the like of which they would never see again, the manager thought, regretting that he had not arranged for a photographer. Monsieur Eugène, ever the fine gentleman, was doling out money to all and sundry ("Thank you, Monsieur Eugène," they said, "See you soon"), distributing alms to those present, just like a saint—that must be why he was wearing the wings, they thought, though they could not help but wonder why they were green.

Wings, what an utterly ridiculous idea, M. Péricourt was thinking, remembering his conversation with Pradelle. He was driving along the boulevard Saint-Germain, traffic was light, only a few automobiles, some hackney carriages, the weather was magnificent. His son-in-law had talked of "whims," of wings, but had there not been some mention of chamber orchestras, too? The relief he felt, M. Péricourt finally realized, was the result of losing a battle he could never have won, because this world, this adversary, they were alien to him. It is impossible to win against something you cannot understand.

What cannot be understood must simply be accepted, the staff of the Lutetia might have said, as they pocketed the blessings of Monsieur Eugène, who, still screeching, strode through the lobby, lifting his knees high, heading toward the doors open onto the boulevard.

M. Péricourt had not even needed to come. Why had he set himself this absurd mission? He would be better off turning back. Since he was already on the boulevard Raspail, he would pass the Lutetia, take the next turning, and drive home. Be done with this. The decision came as a relief.

The manager of the Lutetia was also eager for all the fuss to be over: the other guests found this carnival in the lobby to be in poor taste. And the rain of money turned his staff into beggars, it was indecent, let the man go!

Monsieur Eugène must have sensed this, for he stopped abruptly, like prey suddenly aware of a predator. His contorted posture at odds with the frozen inscrutability of his mask.

Without warning, he stretched his arm out in front of him and gave a loud, distinctive howl: *rrrââhhhhrrrr!* He pointed to a corner of the lobby where a maid had just finished dusting the coffee tables. He ran over to her. Seeing this stone-faced man in a safari suit rushing toward her, she was terror stricken. "I can't tell you how frightened I was, my God, but we laughed about it later . . . it was . . . the broom he wanted.—The broom?—Honest to God!" Monsieur Eugène snatched up the broom, stuck it against his shoulder like a rifle, and still roaring, marched about, soldierly and stiff legged to the rhythm of silent music everyone thought they could hear.

And it was with a military step, his great wings beating the air, that Édouard stepped through the doors of the Hôtel Lutetia and onto the sunlit pavement.

Turning his head, he saw a car speeding toward the corner of the boulevard. He threw the broom into the air and hurled himself into space.

M. Péricourt had been accelerating when he saw the small crowd outside the hotel, and he was passing the entrance when Édouard rushed forward. What he saw was not, as one might imagine, an angel fluttering in front of him since, given his stiff leg, Édouard did not manage to get off the ground. He stood squarely in the middle of the road and flung his arms wide as the car approached, staring at the sky, trying to rise into the heavens; but that was all.

Or almost all.

M. Péricourt could not have stopped. But he could have braked. Panic stricken at the sight of this startling apparition—not the angel in the safari suit, but the face of Édouard, his son, unscathed, unmoving, transfixed, like a death mask, the eyes wide with surprise—he did not react.

The car crashed headlong into the young man.

It made a dull, mournful sound.

Only then did the angel take flight.

Édouard was catapulted into the air. It was an inelegant flight, like an airplane bound to crash, but for a fraction of a second everyone saw the young man hover, his body arched, his eyes turned heavenward, his arms spread wide, like an ascension. Then he fell, plummeting onto the street, his skull slamming against the curb, and that was all.

* * *

Albert and Pauline boarded the train shortly before noon. They were the first travelers to board, she bombarded him with questions and he answered straightforwardly.

To listen to Albert, reality was simple.

Every now and then Pauline glanced at the suitcase she had set on the luggage rack facing her.

On his lap, Albert protectively clutched the hatbox containing the horse head mask.

"So, who is he, this friend of yours?" she whispered impatiently.

"A friend . . . ," he said evasively.

He did not have the energy to describe him, she would see for herself; he did not want her to panic, to run away and leave him now, because all his strength had drained away. He was shattered. Since his confession, Pauline had dealt with everything: the taxi, the station, the tickets, the porters, the inspectors. Had he been able, Albert would have fallen asleep where he sat.

Time passed.

Other passengers boarded, the train began to fill, a waltz of suitcases and trunks hoisted through the windows, children shouting, the thrill of setting off, friends, loved ones, parents on the platform, recommendations, people searching for their seats—excuse me, I'm here, do you mind?

Albert had rolled down a window and stood, leaning his head out, staring toward the back of the train like a dog waiting for his master.

People jostled him as they moved along the corridor, edging sideways since he was blocking the way; the compartment was full now, only one seat was empty, the one for the friend who had still not arrived.

Long before the train departed, Albert realized that Édouard would not come. He felt overwhelmed by grief.

Pauline understood, she snuggled against him, taking his hands in hers.

When the conductors along the platform began to call out that the train was about to depart, Albert bowed his head and cried; he could not help himself.

His heart was broken.

As Mme Maillard would tell it later: “Albert wanted to head off to the colonies, all right, fair enough. But if he acts there like he acts here, blubbing in front of the natives, he’ll never amount to anything, you can take my word for it. But that’s Albert for you. What can you do? He was born that way.”

EPILOGUE

Two days later, on July 16, 1920, at 8:00 a.m., Henri d'Aulnay-Pradelle realized that his father-in-law had played the last move in the game: checkmate. He would have killed him, if he had had the opportunity.

The arrest took place at his home. Given the seriousness of the charges against him, there was no choice but to remand him in custody. He was not released until his trial in March 1923. He was sentenced to five years in prison, two of them suspended, and so was allowed to walk from the court a free—but bankrupt—man.

In the meantime, Madeleine had sued for divorce, a process her father's connections made swifter.

The house at la Sallevière was seized and all of Henri's assets sequestered. After he was found guilty, what with reimbursements to the state, the fines, and the legal costs, there was little left, but there was a little. The state, however, turned a deaf ear to his appeals for the return of his remaining assets. In despair, in 1926, Henri instigated a long legal action on which, over time, he squandered what little he still had without winning his case.

He was reduced to a life of penury and died alone in 1961 at the age of seventy-one.

The estate of la Sallevière, entrusted to an institution under the auspices of the Assistance Publique, was turned into an orphanage and continued to operate until 1973, when it was rocked by a scandal rather too sordid to mention. The institution was closed. Thereafter, since it would have required significant public funds to be renovated, the house was sold off to the private sector, to a company specializing in symposiums and conference centers. In October 1987, it was home to a fascinating seminar entitled "1914–18: The Business of War."

On October 1, 1920, Madeleine gave birth to a son. Contrary to the practice, common at the time, where babies were given the names of relatives who had died in the war, she refused to name the child Édouard. "He already has problems enough with his father, let's not make matters worse," she commented.

M. Péricourt said nothing; he understood many things now.

Madeleine's son never had a close relationship with his father and when he came into his inheritance, granted him only a modest living allowance and a single annual visit. It was on the occasion of his visit in 1961 that he discovered his father's body. He had been dead for two weeks.

M. Péricourt's involvement in the death of Édouard was quickly dismissed. All the witnesses confirmed that the young man had thrown himself under the wheels of the car, something that further deepened the mystery of this astonishing coincidence.

M. Péricourt brooded endlessly on the circumstances of this tragic end. The realization that his son had been alive during all those months when he had longed to hold him for the first time plunged him into abject despair.

He was also overwhelmed by the vast web of contingencies that had led to his Édouard dying beneath the wheels of a car that he drove only four times a year. He had to face the facts: though inexplicable, it was not a misfortune, it was a tragedy. The end—whether this or another—had to come because it had been written long since.

M. Péricourt claimed the body of his son and had him buried in the family vault. On the stone, he had engraved: "Édouard Péricourt 1895–1920."

He reimbursed all those who had been swindled. Curiously, though the scheme had raised 1,200,000 francs, the invoices submitted amounted to 1,430,000 francs—there are crafty devils everywhere. M. Péricourt looked the other way and paid in full.

Gradually, he gave up his professional responsibilities, divested himself of his businesses, sold much of his property, and invested the funds for his daughter and his grandson.

For the remainder of his days he would see Édouard's face in that moment when the car hurled him into the air. He spent a long time attempting to interpret his expression. There had been a joy there, and a relief, too, but there had been something else, something he could not name.

One day, the word came to him: gratitude.

It was idle fancy, of course, but when it comes, such an idea is impossible to dispel . . .

He hit upon the word one day in February 1927. Over dinner. When he left the table, he kissed Madeleine on the forehead as always, went up to his room, lay down, and died.

Albert and Pauline arrived in Tripoli and later settled in up-and-coming Beirut in the Lebanon. An international warrant was issued for the arrest of Albert Maillard.

Louis Évrard, however, had no trouble finding someone to sell him identity papers for thirty thousand francs, a sum Pauline considered ruinously expensive.

She haggled them down to twenty-four thousand.

On her death, Mme Belmont left her daughter the family house on the impasse Pers, which, for want of maintenance, had lost much of its value. In addition, the lawyer sent Louise a considerable sum of money and a notebook in which her mother had scrupulously noted the investments made on her behalf—down to the last centime. It was then that Louise discovered that the original capital was composed of monies left to her by Albert and Édouard (forty thousand and sixty thousand francs respectively).

Louise did not have a particularly remarkable destiny, at least not until we meet up with her in the early 1940s.

This leaves only Joseph Merlin, whom no one remembered.

Probably not even you.

Don't worry: this was the one constant in the life of Joseph Merlin—everyone despised him and, as soon as he was gone, forgot him; whenever his name did crop up, it was invariably an unhappy memory.

He had spent a whole night sticking the bills given him by Henri d'Aulnay-Pradelle onto the pages of a large notepad using gummed paper. Each bill was a fragment of his story, of his failure, but that you know already.

Having submitted the report that would methodically damn Henri, Merlin went into hibernation, his career was over and, he believed, his life was too. In that he was mistaken.

He took his retirement on January 19, 1921. Until then he had been moved from one department to another, but the blow he had dealt the government with his reports and his cemetery inspections was not the sort of thing to be forgiven. The scandal! In the ancient world, when a messenger brought bad news, he was stoned to death. Instead of which, every morning, regular as clockwork, Merlin showed up at the ministry. All of his colleagues wondered what they would have done had they been handed the equivalent of ten years' salary; they despised Merlin all the more that he had not kept even twenty francs to polish his ugly clodhoppers, launder his ink-stained jacket, or buy a new denture.

And so, on January 29, 1921, he found himself on the street. Retired. Given his rank, his pension amounted to little more than Pauline's salary at the Péricourts.

For a long time, Merlin brooded over the night he had turned down a fortune in favor of something less fulfilling but more ethical—though he disliked high-flown words. Even after his retirement, the scandal of the exhumed soldiers continued to trouble him. It was through the pages of the newspapers that he followed Henri d'Aulnay-Pradelle's arrest and the spectacular trial of those dubbed the "profiteers of death." With immense satisfaction, he read the accounts of his own evidence at the tribunal, though they were hardly flattering, the journalists had not taken to this dreary witness who dressed appallingly and shoved past them on the steps of the courthouse when they tried to question him.

And then it was no longer news, everyone lost interest in the affair.

All that remained were the commemorations, the dead, the glory. La France. Guided by some sense of duty, Merlin continued to read the newspapers every morning. He did not have the means to buy them all, and so he would go to various places—libraries, cafés, hotel lobbies—where he could read them for free. It was in their pages that, in September 1925, he saw an advertisement to which he responded. A caretaker was wanted for the Saint-Sauveur military cemetery. Merlin was called for interview, presented his service record, and was appointed.

For many years, if you visited Saint-Sauveur, fair the day or foul, you were sure to see him, big boots driving his spade into the earth sodden with rain, tending the flowerbeds and the paths.

Courbevoie, October 2012

IN CONCLUSION . . .

All those I wish to thank here bear no responsibilities for any infidelities in my "true history" novel.

The war memorial swindle is, to the best of my knowledge, a fiction. The idea occurred to me while reading the famous essay by Antoine Prost about war memorials. On the other hand, Henri d'Aulnay-Pradelle's misappropriation of funds draws, in large part, on the "military exhumations scandal" that broke in 1922, presented and analyzed in the magnificent studies by Béatrix Pau-Heyriès. So one of the plot threads is real, the other is not; the reverse might easily have been true.

I read many books by Annette Becker, *Stéphane* Audouin-Rouzeau, Jean-Jacques Becker, and Frédéric Rousseau, whose insights I have found invaluable.

I owe a more particular debt to Bruno Cabanes and to his fascinating book *La Victoire endeuillée*.

The Great Swindle owes much to the novels of the immediate post-war period, from Henri Barbusse to Maurice Genevoix, from Jules Romains to Gabriel Chevallier. Two novels were particularly useful to me: *Le Réveil des Morts, by Roland Dorgelès,* and *Le Retour d'Ulysse,* by J. Valmy-Baysse.

I don't know what I would have done without the invaluable services of *Gallica,* the Ministry of Culture's *Arcade* and *Merimée* databases, and especially the librarians at the Bibliothèque Nationale Française, to whom I offer my profound thanks.

I also owe a particular debt to Alain Choubard, whose fascinating inventory of war memorials proved very useful; I am grateful to him for his help and support.

It is only right that those who helped me throughout the long process be thanked here: Jean-Claude Hanol for his early readings and his encouragement; Véronique Girard, who always gets to the heart of the matter with such gentleness; Gérald Aubert, for his perceptive reading, his advice, his friendship; and Thierry Billard, an attentive and magnanimous editor. My friends Nathalie and Bernard Gensane, who have been unstinting in their time, and whose observations and comments have always been so constructive, deserve a special mention. As does Pascaline.

Throughout the book, I have borrowed here and there from various writers: Émile Ajar, Louis Aragon, Gérald Aubert, Michel Audiard, Homère, Honoré de Balzac, Ingmar Bergman, Georges Bernanos, Georges Brassens, Stephen Crane, Jean-Louis Curtis, Denis Diderot, Jean-Louis Ézine, Gabriel García Marquez, Victor Hugo, Kazuo Ishiguro, Carson McCullers, Jules Michelet, Antonio Muñoz Molina, Antoine-François Prévost, Marcel Proust, Patrick Rambaud, La Rochefoucauld, and one or two others.

I hope they will consider my borrowing a homage.

The character of Joseph Merlin, freely inspired by Cripure,[15] and that of Antonapoulos, inspired by the character of the same name, are a sign of my affection and admiration for Louis Guilloux and Carson McCullers.

I would also like to thank the whole team at Albin Michel. I am grateful to everyone, first and foremost my friend Pierre Scipion, to whom I owe much.

It is perhaps understandable that my most poignant thoughts are for the unfortunate Jean Blanchard, who quite unwittingly provided the French title for this novel. He was shot for treason on December 4, 1914; his name was cleared on January 29, 1921.

These thoughts extend to all those, of every nationality, who died in the war of 1914–18.

NOTES

1 Clemenceau led the French into World War I, and had been prime minister from 1906–09; Poincaré was prime minister in three governments and president during World War I; Maurras (Charles-Marie-Photius Maurras) was a French author and the leader of *Action Française* who (despite being a socialist) supported Clemenceau and France's entry into World War I; Marshal Joseph Joffre (*Papa Joffre*) was a French *général* during World War I whose strategy led to the allied victory at the Battle of the Marne; Jean Jaurès was the leader of the French Socialist Party, and ardent antimilitarist who was assassinated at the outbreak of World War I; Aristide Briand served eleven terms as prime minister of France during the Third Republic, including a brief period before World War I.

2 Battle of Gravelotte (1870)—the largest battle during the Franco-Prussian War, named after Gravelotte, a village in Lorraine.

3 Robert Georges Nivelle, French artillery officer who served in the Boxer Rebellion, and the First World War; Joseph Simon Gallieni, military commander and administrator in the French colonies and finished his career during the First World War; Erich Friedrich Wilhelm Ludendorff, German général, victor of Liège and of the Battle of Tannenberg.

4 Mikhail Illarionovich Golenishchev-Kutuzov, Russian Field Marshal who served under Catherine II, Paul I and Alexander I.

5 Set up in 1919 by Ernest Vilgrain, under-secretary for agriculture and supplies, the "Vilgrain shacks" were rudimentary shops in makeshift shacks that offered Parisians food and other essentials at 20–30% of the price of other shops.

6 Alexandre Millerand would become president a year later, in 1920.

7 Léon Daudet (no relation to the writer), intellectual and politician of the third republic.

8 Pascal Dagnan-Bouveret, a leading light in the French naturalist school and Georges Antoine Rochegrosse a French historical and decorative painter.

9 A French serial killer of the time—he was arrested and charged in 1919 and subsequently tried and executed in 1921.
10 A center-right coalition that formed the government from 1919 to 1924.
11 Action Libérale or Action Libérale Populaire was a (Catholic) French political party during the Third Republic, and joined the Bloc National after the 1919 election, and thereafter it disappeared.
12 Fédération républicaine, the largest conservative party during the Third Republic, and the senior party in of the Bloc National coalition.
13 Raoul Villan was the man who assassinated the French socialist leader Jean Jaurès on the eve of World War I. Although the facts were not in dispute, he was acquitted by popular jury in 1919, and Jaurès's widow was forced to pay the costs of appealing the verdict.
14 Among the alumni of the École Polytechnique were four of the *générals* who led France to victory: Joffre, Foch, Fayolle and Maunoury. Almost a thousand *polytechniciens* died during World War I. The *polytechniciens* play a major role in celebrations after the war, though their role was controversial since not all in France felt the École Polytechnique had played a major role in the defense of their country.
15 Cirpure is the principal character in the Louis Guilloux's 1935 novel *Le Sang Noir* (translated as *Bitter Victory*), based in Guilloux's memories of his philosophy tutor, Georges Palante, an anarchist thinker who killed himself in 1925.